Robert E. Howard:
Selected Poems

Selections, Introduction, and
Commentary by Frank Coffman

2nd Edition
December 2021

Cover design by Frank Coffman

Thanks

I owe a debt of special thanks to Rob Roehm, who edited the poems herein against the authorized versions as established in the *Collected Poetry of Robert E. Howard*, and who provided much information regarding the source books, "zines," letters, and other documents whence the poems derive. His tireless efforts in Howardian scholarship and textual criticism are much appreciated, and enthusiasts of Howard's work owe him great debts.

Many thanks are due also to both Rob and Paul Herman for their great help in the compilation of Howard's corpus of poems [complete now, as far as we know, but some missing poems and fragments may yet be hiding] and in offering many suggestions for the editing of the present text. Thanks also to Rusty Burke, Barbara Barrett, and Deuce Richardson for their excellent editorial suggestions. Important efforts were also made in the past by Jim and Ruth Keegan and Ed Waterman in early work on the complete poetry.

Acknowledging great contributions to my own early investigations into Howard's poetry, I must thank other researchers into the poetic work of Howard: David Gentzel and Patrice Louinet for providing digital copies of much of the poetry and, of course, a special thanks also to Glenn Lord for providing me with photocopies of the Howard portion of the never-published *Images Out of the Sky* (intended to be a collaborative poetic effort with T. C. Smith and Lenore Preece [the title later used by Smith for an anthology of his own work]).

DEDICATION

For Bob Howard, of course—
and to my parents who helped nurture a love of language
and so much more;
to Connie for her love, patience, and support;
and to George & Ann and George, Jr.—who understand.

Table of Contents

Selected Poems

Selected Poems

INTRODUCTION

Robert E. Howard: The Flame and the Shadow

"My soul's a flame of divine fire, a god's voice ..."
— Robert E. Howard, in a letter to T. C. Smith

Now is the lyre of Homer flecked with rust,
And yellow leaves are blown across the world.
— "Autumn" by Robert E. Howard

In Greenleaf Memorial Cemetery in Brownwood, Texas, one of three inscriptions on a family tombstone bearing the name "Howard" reads:

Robert E.
Author and Poet
1906-1936

Two important things stand out upon the contemplation of this inscription: first and glaringly obvious, that Robert E. Howard died too young—sadly not that uncommon a fate— and his short life and suicide have become the focus of much of the critical attention paid him thus far; second, and perhaps as importantly, that he is proclaimed as both author *and* poet.

Now past the centennial of his birth and more than seven decades since his death, there is no doubt that Howard is established as one of the legendary authors of popular fiction, the founder of "Sword & Sorcery," a writer of the first order among the masters of imaginative literature.

But as too few realize, Robert E. Howard was not only a poet as well as a "fictioneer," but, indeed, a poet of exceptional talent. This talent was demonstrated early, deeply and broadly developed in his youth, and sadly somewhat daunted by the markets of his day and the stark economic necessities that forced him to make fiction his practical priority as a writer.

But there was much poetry in the man, and a slow realization of his poetic skills and the scope and breadth of his poetic achievement has been gathering momentum over the decades since his death.

One great thing about true poets: they cannot help but reveal their souls; they cannot help but give themselves away in their verses. And Bob Howard *was* a true poet. Through these poems and through the many letters to various correspondents now available for study, a picture of Howard emerges not as clearly available through his prose fiction alone.

Most of Howard's poetry has been available only in a few slender, out-of-print, small-press-run volumes, eagerly sought and prized by collectors and enthusiasts. The present volume is presented to help rectify the problem of relative inaccessibility of Howard's poetic work and to offer some brief commentary on its nature and its worth. This somewhat large "selection" is chiefly due to the simple fact that most of Howard's poems are worthy of anthology. Some brief commentaries are included to highlight some of the subjects Howard touched upon in an attempt to show the variety, quality, complexity, and intensity of his poetic achievement.

Several distinct themes are evident in Howard's poetry, a few of them strident. The following text is divided into thirty separate sections, arranged by topic, theme, or poetic type. While the reader may not always agree with my selections for this volume or my division of the text into the several themes, topics, or types as assigned to the sections, I hope that the reader will at least find the selections both representative of a broad spectrum of Howard's poetry and the sections at least reasonable and not arbitrary. I've attempted a fairly daunting task, as this volume—lengthy as it is—was initially much longer and divided into two parts. Indeed, there is so much general merit to Howard's poetry that I've decided to allow this "selection" to err on the side of inclusiveness to show Howard's breadth and depth as a poet, rather than to select what some might call only "the best of the best."

It is also quite clear that there are more than a few lost po-
ems—as indicated from various lists and bibliography headings
by title or by single, intriguing lines and some fragments and
"rough drafting" typescripts. Of what remains to us—far more
than the few who believe they "know" Robert E. Howard's po-
etic work might expect—not all is gold, but there is much gold
therein, and I envy those of you who are about to encounter
Howard's verse for the first time the joys and sublimely intense
experiences that lie awaiting. Those who have some experience
with Howard's poetry might well be beckoned to deeper explo-
rations and discover more than a few surprises along the "read."

Just as Howard was a self-made writer of prose, a pioneer-
ing tale-spinner across several genres, and the acknowledged
originator of "Sword and Sorcery," his poetic abilities were also
largely self-acquired through voracious reading[1] and constant
writing—especially, it seems, around the years of his late teens
through early twenties whence we can date most of the poems
that have survived.[2] He admired the poetry of H. P. Lovecraft
and that of Clark Ashton Smith, as well as some other con-
tributors to *Weird Tales*. Of course, he was also influenced by
poets of the 19th century and by the ancient traditions of poetic
art and practice.

There have been some important observations previously
written about Howard's poetry over the years, several of these
by Glenn Lord in the brief texts of introductions to the few
published collections of verse and some scattered comments in
Lord's *The Last Celt*. Other scholars have published in hard-
to-obtain sources like the small circulation (30 members) Rob-
ert E. Howard United Press Association (REHupa) and other
almost as hard to obtain items like *Savage Sword of Conan* and
in Conan-related or other Howardian "fanzines."

Howardian scholar Fred Blosser published a fine early essay,
which surveys the few scant early forays into REH poetic criti-
cism in his essay "Bard from the Shadows" in *Savage Sword of
Conan* #58, 1980.

There is little doubt that the single most important over-
view and essay-length assessment of Howard's poetry thus far is

Steve Eng's "Barbarian Bard: The Poetry of Robert E. Howard" which appears in Don Herron's pioneering 1984 anthology, *The Dark Barbarian*.

An even earlier comment on Howard as poet is found in Tevis Clyde Smith's "Introduction" to *The Grim Land and Others*, published by Jonathan Bacon in 1976:

> It is unfortunate that Bob, himself, is not alive to chat with those who never had the opportunity to meet him. The goosebumps would have gone up and down their spines to have heard him chant his poems, or the poems of anyone else for that matter, for *he was, certainly at the very first, primarily a poet*. (emphasis added)

I believe that Howard was "primarily a poet" first *and* last. His prose is imbued with rich poetic nuances and virtuosities. His poetic nature was held in check to some degree by economic necessities, but, ultimately, it could not be restrained or repressed. Smith's choice of the word "chant" in writing about the way Howard delivered poetry rather than the more common "recite" or the simple "read" is indicative of much. That primacy as poet—both *at the very first* and fundamentally—will, I believe, be clear to the reader as the pages of this book are turned.

One important thing to note is that the early voices and commentaries on Howard's poetry were all hindered to some degree by the simple fact that they had only about a third of the entire body of his poetic work to examine. This led to some narrowness of assessment, not due to any lack of research or critical perspective, but, rather, to a lack of sufficient material to see Howard's poetic "big picture." As with the criticism of the prose fiction, much of the poetry-related evaluation sees Howard's range too narrowly.

Here again, Eng's masterful divisions in his seminal 1984 essay [which, by the way is also available in (and the divisions of which form the section divisions of) the *Collected Poetry of Rob-*

ert E. Howard, finely edited by Rob Roehm and recently published by the Robert E. Howard Foundation] is quite comprehensive, considering that he did not have the full corpus to examine. Eng's division of the poems into eight classes was visionary. In examining Howard across the *thirty thematic and topical areas* [3] I have suggested, I hope that this text will help to go even further in demonstrating the true breadth and depth of Howard's poetic genius.

We may profitably look at Robert E. Howard the Poet along the lines of both the traditions he upheld and advanced and the range of forms that he adopted and adapted to his own visions.

For one thing, we see in Robert E. Howard a poet of that earliest generation to be affected by the first shocks of the twentieth century's transition from the Age of Print into the Age of Multimedia and Hypermedia.[4] In his teens, he was caught up with several radical visions and causes and characteristics of the epoch: socialism, the Lone Scout Movement, reaction in general against what would later be called "the Establishment."

Almost by definition, intellectuals—which group includes, most creative artists across all the arts—are eccentric. And much has been written about Howard's idiosyncrasies. Indeed, most critical work thus far has been from biographical and psychological avenues of critical approach (even pseudo-psychoanalytical as with L. Sprague de Camp's sadly flawed *Dark Valley Destiny: The Life of Robert E. Howard*). Yet Howard was also solidly grounded upon important heroic and formal traditions and envisioned himself, I believe, in some decidedly "anti-modern" ways, decidedly traditional ways.

I believe he saw himself as a bardic voice born too late for the age of chanted song and almost too late for the last surge of poetic narrative. He was a man who took up the mantle of those mystics and magicians with words of the century before his own—the Romantics and Victorians—who had themselves revived the legendary past and the heroic days of the Classical and Medieval worlds. He saw himself clearly a part of the newly besieged Age of Print (cinema, radio, and other media having already emerged). Howard understood that any new "Homer" would have to be a "singer" in print whose voice needed to boom from the printed page to reach a people caught up in changing times—people at the cusp of yet another communications revolution.

It is here that we find an interesting paradox in Howard's character in the duel between Barbarism and Civilization. He found himself torn between the chaotic nature of a violent and brutal and cynical world vision, fueling his belief in the ultimate triumph of Barbarism on the one hand, and the sophistication of the literary forms and themes of heroism coming directly from the Victorian Age of "cosmic optimism" with its ideals of Progress and "Manifest Destiny" and—to some degree—from the Romantic Age of "natural order" and the "noble savage." He would have this same predicament in trying to zero in on a final vision of his native Texas and "the Old West" in general, fluctuating between the tall and humorous Western yarn (Breck Elkins, etc.) and a West tinged by Horror ("The Horror from the Mound," etc.) or even a West as a setting for Viking incursion and exploration (*Marchers of Valhalla*). Howardian scholar and biographer Rusty Burke has commented upon Howard's "telescoping" of history, of conflating and commingling epochs.

We might well see Robert E. Howard as a man adrift in Time, aware of his own, but not necessarily preferring it to others he studied or envisioned.

Howard's chants of song and story were for "the common ear"—and I mean "common" in the best positive sense. Howard targeted the basic, instinctively human elements of a broad readership. Howard may be seen as a poet of *celebration* of the gamut of human emotions and sensations. In a letter to his friend Tevis Clyde Smith, Howard writes:

```
The thing about a poet—a real poet
feels everything, that's why he can
express himself so powerfully and
```

```
can make other people feel the same
things-but he never really thinks.
For real poetry is sensation and
not conscious thought. . .
```
(*Selected Letters 1923-1930,* 11)

Howard was, despite the radical exuberance of youth, a poetic traditionalist and even a reactionary of sorts in an age when so-called "free verse" was ascendant and a general revolution across all of the arts was rapidly gaining momentum. That period of the rise of nihilism and doubt between the two great World Wars coincided with Howard's formative years and his prime, but—while it may have affected his worldview and overall outlook—it did not alter his admiration and emulation of the poetics of tradition. It did not change the vision he had of himself nor the lasting appreciation and impact he hoped to achieve through his art as a poet. This vision was not kept without moments of self-doubt, but there is always a sense that Howard believed he had potential. In January of 1926, at the age of only 20, he writes to Clyde Smith:

```
All day I've tried to write
poetry. I've worked. Hell, how
I've worked. Changing, revising,
aw hell! My stuff is so
infernally barren, so damnably
small. I read the poems of some
great author and while they
uplift me, they assure me of my
failure. Hell, hell, hell. My
soul's a flame of divine fire, a
god's voice and damn me damn me
damn me, I cant give it a human,
worldly voice. No wonder most
poets drink themselves into the
gutter and out again and into
the mire.
```
(emphasis added)

The idea of the "flame of divine fire" and the notion that poets are the ones who can—literally through divine inspiration—speak with "a god's voice" was, I believe, the driving self-assurance behind Howard's poetry. In the letters, he often demeans his own work—usually with a definite tinge of false modesty in evidence in one of the several personae he puts on in the many correspondences. But the letters are simply packed with poems and experiments, effusions of verse of varying topics and varying quality, but bejeweled with a few gems of dazzling brilliance and evocative power, giving ample evidence of the spontaneity and naturalness of his poetic voice.

In one epigram contained in the poetry-laden letters to Smith, Howard, age 20, writes:

```
Poet

My soul is a blaze
  Of passionate desire
My soul is a blaze
  That sets my pen on fire.
```

—letter of 23 June 1926 to TCS

Deep down, Howard knew himself to be a poet, but the market for verse was far from lucrative compared to that for pulp fiction—and even that was meager enough compared to the money "the slicks" paid. Howard had to work hard at "splashing the field"—as he called it—in many genres of pulp prose to make his way and help support his family and his ailing mother.

Necessity directed the majority of his efforts over the last decade of his life to the yarns that have made him famous. He was a "Singer of Tales"[5] in the old bardic tradition, a minstrel of the magical realms he envisioned.

This poet of the post oak country of central Texas truly had the Flame of inspiration, sadly forced into relative Shadow by the necessities of marketability and his own compulsion to make a living as a writer.

Near the conclusion of "Barbarian Bard," Steve Eng writes: "One day a *Selected Poems* will place Howard in permanent perspective." The purpose of this book is precisely that.

In the final analysis, as I believe the reader will see from the selection of poems herein, Robert Ervin Howard was an accomplished and unique poet whose best work exhibits a range of moods, themes, and poetic techniques. Some of the poems show forth as grim and gray as cold iron, some ring like the singing bronze of blade on blade, some are dark as Death, some hot as Hell, some shine forth as the sparkling and dazzling jewels of sensation and sound in a golden bardic crown.

Though many things worked against what might have been an even more profuse and profound outpouring of his verse, based upon the fine body of poetry he has left us, he will, I believe, eventually be viewed as an important poet at a level equal to his already-established stature as one of the great and inventive storytellers of his age. Indeed, he must ultimately be viewed as "Author *AND* Poet" as his tombstone proclaims.

While his poetic achievement has been kept thus far decidedly in the shadows surrounding the blaze and brilliance of his famous tales and prose fiction, the verses have never been in complete obscurity.

My hope with this book is to help in some way to remove his poetic achievement from that comparative shade and allow it to be placed in full view in a new light of enjoyment, enthusiasm, and examination—ready for both readerly and scholarly appreciation.

But enough of this. Bob's hand rests upon the strings of Homer's rusted lyre; the once-yellowed leaves that follow are miraculously greening again; the music begins and a strong, young voice rises in song . . .

Frank Coffman
Elgin, Illinois
June 2007 (rev. May 2009)

WORKS CITED IN THE INTRODUCTION

Blosser, Fred. "The Bard from the Shadows." *Savage Sword of Conan*, no. 58, November 1980. Marvel Comics.

Eng, Steve. "Barbarian Bard: The Poetry of Robert E. Howard" in *The Dark Barbarian: The Writings of Robert E. Howard: A Critical Anthology*, ed. Don Herron. Berkeley Heights, NJ: Wildside Press, 1984: 23-64.

Howard, Robert E. *Selected Letters: 1923-30* ed. by Glenn Lord. West Warwick, RI: Necronomicon Press, 1989.

- - - - - *Selected Letters 1930-36* ed. by Glenn Lord. West Warwick, RI: Necronomicon Press, 1991.

NOTES ON THE INTRODUCTION

1 "Howard read anything he could lay hands on, including considerable verse. He believed English poetry to be the highest form of English literature, and he named a long list of his favorites including Tennyson, Swinburne, Wilde, Kipling, Alfred Noyes, Chesterton, James Elroy Flecker, De la Mare, Omar Khayyám (presumably Edward Fitzgerald's translation), Rupert Brooke, Siegfried Sassoon, Masefield, Robert Gilbert Vansittart, Francis Ledwedge, Lord Dunsany, George Sylvester Viereck, and the Americans Poe, Longfellow, Bret Harte, Sidney Lanier, Robert W. Service, the Benét brothers (especially Stephen), Nathalia Crane, Henry Herbert Knibbs, Joe Moncure March, and H. P. Lovecraft. He read and admired *Weird Tales* compeer Clark Ashton Smith as well. He commemorated François Villon in a poem, and he liked Verlaine and Baudelaire, though not so well as the best English poets. He praised Sappho at great length, as the supreme woman poet and one of the best poets of all time. But he did not mention Talbot Mundy as a poet, though he may have been Howard's most immediate influence. The poems Mundy interspersed in his fiction have Howard's Kiplingesque cadence and exotic tone" (Eng 24)

2 "*...I'm beginning to believe the poetry business is a lot like the fight game -- most of the poets do their best work early in life....*" —(*Selected Letters: 1923-1930*, 60 emphasis added)
        Likely the greatest authority on the dating of Howard's typescripts—alongside Glenn Lord—is scholar Patrice Louinet who has developed a remarkable amount of information relevant to the dates of creation of various texts, inclusive even of a sense of dating based upon the gradual deterioration of the key faces on Howard's Underwood Model 5 typewriter. It seems certain that the majority of Howard's poetic output was composed between his late teens and early twenties, with a gradual tapering in the few remaining years before his death at age 30,

as he began to devote more and more of his time and talent to the production of his "yarns" across several genres and magazine markets. However, if we are to credit lists of titles and first lines, it also seems clear that many poems have not survived, some of which might well have been composed in the later years of Howard's brief life. Also, most poets work in manuscript and not typescript—at least in early draft stages. We will likely never know the true extent of Howard's poetic output, and dating of most poems will always be in question.

3 The nature and names of the thirty sections into which these selections are classified came to me over the span of a couple months of contemplation following discussions about the possibility of this book begun at the Howard Days celebration in the centennial year of 2006. Some, of course are obvious choices based upon the mere examination of the poems themselves; some are along lines parallel to Blosser's or Eng's distinctions. Some of my 30 divisions are, I hope, serendipitous.

4 Now, in our twenty-first century, of course, "Multimedia" has become "Hypermedia" with ease of access, increasing interactivity, and ever-broadening and inviting horizons for creative intervention. Fr. Walter Ong's discussions on the transitions from Oral Culture to Scribal Culture to Print Culture are especially interesting [Ong, Walter J. *Orality and Literacy*. London: Routledge, 1982]. We are now well past the cusp of the third great communications shift into Hypermedia Culture.

5 The monumental work of Milman Parry, completed by his colleague Albert B. Lord in *The Singer of Tales* is a masterful exploration of oral poetic technique and the power of memory. They studied the oral traditions of the Balkans in the early 20th century while these arts were still vibrantly alive. [Lord, A. B. *The Singer of Tales*. Cambridge: Harvard UP, 1960, 2nd ed. 2000.]

SOME NOTES ON EDITORIAL CHOICES AND FORMAT

Regarding the presentation of poems in this volume, specifically the way in which the type is set generally, the transformation of long line lengths in originals, and the titles ascribed to untitled poems, I have observed the following practices:

A. The indentation of lines in rhymed poems generally follows typesetting traditions for rhymed verse. When clearly defined stanza patterns are observed (and not, for example, long blocks of text as with rhyming couplets in long sections), the indentations follow the rhyme scheme of the poem or stanza. I believe that Howard often wrote "across the page" long lines—especially in those poems that might be well designated "long ballads"—to both conserve paper and, perhaps, allow for inspirational "flow." It is certain that many of the poems eventually set in type for *Weird Tales* and other magazines do not match the typescript. So, this and other "variances" from original typescript in terms of the presentation of lines should not bother the reader.

B. To fit the dimensions of this book, the long-line—poems most of them 6 or 7 accent lines have been arranged into two lines, with a break at the caesura (usually after the third, or more often the fourth foot—especially in the case of the "long-line ballads" where 7 becomes 4-3). If the reader wishes to mentally reconstruct the long lines, the practice has been followed of starting the continuation of a line with a lower case letter, while the beginnings of full lines follow the accepted common practice of traditional verse in beginning with a capital.

C. The poems that were left untitled by Howard have been titled according to the common practice of using the first line of the poem as its title for presentation. These poems can be detected by the practice herein of capitalizing only the first letter of such a title and any other proper nouns that might be in the title, avoiding the normal "title case" of capitalizing all key words—which latter is the practice used herein for presentation of the poems that were given a specific title. It should also be noted that some poems in previous collections were clearly titled by others: editor or agent. The reader should take this into account as well.

SELECT BIBLIOGRAPHY

Blosser, Fred. "The Bard from the Shadows." *Savage Sword of Conan*, no. 58, November 1980. Marvel Comics.

Eng, Steve. "Barbarian Bard: The Poetry of Robert E. Howard" in *The Dark Barbarian: The Writings of Robert E. Howard: A Critical Anthology*, ed. Don Herron. Berkeley Heights, NJ: Wildside Press, 1984: 23-64.

Howard, Robert E. *Selected Letters: 1923-30* ed. by Glenn Lord. West Warwick, RI: Necronomicon Press, 1989.

- - - - - *Selected Letters 1930-36* ed. by Glenn Lord. West Warwick, RI: Necronomicon Press, 1991.

Lord, Glenn. "Introduction" to *Always Comes Evening* (2nd ed.). San Francisco: Underwood-Miller, 1977. [originally published by Arkham House, 1957.]

- - - - - "Introduction" to *Echoes from an Iron Harp*. West Kingston, RI: Donald M. Grant, 1972: 9-10.

- - - - - "Introduction" (pp. 9-12) to *Singers in the Shadows*. New York, Chicago: Science Fiction Graphics, 1977. [originally published West Kingston, RI: Donald M. Grant, 1970 (pp. 7-9)]

- - - - - "Introduction." *Shadows of Dreams*. Hampton Falls, NH: Donald M. Grant, 1989.

Smith, Tevis Clyde. "Introduction" to *The Grim Land and Others*, ed. Jonathan Bacon. Lamoni, IA: Stygian Isle Press, 1976: 1-2 [unnumbered]

Warfield, Wayne. "Introduction" to *Etchings in Ivory: Poems in Prose by Robert E. Howard* (2nd ed.). Aberdeen, MD: Hall Publications, 1975: 1-2.

ROBERT E. HOWARD
SELECTED POEMS

PROEM

Let no man read here who lives only in the world about him. To these leaves, let no man stoop to whom Yesterday is as a closed book with iron hasps, to whom Tomorrow is the unborn twin of Today. Here let no man seek the trend of reality, nor any plan or plot running like a silver cord through the fire-limned portraits here envisioned.

But I have dreamed as men have dreamed and as my dreams have leaped into my brain full-grown, without beginning and without end, so have I, with gold and sapphire tools, etched them in topaz and opal against a curtain of ivory. Like medallions of jade and fire upon a topaz girdle they glitter, and as such I offer them, without beginning and without end, even as scenes carved upon a marble frieze. Scan them here, men of strange eyes and strange souls.

Robert E. Howard

I

Adventure's Call & Wanderlust

Certainly one of the themes that runs through both the prose and poetry of Robert Ervin Howard is what Howard himself calls Adventure's "beck"—that almost visible signal and "come hither" from the Muse of the Age of Epic and Heroic Song. Joseph Campbell has called this "The Call to Adventure" in his writings on the "Monomyth"—the ubiquitous "Hero's Journey" found in the myths and legends and heroic tales of all nations. Howard certainly understood this "Call," rooted in the very essence of heroic story and song—likely instinctively or innately known, but reinforced through his voracious and broad readings of myth, legend, and history. He knew it, not only as a necessary early element of an heroic tale, but felt it quite keenly as a man who lusted for experience and the chance to wander, a would-be traveler whose physical travels were never to be as extensive as he hoped, but whose imagined journeys opened doors to whole new worlds. Unfulfilled *Wanderlust* was replaced by a fulfilled "*Wonderlust.*"

"Adventure" has movement built into the very root of the word. The "-ven-" infix is the same that we find in Caesar's "Veni, vidi, vici" and also in the ancient English "wend" (present tense of "went"). It has to do with motion, action, a going forth as modified by the "ad-" prefix. The word implies travel and action—things that fill Bob Howard's poems and tales.

Of special lure for Howard was The Sea. While only actually experiencing the genuine article at places like New Orleans and Galveston, it seems to have called to Howard like a Siren's Song. It's no wonder that so many of his stories and poems are about this love of the sea—about Vikings, Pirates, and various heroes sailing off to new and exotic places.

This section features poems that touch upon "The Call."

ADVENTURE

I am the spur
That rides men's souls.
The glittering lure
That leads around the world.

ADVENTURE, I HAVE FOLLOWED YOUR BECK

Adventure, I have followed your beck
Through all the ages, I have sought no other lover.
I have followed o'er land and sea,
    dim vale and mystic moon mountains.
I have heard Pan's pipes amid moon-dappled woodlands
    and have seen the satyrs frolicking with nymphs upon
The fragrant swards, while the night-breezes
    murmured among the leaves.
I have watched your lateened feluccas
    a-leap upon turquoise seas of morn,
And I have stood upon your snow-browed peaks
    and seen the lavender slopes of your brooding mountains
Stretching away to the amethyst sky-line.
I have heard the berg song of your Arctic floes
    and have watched
Your Northern Lights flaring
    in god-like grandeur from the Pole.
I have sailed your seas. And I have seen the boundless desert
    sands, all purple in the sunset, spread to
The brooding horizons. I have trod your nameless jungles,
    dared your turbid rivers;
Harked to the shadowy jungle, where it brooded, bestial chin
    on midnight hand, like a sullen giant of darkness.
And I've seen your nameless mountains rise from the sea
    of tangled forest, and stand like sightless somber gods
Against the twilight. Adventure, I desire no other lover.

I have followed your ways about the world and yet again.
All the ages that have clanged to your stride,
  have known my step.
My feet are dusty with the musk of antiquity,
  my hands clutch the stars from their sockets.
Adventure, you are wondrous with mystic beauty.
  Your tresses snare the stars and you are dusky-breasted
As Egyptian dawns. Your eyes are soft twin planets of mystic
  allure, speaking of all the wonders of all the eons.
Your voice is as soft, as melodious as the harp of Arion and
  there runs in haunting refrain a thousand minor notes.
The song of Circe is there, the whisper of the dawn-winds.

THE ADVENTURER'S MISTRESS

The scarlet standards of the sun
  Are marching up the mountain pass;
The whispers of the dawn winds run
    Across the oxen-booming seas—
  And shimmering in the waving grass
Are webs the ghostly spiders spun
    When strange shapes glided in the trees
And shadows dusked the silent leas.

My castle stands upon a shore
  Where waves are placid as a lake.
My galleons bring their golden store
    As drowsy days drift idle by;
  No gales make spar or top mast shake.
Here seas on shoals forever roar
    And here the trees loom weird and high
And gaunt crags lift in the sky.

Why should I leave my towering walls
  To tread the path about the earth?

Fair girls are dancing in those halls,
    Their breasts are round, their arms are white,
  And light and luring is their mirth,
And yet, for lust that ever calls
    I tread the trails of eerie light
    A phantom, through the phantom night.

For this, my lust is stronger far
  Than demon's charm or witches' spell.
It heeds not wall nor dungeon bar
    Nor anything that hindereth.
  For it was born for One from Hell;
And she rides her Yellow Star
    She fires my love with Hades' breath—
    My ancient mistress, beldame Death.

She beckons me from every hill,
  I see her standing by the sea;
I follow fast, I follow still
    By horse and foot, by keel and sail
  With all the winds that drone or dree.
I match her cunning with my skill
    As fierce, alert, I keep the trail
    Through desert sands and ocean gale.

My flaming beard is streaked with snow,
  My arm is slower than of eld,
That once wreaked havoc on the foe;
    And slower, too, these steel-clad hands
  That in days gone by have felled
A lord of Mecca with one blow—
    What time I wooed with clashing brands
    From sunset to the Holy Lands.

The combers crash along the shale;
  The seas are crimson with the dawn.

A ship with scarlet-spreading sail
 Swings into view with lurch and list.
 Somewhere the red abysses yawn
And though the slain years have their tale
 Of broken swords and spears that missed,
 Somewhere we have a secret tryst.

Soon I shall leap from shore to deck
 And ride into the sky-line's haze
To follow my old lover's beck.
 Aye, swift will fade the hill, the tree;
 And moons will wane and suns will blaze
And stars will leap, nor shall I reck—
 For she waits on some distant lea
 And at the last will come to me. . .

THE CALL OF THE SEA

White spray is flashing
 O'er the grey sea
White waves are lashing
 Calling to me,
"Follow the sea-ways,
 "Follow the sea."

Tall masts are dipping,
 Now the gulls fly
White, smoothly slipping,
 'Tween sea and sky,
See where the albatross
 Hovers on high.

White surf is beating
 On the grey shore
Wave hordes, fierce meeting,
 Savagely roar,

Where the white surf fiends
   Screech evermore.
Now the tide surges
   Far out to sea
Wave with wave merges
   Where ocean-winds dree.
Hark to the wild wind,
   Fierce, roaring, free!

Swift scudding ocean breeze
   Leap from the shore!
Bear me to bounding sea,
   Where the waves roar,
Over your wild ways
   To roam evermore.

THE DAY THAT I DIE

The day that I die shall the sky be clear
   And the east sea-wind blow free,
Sweeping along with its rover's song
   To bear my soul to sea.

They will carry me out of the bamboo hut
   To the driftwood piled on the lea,
And ye that name me in after years,
   This shall ye say of me:

That I followed the road of the restless gull
   As free as a vagrant breeze,
That I bared my breast to the winds' unrest
   And the wrath of the driving seas.
That I loved the song of the thrumming spars
   And the lift of the plunging prow,

But I could not bide in the seaport towns
  And I could not follow the plow.
For ever the wind came out of the east
  To beckon me on and on,
The sunset's lure was my paramour
  And I loved each rose-pale dawn.

That I lived to a straight and simple creed
  The whole of my worldly span
White or black or yellow I dealt
  Foursquare with my fellow man.

That I drained life's cup to its blood-red lees
  And it thrilled my every vein,
I did not frown when I laid it down
  To lift it never again.

That ever my spirit turned my steps
  To the naked morning lands
And I came to rest on an unknown isle—
  Jade cliffs and silver sands.

And I breathed my last with a simple tribe,
  A people savage and free,
And they gave my body unto the fire
  And my soul to the reinless sea.

TO THE CONTENTED

Bide by the fluted iron walls
 Take ye a serving wench to wife;
Drown in the pot the bugle's calls,
 Trade your spear for a peddler's knife.
 Turn to the vendor's paltry strife,
  Gird ye round with doors and bars
 Safely snore in the lap of Life—
  I must follow the restless stars.

Wait at the doors of your master's halls
 —For the faithful server, boards are rife—
Make no oath when the whip-lash falls—
 Hark to the counsel of your wife;
  Trade your harp for a peddler's fife.
  But gods, the spray and the plunging spars!
 Here is my heart—in the heart of Life
  And I must follow the restless stars.

Envoi
King, there are stallions in golden stalls,
 But bars of sapphire are only bars!
Bide in peace in the high safe halls—
 I must follow the restless stars.

ROADS

I too have strode those white-paved roads that run
 Through dreamy woodlands to the Roman Wall,
Have seen the white towns gleaming in the sun,
 And heard afar the elf-like trumpet call.

II

Barbarism Ascendant

One theme that seems clearly dominant in Howard is his deeply-rooted and often-articulated belief that civilization is and must be forever only a veneer, possible to sustain to some degree over brief epochs, but always, ultimately falling to the barbaric, overcome by mankind's natural inclination. Howard quite often plucked notes and chords from what Fred Blosser has called "the Dark Harp of Conan's creator. . ."

The titles of Don Herron's two important anthologies emphasize this theme: the seminal collection, *The Dark Barbarian,* and the recent important collection *The Barbaric Triumph.* The former of these takes its title from lines in one of Howard's key poems on this theme, "A Word from the Outer Dark":

> *I am the Dark Barbarian*
> *That towers over all.*

Howard was, on occasion, eerily prophetic. On this theme in his poem, "A Warning," Howard concludes:

> *But Life, the tigress that bore you all*
> *Has never changed her shape . . . .*
> *But you will not know and you will not heed*
> *Till your towers come tumbling down.*

This theme is certainly common with Howard, but although strident and glaringly clear in his work, it has to some degree been overemphasized in critical attention. Some of his other themes and perspectives have been overlooked—or at least undervalued and under-discussed as a result. Nevertheless, the poems in this section chant loudly for themselves.

ASTARTE'S IDOL STANDS ALONE

Astarte's idol stands alone
  With eyes that hold the ravished years;
Baal-Pteor's shrine is shattered stone
  Where through the night the jackal leers.

No more Bab-Ilu's women sit
  Beneath Mylitta's mistletoe;
No more grim Moloch's eyes are lit
  By torches flaming row on row.

* * * * *

Across the stars their doom was writ:
  "The dark before the dawn must go."

Yet Baal, unseen, sits still enshrined
  Along the world's broad thoroughway;
Bubastes' tendrils still are twined
  About the dreams of men today.

For man still wears, from birth to dust,
  The seal of Chiron's neighing foal
And fires of Moloch's darksome lust
  Still light the windows of the soul.

BLACK CHANT IMPERIAL

Trumpets triumph in red disaster,
   White skulls litter the broken sod,
And we who rode for the one Black Master
   Howl at the iron gates of God.

Temples rock and the singers falter,
   Lights go out in the rushing gloom—
Slay the priest on this blackened altar,
   Rip the babe from the women's womb!

Black be the night that locks around them,
   They who chant of the Good and Light,
Black be the pinions that shall confound them,
   Breaking their brains with a deadly fright.

Praised be the Prince that rules forever
   Throned in the shadows stark and grim,
Where cypress moans by the midnight river—
   Lift your goblets and drink to him!

Virgins wail and a babe is whining
   Nailed like a fly on a gory lance;
White on the skulls the stars are shining,
   Over them sweeps our demon's dance.

Trumpets bray and the stars are riven!
   Shatter the altar, blot the light!
From the bursting hells to the fallen heaven
   We are kings of the world tonight!

THE DUST DANCE [VERSION 2]

For I, with the shape of my kin, the ape,
   And the soul of a soaring hawk,
I fought my way from the jungle grey,
   Where the hunting creatures stalk.

For I was made of the dust and the dew,
   The dust and the clouds and the rain,
The snow and the grass, and when I pass,
   I'll fade to the dust again.

I laughed when Nero's minions sent
   Fire tortured souls to the sky.
Without the walls of Pilate's halls,
   I shouted, "Crucify!"

I roared my glee to the sullen sea
   Where Abel's blood was shed.
My jeer was loud in the gory crowd
   That stoned St. Stephen dead.
You say God's spark has kindled my eye,
   As the sun-rise reddens the east;
Into your beards I roar the lie—
   'Tis the gleam of the stalking beast.

Oh, ye prophets, men of Israel,
   Doff the sandal and the staff—
Moons rise silver over Kabul—
   Follow me and learn to laugh.

*   *   *   *   *   *   *   *

The men go up and the men go down
   And who shall follow the track of men?
The dust spins slow in the desert town,
   And a fog drifts white on the silent fen.

The sword is broken, the shield is bent—
　　Our backs are at the wall;
　Stark and silent they lay who went
　　To harry the coasts of Gaul.

From the north's blue deeps our galleys sweep
　　To south and west and east;
We bring our bows from the northern snows
　　That the great grey wolves may feast.

　　*　*　*　*　*　*　*　*

Grim, grim, grim the elephants were chanting,
　　Chanting in the jungle in the dim, dark dawn;
Through the waving branches were the late stars slanting,
　　Beating up the morning ere the night was gone.

Lion in the morning, crouching by the river.
　　Red birds flitting with a sing-song shrill.
Morning like a topaz, the green fronds a-quiver.
　　Scent of lush a-wafting in the dawn air still.

Moses was our leader when we came up out of Egypt—
　　Came up out of Egypt so many years ago—
When I think of magic, I always think of Moses,
　　Riding down to glory while the hautboys blow.

Oh, the plain was dusty—how the heathen roar!—
　　Joshua and Israel! Hear the trumpets blow!—
How we shook the desert!—thank a Canaan whore—
　　Roaring in our triumph at the walls of Jericho.

　　*　*　*　*　*　*　*

　Oh, Jezebel, oh, Jezebel,
　　They hurled you from the wall,
　And all the priests and prudes of Israel
　　Gave thanks to see you fall.

But I could laugh with Jezebel,
   And kiss her on the lips,
And strip the scarf from off her breasts,
   The girdle from her hips.

For I foreswear Elijah,
   Forget that Adam fell,
To press the waist of Lilith
   And laugh with Jezebel.
Oh, brother Cain, oh, brother Cain,
   I take you by the hand,
For Abel was the first prude
   To cumber Eden's land.

Then down the road that leads to hell,
   We strode, a merry band—
Sargon, Belshazzar, Jezebel,
   Cain with his bloody hand.

THE FLOOD
(To All Evangelists)

Rise in your haughty pulpits;
  Preach with a godly ire!
You turn my blood to venom;
  You turn my soul to fire.
Lords of the fading darkness,
  Nursing a crumbling race,
This is the bitter gauntlet
  I hurl into your face:
That the day of your rule is over,
  And the tribes begin to rise,
As a sleeping giant, stirring,
  Opens his drowsy eyes.
Under the ice are gathering
  Floods that were born in hell,
And the slow, great waves are coiling,
  With the power to rebel.
You dance with a broken sceptre,
  You squeak on a barren throne,
And your temples rise and topple
  And crumble to shattered stone.
The day of the light is coming,
  But you would bide within the dark;
You seek to drag us backward—
  Men of the darkness, mark!
The day shall come of our fury
  When we hurl all chains aside,
And the flood will beat you under
  With the fury of its tide.

UNTAMED AVATARS

They break from the pack and they seek their own track,
  They are swifter than cormorants flying;
They range far and wide, they are fierce in their pride,
  And they glory in slaying and dying.

Their love is a breath that is withering as death,
  They take, but they never are giving.
Their hate is as fell and eternal as Hell.
  Yet, gods, how they revel in living.

They jeer at the pack and they bend not the back
  To the rule of the weak and the many;
From beginning to end they've no lover nor friend,
  Nor feel they the needing of any.

They are beasts hard and lean and their talons are keen
  To rage and to rend and devour—
Oh, mocking their mirth, for the best of the earth
  Is laid at their feet in their hour.

Oh, they never can win, but the one single sin
  That they shun is the sin of the dastard.
And they grin as they die, in their conqueror's eye,
  And he trembles, the small yellow bastard.

For these are the men who know all of sin,
  Save the sinnings of fear and forgiving—
Untamed avatars, they have broken the bars—
  And gods, how they revel in living!

Robert E. Howard

A WARNING

You have built a world of paper and wood,
　　Culture and cult and lies;
Has the cobra altered beneath his hood,
　　Or the fire in the tiger's eyes?

You have turned from valley and hill and flood,
　　You have set yourselves apart,
Forgetting the earth that feeds the blood
　　And the talon that finds the heart.

You boast you have stilled the lustful call
　　Of the black ancestral ape,
But Life, the tigress that bore you all,
　　Has never changed her shape.

And a strange shape comes to your faery mead,
　　With a fixed black simian frown,
But you will not know and you will not heed
　　Till your towers come tumbling down.

A WORD FROM THE OUTER DARK

My ruthless hands still clutch at life—
   Still like a shoreless sea
My soul beats on in rage and strife.
   You may not shackle me.

My leopard eyes are still untamed,
   They hold a darksome light—
A fierce and brooding gleam unnamed
   That pierced primeval night.

Rear mighty temples to your god—
   I lurk where shadows sway,
Till, when your drowsy guards shall nod,
   To leap and rend and slay.

For I would hurl your cities down
   And I would break your shrines
And give the site of every town
   To thistles and to vines.

Higher the walls of Nineveh
   And prouder Babel's spires—
I bellowed from the desert way—
   They crumbled in my fires.

For all the works of cultured man
   Must fare and fade and fall.
I am the Dark Barbarian
   That towers over all.

III

Celtic Connections, Heritage, Ancestry, and the "Northern Thing"

Despite the decidedly Anglo-Saxon surname, Bob Howard felt more deep affinity with his mother's Ervin ancestry and the Scots-Celtic lines of the family. As far as the Germanic lines went, for some reason Howard transmuted his English heritage into a love of things epitomized by the Viking tradition, this in combination with the age-old Celtic antipathy toward the *Sassanach*. Thus there was a shift from Western to Northern Germanic, a love of what Tolkien and Lewis and the other *Inklings* called "The Northern Thing."

Several of his poems and notable fictional characters (the Pictish king Bran Mak Morn, Turlough Dub O'Brien, and others) and even some of his various *noms de plume* (Patrich Howard, Patrick Ervin, etc.) clearly show this bent and his love of things Celtic. A few of his poems seem to be formed with a nod to the complexities of Irish or Welsh metrics, although he did not experiment much in this direction.

Behind many of Howard's dark-haired, blue- or grey-eyed heroes in fiction is this inherited and developed mood combining Celtic exuberance and Norse ferocity, both roiling beneath the lowering skies of the North of the World.

An oft-quoted passage from G. K. Chesterton, who was himself one of Howard's poetic inspirations, sums up Howard's Celtic affinities and attitudes quite nicely:

> *The Great Gaels of Ireland*
> *Are the men that God made mad,*
> *For all their wars are merry,*
> *And all their songs are sad.*

This merry sadness can be felt in the poems to follow.

ALIEN

My brothers are blond and calm of speech,
  Placid and slow of ire,
But all my blood is the heritage
  Of one grim great-grandsire.

He came by night when the river-plain
  Was wild with storm and flood,
To mix with the stolid Saxon strain
  His searing alien blood.

His hair was black as the wings of night,
  Coarse as a black bear's fell;
His eyes were blue as the fire that roars
  On the molten floors of hell.

My hair is black as a midnight sin,
  My eyes are blue bale-fire;
My heart would sear a naked stone
  With its hate and mad desire.

BLACK HARPS IN THE HILLS

Let Saxons sing of Saxon kings,
  Red faced swine with a greasy beard-
Through my songs the Gaelic broadsword sings,
The pibrock skirls and the sporran swings,
For mine is the blood of the Irish kings
  That Saxon monarchs feared.

The heather bends to a marching tread,
  The echoes shake to a marching tone-
For the Gael has supped on bitter bread,
And follows the ghosts of the mighty dead,
And the blue blades gleam and the pikes burn red

In the rising of the moon.
  Norseman reaver or red haired Dane,
    Norman baron or English lord—
Each of them reeled to a reddened rain,
Drunken with fury and blind with pain,
In the black fire spilled from the Gaelic brain
    And the steel from the broken sword.

But never the chiefs in death lay still,
  Never the clans lay scattered and few-
But a new face rose and a new voice roared,
And a new hand gripped the broken sword,
And the fleeing clans were a charging horde,
  And the old hate burned anew!
Brian Boruma, Shane O'Neill,
  Art MacMurrough and Edward Bruce,
Thomas Fitzgerald-ringing steel
Shakes the hills and the trumpets peal,
Skulls crunch under the iron heel!
  Death is the only truce!

Clontarf, Benburg, and Yellow Ford-
  The Gael with red Death rides alone!
Lamh derg abu! And the riders reel
To Hugh ODonnell's girding steel
  And the lances of Tyrone!

Edward Fitzgerald, Charles Parnell,
  Robert Emmet—I smite the harp!
Wolfe Tone and Napper Tandy—hail!
The song that you sang shall never fail
While one brain burns with the fire of the Gael
  And one last sword is sharp-

Lamh laidir abu! Lamh derg abu!
  Munster and Ulster, north and south,
The old hate flickers and burns anew,

The heather shakes and the pikes gleam blue.
And the old clans charge as they charged with you
   Into Death's red grinning mouth!

We have not won and we have not lost-
   Fire in Kerry and Fermanagh-
We have broken the teeth in the Saxon's boast
Though our dead have littered each heath and coast,
And by God, we will raise another host!
   Slainte—Erin go bragh.

Robert E. Howard

"FEACH AIR MUIR LIONADHI GEALACH BUIDHE MAR OR"

Mananan Mac Lir
  The son of the sea
  Is sib unto me
At the break of the year.

In the white autumn tides
  The ghost drums call
  When the midnights fall,
And the ghost ship rides
  Where the green waves crawl.

I break the loam
  By a Kerry hill—
  They beckon me still
Through the purple gloam;
Strange eyes in the foam.

The sea-wind chills
  The crumbling stones,
  And a ghost harp moans
In the shadowy hills.
But a white sail fills
  And a sweep-head drones.

The great white oars
  They gleam and bend
And the west wind roars
  From the blue world's end;
  They call me like a friend,
Forgotten shores.

HERITAGE [VERSION 1]

My people came from Munster
    and the cold north Nevis side.
Their hearts were black with ancient wrongs
    and hate and bitter pride.
Their souls were wild and restless
    with swift and changing moods;
They knew red border forays
    and dark unholy feuds.
And first within my cradle
    on the day that I was born
I heard the songs the rebels sang
    to give the gallows scorn.

But when the springtime standards march
    in a great green waving host,
I never dream of Inverness
    or the rugged Kerry coast.
I never dream of a barren shore
    where the sea wind keens and shrills;
My dreams are all of Devon downs
    and the good green southern hills.
I never see the surging Lorne
    or the sullen Kenmare' flow,
But I have walked through Dartmoor nights
    with all the winds that blow.

I know the quaint ale houses
    beneath the oaks whose shade
Was flung when lost Lundinium fell
    before the Roman raid.
I know the croon of sleepy streams,
    and the brown time-carven towns,

But best of all the fall of night
   across the dreaming downs.
I have not walked there waking,
   but dream roads I have trod,
And Devon is my heritage
   by tree and hill and sod.

Beyond the years of yearning,
   and lust and blood and flame,
My people rode in Devon
   before the Saxon came.
Oh, wattle hut and barley,
   oh feast and song and tale!
Oh, land of dreamy legend
   and the good brown British ale.
My heritage is barren,
   my feet are doomed to roam;
I may not drink from Devon springs
   or break the Devon loam.

But when the kings are fallen
   and the when the empires pass
And when the gleaming cities
   are wasted stone and grass;
When the younger peoples totter
   and break their gods in vain,
They who were first of all the earth
   may get them home again.
Gods, hurl the haughty deathwards
   and shake the iron thrones
That my kin shall ride in Devon
   above the Saxon's bones.

MARCHING SONG OF CONNACHT

The men of the East are decked in steel,
  They march with a trumpets' din,
They glitter with silk and golden scales
  And boast of high kings' kin—
We of the West are clad in hides
  But our hearts are steel within.

They of the East ride gallant steeds,
  And each knight wears a crown—
We fight on foot as our forebears fought
  And we drag the riders down.

They of the East are full of pride,
  Cubs of the lion's den.
They boast they breed a race of kings—
  But we of the West breed Men.

ONE BLOOD STRAIN

Now autumn comes and summer goes,
  And rises in my heart again,
As witchfire glimmers through a pool,
  The mystic madness of the Dane.

Blue thunder of a foaming sea
  Reverberating through my sleep,
White billowing sails that fill and flee
  Across a wind-swept restless deep—

They speak to me with subtle tongue
  Of blue-bright ways my forebears trod,
When time the bearded Vikings bent
  Their oars against the winds of God.

And I am but a common man
  Who treads a dreary way ashore,
But oceans thunder in my dreams,
And blue waves break on creaking beams,
And foaming water swirls and creams
  About the strongly bending oar.

When summer goes and autumn comes
  To paint the leaves with sombre fires,
I feel, like throbs of distant drums,
  The urge of distant nameless sires.

RETRIBUTION
[THE SONG OF MURTAGH O'BRIEN]

The moon above the Kerry hills
    had risen scarce a span
When we went forth from Knocknaroe
    to card a Saxon man.
We stretched him naked on the ditch—
    God save this soul of mine!
The howls of him as hard we dragged
    the cats along his spine.

A great, full-bodied man he was,
    that beat poor Tom O'Rourke,
The hardest English landlord now,
    from Donegal to Cork.
'Twas, "Damn your eyes! Pay rent or starve!
    Get out with all your brats!"
But, faith, the howling of him now
    was louder than the cats.

It's maybe he remembered then,
    the swelling Saxon toad,
How he evicted Biddy Flynn
    to die beside the road.
I hope that he remembered, too,
    the while the tomcats clung,
MY cousin Mike O'Flaherly
    his testimony hung.

He cursed the king in agony
    and damned the penal laws—
Oh, quite a different man he was
    beneath those ripping claws.

His squealing dwindled to a moan,
   his back was bloody beef;
We flung him in the thorny ditch
   like, any common thief.

The mist was stealing from the sea,
   the night was strange and still.
We heard him weeping like a child
   as we went down the hill.
And then, above our oaths and jests,
   there sounded from the wood
A cry so wild and sweet and sad
   it chained us where we stood.
Some nightbird rended by an owl—
   I felt black sorrow rise;
I turned to speak to Dermod Shea,
   and tears were in his eyes.

SONG BEFORE CLONTARF

Lean on your sword, red-bearded lord,
  and watch your victims crawl.
Under your feet they weakly beat
  the dust with their dying hands;
The red smokes roll from the serf's roof-pole
  and the Chieftain's shattered hail—
But there are fires in the heather
  and a whetting of hungry brands.

The peaked prows loom like clouds of doom
  along each broken port.
The monks lie still on the heathered hill
  among the fallen stones.
Over the land like a god you stand,
  our maidens howl for your sport—
But kites await in the heather
  to tear the flesh from your bones.

Clouds and smoke for a broken fold,
  a lash for the bended back—
Thus you roared when your crimson sword
  blotted the moon on high
But sea breaks and the world shakes
  to the battle's flying wrack
And Death booms out of the heather
  to nail you in the sky.

THE SONG OF THE LAST BRITON

The sea is grey in the death of day,
   Behind me lifts the night.
I'll flee no more from the ancient shore
   Where first I saw the light.

The Saxons come and the Saxons go
   With the ebb and flow of the tide;
Their galleys loom, grim shapes of doom,
   But here shall I abide.

My castles rust in crimson dust,
   Red ruin tossed in the drift—
But the sea is grey, and the wolf's at bay,
   And the ravens circle swift.

Come from the mists of the Northern Sea
   Where the smoke-blue hazes melt.
Your dead shall lie where here I die,
   The last unconquered Celt.

TO HARRY THE OLIAD MEN

When the first winds of summer the roses brought,
  And the fields were a-blossom again,
The warriors went riding from green Connacht
  To harry the Oliad men.

Cail of the Sword, we called our lord,
  He harried the East and the North—
Oh, the blades dripped red and the ravens fed
  When Cail and his wolves went forth.

The war-cloud rolled like the wind before—
  And the gods of the North were old—
The sea-folk fled from the purple shore
  As the white birds flee the cold.

IV

Cosmic Visions

In several of his poems, Robert E. Howard contemplates and meditates and pronounces upon questions regarding the great nature of things universal. If not finding answers, he at least questions and surmises.

Nodding a bit to Howard's literary "pen-pal," H. P. Lovecraft, we can say that Howard often thought and sometimes wrote about things "cosmic": Eternity, Destiny, Origin or Creation, Destruction, Life, Death, Good, Evil.

These themes are found also in his letters, but they appear in a few significant examples in the poetry, and they are touched upon by many other poems that have been arranged under different, more specific themes in this anthology.

Contrary to what many suppose and several have stated, Robert E. Howard's work, not only in the fiction, but most certainly in the letters and in the poems, reflects a *mind* that "splashed the fields" of deep thought as well as those more practical fields of varied publication markets and genres.

Howard has too often been looked upon as a writer of limited range, marvelous in a very few select genres, originator of one, sadly limited by environmental circumstances and his choice—at least act—of early suicide. But this is far too narrow a view of both Howard and his work. His poetry covers a broad spectrum, remarkable for one who only lived thirty years and shared his visions and perspectives through literature for less than the latter half of that.

HYMN OF HATRED

O, brother coiling in the acrid grass,
   Lift not for me your sibilant refrain:
Less deadly venom slavers from your fangs
   Than courses fiercely in my every vein.

A single victim satisfied your hate,
   But I would see, walled cities crash and reel,
Gray-bearded sages blown from cannon-mouths,
   And infants spitted on the reddened steel.

And I would see the stars come thundering down,
   The, foaming oceans break their brimming bowl
Oh, universal ruin would not serve
   To glut the fury of my maddened soul!

AN OPEN WINDOW

Behind the Veil what gulfs of Time and Space?
   What blinking moving Shapes to blast the sight?
I shrink before a vague colossal Face
   Born in the mad immensities of Night.

SERPENT

I am the symbol of Creation and Destruction.
I am the beginning and the end.
With my tail in my mouth
I am the Circle of Eternity.
Wisdom is in my eyes
And the dusk of wisdom lurks amid my coils.
My track circles the world
And I loop my coils about the Universe.
My head waves among the stars
And the nations fall prostrate before me.
Coiled, head upright, I am the spirit of the sea.
The world-shaking dinosaur was my henchman
And the flying dragons were my footmen.
The ancients knew me.
They reared shrines and altars
And I taught them dim, dusky wisdom.
I coiled in the ruins of Troy and Babylon
And on the forgotten streets of Nineveh.
The Norse called me Midgaard and built their galleys
Like a sea-serpent.
The Egyptians and the Indians called me Ysis
And the Phoenecians Baal.
I am the sea that girdles the world.
I am the first and I shall be the last.
I am the Serpent of the Ages.

THE WHEEL OF DESTINY

The day of man's set doom is come,
   The altars break, the idols fall;
The shattered oracles are dumb
   And utter stillness ruleth all.

Across the great world's silent girth
   The grass-grown cities rot and rust:
Still are the rulers of the earth—
   Men and their worth sink back to dust.

Man fades without a trace to tell;
   Where seas roar on the primal plain
The mindless, living, single cell
   Begins the long, slow climb again.

V

Howard's World

Bob Howard frequently wrote about HIS world—that is the "real" world he lived in and passed through, not the many other worlds of his creative imagination. A thus-far decidedly neglected area in the study of Howard's poetic and fictional work is his interest in and commentary upon the people, the social conditions, the historical events of his own days.

This only makes sense. One could not possibly grow up through the Great War and the Great Depression, through the rise of cinema and radio and air travel and the Roaring Twenties and not be influenced by world events—even in a tiny town in Texas.

The poems in this section show a Bob Howard involved in the world. That he frequently traveled out of it to create and explore worlds of his own was, simply, the perpetual problem of the artist: whether to live in this world (what Tolkien calls the "Primary World"[5]) or the worlds of his art ("Secondary Worlds" according to JRRT).

As noted by other poets like Browning and Tennyson (from the age of heroic narrative echoed in much of Howard's verse), this dilemma—whether to be committed to ones Life or to ones Art—presents a real quandary for the true artist. Committing to one, all too often detracts from or even virtually eliminates, or at least severely restricts, the other.

Perhaps this goes some way to explaining some of the issues concerning Howard's personal relationships with which the biographical critics have been so occupied. In any event, the following poems show a Bob Howard affected by and reacting to his world and his times.

Included in this section are two poems that might be called "juvenilia"—if such a term can apply to one who died so young: "Parody," Howard's first known poem, and "Private Magrath."

AN AMERICAN

Sing of my ancestors!
  Sing of them with pride!
Sing of fair America,
  Green prairies and blue tide!
One was born in County Cork!
  Hail the shamrock green!
(One was named Abraham
  Simeon Levine.)
One held rule in Dundee,
  Friend of the Montrose.
(One sold nuts and apples
  Where the river Tiber flows.)
One drank ale in Devonshire,
  One scaled Lomond's crags.
(One grew up in Warsaw
  And peddled clothes and rags.)
One sailed out from Liverpool,
  Bold and free and glad.
(One lended cash at high
  Rates in Petrograd.)
Och, oi oi, and hoot mon!
  Gott sie dank go bragh!
Gevald! Be dommed! Diavoli!
  America iss braw!
Shure, its mesilf thot loves the land,
  Vy shouldn't I? Oi oi!
Some fellow he no lika diss,
  I'm nae yon kind o' boy!
Its aiche mon for his ain, py hell!
  A feller got to stand
An' tella peoples who he iss
  And brag on his own land!
Vun nation unt vun langvitche!
  Oi! And go for business fine
To Michael Israel Malcolmsky
  Gammettio O'Stein.

THE CAMPUS AT MIDNIGHT

Starlight gleams through the windows
    Night dew jewels the grass
Winds creep through the sky-limned branches
    Rustling the leaves as they pass.
Silent the buildings are sleeping,
    White comes the moonlight soon;
Etched in soft fire the shadowy spire
    Looming against the moon.

A DAWN IN FLANDERS

I can recall a quiet sky once more,
    And splintered trees carved black against the dawn,
And guns whose melted steel forgot their roar,
    And walls that sagged, their rafters being gone.
The dead lay silent where the hill sides sloped;
    Blackened and charred, they slumbered heap on heap.
And in the dawn the living stirred and groped
    As men that waken from a frozen sleep.

THE DRUM

I heard the drum as I went down the street,
  Its thunder above the people's din.
  I shivered in the cold; my clothes were thin—
The drum—my brain reeled dizzy to its beat,
Lending a rag-time to my freezing feet,
  Soaked with the rain my torn shoes let in.
  "Enlist for home and country!" crazed for gin,
I heard the grim drum challenge and repeat.

Here in the bloody frozen mud I lie,
  My brains are oozing out to stain the mire—
    I never knew a woman or a home—
  I heard the drum—it set my brain on fire—
    I don't accuse—I guess I had to come—
But I am dying here—I'm wondering why.

Robert E. Howard

HATE'S DAWN

I pinned him hard in a vacant trench,
  The corporal who had my hate.
The rats ran through the reeking stench,
  And he blanched before his fate.

The skies were dim with the birth of dawn,
  And the wind was thin and bitter.
The stars were bleak as a woman's lies,
And he shrank from the horror of the skies
And the red death in my bitter eyes,
  And my bayonet's cold glitter.

Long be the trail of vengeance,
  But the spurs of hate thrust on!
"This is the curse at Ypres,
  This is the blow at Toulon!"

The blood burst from his sagging lips.
  The stars dimmed and were gone;
And over the wastes of No Man's Land,
  The wind blew up the dawn.

LITTLE BROWN MAN OF NIPPON

Little brown man of Nippon
   Who apes the ways of the west,
You have set the sword on your standard,
   And the eagle on your crest.

Little brown man of Nippon,
   You have dreamed a deadly dream;
You have waked the restless ravens
   And the rousing vultures scream.

Oh, lines of an unborn empire,
   Foam of a rising flood,
Your bones shall mark the borders,
   The tide shall be your blood.

Little brown man of Nippon,
   Though the star of the West be set,
And the last of the fair-haired strew the field
   Where East and West be met—

Though you herd us down like cattle,
   And hew us down like corn,
Our blood shall drown your vision
   Of the empire yet unborn.

In utter desolation, and despair
   At the end, on a blackened hill,
You shall sit and view your empire,
   Broken and charred and still.

The beams of shattered houses,
   Reared stark against the sky,
And fields wherein, for waving grain,
   Long waves of dead men lie.

We will set the torch with our own hands
  To wall and roof and spire;
We will cut the throats of our women,
  And feed our babes to the fire;

We will fling our naked bosoms
  Against your bloodied steel;
As you tread us under, dying,
  Our teeth shall rend your heel.

But, little brown man of Nippon,
  Should the dice fall otherwise,
And the gods of the fair-haired triumph
  When the battle-dawns arise—

We will give your flesh to the sea-gulls
  And your cities to the flame,
Till the world forgets your visions,
  And the years forget your name.

Over your island empire
  Shall our steel-clad squadrons fly
Till the land lies black and silent
  Under a flame-ripped sky.

Till the hungry wolf goes slinking
  Along your shattered streets,
And the kite in your ruined palace
  Tears at the crimson meats.

And over the crimson gutters
  Which infant bodies choke
The raven flaps and strangles
  In the drifting shreds of smoke.

No plough shall break your valleys,
   No song shall rouse your hill—
Still and silent the ploughmen,
   The singers silent and still.

And your nation's only emblem,
   Oh, man of the crimson dream—
Save corpses in the broken streets
   And the death-fires' baleful gleam—

Shall hang at the prow of a cruiser,
   That furrows the flying foam,
Bearing the spoils of conquest
   To the fair-haired people's home.

Shall hang at the prow of a cruiser,
   Grinning and dripping red,
The price of a dream of empire—
   Little brown man, your head.

MATCH A TOAD WITH A FAR-WINGED HAWK
[BOB AND CLYDE*]

Match a toad with a far-winged hawk,
A scarlet rose with a thistle stalk;
A stagnant pond with the white sea-tide—
You match the friendship of Bob and Clyde.
Clyde was a plucker of gems divine—
Bob was half poet, half devil-swine.
One of them mounted the gods' own peak,
Out of the world's vile muck and reek,
Up from the world-path's ruck and slime,
Climbed on a ladder of godlike rhyme.—
One of them made his bid for fame,
Scorched his wing at the Muses' flame,
Warped his soul like a brooding devil
Found at last, and kept to, his level.
A friendship strange—yet it lasted on
Till their lives had faded to dusk from dawn.
Friendship of a falcon for a mugger—
Gods' own poet and third-rate slugger.
Lived their lives, friend unto friend—
Each in his own way met his end.
One of them passed like a Median king—
One of them died in a boxing ring.
One of them passed on a distant shore
Where the breakers answered the sea-wind's roar.
High on the crags he stood at bay,
Laughed like a god o'er the din of the fray;
Crimson the cliffs and red his sword,
One man facing a blood-crazed horde;
Man after man fell to his blade,
Laughed as he faced them, unafraid.
They swarmed like demons; what did he care?

Beauty and glory and pride were there;
Crag and mountain, ocean and sky,
Glorying to see a strong man die.
Laughed on the crags like a white limbed god,
For he knew the ways that the godlings trod—
He had scaled all peaks of glory. Last
With a snatch of a song on his lips he passed.
One heard the tumult of throngs outbreak
As he writhed on the matt like a wounded snake,
Striving to get his legs beneath—
Red oaths ebbed through his broken teeth—
Above him the ring-light's garish blaze,
Sordid faces leered through the haze,
Foreign voices venting foul spleen,
Scents of unwashed forms obscene—
Shouts that flickered the ring-light's shine
"Stand up and fight, you yellow swine!"
Then the darkness loomed like a mighty tide
And he gasped out a crimson curse and died.
Thus they lived their lives friend unto friend,
And each in his own way met his end.
Match a toad with a far-winged hawk,
A crimson rose with a thistle stalk;
A stagnant pond with the ocean's tide—
You match the friendship of Bob and Clyde.
Friend unto friend, they lived their days,
Friend unto friend they walked their ways.

[*editor's suggested title]

NIGHT MOOD

It is my mood to walk in silent streets
Where lone and shadowy cats prowl lonesome beats.

Old sidewalks, rough and worn from years of shoes;
Past picket fences, garbage and refuse.

Old trees, whose shadowy forms the starlight weaves
With dim, white splashes filtering through their leaves.

And a lone arc light, guttering through the night
While countless moths fly 'round and 'round its light.

NIGHTS TO BOTH OF US KNOWN

The nights we walked among the stars
    When dusky trees were still
And saw the slender crescent moon
    Stretch naked on the hill.
The days when youth was golden fire
    And dreams in dreams were won
And visions came on flaming wings
    From night and setting sun,
Of oceans greater than our seas,
    Long leagues of emerald green,
That broke on shadow haunted shores
    In jade and crystal sheen.
And lands that lie along the sky
    When twilight breaks the day,
Blue hills that hold enchanted lakes,
    Ah, God, how far away.
And purple galleons aflame
    With gems and frozen gold,

Red islands haunted by the ghosts
   Of mariners of old.
And shadows gliding o'er the deep
   With mystic echoed song—
Ah, God, the years, the crawling years,
   How slow and lean and long,
Ah, days that swept on eagle wings,
   Oh, nights to which we sung;
Oh years, long faded into night,
   That worlds and we were young.

NO MAN'S LAND

Across the wastes of No Man's Land,
   the grey clad slayers came
Like phantoms of the lifting night,
   steel-tipped and crowned with flame.
We met them at the parapet
   before the dawn was red
And ere we closed we trampled on
   a carpet of the dead.
The dark smoke veiled us like a fog,
   lit up by crimson flame
Our powder flashes scorched their eyes,
   yet grimly on they came.
And up and down along the trench
   the grim battalions swayed
As reddened fingers sped the ball
   and drove the dripping blade.
The zooming shells came swooping down,
   the rockets flashed and streamed.
Beneath our feet the wounded writhed
   and shrieked and cursed and screamed.

I heard the shells that flashed and crashed,
   I heard the bullets' dree,

When from the gory, writhing muck,
    a face looked up at me.
A German face, the face of one
    that I had seen before,
A lad I knew in San Ferez
    before we went to war.
Now up he leered with ghastly grin,
    his blonde hair dyed with blood
Till in that face I set my heel
    and crushed it in the mud.
Then I was jostled far aside
    by clumps of battling men—
And just in time, I ducked and leaped—
    a shell roared midst them then.
They vanished in a crimson cloud
    from which things frightful sprung
Festooned about their comrades' limbs,
    their gory entrails hung.

A charging ape, a sudden shape
    came ploughing through the muck,
His shoulders hunched, his eyes were shut,
    he grunted as he struck.
I did not feel the tearing steel
    and yet a flame of Hell
Speared through me as I raised my gun
    and killed him as I fell.
As in a far forgotten land,
    I heard the battle rout.
I seemed to ride on swaying clouds
    and then the world went out.

Red shapes of shadows came and went
    and leered and jeered at me
Ere I came back and found a world,
    war-spent, but calm and free.

PARODY

[Howard's First Poem?!
written for a Cross Plains H.S. Class
on description of June in "Sir Launfal"
Jan. 28, 1921 (Howard had just turned 15)]

What is so vile as a February day?
When it rains and snows together,
And muddy and wet is every roadway.
Whether we walk on the side of the street,
We cant hardly step for the mud on our feet.
Every man feels a stir of hate,
And swears at the mud that clogs his gate.
And people are tired of mud and life
And think, "Why all this toil and strife?"
For melting snow is everywhere seen
All over the hill and the swamp
And mud-puddles so stagnant they're green,
And the earth is moldy and damp.
The bullfrog sits on a log in the lake
Like a mossy bump on the rotten old log,
And sees what a dismal croak he can make.
The old cat stands on the fence like an owl
And loud, lonely and dismal is her howl.
With the frog and the cat is mankind accursed,
In the sore ear of Nature which song is the worst?

Robert E. Howard

PRIVATE MAGRATH OF THE A.E.F.

(As an aid to remembrance of November 11th, 1918)
[another early poem]

The night was dark as a Harlem coon
Smoke and clouds once lin' the moon;
Flares goin' up with a venomous sound,
Bustin' and throwin' a green light around.
An', yeah, there was me, a cursin' my soul
For losin' meself from the raidin' patrol.
Creepin' along in the mud and the slime,
Cussin' and havin' the Devils own time.
Smeared and spattered with Flanders mire,
Tearin' me clothes on the loose barbwire.

I'm crawlin' along, keepin' close to the ground,
When all of a sudden I hears me a sound.
I halt and I listen, it's too dark for sight
But some bird's ahead of me there in the night.
I reached for me gun—then I swear through me teeth
For somewhere the thing's fallen out of its sheath.
But before I can move, I hear feet a-slush
And something to meself: "Come right ahead, Fritz,
I've lost me gat but I've got me mitts."

I sidestep quick as he makes his spring,
His bay'net flashes, I duck, I swing!
Flush on the jaw my right he stops,
Down in the muck on his face he flops.
I'm cursin' him for a bloody Hun
As I loosen the bay'net off his gun.
I feel for his ribs 'neath his tunic drab
For I've only time for a single stab.
I feel a locket a-dangling there,
I jerk it out, then a rockets flare
Limns it in light like a crimson flame

And I see the face of a white haired dame
And German letters beneath it run,
Which I take it to mean, "To my darlin' son."
I haul that Hun up onto his pegs,
And I says, "Get goin'; and shake your legs.
Your lines are that way, now get gone."
And I hands him a boot to help him on.
Saying, "Make tracks on your homeward path,
    With the compliments of Monk Magrath."

SHALL WE REMEMBER,
FRIEND OF THE MORNING

Shall we remember, friend of the morning
    Dusk of the twilight and rose of the dawn?
— Laughing we fared in our youthfulness scorning—
    Mornings as golden shall lift when we're gone.
Oceans are eld and the mountains are hoary
    Ancient forgetfulness leaves them apart;
We shall remember our youth and the glory
    We breathed when our race was just at its start.
Soon shall we fade as the twilight's red splendor
    Fades to the misting of magical dusk
Soon to the eons our souls shall surrender—
    Ghosts dim at twilight, a faint breath of musk.
We shall remember, our ghosts shall remember
    Sunsets of glory and pale rose of dawn
We shall remember, our ghosts shall remember
    Ages and ages long after we're gone.

Robert E. Howard

A SON OF SPARTACUS

"If we must slaughter…"—*Kellogg*
[ed. note: compare this poem to "Hate's Dawn"]

I pinned him hard in an empty trench,
  The sergeant who had my hate;
The rats ran through the reeking stench
  And he blenched before his fate.

The skies were pale with the birth of dawn,
  The wind was thin and bitter;
The stars were black as a harlot's lies,
And he shrank from the horror of the skies,
And the black hate in my bitter eyes
  And my bayonet's cold glitter.

Wildly and strange he mumbled and stared,
  As one whose wits are scattered,
And drooled at the mouth as he strove to rise
  On the shards of a leg shell-shattered.

"Long be the trail of vengeance,
  "But the spurs of hate thrust on!
"This for the curse at Ypres!
  "This for the blow at Chalon!
"And a last stab through your rotten heart
  "For the girl at Montlucon."

The blood burst from his sagging lips;
  The stars paled and were gone;
And over the wastes of No-Man's Land
  The wind blew up the dawn.

A STIRRING OF GREEN LEAVES

I long for the South as a man for a maid,
  The rose at the window bar,
The stars and the palm-trees' velvet shade
  And the strum of a Spanish guitar.

My people laughed at the frost and cold,
  And the blast from winter's mouth,
But my soul is worn and thin and old
  And it reaches blind to the South.

Why should I yearn for a gypsy trail
  Through the olive trees of Spain?
Mine is the race of the Western Gael
  And the cold, slow blood of the Dane.

But never the restless leaves are stirred
  By a breath from summer's mouth
But like the soul of a wandering bird
  My soul is yearning South.

SYMBOLS

Scarce had the east grown red with dawn
  Or the moon-born day begun
Ere three of us went up a winding road
  In the face of the rising sun.
One of us plucked a red rose
  One of us plucked a white
One of us turned from the rising sun
  And reached his hands to the night.

THERE WERE THREE LADS

There were three lads who went their destined ways
  Bewildered by this thing that men call Life
Toiled through the week and idled leisure days.
  And cursed the world but knew the world was rife
With things of beauty. Even they could see.
  They reveled in old tales of ages hoary
  And plagued by souls vague reaching out for glory,
But knew a dim, uncertain longing to be free.

They saw, they felt but could not put in words
  The things of beauty that oft met their eyes,
Waving of blossoms and the flight of birds,
  The tints of sun-set fading from the skies.
    They dimly glimpsed the sky-kissed mountain crest
    And felt chagrin of failure, dim unrest.

Blasphemous, showing their deep joy at verses,
Praising an artist with deep, sulphurous curses.
When their souls thrilled they knew but naught to swear
  Admiring cursed at lakes by breezes kissed,
"Say, look at that damned elm waving there."
  And vaunt its praise with oaths that fairly hissed.
They named, if chose, a demi-god a lout

Sneered at the thought that man-kind was their brother
Yet they could see a pretty girl without
   Licking their lips and elbowing each other.
And they could see young saplings in the shade
   And think of dancing girls. Could see
The sapling's litheness in a tender maid.
   Could revel in the winds that whisper free.

"Say, boy, you see that moon just coming up,
   Throwing its banners like long, silver teeth,
Say, I can think that it's some sea-king's golden cup—
   Look there, white clouds above and purple hills beneath.
You know old pard, I guess that I'm a fool.
   But I have got a lot of thoughts in me—
But what's the use? There never was a school
   Could teach a fellow to write poetry.
And yet it's in my soul. I'd like to tell
   The things I feel and see and sometimes think
Yet I can't catch and put them into ink—
   My thoughts are great—my speech so barren. Hell!"

And in impotent anger, kick the sand
And gesture vaguely with a toil-worn hand.

And sometimes they would put on leather gloves
   And therewith deal each other manful blows,
   Pausing perchance to shake a bleeding nose,
   Admire a leafy bough or budding rose,
Through loosened teeth quote poets songs of loves.
They took delights in rough and savage games,
Strong drink, and called each other scorching names.
Yet they would turn aside to smell a flower. Oftentimes
Would sit them down and seek to make some rhymes.

Then feeling their dim soul-glories wane, morosely go
To see a prize-fight or a picture show.

THE VIKING OF THE SKY

The skies are red before me
  And the skies are red behind,
Crimson clouds are roaring o'er me
  On the shouting of the wind.
And the world below is swinging
  Like a planet all a-fire
But I laugh, for I am winging
  Far above the stench and mire.

Slither and crawl
  In the gory muck
Writhe and fall
  In the battle ruck,
Muddy and bloody, curse and die!
I am aswing on the wings of the sky!

I rend through the veil that batteries cloak
I soar through the swirling world of smoke.
The flame-bursts leap like a fiery fount,
But I laugh, I laugh and I mount! I mount!
Into the oceans of white and blue
Where the wild wind giants hammer and hew.
Where air-fleet crashes on reeling fleet
And Death is racing on flaming feet.
Mid a sea of flame and a roar of strife,
This is Valhalla! This is Life!
Below the batteries hammer loud,
A lean plane leaps from a racing cloud!
The wide wings roar like a brazen drum,
On with the speed of the winds we come!
Death is my lover, Death my bride,
On my roaring wings she rides astride!
This is glory! My chest is bare
The wind-whips rip through my flying hair!
Over the smoke-cloud's crimson reach,

With the thrum of the Maxim's ripping screech!
Through clouds as fleecy and white as snow,
Till I see the face of the frenzied foe!
The flame spurts red and the smoke leaps blue
And a spear of Hell's-fire sears me through.
Ships so close that the flame jets cross,
His face turns blank as a Chinese joss!
His struck plane staggers, it dips to fore
And down he goes with a ripping roar!
Down, with a screech of loosened stays,
And a fusilage that leaps-ablaze!
And the red god roars on the shouting gale
As he rides that last, long, crimson trail!
The red smoke spirals where he fell
And he'll never stop till he lands in Hell.

This is glory! All else is chaff!
My chest is red but I laugh! I laugh!
Now to nose my ship for the fray,
I pass—but before I die—I'll slay!
Out where the surging smoke-fogs crowd
Into the depths of a red-fringed cloud!
In with a roar and out with a rip!
Straight for that circling enemy ship.
Cuddle that Maxim like girl or child,
Racing and roaring, glory wild!
All the firmament's reeling red
On we are racing head on head!
You and I and the bellowing skies!
Cuddle that Maxim, curse your eyes!
Now his frenzied volleys answer mine—
Got you center, you son of a swine!
The cannon peals and the wild wind brawls
He dips, he reels! He sways, he falls!
With a yell of stays ripped loose by the wrench
Down to fall in his comrades trench.
Now their batteries thunder loud,

Now their smoke leaps up like a cloud.
The great shells flash like living things
The shrapnel rips through my tattered wings.
I've known glory! I'm ready now!
Straight for the stars I turn my prow.
And a flame of Hell-fire follows me—
Little I care, I'm gloried, free!
I've known red living o'er man's weak law—
Smite! I'm ready—I'm ready—Ha!

VI

Human Baseness & Natural Depravity

While some have suggested this as a dominant theme in Howard—a close companion to the ascendance and necessary ultimate triumph of Barbarism—it is, after all, but one of many, as this overall selection of poetry is intended to demonstrate. But the theme is undeniably present and strongly represented. Howard's darker moods can gloom so darkly that they have, perhaps, dulled his multifaceted complexity—as if a jeweler were to have put a black opaque backing behind the set of a diamond instead of the usual reflective and enhancing surface of bright metal.

The theme that mankind is "Never Beyond the Beast" is, nonetheless, frequently expressed in Howard's poetry. It is the alter-ego to his less-known (certainly less critiqued) Biblical-inspired poetry, his light verse, and his praises of life, love, friendship, and creative inspiration. This theme is the grim nemesis to the occasional brighter moods that are also evident in his complete poetic opus.

THE CHANT DEMONIAC

I am Satan; I am weary,
  For my road is long and hard
And it lies through regions dreary
  Since the Golden Gates were barred.
    (I wait, I wait at the Flaming Gate
    I give men death and they give me hate.)
I am Satan, never resting
  For the scourge is at my back.
Yonder soul, his crimes attesting,
  To the fire, to the rack.
Yet another and another
  Will the tally never cease?
Turn from sin, I beg, my brother,
  Give a weary demon peace.
I am Satan, I am weary,
  By the ever flaming sea;
Ye who tread my regions dreary,
  Sinners, sinners, pity me.

DESTINY (2)

What is there real, my girl?
  Fair hair and a sparkling eye?
See, where the dust a-whirl
fades in a sombre sky.
What is there real, my love?
  Red lips and pearly teeth?
Ah, they are fair above,
  But a skull is grinning beneath.

A HAIRY-CHESTED IDEALIST SINGS

I was drunk, drunk, drunk!
Roaring drunk—wild drunk—raving drunk—killing drunk.
The blood hummed in my veins,
   and the muscles stood out on my arms.
My brain seethed inside my skull, and I was drunk.
I leaned against the bar and sang wild, rotten songs.
Spike opened his great empty slab of a face
And laughed like a mule bellowing.
I yelled, "Damn you, I've always wanted to do this!"
And I drove my iron fist into his face,
My fist into his face, with a hundred and eighty pounds
   of drunken Irish muscle behind it.
Down he went with a crash,
Down into the sawdust, down among the muddy feet,
Down among the spitoons,
And I split a keg of beer with my fist, and roared:
"Life! And the sting of Life! Laugh, you sons of Adam!"

I reeled out into the night,
And I saw lights and heard music.
   I saw men and women dancing;
Dancing, dancing—hip wriggling, shoulder shaking;
Dance and leap, proud dancers in the lamp light.
Each of you holds a skeleton—
   nod your bare skulls in the white light!
I watched them rasping their bodies against each other;
I watched them drink and go forth together
   into the darkness—
Men and Women, always into the darkness.
And I roared:
"Life! And the sting of Life! Laugh, you sons of Adam!"

I sat at the ringside and watched two young men,
Fierce and proud and strong in their youth,

Smash and batter each other.
They broke each other's jaws—
   they smashed each other's ribs,
They caved in each other's faces, blood drenched them;
They stood in blood.
And one felled the other with a blow
   that would have killed an ox.
And the loser fell close to the edge of the ring,
   and his skull gave way, and his brains came out.
And I plunged my hands deep into the blood
   and the brains, and I roared:
"Life! And the sting of Life! Laugh, you sons of Adam!"

I went into the brothels and saw the women.
The rooms were full of man-stench and woman-stench;
Rot-gut whisky perfumed the air, and unwashed bodies,
Sweat and tobacco smoke and stale beer.
Their laughter rose high and thin,
   and their kisses were slurring and empty.
And I roared:
"Life! And the sting of Life! Laugh, you sons of Adam!"

I staggered out into the red dawn.
Men crawled like ants along the ridges and the cliffs of
The brazen-souled buildings. And a scaffolding gave way.
Down they came, screaming and cursing,
Down four hundred feet like new-born souls coming to earth;
Their skulls broke, their brains flowed out,
   their blood splashed,
Their bones shattered. And again men crawled like ants
Along the ridges and the cliffs of the buildings.
And I roared:
"Life! And the sting of Life! Laugh, you sons of Adam!"

MARK OF THE BEAST

Kissing the lips of the morning
  The stars pale out in the East;
And my heart is grown cold with scorning
  The ancient mark of the Beast.

It is here, in my heart's red cavern,
  Black as a harlot's hate—
In cave and tower and tavern
  It has gripped me close to my Fate.

Over the verdant meadows
  Dawn comes out of the East—
Would with the fading shadows
  Faded the Night of the Beast.

His hands are set in my heart strings,
  His talons sink in my brain;
Shaking and silent his art sings
  Ever a red refrain.

Time nor the tunes may alter,
  Primitive, hairy, and nude—
Realm and race may falter
  Back to the solitude.

Back to the primal beaches,
  Back to the cave of the Ape;
Ever beyond there reaches
  A huge and abhorrent Shape.

Robert E. Howard

THE MEN THAT WALK WITH SATAN

The men that walk with Satan, they have forgot their birth.
Their dreams are lost in stillness in the ages of the earth.
White ghosts are in their sighing and death is in their mirth.

The men that walk with Satan, their years are as a day;
They know each generation as a dream that drifts away.
And they bid mankind make merry and revel while they may.

The men that walk with Satan, their eyes are ghostly meres;
They know no more the passions, the hatreds and the fears.
Their souls have turned to sea fog in the drifting of the years.

The men that walk with Satan, they know the gods are small
For they have trod the eons and seen the idols fall.
Their footsteps waked the echoes
   through proud Belshazzar's hall.

The men that walk with Satan,
   they feign would turn and sleep
But through their drowsing visions
   flames fierce and scarlet leap.
So they tread the years forever—
   and their eyes are strange and deep.

The men that walk with Satan, they sit where glories shine,
Where kings and lovely women grow radiant with wine;
But they see forgotten cities where the desert mosses twine.

The men that walk with Satan, they know that gold is rust,
No more they lash their spirits to stir their ancient lust;
Their sins are of the ages long crumbled to the dust.

The men that walk with Satan, they dream of ancient wars.
They stride the skies at even on sunset's burning bars.
The men that walk with Satan, their eyes are in the stars.

NEVER BEYOND THE BEAST

Rise to the peak of the ladder
   Where the ghosts of the planets feast—
Out of the reach of the adder—
   Never beyond the Beast.
He is there, in the abyss brooding,
   Where the nameless black fires fall;
He is there, in the stars intruding,
   Where the sun is a silver ball.

Beyond all weeping or revel,
   He lurks in the cloud and the sod;
He grips the doors of the Devil
   And the hasp on the gates of God.
Build and endeavor and fashion—
   Never can you escape
The blind black brutish passion—
   The lust of the primal Ape.

VII
Light & Risque Verses

We can be certain that many of the poems, fragments, and ditties Howard included in his letters to Tevis Clyde Smith (and a few other extant verses) were never intended for a broader readership than the recipient of the letter. However, as all writers learn, it is a potentially dangerous thing to commit ones thought to the page—it is giving something of oneself away.

In the case of authors and artists—actually, of all—who become famous, everything becomes "fair game" for critics and researchers who yearn for and learn—chiefly through extant jottings, poems, journals, and letters—the nature of their subject through often personal, private, or privileged writings. Such is the case with Howard's less–than–serious verse.

Bob Howard was no prude, and, by all accounts, he was well-accomplished in the remark "not for polite company" or the off-color joke or song. This can be seen from the poems in the following selections [which, as the *Complete Poetry* attests, is actually somewhat pale in comparison to a few poems that are <u>not</u> herein selected]. I have not included, for example, "The Inn of the Gory Dagger" and others of that ilk.

Both his light and humorous verses and the more bawdy renditions to follow exhibit frequent use of parody, spinning off the originals of Robert W. Service, Rudyard Kipling, Edward Fitzgerald, and others. Howard was a masterful parodist. It was one of the developing characteristics of his virtuosity and range as a poet that he enjoyed mimicking poetic styles and forms.

Howard also shows a distinct talent for capturing dialect and poetic "tone of voice." Dialect especially is a difficult thing to bring off through text on the page—at least as difficult as mimicking voice patterns in oral declamation, since the text needs to force the reader to "hear" the dialect.

AN AMERICAN EPIC

The autumn sun was gettin' low, the day was mighty windy,
When Hiram shot the hired man that kissed his girl Dorindy.
Them two was in the orchard there,
    for apples birds was peckin'
When old man Hiram hove in view
    and busted up their neckin'.
The hired man he took it out across the fields and ditches
But Hiram drawed a perfect bead
    and shot him in the breeches.
The hired man he flagged it on, for he knew other ladies—
But Robert Frost can write the rest, or he can go to Hades.

ANCIENT ENGLISH BALLADEL

O come, friend Dick, go whoring with me!
    The summer moon is ripe.
The trees dream by the crescent lea,
The ships sail on the silver sea—
Oh come, good Dick, go whoring with me!
    For life is a lot of tripe.

Over the waste we 'ull go in haste,
    And over the barren down;
There's many a whore that waits by her door
    In the streets of the sea-port town.

There's many a white rump ripe, Dick,
    In the tavern and the town;
Girls that are rosy and white, Dick,
    To fill your soul with delight, Dick,
And surely you have the right, Dick,
    So over the hill and down!

They have given their bloomers to charity
   For them they will need no more.
They wiggle their hips along the quay
   And the outbound sailors roar,
They wiggle their hips at the port bound ships
   And the seamen swim to the shore.

We will join the dames in their blithesome games
   And add to their natural heat,
And they will be true to us, Dick,
   And the Asiatic fleet.

I know the girl for you, Dick,
   She will wake in you a song,
For seventy million Frenchmen
   Can't be wrong.

The moon dreams on the silver lea,
   Each star, gold wings unfurls;
The moon road carves the ivory sea.
   Come, let us go to our girls.

A BALLAD OF BEER

I was once, I declare, a grog-shop man
   And I lolled in the cool of a bar;
I have known, I will swear, in a new life's span,
   A desert where no springs are.
For far over all that folks hold dear
   In me there lives and leaps
A love of the lowly stuff called beer,
   A passion for foaming deeps.
To fill my glass with no paltry plan,
   To guzzle and swig at will,
To mock at the raging revenue man
   And steep my soul in swill.
To scorn all strife and view all life
   With the goofy eyes of a drunk,
From the dizzy sea to the hangman's tree,
   From the saint to the heart of the skunk.
From the boozy king to the beggar stewed,
   From gin to the saki stall,
For I know that the beer for good was brewed
   And I want to drink it all.
To drink it all! The good brown beer,
   From the pub to society ball,
With never a bouncer to kick my rear
   Or slam me with a maul.
With pink D.T.s I will pay the wage,
   But leave my guzzling free,
For once I know in a bygone age
   They made a Dry of me.

Robert E. Howard

THE BAR BY THE SIDE OF THE ROAD

There are liquorless souls that follow paths
    Where whiskey never ran—
Let me live in a bar by the side of the road
    And drink from the old beer can.

Let me live in a bar by the side of the road
    Where the race of man goes dry,
The men who are "drys" and the men who are "wets"
    (But none are so "wet" as I.)

I see from the bar by the side of the road,
    A land with a drouth accurst;
And men who press on with the ardour of beer,
    And men who are faint with thirst.

I know there are bars in Old Mexico,
    And schooners of glorious height.
That the booze splashes on through the long afternoon,
    And floods through the gutters of night.

But still I take gin when the travellers take gin
    And Scotch with the whiskey man,
Nor ever refuse a thirsty soul
    A swig from my old beer can.

For why should I praise Prohibition's restraints,
    Or love the revenue man?
Let me live in a bar by the side of the road
    And drink from the old beer can!

THE KISSING OF SAL SNOOBOO

(editor's note: a parody of Robt. W. Serives's poem
"The Shooting of Dan McGrew")

A bunch of the girls were whooping it up
  In the old Lip-stick saloon,
And the kid at the player-piano
  Was twanging a jazzy tune,
When out of the night with perfume on his shirt
  And Stacomb upon his hair,
A young man staggered inside the door
  And meowed like a grizzly-bear.
He kicked the kid off the piano stool
  And sat him down to play.
The piano yowled like an old tom cat
  To the tune of "Hip! Hurray!"
Says he, "Gals, you don't know me,
  But, by gosh, I know you,
And one of you is a classy dame,
  And that one is Sal Snooboo!"

She squawked and somebody turned the lights,
  Something went "Smack!" in the dark.
There was nothing for anybody to do
  But to stand still and snigger and hark.
Somebody turned the lights on,
  And Sally was standing there,
But the stranger wasn't; he was done,
  And Sal was arranging her hair.

Robert E. Howard

THE MAIDEN OF KERCHEEZER

She was snoozing on her sweezer,
  Many a goofish year ago,
And a smile was on her beezer,
  As she gently scratched her toe.

She, the Maiden of Kercheezer,
  Hair as black as a harness tug,
As it fluttered in the breezer,
  O'er her lovely, girlish mug.

Evening dress of green and yeller,
  What a shoulder she could shake
And she had a nifty feller,
  Hight the knight of Duckandrake.

He was knock-kneed, she was cross-eyed,
  Oh, they were a lovely pair,
How he'd fondly knock her hoss-eyed,
  As she gently pulled out his hair.

And her folks didn't like his beezer,
  But what difference did that make?
And the maiden of Kercheezer, ever
  Eloped with noble Duckandrake.

NECTAR

When I stand at the gates of Paradise
  I will wipe my brow and say:
"It's a long path and a dusty path
  The path I have walked today.

"It's a hot path and a dry path
  From Hell to Paradise—
Oh Peter, my boy, have ye never now
  A bit of a bottle on ice?"

"Patrick, me lad, I've saved ye wan,
  It's thirsty ye'd be, I knew!"
And he'll fetch me a bottle black and cold,
  Of the paradisal brew.

Oh, a bottle black and beaded cold,
  And the liquid amber and clear,
With the sparkling foam and the right sharp tang—
  And I'll drink his health in the beer.

And when I pass through the Golden Gates
  I'll see ten thousand signs:
"Judas & Co.," "Sargon & Cain"—
  "Liquors and Ales and Wines"!

Lined each side of the silver streets,
  Gemmed with many a star,
With flaming moons for electric lights—
  Each building in heaven a bar!

Robert E. Howard

THE PASSIONATE TYPIST

My love, to you this verse I pen,
　　Without you I am dust—
With you, I am most blest of men—
　　Oh, Lord, a key has bust.

Oh, seize our hour while we may!
　　Live while we yet are young!
Oh, come, my love, let's waft away—
　　Oh, gosh, the space bar's hung.

Oh, come, the city's clamor flout!
　　Come to some grassy bank!
Oh, Hell, the ribbon's worn out,
　　Oh, blank-blank-blank-blank-blank!

A POET'S SKULL

My empty skull is full of dust,
  I have no beer to drink;
I would the Queen her rump would bust
  Upon a skating rink.

As I was going down the street
  I met with Rabelay;
Said he, "I have no dung to eat
  "Upon my wedding day."

"Be of good cheer, my boy," said I,
  And smote him in the back.
"On yonder horizon I spy
  An oscillating jack."

With loud acclaim he praised my name
  With fame that should endure;
I left him singing like a child,
  While fishing in the sewer.

And down the street, by merest chance,
  I met de Maupason;
Quoth I, "My friend, where are your pants?
  "You have not got them on."

He smiled a Mona Lisa smile.
  "Sacre by damn!" said he.
"The lousy wop is full of guile,
  "And likewise the Chinee."

"But now," his eyes with ardour shined,
  His shirt waved like a sail,
"I go in woodland lanes to find
  "Material for a tale."

"Material for a—what?" I said.
  He briskly marched away.
The bawdy lamps were glowing red;
  I heard a street-band play.

And hand in hand, the stars they ran,
  The seas were full of beer;
And down the street an aged man
  Came spinning on his ear.

Around, around, around he spun,
  And never a word he spake,
With awful leers he ate a ton
  Of fish and ginger cake.

His foot was on a hell-cat's tail,
  Her back a Gothic arch;
The stars came down like blazing hail,
  And sang the Wedding March.

With evil grin he wagged his shin,
  And round and round he whirled;
His hair was combed by all the winds
  That roam around the world.

A figure whipped along the street,
  Like a sparrow in the rain;
Such boots were his as case their feet
  Who tramp the Spanish Main.

He strode to sound of magic lutes,
  Oh, red the wine he drank!
Kit Marlowe in his Spanish boots
  With rapier at flank.

A SAPPE THER WOS
AND THAT A CRUMBE MANNE

[ed. note: Move over Chaucer!]

A sappe ther wos and that a crumbe manne
Whoe from the timee that he firs beganne
To jazzen oute he loved rapery,
And many a damsel sat himme on his knee.
As far as goeth manne he had wente,
And many a virgin's gude name hadde bente.
Betimes among the dames of seventeen,
And jazzen all the nighte at Racine.
To Philadelphia hadde been alsoe
Ageyne another trull in Chicagoe.
And many a damsel hadde proved fickle,
"Gude sirs," quothe, "A maiden for an ickle
"Her pantys taken down for any manne,
"I hode you sirs, ageyne the whole damn clanne."
And forthwith bought a ticket to New Yorke
Because Hisse wife expected ther the storke.

VIII

Love, Lust, & Sensuality

Those who have seen Howard as a poet of little range and a soul obsessed with a nihilistic and cynical outlook have read neither the letters nor the poems carefully enough.

As the present text and its various sections hope to prove, Howard was a poet with a broad range of topics, thoughts, and emotions. Some of the most interesting of Howard's verses are on the topics of Love, Sensuality, and Lust. Despite what some critics and amateur psychologists have alleged regarding Howard's libido, romantic escapades—or the lack thereof—there is ample support in the poetry to suggest a very typical—and normal—young man (despite the obviously abnormally active imagination and acute creative abilities) with very typical urges.

There is also ample textual evidence, to suggest at least, that Howard acted upon those urges, knew passion, and certainly knew love—albeit the likelihood that these were often competing against and frequently losing to the necessities of making a living, honing his art, and attending to family matters, including, of course, his mother's failing health.

Some of the poems in this section, including: the hauntingly significant "Bride of Cuchulain," the sensuous and finely-wrought sonnets like "Desire" and "Flaming Marble," the confessional tone of "And so his boyhood wandered into youth,"* the fantastic vision of "Heart of the Sea's Desire," and in such (for his era) taboo topics as we find in "Lesbia"—all should suffice to convince the reader that Howard's poetry covers at least as broad and perhaps even a broader spectrum of topic, theme, thought, and emotion than does his fiction.

[*entitled "Fragment" in all previous collections]

AND SO HIS BOYHOOD
WANDERED INTO YOUTH*

And so his boyhood wandered into youth,
   And still the hazes thickened round his head,
   And red, lascivious nightmares shared his bed
And fantasies with greedy claw and tooth
Burrowed into the secret parts of him—
   Gigantic, bestial and misshapen paws
Gloatingly fumbled each white youthful limb,
   And shadows lurked with scarlet gaping jaws.

Deeper and deeper in a twisting maze
   Of monstrous shadows, shot with red and black,
Or gray as dull decay and rainy days,
   He stumbled onward. Ever at his back
He heard the lecherous laughter of the ghouls.
Under the fungoid trees lay stagnant pools
   Wherein he sometimes plunged up to his waist
   And shrieked and scrambled out with loathing haste,
Feeling unnumbered slimy fingers press
His shrinking flesh with evil, dank caress.

Life was a cesspool of obscenity—
   He saw through eyes accursed with unveiled sight—
   Where Lust ran rampant through a screaming Night
And black-faced swine roared from the Devil's styes;
Where grinning corpses, fiend-inhabited,
   Walked through the world with taloned hands outspread;
   Where beast and monster swaggered side by side,
And unseen demons strummed a maddening tune;
   And naked witches, young and brazen-eyed,
Flaunted their buttocks to a lustful moon.

Rank, shambling devils chased him night on night,
  And caught and bore him to a flaming hall,
Where lambent in the flaring crimson light
  A thousand long-tongued faces lined the wall.
  And there they flung him, naked and a-sprawl
Before a great dark woman's ebon throne.
How dark, inhuman, strange, her deep eyes shone!

[*entitled "Fragment" in all previous collections]

THE BRIDE OF CUCHULAIN

Love, we have laughed at living,
  Love, we have laughed at death;
  At ecstasy and giving, and all vain things of breath.

We know, for we rent the curtain
  To gaze behind the lure,
  That naught but death is certain,
    that naught but death is pure.

From our thrones of ivory, flattered
  The scarlet courtiers come;
  Challenging ages hoary, pulses the regal drum.

But the breeze of the night is dreary
  And the moon is bent and old
  And your head on my breast is weary
    and my soul is thin and cold.

Come to the upland meadows,
  Come to the ocean grey;
  We and the world are shadows swiftly drifting away.

There, where the grey sea crashes
  Along the ancient shore,
  There where the spent spray lashes white sands forevermore,

I will weave the pale sea flowers
  To twine on your pallid brow
  That you may forget lost hours and Time be only Now.

Then all Earth's joys and sorrows
  Shall pass like ocean spray
  Till all the sad tomorrows fade in one dim Today.

Robert E. Howard

A CHALLENGE TO BAST

Come not to me, Bubastes,
  With agate talons hid,
Veil not the fury of your eyes
  Beneath the drooping lid.

Save all your gentleness for those
  Mad passion makes aghast,
For they who are too frail to face
  Your love's unholy blast.

But come to me as you of old
  Your demon lovers met—
A black, stark naked frenzied thing
  Of ebony and jet.

Where jackals haunt the shadows
  In the star-light's yellow glow
With bodies writhing savagely,
And teeth that gnash in ecstasy,
We'll glut all hidden splendors
  That maddened passions know.

THE DAY BREAKS OVER SIMLA

Near a million dawns have burst
  Scarlet over Jakko's hill
Since our burning kisses first
  Mingled in the twilight still,
  In the magic, sapphire dusk
    when our passions drank their fill.

I remember how the moon
  Floated over shadowed dells
And the mellow mystic tune
  Of the tinkling temple bells—
  Ere Siddertha's people turned
    to the braying sea-conch shells.

Lips to scarlet lips we pressed
  Ah, your eyes were star lit meres
As your tresses I caressed
  Calmed your modest virgin fears—
  Love upon an Indian night,
    love to last a thousand years.

Fades the rosy dawn as slow
  Morning flames across the plain;
With a sigh I turn and go
  Humming some old time refrain
  To the consul house as day
    over Simla breaks again.

DESIRE

"Turn out the light." I raised a willing hand
  And plunged the room into the silken, cool
  Darkness in which the deeper passions rule;
Your tresses snared me with each moon-lit strand,
Your soft breasts sent warm raptures through my hand.
  I felt your slim, fresh body close to mine,
  The blood went racing through my veins like wine
And my desire was like a flaming brand.

The pulsing world was as a couch for us;
  The brittle moon that flung her silver down
A jewel mystical and luminous
  Enshrined and fashioned in our passion's crown;
    The dusky, deep sapphirean sky above
    A star-ensplendored canopy for love.

EGYPT

Bubastes! Down the lank and sullen years
  Your magic haunts my dreams in distant lands,
  My old desire assails me with red brands;
I see the god that o'er your shoulder leers,
Your eyes, your eyes like mystic midnight meres—
  Your body quivering to my questing hands—
  Why do you beckon me across the sands?
Have you not other victims to your spears?

There is no dream, but your long narrow eyes
Bring back the days of Egypt's dusky skies.
  Fair Bast! I come! I know you wait me there,
    And I must feel again, like singing wine,
  Your slender fingers flutter through my hair,
    Your slim, white body nestling close to mine.

FLAMING MARBLE

I carved a woman out of marble when
  The walls of Athens echoed to my fame:
  And in the myrtle crown was shrined my name.
I wrought with skill beyond all earthly ken;
And into cold, inhuman beauty then
  I breathed a mist of white and living flame—
  And from her pedestal she rose and came
To snare the souls and rend the hearts of men.

Without a soul, without a human heart
  She broke the crystal gong of mortal pride.
And even I fell victim to my art:
  With bitter, joyous love I claimed my bride.
   And still with frozen hate that never dies
   She sits and stares at me with icy eyes.

THE GLADIATOR AND THE LADY

When I was a boy in Britain
   and you were a girl in Rome,
Forests and mountains lay between,
   and the hungry, restless foam.
Today naught lay between us,
   only the wall, at least,
That guards the proud patrician
   from the slave and the dying beast.
Our hearts we read that instant
   my eyes with your eyes met,
But there were swords to sunder
   and life blood to be let.
And you will marry a consul
   and live on the Palatine
And I will take some slave girl
   from the Garonne or the Rhine.
But you will dream at the banquet,
   while the roses scent the air
Of a blazing eyed barbarian
   with a shock of yellow hair.
And through the roar of the lions
   and the clang of sword and mace,
I'll dream of a pair of dark deep eyes
   and a proud patrician face.
We still are as far asunder
   as the hut and the arch and dome
When I was boy in Britain
   and you were a girl in Rome.

THE HEART OF THE SEA'S DESIRE

The stars beat up from the shadowy sea,
  The caves of the coral and pearl,
And the night is afire with a red desire
  For the loins of a golden girl.
You have left your girdle upon the beach,
  And you wade from the pulsing land,
And the hot tide darts to your secret parts
  That have known one lover's hand.
The hot tide laves your rounded limbs,
  That his subtle fingers part,
And the sea that lies between your thighs
  Is the heart of the Night's red heart.
In the days to come and the nights to come,
  And the days and the nights to be,
A babe you shall hold to your breast of gold
  As you croon a lullaby;
A babe with the cry of a wind-racked gull,
  That shall grow to a round-limbed girl
With strange cold eyes like the sea that lies
  In the caves of coral and pearl.
Her soul shall be as an ocean wind,
  Restless her feet shall be,
And she shall be part of the Night's red heart,
  And the heart of the sounding sea.
And the man who lies by your side at night,
  He is not your daughter's sire;
For she is the babe of a hungry Night,
  And the heart of the sea's desire!

KERESA, KERESITA

Keresa, Keresita,
  An echo shivers far
To the whispering groves and the star-lit pools
  Where the woodland shadows are
And over the crest of the silver hills
  Hovers a quivering star.

There are eyes in the curve of the river
  Where the night-veiled willows mass
There are feet that are lighter than forest deer
  Through the dim, tall, waving grass
And ruffling the waves of the silver lakes
  The murmuring night winds pass.

Keresa, Keresita,
  Follow the night winds track.
There's a strange, wild thrill on the wings of night
  And the wind that comes not back.
Come to blue of a star-flecked sky
  And the forest's silver and black.

Keresa, Keresita,
  Great Pan's abroad this night,
I hear them whisper among the leaves
  Dryad and nymph and sprite,
Come to my arms and the couch of ferns
  And the mellow silvery light.

LESBIA

From whence this grim desire?
  What was the wine in my blood?
What raced through my veins like fire
  And beat at my brain like a flood?

Bare is the desert's dust,
  Deep is the emerald sea—
Barer my deathless lust,
  Deeper the hunger of me.

Goddess I sit and brood—
  They cringe to my Hell-lit eyes,
The wretched women nude
  I have gripped between my thighs.

As they writhed between my hands
  And the ocean heard their screams
Firing my passion's brands
  As I dreamed my lurid dreams.

Their breath came fast and hot,
  Their tresses were Hades' mesh;
World and the worlds were not;
  Flesh against pulsing flesh.

Their white limbs fluttered and tossed,
  They whimpered beneath my grasp
And their maidenhood was lost
  In strange unnatural clasp.

Hours my pleasure beguiled
  The green Arcadian glades,
As idle mornings I whiled
  With free-hipped country maids.

Under the star-gemmed skies
  That looked upon curious scenes
I have spread the round white thighs
  Of naked and frightened queens.

What was it turned my face
  From brown-limbed Grecian boys,
Weary of their embrace
  To darker and barer joys?

A miser weary of coins
  I wearied of early charms,
Of youths who ungirt my loins,
  Restless sighed in their arms.

With many a youth I lay,
  But their wine to me was dregs.
I found scant joy in they
  Who parted my supple legs.

I turned to the loves I prize;
  Found joy amid perfumed curls,
In a maiden's amorous sighs,
  In the tears of naked girls.

These are the wine of delight—
  A girl's ungirdled charms,
A woman's laugh in the night
  As she lies in my eager arms.

Goddess I sit and laugh,
  Nude as the scornful moon—
World and the worlds are chaff.
  Say, shall my day be soon?

LOVE

I have felt your lips on mine
  Your hair has veiled my eyes
When my blood was wild as singing wine
  And star-gold flecked the skies.

We have watched the moonlight dance
  On the breast of the still lagoon
But now I am tired of your changeless glance
  In the eye of the wrinkled moon.

What have you given me
  To name as an ultimate bliss?
Am I more strong, more free?
  What slavery is this?
For a single star on the dusky sea
  I would barter your hottest kiss.

Robert E. Howard

LOVE'S YOUNG DREAM

I saw the evil red light gleam
  Above the brothel door;
I entered in as in a dream
  And climbed the stair once more.

I caught the stench of hairy men
  And sweat and smoke and beer,
And cutting through the smudgy din
  Her empty laugh rose clear.

I stood within her littered room
  That opened on the hall;
I saw the flasks of cheap perfume
  And the pictures on the wall.

Her hat was tossed on a broken chair,
  A coat lay on the floor;
Cheap cigarettes made sick the air
  That seeped through the sagging door.

And all my dreams sank down to fade,
  And yet the girl stood there,
That I had visioned a laughing maid
  With a blossom in her hair.

The girl I dreamed she might have been
  Fades before she that is—
But I'll forget as do all men
  In passion's barren bliss.

For she runs with Life a parallel—
  The dream and its rotten core—
For Life's a harlot out of hell
  With a red light over her door.

THE MYTH

Sages have said, we leave our sex on earth
   When take we our departure through the skies;
And that a soul is done with sensual mirth,
   When from this worldly sphere the ego flies.

We soar with white, unpassioned wings, and placid feet
   Lead ne'er o'er ways that we have trod before,
And up and down and o'er the Golden Street,
   We twang our harps and chant forever more.

They say that Passion's kiss there none will know;
   No eager-breasted girl, nor clean-limbed boy;
The sages sing a tedious land, I trow,
   For when ye steal the sex, ye steal the joy.

For all of worldly life is versed in Sex,
   All that is fair and foul, or fine or fell,
It may fling down, uplift or merely vex,
   Yet tis the wine of gods and flame of Hell.

We polish Vice, we scoff it and we hide,
   And yet it is the wine of Life, the spice,
I cannot see how human soul might bide,
   Forever in a barren Paradise.

Nay, this bare myth doth mock the very Name
   For He made Beauty, strong, and clean and lithe,
But eld, self-righteous sinners, failed in shame,
   They hated Beauty, so they built the myth.

REPENTANCE

How is it that I am what I am
  How did I come to fall?
Who was the man my soul to damn
  Black in the sight of all?
Who was it came in my virgin hood
  And in some evil hour
Turned all my life to bad from good
  Bruising the tender flower?
I cannot remember the fellow's name
  I had long ago forgot;
I was young and my blood was flame
  The person mattered not.
I was hot as a blazing brand
  Blood and body and nerve
Ripe to be plucked by the first man's hand
  And any man would serve.
I have had my day, I have had my fling
  Men have bowed at my knee.
I sit in the bars where the harlots sing
  To sailors hot from the sea.
Sallow my cheeks and my lips have faded
  Life's roses slip my clutch
But my blood is still hot and still unjaded
  I can thrill to a deck-hand's touch.
Still I thrill to the hands of men
  I love the contact yet
The breath that is laden with wharfside gin
  The scent of tobacco and sweat.
Bristly jowls on my painted cheek
  The obscene, whispered jest,
Calloused hands that lustfully seek
  My out-worn charms to quest.
My by-gone life is dim and far;
  I am content with gin,
A slug of wine, sometimes at the bar,
  A room for the sailormen.

THE ROBES OF THE RIGHTEOUS

I am a saintly reformer,
   basking in goodly renown
Sure of applaud of the righteous,
   cinctured in purity's gown.
Young men and old men revere me,
   women and girls out of school
Come to me telling their secrets,
   seeking my counseling cool.
Little they know of my story
   when I was the water-front's toast.
Back in the days of my glory
   down on the Barbary Coast.
Young and my lips full and crimson,
   flaming with passionate blood,
My love was the leap of an ocean,
   my passion the swing of a flood.
Changing and varied my fancies
   yet no woman ever gave more
For I joyed in the man on my body
   just as much as the one just before
Ah, nights that were lurid and gorgeous,
   under the bar lamps blaze
Flutter of cards on the table,
   faces that leered through the haze
Of smoke drifting up from the stogies,
   the red liquor flowing free
And the shout of the salty ballads
   that sailors sang from the sea.
The money scattered like water,
   the pagan thrill of the dance
The hand that groped in my clothing,
   the burning and meaning glance
Then the look as the stair I mounted,
   the man that left the floor,

The joyous and panting waiting,
    the stealthy knock at my door—
What if they knew, the elders,
    that I was a Barbary whore?
Hiding my charms with meekness
    under purity's gown
Sure of applaud of the righteous,
    basking in goodly renown.

A ROMAN LADY

There is a strangeness in my soul
    A dark and brooding sea.
Nor all the waves on Capri's shoal
    Might stay the thirst of me.
For men have come and men have gone
    For pleasure and for hire.
Though they lay broken at the dawn
    They did not quench my fire.
My pity is a deathly ruth
    I burn men with my eyes.
Oh, would all men were one strong youth
    To break between my thighs.
And many a man his fortune spread
    To glut my ecstasy
As I lay panting on his bed
    In shameless nudity.
But all of ancient Egypt's gold
    Can never equal this,
Nor all the treasures kingdoms hold,
    A single hour of bliss.
Within my villa's high domain
    Are boys from Britain's rocks
And dark eyed slender lads from Spain
    And Greeks with perfumed locks.

And youths of soft and subtle speech
   From furtherest Orient,
Wherever arms of legions reach
   And Roman chains are sent.
Why may I not be satiate
   With kisses of some boy—
They only rouse my passions spate
   I never know such joy
As when through chambers filled with noise
   Of wails and pleas and sighs
I stride among my naked boys
   With whips that bruise their thighs.
I drift through mists red flaming flung
   On hills of ecstasies
As shoulder-wealed and buttock-stung
   They shriek and kiss my knees.

SCARLET AND GOLD
ARE THE STARS TONIGHT

Scarlet and gold are the stars tonight,
   The river runs silver below the bridge—
But the hour shall come when the dawn grows white
   Over the eastern ridge.

Your face is a dim white flower of night,
   In your arms unheeded the hours fall—
But the dawn makes hearts grow strange and light,
   And the far lands call.

Robert E. Howard

THE SEA GIRL

My love is the girl of the jade green gown
  And strange, inscrutable eyes;
She is slower far to smile than to frown
  And her laugh is the wrath of the skies.

Her footsteps fall where the wild winds flee,
  Her kiss is the touch of Fate;
And her love, the love that she gives to me
  Is crueler than her hate.

The beautiful women of human ken,
  They ravish man's love away;
But my girl tramples the bones of men
  And mingles their souls with spray.

Pensive and quiet and fraught with guile
  She dreams when the gulls drift free,
But her strange lips bide white teeth and her smile
  Is the song of the Lorelei.

Yet her wind-blown voice is an urge and a spur
  That bids me follow her fast
Though I know that I, through my love of her,
  Shall come to my death at last.

Shall lie in her arms mid the sea-deeps green
  Where the dim, lost tides go down,
Yet I would not trade for a white-armed queen
  My girl of the jade green gown.

THUS IN MY MOOD I LOVE YOU

To a Woman (3)

Thus in my mood I love you
  In the drum of my heart's fast beat,
In the lure of the skies above you
  And the earth beneath your feet.

Now I can lift and crown you
  With the moon's white empery,
Now I can crush and drown you
  In my passion's misty sea.

I can swing you high and higher
  Than any man of earth,
Draw you through stars and fire
  To lands of the ultimate birth.

Were I like this forever
  You'd only too little to give,
But here tonight we sever
  For life loves life to live.

And the higher a man may travel
  The lower may he fall
And the skein that I must unravel
  It was never meant for all.

TO A NAMELESS WOMAN

1

Hard shadows break along the smoky hills,
  Clear etched against a cold blue marble sky.
  Along the north the purple lances lie.
To hint the gems that hoard of winters spills,
Glimmering treasure from some earth-troll's tills.
  A thin and bitter wind is whispering by;
  And in my heart a dream that will not die,
Shatters my crystal soul with tremored thrills.

Scarcely a breath divides us, yet apart
  We stand as though an ocean lay between.
    A silence falls—and you seem strange and cold.
Perish, my dream, and die, my empty heart.
  For in your eyes I see a mystic sheen
    Inhuman wondrous and inhuman old.

2

I am a breath upon a summer sea,
  My feet have never trod these ways before,
  Forgotten, I shall tread these roads no more.
But in your heart pulse throbs Eternity.
You were, you are, and evermore shall be;
  And you have heard the emerald oceans roar
  On many a dim and naiad-haunted shore,
And ghostly kings have worshipped at your knee.

I am an infant wailing in the night,
  Trembling before the knowledge that is yours.
    Under your heart unborn Tomorrow sings.
  And not for me your eon lent allures.
Since I have seen your dusky eyes alight
    With sudden memory of forgotten things.

IX

Nihilism, Futility, & Disillusionment

While the preceding section offered a sampling of some of Howard's sensual, erotic, even romantic moods and reflections, it must be acknowledged that his often-stated and variously expressed world view gives clear evidence of a sense of disillusionment and futility. The inescapability from an ultimate barbaric triumph and the notion that humankind in general has never gone and, ultimately, can never go "beyond the beast" are frequently encountered in his poetry as well as thematically in his prose.

Some of his poems go so far as to express a stark nihilism—not that uncommon in the disillusioned years following "The Great War," and a sense that affected many artists across the many arts.

The term "Great Depression" applies to much more than an economic crisis. And, as Henry Adams had envisioned and pronounced as early as the beginning of the century, we had likely unleashed forces through technology and science that would prove to be beyond human control.

The old order was changing, giving place to new, but it wasn't the change foreseen in the "Cosmic Optimism" of the Age of the Victorians, believers in the ideals of Progress and Manifest Destiny; it was the new order of Yeats's beast that "slouches toward Bethlehem to be born."

AFTER THE TRUMPS ARE SOUNDED

After the trumps are sounded
　　Over the fading world
After the drums are silent
　　And the lastmost flag is furled,
May we enjoy what we long for
　　A boon that we sinners may tell
The most that we have to hope for
　　A comfortable berth in Hell.

ALWAYS COMES EVENING

Riding down the road at evening
　　with the stars for steed and shoon
I have heard an old man singing
　　underneath a copper moon;
"God, who gemmed with topaz twilights,
　　opal portals of the day,
"On our amaranthine mountains,
　　why make human souls of clay?

"For I rode the moon-mare's horses
　　in the glory of my youth,
"Wrestled with the hills at sunset—
　　till I met brass-tinctured Truth.
"Till I saw the temples topple,
　　till I saw the idols reel,
"Till my brain had turned to iron,
　　and my heart had turned to steel.

"Satan, Satan, brother Satan,
　　fill my soul with frozen fire;
"Feed with hearts of rose-white women
　　ashes of my dead desire.

"For my road runs out in thistles
  and my dreams have turned to dust.
"And my pinions fade and falter
  to the raven wings of rust.

"Truth has smitten me with arrows
  and her hand is in my hair—
"Youth, she hides in yonder mountains—
  go and see her, if you dare!
"Work your magic, brother Satan,
  fill my brain with fiery spells.
"Satan, Satan, brother Satan,
  I have known your fiercest Hells."

Riding down the road at evening
  when the wind was on the sea,
I have heard an old man singing,
  and he sang most drearily
Strange to hear, when dark lakes shimmer
  to the wailing of the loon,
Amethystine Homer singing
  under evening's copper moon.

AND SO I SANG

They bade me sing, but all I could sing,
  in the glory and the shine,
Was: "Man is a toy on a tinsel string,
  and Life is a broken shrine."
But the women's laughter drowned me out,
  and mirth went rattling through.
"And once again you must sing, my friend,
  and let your songs be true!"
But while skulls leered from a woman's eyes,
  and hunger looked from the wine:
And I sang: "Mankind is a blinded toy,
  and Life is a broken shrine."

And the music blared and the women laughed
   and a song rattling through.
And the dancers whirled through the scarlet mist,
   scarlet and white and blue.
But a strange voice sang through the din and mirth
   for a symbol and a sign:
"Man is a toy on the string of the gods,
   and Life is a broken shrine."

A BEGGAR, SINGING WITHOUT

A beggar, singing without:
   "Now are the stars upbraiding!
   Strange and futile and fading—
This is a moon-mazed world!
   Ere ever the stars were raiding
Or the first faint sail unfurled,
   The gods were mazed at the riddle
And the priests made dreams and lies
   That man should fry on the griddle
Or ride the horse of the skies.
   And what is life but a vision,
And what are the rules of the game
   But a cynical high derision
That laughs at glory and shame?"

I PRAISE MY NATIVITY

Oh, evil the day that I was born,
  like a tale that a witch has told;
I came to birth on a bitter morn,
  when the sky was dim and cold.
The god that girds the loins of Fate
  and sends the nighttime rain,
He diced my game on an iron plate
  with dice carved out of pain.
"This for the shadow of hope," laughed he,
  as the numbers glinted up,
"This for a spell and this for Hell,
  and this for the bitter cup."
A Shadow came out of the gloom of night
  and covered me with his cowl
That carried the curse of The Truer Sight
  and the blindness of the owl.
Oh, evil the day that I was born,
  triply I curse that day,
And I would to God I had died that morn
  and passed like the ocean spray.

LIFE [VERSION 1]

About me rise the primal mists
  The road is eerie, dim and grey
Strong shackles load my weary wrists
  I see no light to lead my way.
    No gleam that heralds coming day.
      Far out, far out beyond my ken
    The mazy stars, they whirl and sway
      But I must tramp a sullen fen
   That clogs my weary feet with clay.
     Oh, world of men, oh, world of men.
     I laughed, I dreamed my dreams and then
I started on my road, the way
  O'er which my feet ever must stray,
  Must tread forever and for aye.

LONGFELLOW REVISED

[ed. note: a reply to Longfellow's "Psalm of Life"]

Tell me not in senseless numbers,
  Life is not an empty dream,
If there is a soul, it slumbers,
  Things are sordid as they seem.

Fame and fortune, take no heeding,
  In this round of greed and lust,
But to work—each day succeeding,
  Finds us nearer—to the dust.

Lives of great men all remind us,
  We can make our lives sublime.
And departing leave behind us,
  Dust upon the sands of time.

A MAN

I tore a pine from the mountain crag
  I plunged it into the sea
And I wrote my name across the stars
  For all of Eternity.
I rocked the world with my chariots
  I shook the seas with my pride
And at last I looked at my name in the stars
  And I laid me down and died.
The morns gave birth to the surging years
  Year rose on dying year
But ever above in the flaming stars
  My name stood blazing clear.
And the people came and the people went
  With their fetters and chains and bars,
Saying, "I wonder what unknown man
  "Those strange words wrote on the stars?"

MEN ARE TOYS ON A GODLING'S STRING

Men are toys on a godling's string;
  All of the world is chaff.
Glory and honor, let them sing:
  I am content to laugh.

MONARCHS

These be the kings of men,
  Lords of the Ultimate Night,
Kings of the desert and fen—
  Jackal, vulture and kite.

REBEL SOULS FROM THE FALLING DARK

Rebel souls from the falling dark,
  What are the crowns you gain?
The quenching night of a dungeon stark
  And the brine of the rusty chain.
The taunt and the tang of the bitter blood,
  And the grim of the grisly bars,
The friar's chant and the hangman's hood—
  And a star amid the stars!

X
Poems On Poetry Itself, Poets, Inspiration, & the Imagination

Some of the most interesting and well-wrought of Howard's verses are on the topics of the imagination itself and poetic inspiration and its sources. Some other poems also address the nature of poetry or comment on other poets—or, in the case of "Another Hymn of Hate," as scholar Rusty Burke notes, we find an amusing take on the poet's experiences with critics and editors.

It is clear that he thought a great deal about the origins and nurturing of poetic art. It is also completely clear through the poems and the letters that Howard was a voracious reader of poetry and a self-taught practitioner of its mighty and mystical ways.

Howard was one of those essential artists of any period, but certainly of those periods of great upheaval and transition like the early twentieth century. With his grounding solidly in traditional forms and methods of poetic composition, he was also a poet unafraid to try new things, to tinker with old forms and make then new again, to take liberties with the old and established and to try new permutations and variations.

His comments on other poets are both serious and parodic at times. He sees in poetry itself both its potential power and the futility of hoping it will reach a broad audience.

As much as in any other theme or topic, we see Howard as one of the last minstrels of the age of narrative song, a man who saw "the harp of Homer flecked with rust" as he notes in the one of his essential poems, "Autumn." I believe that Howard saw himself as one whose goal was to take up Homer's harp, burnish, and tune it for a new age and accompany its new chords with new words.

In poems like "The Adventurer" and "Stay Not from Me" we find something of the urgency to "get it all said" expressed by Keats: *"...I behold, upon the night's starr'd face,/Huge cloudy symbols of a high romance,/And think that I may never live to trace/Their shadows, with the magic hand of chance."* As Howard puts it:

> *Time strides and all too soon shall I grow old*
> *With still all earth to see, all life to live*

Of course, sadly, the "growing old" was not to be.

Robert E. Howard

THE ADVENTURER

Dusk on the sea; the fading twilight shifts;
  The night wind bears the ocean's whisper dim—
Wind, on your bosom many a phantom drifts—
  A silver star climbs up the blue world rim.
Wind, make the green leaves dance above me here
  And idly swing my silken hammock—so;
Now, on that glimmering molten silver mere
  Send the long ripples wavering to and fro.
And let your moon-white tresses touch my face
And let me know your slim-armed, cool embrace
  While to my dreamy soul you whisper low.

Dream—aye, I've dreamed since last night left her tower
  And now again she comes on star-soled feet.
Welcome, old friend; here in this rose-gemmed bower
  I've drowsed away your Sultan's golden heat.
Here in my hammock, Time I've dreamed away
  For I have but to stretch a hand out, lo,
I'm treading languorous Shores of Yesterday,
  Moon-silvered deserts or the star-weird snow;
I float o'er seas where ships are purple shells,
I hear the tinkle of the camel bells
  That waft down Cairo's streets when dawn winds blow.

South Seas! I watch when dusky twilight comes
  Making vague gods of ancient, sea-set trees.
The world path beckons—loud the mystic drums—
  Here at my hand the magic golden keys
That fit the doors of Romance, Wonder, strange
  Dim gossamer adventures; seas and stars.
Why, I have roamed the far Moon Mountain range
  When sunset minted gold in shimmering bars.
All eager eyed I've sailed from ports of Spain
And watched the flashing topaz of the Main
  When dawn was flinging witch fire on the spars.

I am content in dreams to roam my fill
   The vagrant, drifting sport of wind and tide,
Slave of the greater freedom, venture's thrill;
   Here every magic ship on which I ride.
Gold, green, blue, red, a priceless treasure trove,
   More wealth then ever pirate dared to dream.
My hammock swings—about the world I rove.
   The sunset's dusk, the dawning's glide and gleam,
Moon-dappled leaves are murmuring in the wind
Which whispers tales. Lo, Tyre is just behind,
   Through seas of dawn I sail, Romance abeam.

AGE COMES TO RABELAIS

Judas Iscariot, Saul and Cain,
   Pharoah and Jezebel—
Is it lost away, the blind black strain
That stabbed me cold with a blinding pain,
That carried me up to the spires of Spain
   And down to the halls of Hell?

Winter is tinting the skies with steel,
   The air is slashed with wine.
I should be looting strange gems from mire,
Ripping the stars with a blasting fire—
But the soul is gone from the looted lyre
   And the song from the heart of mine.

Robert E. Howard

ANOTHER HYMN OF HATE

No heavens for me with their streets of gold
    and harps electro-plated,
With their pearly gates all carved and scrolled
    and their angels glory sated.
For Eternity is a weary time
    and manna's a weary ration.
And when I have scribbled my last sad rime
    and have died of slow starvation—
They will pry me loose from the standard keys
    and the last unfinished story,
And my ghost—distinctly smelling of cheese—
    will mount to real shores glory.
Where magazine souls race to and fro
    like sheep without a herder
And there'll be critics to lay low
    and editors to murder.

My rejection slips will all be there
    of all the forms and genders;
Of them will I build a gibbet rare,
    and hang thereon the senders.
I'll slaughter the shades of the magazines
    with never a man to censure,
I'll chase the ghost of the *SATURDAY POST*
    and torture the wild *ADVENTURE.*
I'll finish *LIBERTY, VANITY FAIR,*
    in a manner rude and gory;
I'll plunge my fists clear up to the wrists
    in the blood of *DETECTIVE STORY.*
I'll batter *TRUE STORY* fore and aft
    and stab him with forty lances;
I'll put *WILD WEST* to a fiery test
    and I'll massacre *TRUE ROMANCES.*
One man of all the gang I'll spare
    (and the rest I'll carve to salad)
Whatever noble man may dare
    to publish this soulful ballad.

AUTUMN

Now is the lyre of Homer flecked with rust,
 And yellow leaves are blown across the world,
And naked trees that shake at every gust
 Stand gaunt against the clouds autumnal-curled.

Now from the hollow moaning of the sea
 The dreary birds against the sunset fly,
And drifting down the sad wind's ghostly dree
 A breath of music echoes with a sigh.

The barren branch shakes down the withered fruit,
 The seas faint footprints on the strand erase;
The sere leaves fall on a forgotten lute,
 And autumn's arms enfold a dying race.

ECHOES FROM AN ANVIL

I leave to paltry poets
 The labor and the lute;
I sing in drums and tom-toms
 The black abysmal brute—
My voice is of the people,
 That giant wild and mute.

(With blood of all the ages
 His broken nails are black,
The whole world weights and burdens
 His hairy, bestial back;
He shambles down forever
 A blind and tangled track.)

I bring no polished diamonds,
 No gems from London town;

No cultured whim or fancy
 My rugged verses crown;
You find here nought but power
 That breaks a city down.

I spill no words of beauty,
 Coins from a silver purse.
My hands are built of iron,
 And iron is in my verse.
I bring no love but fury,
 No blessing but a curse.

My low pitched brow is slanting,
 My eyes are burning red
With fierce black primal visions
 That thunder in my head.
Behind my heart the rivers
 And all the jungles spread.

I slaved in star-girt Babel
 And labored at the wall;
I watched the birth of pavements
 Beneath my slugging maul—
And in a frenzied dawning
 I saw her towers fall.

I toiled in Tuscan vineyards,
 I broke the beaten loam,
I strained against the mallet
 That drove the chisel home,
I sweated in the galleys
 That broke the road to Rome.

Oh, khan and king and pharaoh!
 In cold and drouth and heat
I bled to build your glory,
 An ant beneath your feet—

But always rose a morning
  When blood ran in the street.

The world upon my shoulders,
  Knee-deep in muck and silt,
My hand beneath my tatters
  Still grips the hidden hilt—
Who fed the ancient rivers
  With blood rebellions spilt?

A FABLE FOR CRITICS

Now come the days of high endeavor and
The blare of brazen trumpets through the land.
Now George Sylvester Viereck from his den
Roars forth and Untermeyer rides again.
Across the mountains comes the blast of Hecht
And all the critics get it in the neckt.
Jack London's ghost still haunts a rum-shop's door
And Rupey Brooks pursues a phantom whore.
But who is this who rides in silver white
Attire that shames the stars across the night?
Helmet and shield and corselet all a-gleam,
Like some crusader from a drifting dream,
Upon a prancing jackass shod with flame—
Rise, heralds of the past, bray forth his name!:
That bulging brow, that iron-plated jaw—
Those dagger eyes—that stabbing nose—hurrah!
Shades of Don John! Who else would rise and dare?
Is it? It is! T'is he! T'is Up. Sinclair!
Gaze on the ëcoutrements of war and strife!
Weapons more deadly than the gat or knife!
A pack horse loaded with munitions fell
By he and John Dos Passos and Floyd Dell.
Tremble ye tyrants, flee with leaps and bounds!
For every book he writes weighs forty pounds!

Ye who but laugh at poets' rhymes and rages
—Ware the statistics in these deadly pages!
Now Upty paused awhile and sat alone,
Resting his rump upon a patient stone.
The solitude was tingling in the air
And Rupert Hughes came snooping from his lair.
The hunting beasts were out to make their kills,
J. Ogden Armour's bellow shook the hills.
Now Upty yawned and eyed the timid air,
Thumbing the shin bone of a millionaire.
He closer drew his cape of artist's fur,
A present from George Horace Lorrimer.
Now all the modern school who drank and whored,
Fell on their faces when he rose and roared:
(And even Cabell's knees began to knock)
"God send us other men like Edward Bok!"
Stars gleamed across the chasms of the sky
And Arthur Brisbane trumpeted reply.
Sir Upty paused; the hour was dim and late;
A Soviet was calling to its mate.
And from the caverns of the vale and fen
There slunk the young and bright eyed working men.
Sir Upty heard them going from the knoll
And shook within his boots despite "King Coal."
A bat came whirling in the silent air,
And all the mountain peaks echoed, "Sinclair!"
"Aha! he muttered as the sounds sighed past,
"The syndicated press awakes at last!"
But even as he spoke a rattlesnake
Came flying with its rattles all a-shake.
"Stand, scaly varlet, wherefore dost thou flee?
"Nor halt to make obeisience to ME?"
"Go sit upon a tack," the snake replied,
"There follows close with long and lengthy stride,
"One who would make me listen, if he could,
"To words defined according to his mood."
The scornful snake went tooling down the plains

And Upty's blood congealed within his veins.
For in the moonlight bulked a mighty form
That beckoned with a silent tree-like arm.
"Avaunt, foul ghost!" Upty in panic said,
And hurled "The Goose Step" at the phantom's head.
"Heh heh!" the spook responded with a roar
That woke up G.B. Shaw on Erin's shore.
"I know you," Upty said, with accent fierce,
"You are that tough art-saker, Ambrose Bierce!
"Did Villa's bullets find their fatal mark,
"Or what was it that sent you to the dark?"
(His strong right arm upheld in direful threat
"The Money Changers"—deadly arm! And yet
Through many a man has trembled at his ruth,
The phantom snickered with a mirth uncouth.)
"Think not to dent my hide with any such
"Though it may be translated into Dutch.
"No, Villa's bullets bounced from off my brow,
"For I had listened to you telling how
"The bright millennium would dawn some day,
"And heard you through and lived to walk away.
"But finally in the game of life I lost—
"I tried to read a rhyme by Robert Frost."
At this same moment came a fearsome yell,
As of some lost soul shooting craps in Hell.
"E. Haldeman," said Ambrose, "Lord of earth,
"To another little blue book's given birth.
"Or Mencken splits a mild infinitive,
"Or questions Sara Teasdale's right to live."
And then he blenched," Flee for your life," he cried,
"Behold who comes along the mountain side!"
"The air for us, by gosh!" and hand in hand,
Ambrose and Upty fled across the land.
There came, a-thrumming on his mighty chest,
And walking on his knuckles, Eddie Guest.
George Nathan raised his antlers to the breeze.
And H.L. Mencken chattered in the trees.

Robert E. Howard

MAN AM I

Man am I, man, and less than a beast,
    man, and more than a god;
For I have followed the flaming trails
    that deities never trod;
And in my soul there are secret fire
    and the curse of the leper's spot,
And passions smolder, such hidden lusts
    as the lowest beasts know not.

Man am I, wolf of a wolfish world,
    with a soul that I only sell
And a whirlwind maze of sin and lust
    from the furnaces of Hell.
My Fate was forged on the anvils of Hell
    and riveted 'bout my soul,
And the demons brought worn-out fags of Lives
    to make a sardonic whole.

My soul is a spire of living flame,
    my soul is a soaring fire
That gives no heed to Satan's mead
    or Hades' ultimate ire;
For I've known Labor with no reward
    and Toiling with never a gain,
And the flames that tormented Oscar Wilde
    and tortured Paul Verlaine.

My soul is a spire of living fire,
    a leaping flame divine;
But I live my days and I tread my ways
    in the Deserts of the Swine.
My soul is a strange and far-winged bird,
    out of the Mystic whirled,
But I must tread the wandering trails
    of a mazy, sordid world.

MOONLIGHT ON A SKULL

Golden goats on a hillside black,
  Silken gown on a wharf-side trull,
Screaming girl on a silver rack—
  What are dreams in a shadowed skull?

I stood at a shrine and Chiron died,
  A woman laughed from the purple roofs,
And he burned and lived and rose in his pride
  And shattered the tiles with clanging hoofs.

I opened a volume dark and rare,
  I lighted a candle of mystic lore—
Bare feet throbbed on the outer stair
  And book and candle sank to the floor.

Ships that reel on the windy sea,
  Lovers that take the world to wife,
What may the Traitress hold for me
  Who scarce have lifted the veil of life?

MUSINGS [VERSION 1]

The little poets sing of little things:
Hope, cheer, and faith, small queens and puppet kings;
Lovers who kissed and then were made as one,
And modest flowers waving in the sun.
The mighty poets write in blood and tears
And agony that, flame-like, bites and sears.
They reach their mad blind hands into the night,
To plumb abysses dead to human sight;
To drag from gulfs where lunacy lies curled,
Mad, monstrous nightmare shapes to blast the world.

THE POETS

Out of the somber night the poets come,
  A moment brief to fan their lambent flame;
Then, like the dimming whisper of a drum,
  Fades back into the night from whence they came.

The gray fog, swirling cloak of cynic Time,
  Meshes achievement in the ages' gloom,
A moment's mirth, a breath of lilting rime,
  And then—the gray of old oblivion's womb.

Weaver of melodies all golden-spun
  The singer sings his song—and passes on.
The poets strum his lyre—then is one
  With gray-hued dusk and rose of fading dawn.

A moment's laughter on the winds of Time,
  A moment's ripple on Time's silent sea,
A golden riffle in the river's slime,
  And then—the silence of Eternity.

Gray dust and ash where leaped the mystic fire,
  Mingled with air and wind the once-red flame;
Breeze-born the tune, but now forgot the lyre—
  Remains?—the musty thing that men call Fame.

Half-curious eyes that scan the yellowed page,
  All heedless of the makers of the feast—
Why, Pierrot might have been a musty sage,
  Francois Villon a stoled and sour priest.

Who penned this lyric? Who this sonnet? Whence
  The soul of fire that snared these stars in song?
Who knows? Who cares? A vast indifference
  Is all the answer of the marching throng.

RECOMPENSE

I have not heard lutes beckon me,
  nor the brazen bugles call,
But once in the dim of a haunted lea
  I heard the silence fall.
I have not heard the regal drum,
  nor seen the flags unfurled,
But I have watched the dragons come,
  fire-eyed, across the world.

I have not seen the horsemen fall
  before the hurtling host,
But I have paced a silent hall
  where each step waked a ghost.
I have not kissed the tiger-feet
  of a strange-eyed golden god,
But I have walked a city's street
  where no man else had trod.

I have not raised the canopies
  that shelter reveling kings,
But I have fled from crimson eyes
  and black unearthly wings.
I have not knelt outside the door
  to kiss a pallid queen,
But I have seen a ghostly shore
  that no man else has seen.

I have not seen the standards sweep
  from keep and castle wall,
But I have seen a woman leap
  from a dragon's crimson stall,
And I have heard strange surges boom
  that no man heard before,
And seen a strange black city loom
  on a mystic night-black shore.

And I have felt the sudden blow
  of a nameless wind's cold breath,
And watched the grisly pilgrims go
  that walk the roads of Death,
And I have seen black valleys gape,
  abysses in the gloom,
And I have fought the deathless Ape
  that guards the Doors of Doom.

I have not seen the face of Pan,
  nor mocked the Dryad's haste,
But I have trailed a dark-eyed Man
  across a windy waste.
I have not died as men may die,
  nor sin as men have sinned,
But I have reached a misty sky
  upon a granite wind.

ROMANCE

I am king of all the Ages
I am ruler of the stars
I am master of Time's pages
And I mock at chains and bars.
Now, as when I sailed the world
Ere the galley's sails were furled
And the barnacles had crusted on their spars.

I am strife, I am Life,
I am mistress, I am wife!
I am wilder than the sea wind, I am fiercer than the fire!
I am tale and song and fable, I am Akkad, I am Babel,
I am Calno, I am Carthage, I am Tyre!

For I walked the streets of Gaza
    when the world was wild and young,
And I reveled in Carchemish when the golden minstrels sung;
All the world-road was my path, as I sang the songs of Gath
Or trod the streets of Nineveh where harlots roses flung.

I swam the wide Euphrates
    where it wanders through the plain
And I saw the dawn come flaming over Tyre.
I walked the roads of Ammon
    when the hills were veiled in rain,
And I watched the stars anon from the walls of Askalon
And I rose the plains of Palestine beneath the dawning's fire
When the leaves upon the trees danced
    and fluttered in the breeze
And a slim girl of Juda went singing to a lyre.

Robert E. Howard

STAY NOT FROM ME

Stay not from me that veil of dreams that gives
   Strange seas and skies and lands and curious fire,
   Black dragons, crimson moons and white desire,
That through the silvery fabric sifts and sieves
   Strange shadows, shades and all unmeasured things,
   And in the sifting lends them shapes and wings
    And makes them known in ways past common knowing—
Red lands, black seas and ivory rivers flowing.

   How of the gold we gather in our hands?
    It cheers, but shall escape us at the last,
    And shall mean less, when this brief day is past,
   Than that we gathered on the yellow sands,
   The phantom ore we found in Wizard-lands.

   Keep not from me my veil of curious dreams
    Through which I see the giant things which drink
    From mountain-castled rivers—on the brink
   Black elephants that woo the fronded streams,
   And golden tom-toms pulsing through the dusk,
    And yellow stars, black trees and red-eyed cats,
   And bales of silk and amber jars of musk,
    And opal shrines and tents and vampire bats.

   Long highways climbing eastward to the moon,
    And caravans of camels lade with spice,
   And ancient sword hilts carved with scroll and rune,
    And marble queens with eyes of crimson ice.

   Uncharted shores where moons of scarlet spray
    Break on a Viking's galley on the sand,
    And curtains held by one slim silver band
   That float from casements opening on a bay,
    And monstrous iron castles, dragon-barred,
    And purple cloaks with inlaid gems bestarred.

Long silver tasseled mantles, curious furs,
  And camel bells and dawns and golden heat,
And tuneful rattle of the horsemen's spurs
  Along some sleeping desert city's street.

Time strides and all too soon shall I grow old
  With still all earth to see, all life to live:
  Then come to me, my silver veil, and sieve,
Seas of illusion beached with magic gold.

SLUMBER

A silver scroll against a marble sky,
  A brooding idol hewn of crimson stone,
  A dying queen upon an ebon throne,
An iron bird that rends the clouds on high,
A golden lute whose echoes never die—
  A thousand dreams that men have never known
  Spread mighty wings and fold me when alone
Upon my couch in haunted sleep I lie.

Then rending mists, the spurring whisper comes
  "Wake, dreamer, wake, your tryst with Life to keep!"
Yet, waking, still a throb of phantom drums
  Comes hauntingly across the mystic deep;
Their echo still my thrilling soul chord thrums—
  Which is the waking, then, and which the sleep?

Robert E. Howard

A SONNET OF GOOD CHEER

Fling wide the portals, rose-lipped dawn has come
  To kiss our drowsy visions into life;
  Let me arise, a-lust for love and strife
To follow far some distant, pulsing drum.
Upon my vibrant soul-chords passions strum;
  With hot, red, leaping blood my veins are rife.
  Gods, let me take the universe to wife!
Ere Death, the cold accountant, close my sum.

Then as I spake, methought fierce laughter came
  Across the dying hills where sunrise shot;
"Fool, fool, you came unbidden to this game,
  "And Death that takes you hence shall ask you not.
"From life, this and only this , may you claim;
  "Living, to die, and dying, be forgot."

THE TIMES, THE TIMES STRIDE ON
APACE AND FAST

The times, the times stride on apace and fast
  They baffle our uncertain questing hands;
  Our feet are straying 'mid illusion's sands
Our day is over and our Time is past.
We knew an Age of thrones and trumpet peal
  Through all our dreams the bygone Ages speak
  To foil the powers drab that ever seek
To bind our restless spirits to the wheel.

Selah. Through all the pipes of Pan be mute
  Yet shall we sail to seek the Golden Fleece
  If we may dream awhile amid some trees
  And through the drowsy hum of summer bees,
Faintly and far, hear yet again the lute
  We heard upon the sapphire hills of Greece.

TO ALL SOPHISTICATES

You who with pallid wine still toast
The black decay of a dusty host—
You who pray to a mist and a ghost—
   Stand back—give me room!
Out of the dregs and the bitter mire
With an iron brain and a heart on fire
To rend the altar and break the spire,
   I come like the crack of Doom.

Sing of the rose, the moon and the vine—
I bring you fury and gall and brine,
The black coins cast from the heart of mine,
   The blast of a black despair.
Terror and tears to trample your trust,
Madness to bludgeon you into the dust,
Death and decay and mold and rust—
   Skulls to champ and to stare.

Sing of the pride of your bloodless art—
I bring the winds of a blazing heart,
And a song to sing on the hangman's cart,
   And an answer for Hell's red roll;
I chant no sultan or queen or Cid,
No tender kiss that the roses hid—
My songs are nails for a coffin lid,
   Each rhyme is a charring coal.

You who polished and pale and proud,
White hand devotees, sworn and vowed,
You fold your hands and wait for your shroud
   And quack in a faultless tongue;
Rude on your ears my clamor falls
As you lounge in silk and the marble halls—
Well, I was bred in Life's stable stalls,
   Battered and scarred and stung.

By Life that battered and took and gave—
By God, I have been a rebel slave!
With my bleeding hands I dig my grave!
    But others shall dig for you.
You have set up men and called them gods,
You have taken their words to fashion rods—
You will know, when you hear the falling clods,
    Your gods have never been true.

Wolves at the wicket, worms at the gate—
But still you squeak in the path of Fate—
Belly-hunger and lust and hate,
    These are the truths and the facts!
Bow to your blind little idols of rhyme,
Prattle of seasons, tide and time—
I come from the filth and the jungle slime,
    With the torch and the bloody axe.

TO LYLE SAXON

Like some Arcadian legend
    From misty Time withdrawn,
We see a shadow drifting
    Across a Creole lawn.

As ghosts we know the silence,
    The moon's white silver shard,
The stars above New Orleans,
    The hoofs upon the sward.

Dark Time erased the symbol
    In blood and bitter tears,
Yet still an echo's echo
    Floats down the dusty years.
          . . . . .
The river broke the silence,
    The cypress sighed above;
A dark eyed woman plighted
    Her strange mysterious love.

Her eyes were pools of shadows
    Until the red dawn burst;
Her memory still lingers,
    Her name a name accurst.
          . . . . .
Still stand around dreaming fountains
    Grey trees in brooding rings,
And still along the levee
    The dusky river sings.

But dawn's red rose shall wither
    And God's domain shall pass
Before we shall see the Centaur
    Come neighing o'er the grass.

TO MODERNS

Little poets, little poets,
  Your star is growing dim—
A wind is coming out of the East
  To rend you life from limb.

Oh, you that sit in the rhymer's seat
  And prattle of little things,
Turn your faces from the gilded scroll
  And see what the black wind brings!

Your verse is smooth as a windless brook,
  Your words fall well in line;
You have trimmed your accents carefully
  And polished them till they shine.

Just so the workers in Babylon
  Rubbed gem and gleaming ore,
    Lit little lamps in the burnished hall,
    Forgetting that rough stones hold the wall—
'Til the riders swept on Babylon
  And Hell ran red before.

Little poets, little poets,
  The people praise your rhymes;
You sing of kisses and spring and love,
The budding rose and the maiden's glove,
  Like a thousand tinkling chimes.

But a great bell booms in the deadly East
  Where a fearsome people lurk;
There are shapes of doom in the gathering gloom
  And monsters in the murk.

Gods of all Hells, can you not see
  Before it is too late
That rhyme is the speech of the grisly dark—
  The ghouls that haunt the Gate?

Oh, jingle your foolish, petty songs—
  Jeer at the Talon and Tooth;
   Till the portals break and the towers fall
   And the terrible people nail you all
  To a cross of iron truth.

What has the true rhyme to do with light,
  Love or a flower's smell?
The poems that set the sky on fire
  Were born in the pits of Hell.

Murder and madness, hate and lust,
  Gibbering heresies,
   These are the tales that poets tell;
   Of the seething brain in the rotting shell.
   Loose the abhorrent hordes of Hell,
Then carve your poems in blood and rust,
  Abysms and blashphemies.

TO THE STYLISTS

Hammer your verses, file your songs;
  Shackle your soul with brazen bars;
To the unchained troubadour belongs
  The heritage of the stars.

WHICH WILL SCARCELY BE UNDERSTOOD

Small poets sing of little, foolish things,
  As more befitting to a shallow brain
That dreams not of the pre-Atlantean kings,
  Nor launches on that dark uncharted Main
    That holds grim islands and unholy tides,
    Where many a black mysterious secret hides.

True rime concerns her not with bursting buds,
  The chirping bird, the lifting of the rose—
Save ebon blooms that swell in ghastly woods,
And that grim, voiceless bird that ever broods
  Where through black boughs a wind of horror blows.

Oh, little singers, what know you of those
Ungodly, slimy shapes that glide and crawl
Out of unreckoned gulfs when midnights fall,
  To haunt the poet's slumbering, and close
    Against his eyes thrust up their hissing head,
    And mock him with their eyes so serpent-red?

Conceived and bred in blackened pits of hell,
  The poems come that set the stars on fire;
Born of black maggots writhing in a shell
Men call a poet's skull—an iron bell
  Filled up with burning mist and golden mire.

The royal purple is a moldy shroud;
  The laurel crown is cypress fixed with thorns;
    The sword of fame, a sickle notched and dull;
    The face of beauty is a grinning skull;
And ever in their souls' red caverns loud
  The rattle of the cloven hoofs and horns.

The poets know that justice is a lie,
  That good and light are baubles filled with dust—
The world's slave-market where swine sell and buy,
This shambles where the howling cattle die,
  Has blinded not their eyes with lies and lust.

Ring up the demons from the lower Pit,
  Since Evil conquers goodness in the end;
Break down the Door and let the fires be lit,
  And greet each slavering monster as a friend.

Let obscene shapes of Darkness ride the earth,
  Let sacrificial smokes blot out the skies,
  Let dying virgins glut the Black God's eyes,
And all the world resound with noisome mirth.

Break down the altars, let the streets run red,
  Tramp down the race into the crawling slime;
Then where red Chaos lifts her serpent head,
  The Fiend be praised, we'll pen the perfect rime.

XI

People Poems: Vignettes of Humanity

Especially in one long and poetry-laden letter to T. C. Smith [23 June 1926] but elsewhere as well, Howard creates short poems that present portraits of various personality types—some typifying occupations. These "people poems," as I call them, are reminiscent of [perhaps influenced by?] the poems of Edgar Lee Masters in his *Spoon River Anthology* or of Edwin Arlington Robinson in his poems of Tilbury Town—a thinly-veiled collection of vignettes about characters and types from Robinson's home town of Gardner, Maine ("Richard Cory" being the most famous example).

The people poems by Howard form a small but interesting collection, providing good insights into Howard's world view and frame of mind.

Considering so many of them are bunched in the letter to Smith noted above, Howard is likely to have gone through a period of effusions of poetic energy focusing on this type of poem. Whether he had recently read or reread Robinson or Masters is conjectural. I suspect he had. At least one of these short poems ["Nun"] is almost certainly inspired by a short lyric by Gerard Manley Hopkins, another poet whom, I suspect, Howard admired—at least for the music of his language if not the strident Christian themes.

Each of these tiny windows into Howard's perceptions and estimations of the world around him might, in and of itself, offer no great insight. Taken together, I believe they allow a great deal of light to pour in.

THE ACTOR

I am an actor and have been an actor since birth.
There is a saint in me and a villain.
Few of the things I do, the words I say,
Are unpremeditated.
I meditate upon the effect of my actions on men,
And cloak myself with a romance and a mystery
Which I do not deserve.
At times the hardness of me seems deeper,
And at times, the softness.
I am one of many moods and many minds.
I do not know myself, and I am an actor,
But which of myselves is the true and deeper self?

THE BUILDERS [VERSION 1]

We reared up Babel's towers
   Flung Sidon's turrets high;
We set the wall of China
   To parapet the sky.

The mountains chant our glory,
Oh, pharoah, khan and king,
The years forget the story,
   The seas our anthems sing.

The towers stand recorders,
   Star written names of gilt,
Of king and khan and pharoah—
   What of the men who built?

THE BUILDERS [VERSION 2]

The towers stand recorders,
　　Star written names of gilt
Of king and khan and pharaoh—
　　What of the men who built?

We reared up Babel's towers
　　Flung Sidon's turrets high;
We set the wall of China
　　To parapet the sky.

They set their names to burnish
　　Their purple pride and lust
Who sate enthroned and drove us—
　　Our fame is with the dust.

The years forget the story,
　　Oh, pharaoh, khan and king,
But the mountains chant our glory
　　The seas our anthems sing.

CASTAWAY

I have drowned my soul in the rain
　Where the dawn and the twilight sever;
I have fashioned a crown of pain
　To rest on my brow forever.

The tides go out to the sea
　And the marsh and the grass surround me;
I haunt the bare salt lea
　Where the bursting breakers hound me.

Gulls that lair in the blue,
  Cranes where the ripples quiver,
The great tides thunder through
  But the mist is chained to the river.

My heart tugs to be gone
  And the far winds break the billows,
But I watch each dreary dawn
  From the hummocks in the willows.

Oh, the winds and the deep sea rain,
  And the endless surges sweeping;
My heart is hollow with pain
  And my eyes are blind with weeping.

Oh, the dream behind my eyes
  And the flames in the brain that burn it!
But the curse I hurl to the skies,
  The wandering gulls return it.

I have drowned my soul in the rain
  Where the dawn and the twilight sever;
I have fashioned a crown of pain
  To rest on my brow forever.

THE CHOIR GIRL

I have a saintly voice, the people say;
　With Elder Blank I send the music winging—
　I smile and compliment him on his singing—
By God, I'd rather hear a jackass bray.
　I nod and smile to all the pious sisters—
　I wish their rears were stung with seven blisters.
That youthful minister, so straight and slim—
I'd trade my soul for one long night with him.

COWBOY

Poets and novelists have sung of me;
　Made me a bronzed-faced Centaur, leather-girt.
The real man they all have failed to see;
　A weary, ignorant man in an unwashed shirt.

DREAMER

I live in a world apart
　A world that has no link with this drab earth.
A vague, melodious world, where breezes start
　Soft joys and gay-hued mirth.

NUN

I have anchored my ship to a quiet port;
　A land that is holy and blest.
But I gaze through my bars at the tempest's sport
　And I long for the sea's unrest.

EMANCIPATION
[THE TRAMP*]

The couplers lock and the air-brakes grate—
And I'm headed West on a Red Ball freight,
The rain can fall and the wind can moan,
For I chucked the grind, and I'm on my own.
No more figures to check and add,
Till my eyes go blind and my brain goes mad.
No more bosses to hem and say:
"We have been forced to reduce your pay.
"Just be thankful you've got the job."
No more cringing to some fat slob
Who holds my fate in his grubby hand—
I'm marked no more with the wage-slave's brand!
What do I care if my shoes are thin
And the holes in my clothes let the rain soak in?
I've served my time and I'm overdue,
Just a poor sap who used to stew
With the other poor worms that buy and sell;
But I've told the boss he can go to Hell.
I've left him singing his hymn of Hate—
And I'm headed West on a Red Ball freight!

[*editor's suggested title - in keeping with these
"People Poems]

Robert E. Howard

THE FOLLOWER

I am the man who followed,
  Never the man who led,
Many a chief I've followed,
  In many a fray I've bled.

I was with Sargon of Akkad,
  When he hurled his nomad hordes,
Against the host of Sumer,
  And they fell before his swords.

Armor-bearer and captain,
  Councilor to the king,
Never my praise they utter,
  When the monarch's name they sing.

Who speaks of Aristotle,
  Before Alexander the grand?
Shades of Le Chutsai Mingan,
  Councilor of Genghis Khan.

No fame to the man who followed,
  Unknown on land and sea,
Yet the kings of all the ages
  Have owed their thrones to me.

GIRL

Gods, what a handsome youth across the way.
  What shall I do to make him notice me?
I must not be too obvious—there
  I'll shift my dress, demurely and let him see
A quick glance of an ankle very trim;
  Then blush and smooth my skirts down hastily
As if 'twere unintentional and—Hell!
  The fool's not even got his eyes on me.

A GREAT MAN SPEAKS

They set me up on high, a marble saint,
  As if to guard the virtue of the park.
  My flanks are gaunt, my gaze is cold and stark,
For I must look the part the liars paint,
They've cleansed my history of fleshly taint.
  The elders bid the younger people mark
  How virtuous I gleam against the dark—
Could I but speak I'd make the bastards faint.

Great God, how could they know the lusty zest,
  The love of life that made my sinews dance?—
  Below me now, against my base, inert,
A lousy tramp, a sleeping house-maid rest.
  I yearn for that square flask in his old pants.
  My fingers burn to feel beneath her skirt.

HARVEST

We reap and bind the bitter yield
   Of seed we never sowed,
To buy the meat that others eat,
   To pay the debts by others sealed—
Theirs was the fatness of the field,
   Ours the barren road.

LIBERTINE

I set my soul to a wild lute
   And taught my feet to dance.
I float, a broken straw,
   Upon the Sea of Chance.

THE PEASANT ON THE EUPHRATES

He saw old Sumer reel before the hoofs
Of Sargon; and the Babylonian roofs
Go up in flames to quench the Mede's hot ire;
He knew the Persian's and the Greek's desire;
He saw red kingdoms born and pass away,
Like clouds upon a dreamy summer day.
Patient, he toils along the changing years,
Captive, he hardly know to what lord's spears.
Roman or Arab, Turk, or Briton—all,
All one to him, the evelasting thrall.

PRUDE

I dare not join my sisters in the street;
   I think of people's talk, the cynic stare.
Fierce envy makes me scornful of their play,
   And hide my lust behind a haughty air.

SAILOR

I saw a mermaid sporting in the bay,
  Far down, far down where blew no roaring gale;
About her snowy shoulders flashed the spray,
  The waves played emerald at her sinewy tail;
She swam a jade and golden, star-set way,
Where all the rainbow colors seemed to play—
  She vanished at the Swedish captain's hail
  Who bid me go to Hell and furl a sail.

TOPER

Toil, cares, annoyances all fade away;
  I care not who may run for President.
I drowse and swig my rum the live-long day,
And watch the shallops skimming o'er the bay.

XII

The Realms of Gold:
Exotic Places Real and Imagined

Robert E. Howard developed the art of transporting his readers both Elsewhere and "Elsewhen." In the poems, he often depicts the exotic and intoxicating real world places he had read about and he frequently takes us to the many wondrous places of his artistic and imaginative vision.

Howard was a great student of both History and Legend, of both Mythology and the marvels of the Mundane (primary definition as in the Latin *Mundus*). He lived in worlds of wonders both real and imagined. It is difficult to place some of Howard's fiction in precisely that category that can be called "Mythopoeic" (*Myth and World Creating*, from the Greek word *poesis* / creation. It has so much basis in dim history and legend that the word "Mythomorphic" (*Myth and World RE-Shaping*) might well be used. Such is also true of many of the places depicting in his poetry.

Keats used the phrase "realms of gold" to describe the journeys that one can take traveling through the gilt-edged pages of old books. Emily Dickinson later wrote that *"There is no Frigate like a Book / To take us Lands away / Or any Coursers like a Page / Of prancing Poetry."* Such travel was well-known and well-loved by Howard.

These poems show Howard's virtuosity at imagery and vivid description. The words paint us worlds that the mind can enter and by which we are enthralled.

THE CATS OF ANUBIS

The stars come blinking in a dusky sky,
  Like yellow eyes of vast Bubastes cats
  And dim and shadowy the restless bats
Against the creeping twilight wheel and fly.
Grey shadows mask the sands, the desert shrinks,
  And yet, unseen, seems still more dim and vast,
Against the stars rears up the silent Sphinx
  A brooding monster of forgotten past.

A shadow 'mid those ruins glides and creeps,
A thing from which the shuddering moonlight leaps:
  Like witch-rid wind from out of the hinterlands
  A fog-like aura haunts the sombre sands.
Grim, dreaming monstrous dreams; of naked feet
  That danced in worship; many a frightful feast;
Unhallowed rites that for such god were meet,
  Unholy neophyte and grisly priest

Egypt, thou land still chained unto the past,
Thy ghost gods in the deserts still are massed
  And many a fearful shape still glides and leers.
  The phantom, stealing down the slaughtered years
From out the fastness of some unthought Thule,
Brooding upon his ancient bestial rule—
  Freedom is naught, till men have conquered this,
  This undying fiend, the Cat of Anubis!

CRETE

The green waves wash above us
  Who slumber in the bay
As washed the tide of ages
  That swept our race away.

Our cities—dusty ruins;
  Our galleys—deep-sea slime;
Our very ghosts, forgotten,
  Bow to the sweep of Time.

Our land lies stark before it
  As we to alien spears,
But, ah, the love we bore it
  Outlasts the crawling years.

Ah, jeweled spires at even—
  The lute's soft golden sigh—
The Lion-Gates of Knossos
  When dawn was in the sky.

DEEPS

There is a cavern in the deep
  Beyond the sea-winds brawl;
Where the hills of the sea slope high and steep,
And dragons sleep
And serpents creep
There is a cavern in the deep
  Where strange sea-creatures crawl.

DESERT DAWN

Dim seas of sand swim slowly into sight
  As if from out the silence swiftly born;
  Faint foremost herald of the coming morn,
Red tentacles reach out into the night;
The shadows gray, then fade to rosy white.
  The stars fade out, the greatest and the least;
  Now a red rose is blooming in the east,
And from its widening petals comes the light.

While, fleecy clouds are fading from on high,
  The sun-god flings afar his golden brands;
    A breeze springs up and races 'mid the dunes,
    A-whisper with old tales and mystic runes;
Now blue and gold ride rampant in the sky,
  And now full day comes marching o'er the sands.

Robert E. Howard

EASTER ISLAND

How many weary centuries have flown
  Since strange-eyed beings walked this ancient shore;
  Hearing, as we, the green Pacific's roar,
Hewing fantastic gods from sullen stone!
The sands are bare; the idols stand alone.
  Impotent 'gainst the years was all their lore:
  They are forgot in ages dim and hoar;
Yet still, as then, the long tide-surges drone.

What dreams had they, that shaped these uncouth things?
  Before these gods what victims bled and died?
   What purple galleys swept along the strand
That bore the tribute of what dim sea-kings?
   But now they reign o'er a forgotten land,
  Gazing forever out beyond the tide.

A FAR COUNTRY

A granite wind sighed from the crimson clay desert.
A witch laid her shoon
On the horn of the moon;
The stars in the east
Were the robes of a priest,
And a granite wind roared from the crimson clay desert.

A king on a sapphire hill brooded forever.
A queen glimmered cold
In opal and gold;
Kissing white mice
With eyes of red ice,
And a king on a sapphire hill brooded forever.

A jester in motley held revel with spectres.
Ghostly white petals
Grew out of the nettles;
Gleaming like gems
On amaranth stems,
And a jester in motley held revel with spectres.

A golden-winged serpent laughed in the silence.
The mountains lay white
Like saints in the night;
The valleys were filled
With the gold rivers spilled.
And a golden-winged serpent laughed in the silence.

Robert E. Howard

THE GODS OF EASTER ISLAND

Long ere Priapus pranced through groves
   Arcadian sunlight kissed
The gods of Easter Island were born out of the mist.
Before the Elder deities from Egypts fogs were born
The gods of Easter Island stood up to greet the morn.
Before Mylitta knew the light or ever Bel had birth
The gods of Easter Island were rulers of the earth.
Before the bulls of Nineveh were hewn out of their stone
The gods of Easter Island stood silent and alone.

The gods of Easter Island saw kingdoms come and go
And shrines and idols shattered
   as tides that ebb and flow.
They saw the kite-winged Horus
   sweep down the beach to drink.
They saw Atlantis topple and Lemuria sink.
They brood through topaz eventide
   when tropic day is done;
I see them o'er the ocean, black in the dying sun.

THE GODS OF THE JUNGLE DRUMS

Mutter of drums, Jungle drums!
Over the bay their murmur comes;
  The dark waves ruffle unto their beat
  As over the water on unseen feet,
  Eery and phantom, spectre fleet,
    They glide and float, each ghostly note—
    Eyes in the shadows that gleem and gloat—
The gods of the jungle drums.

Spears will flash in the crimson dawn
   —Boom! Boom!—say the hidden drums—
  Boats will leap from the dusky shore
Steered by Satan's own yelling spawn.
    Then red assegai and flying oar
    And the battle yell and the war horn's roar
Will drown the sound of the drums.

Fires will gleam in the kraal tonight—
   Boom! Boom!—say the jungle drums—
Crimson and fierce their leaping light
Red as the spears that swept the fight.
There will the warriors boast their might
    And shout their fame as about the flame
    They leap in a dance that fiends would shame.

For the cooking pots are brimming o'er
And the red-stained war-spears clash no more;
Stilled is the giant war conch's roar!
And the drums held sway as they did before—
  The magical jungle drums.

HIGH BLUE HALLS

There's a kingdom far from the sun and star
  With never a wind to dree;
Where the golden balls of the silence falls
  In the high blue halls of the sea.

There's death to change in that kingdom strange,
  For its days are all the same;
Its blue floors blaze in a golden maze
  Through a purple haze of flame.

Through an emerald sheen dim shapes careen
  And white limbs trail and quiver;
In rose pale fire 'round spear and spire
  In white desire they shiver.

There's never a tree for eye to see
  But ever in ghostly showers
Great petals white drift down the night
  Like a wild delight of flowers.

There's a kingdom dim 'neath a ghost tree's limb,
  That throbs eternally,
Life's furtherest halls where magic calls
  In the high blue halls of the sea.

HILLS OF THE NORTH! LAVENDER HILLS

Hills of the North! Lavender hills.
Blue hills, tipped with crystal
Defying the ages.
Hills, high peaks where eagles wheel,
Where wild winds shout forever,
Whirling the snow
Like a mad dervish.

THE ISLE OF HY-BRASIL

There's a far, lone island in the dim, red West
Where the sea-waves are crimson
   with the red of burnished gold,
(Sapphire in the billows, gold upon the crest)
An island that is older than the continents are old.

For when in dim Atlantis a thousand jeweled spires
Burned through the twilight in the ocean's dusky smile,
And when mystic Lemuria glowed
   with myriad gemming fires
Strange ships went sailing to seek the wondrous isle.

And when the land of Britain was a forest for the deer
And the mammoth roamed the mountains
   and the plains were veiled in snow,
When the dawn had swept the ocean
   and the air was crystal clear
The ape-man looking sea-ward caught
   the distant topaz glow.

When Drake went down to Darien
   and Cortez sailed the Main
And the wide blue Pacific lay like a summer dream,
From the gold-decked bridges of the galleons of Spain
Far upon the skyline they saw the island gleam.

It flashes in the Baltic,
   dimly glimpsed through driving snow,
And it lights the Indian Ocean
   when the waves are lying still,
It dreams along the sea-rim
   in the twilight's golden glow,
And mariners have named it The Isle of Hy-Brasil.

For sailing ships are anchored close,
   about that ancient isle,
Ships that roamed the oceans in the dim dawn days,
Coracles from Britain, triremes from the Nile,
Anchored round the harbors, mile on countless mile,
Ships and ships and shades of ships, fading in the haze.

And there's a Roman galley with its seven banks of oars,
And there's a golden barge-boat
   that knew the Caesar's hand,
And there's a sombre pirate craft
   with shattered cabin doors,
And there's a sturdy bireme
   that sailed to the Holy Land.
Main masts lifting like a forest of the south,
Beaked prows looming and the scarlet courses furled,
Dim decks heel-marked, warped by rain and drouth,
Rift in the cross-trees, drift of the southern seas;
Dim ships, strong ships, from all about the world.

High ships, proud ships, towering at their poops,
Galleons flaunting their pinnacles of pride,
Battleships and merchantmen and long, lean sloops,
Flagships floating with the schooners on the tide.

And there's a Viking Serpent that sailed the northern seas,
That knew the stride of giants, ferocious gods of brawn,
And there's a lateened rover that billowed to the breeze,
There a ship that sailed from Tyre
   when the waves were tinged with fire
And the first skies of history were rosying to dawn.

The Good St. Brandon knew it
   when he turned him to the West
When he left the world behind him
   as he ventured far away,

And his fearless keel went plowing
  the ocean's sapphire crest
Till he won unto Hy-Brasil which no other mortal may.

For the island is Hy-Brasil, the paradise of ships,
Where the dim ghost crafts lie anchored and at rest,
Where the sea wind never rages
  and the sea rain never drips,
There they dream away the days
  in the mystic, sapphire haze
About the isle of Hy-Brasil, far off amid the West.

Robert E. Howard

NOCTURNE

Night falls
On ruined walls
  And towers hoary;
A star gleams
On vanished dreams—
  Forgotten glory.

Dim shades
Haunt the glades
  For Trystery.
The pale night
Glitters white
  With mystery.

Breezes shake
The silver lake
  Waves quiver.
Shadows leap
Sway and sleep
  Along the river.

OCEAN-THOUGHTS

[ed. note: an interesting variant of the villanelle form]

The strong winds whisper o'er the sea,
   Flinging the gray-gnarled ocean's spate;
The gray waves lash along the lea.

The lone gulls wings are high and free,
   The great seal trumpets for his mate;
The high winds drum, the wild winds dree.

The gray shoals roar unceasingly,
   Where combers march in kingly state,
The crest-crowned monarchs of the sea.

And now, along the lone, white lea,
   The surges fade, the winds abate.
And the wide sea lies silently.

But far to islands, restlessly
   Surges the tide, unreined and great,
Forever roaming and forever free.

And thus my soul, forever restlessly,
   Longs for the outworld, vast, unultimate,
The vasty freedom of the swinging sea,
Forever roaming and forever free.

REBELLION

The marble statues tossed against the sky
  In gestures blind as though to rend and kill,
  Not one upon his pedestal was still.
Stiff fingers clutched at winds that whispered by,
And from the white lips rose a deathly cry:
  "Cursed be the hands that broke us from the hill!
  There slumber of unbirth was ours till
They gave us life that cannot live or die."

And then as from a dream I stirred and woke—
  Sublime and still each statue raised its head,
    Etched pure and cold against the leafy green,
No limb was moved, no sigh the silence broke;
  And people walked amid the grove and said:
    "How peaceful these white gods!—aye, how serene."

SHIPS

[ed. note: variant of "The Isle of Hy-Brasil]

There's a far, lone island in the dim, red West,
  Where the sea-waves are crimson
  with the red of burnished gold
(Sapphire in the billows, gold upon the crest),
  An island that is older than the continents are old.

Sailing-ships are anchored about that ancient isle,
  Ships that sailed the oceans in the dim dawn days,
Coracles from Britain, triremes from the Nile.
Anchored round the harbors, anchored mile on mile,
  Ships and ships and shades of ships fading in the haze.

And there's a Roman galley with its seven banks of oars,
  And there's a golden bargeboat that knew the Caesar's hand,
And there's a somber pirate craft with shattered cabin doors,
  And there's a sturdy bireme that sailed to Holy Land.

Main-trees lifting like a forest of the south,
  Beaked prows looming, and the wide courses furled,
Dim decks heel-marked, marked by rain and drouth,
Spindrift in the cross-trees, drift of southern seas,
  Dim ships, strong ships from all about the world.

High ships, proud ships, towering at their poops,
  Galleons flaunting their pinnacles of pride,
Schooners and merchantmen, and long, lean sloops,
  Kings' ships riding with galleys on the tide.

Robert E. Howard

TWILIGHT ON STONEHENGE

Great columns loom against the brooding sky
  Like giants of another world they stand
  Flinging their shadows far across the land—
Across the sunset's path their shadows lie;
Above, between, the lone, gray sea-gulls fly.
  And now the moon rides like a smoldering brand
  And mid those shadows, hewn by Titan's hand
Glides shades of eld, ghost shapes, dim-seen and sly.

The crimson moon rides higher o'er the brake,
  The darkness fades, the shadows merge and melt;
    Across the fen the sea-wind's whisper comes
    Bearing the discord of forgotten drums—
That speak to ghosts alone where bird and snake
  Drowse in the last, lone stronghold of the Celt.

[TWILIGHT STRIDING O'ER THE MOUNTAIN]

L'ENVOI

Twilight striding o'er the mountain,
Morn is whispering o'er the desert.
Mid the leaves the sea-breeze murmurs,
From the woodlands dryads beckon,
Come with me and learn the glory
Of the desert in the morning,
Of the ocean in the dawning.

XIII

Reflections & Introspections

Often Howard's poems are quite reflective and introspective, seemingly pronouncements after meditation and contemplation. Soul-searching is always a monumental task for a complex soul. There is so much to explore, so little time.

Some of the poems that follow will, I hope, go some significant way toward demonstrating the problems that some critics have encountered through the oversimplification of Howard and his body of work. He is not a writer easily pinned down or pigeon-holed in some neat category.

Some of the poems in this section show some derivation from the important poetic predecessors encountered in Howard's broad readings. It is difficult, for example, to not see some influences from both Shakespeare and Yeats in "On with the Play"; others provide more innovative and original perspectives.

ON WITH THE PLAY

Up with the curtain, lo, the stage is set;
  The mimes come trooping for their destin'd parts,
  The Devil swings his hand, the music starts;
But the main star has not arrived as yet,
And all the players wait and swear and fret.
  He comes! The tamborine with empty clack
  Greets the proud brow, the eye, the unbent back;
On with the play of broken dreams and sweat!

Aye, play their game if you would wish to rise,
  Conform yourself to standard rote and rule,
    But when you've reached the pinnacle of pelf
    Some day take down an old book from the shelf,
And scanning pages, years, with curious eyes,
  Remember one who signed himself A Fool.

RED THUNDER

Thunder in the black skies beating down the rain,
Thunder in the black cliffs, looming o'er the main,
Thunder on the black sea and thunder in my brain.

God's on the night wind, Satan's on his throne
By the red lake lurid and the great grim stone—
Still through the roofs of Hell
the brooding thunders drone.

Trident for a rapier, Satan thrusts and foins
Crouching on his throne with his great goat loins—
Souls are his footstools and hearts are his coins.

Slave of all the ages, though lord of the air;
Solomon o'ercame him, set him roaring there,
Crouching on the coals where the great flames flare.
Thunder from the grim gulfs, out of cosmic deep
Where the red eyes glimmer and the black wings sweep,
Thunder down to Satan, wake him from his sleep!

Thunder on the shores of Hell, scattering the coal,
Riding down the mountain on the moon-mare's foal,
Blasting out the caves of the gnome and the troll.

Satan, brother Satan, rise and break your chain!
Solomon is dust and his spells grow vain—
Rise through the world in the thunder and the rain.

Rush upon the cities, roaring in your might,
Break down the towers in the moon's pale light,
Build a wall of corpses for God's great sight,
Quench the red thunder in my brain this night.

THE SKULL IN THE CLOUDS
[REUBEN'S BRETHREN]

"Unstable as water, thou shalt not excel."

Drain the cup while the ale is bright,
  Brief truce to remorse and sorrow!
I drink the health of my friend tonight—
  I may cut his throat tomorrow.

Tonight I fling a curse in the cup
  For the foe whose lines we sundered—
I may ride in his ranks when the sun comes up
  And die for the flag I plundered.

Kisses I drank in the blaze of noon,
  At eve may be bitter as scorning—
And I go in the light of a mocking moon
  To the woman I cursed this morning.

For deep in my soul the old gods brood—
  And I come of a restless breed—
And my heart is blown in each drifting mood
  As clouds blow over the mead.

Robert E. Howard

A RIDING SONG

Blast away the black veil,
  Blast away the blue;
Fill with wind the slack sail,
  Stars are blinking through.

Hammers pound, hammers pound,
  Ghosts are in the hall;
Out beyond the dim sound
  The green seas call.

What of hearts can men lend
  Beg or buy or borrow?
Joy and hope and pain end
  Riding down Tomorrow.

Shadows haunt the still house—
  Lock the doors forever;
Fling the key in the sea,
  Riding from the river.

Lock the Door behind the doors
  On all joy and sorrow;
Drown them where the sea roars,
  Riding down Tomorrow!

UNIVERSE

My face may be a Universe peopled
   by billions and billions
Of lives which flame up and are extinguished
   while I draw a breath
There may be continents and rivers,
Mountains and valleys.
I writhe the cosmic expanse of my lips
And earthquakes shake the nations and men die.
I clench my jaws and the muscles bulge—
Like Atlantis above the smooth oceans of my skin.

And while I clench my jaws
On the Atlantises of my jawbone muscles,
Generations thrive and live and die, all in a second.
I relax my jaws, my bulging muscles smooth out,
And continents have sunk into the depths
Bearing millions of screaming lives to oblivion.
I wonder if our universe is a man's face and if
Men, seeing afar the reflection of that face in some
Cosmic mirror, have dreamed of the face of God?

VISIONS

I cannot believe in a paradise
   Glorious, undefiled,
For gates all scrolled and streets of gold
   Are tales for a dreaming child.

I am too lost for shame
   That it moves me unto mirth,
But I can vision a Hell of flame
   For I have lived on Earth.

XIV
Reincarnation

It is quite clear from the letters and frequent references to it in both the fiction and the poetry that Bob Howard often contemplated reincarnation and deeply examined its implications and possibilities—whether he himself finally or firmly believed in it or not. There is no doubt that the subject intrigued him. There is ample record that he at least stated openly and wrote on occasion—seemingly sincerely—that he believed he had experienced prior existences.

His various musings on Life and Death in the letters would, perhaps, also seem to go some way toward explaining his views on suicide. In at least one letter, he seems to present a view that there is a sort of conservation of Life Force at work in the Universe. In other letters he freely suggests previous or future existences. But then again, frequent consideration of a philosophy does not require commitment to it.

In any event, the poems give ample testimony to Howard's interest in the topic.

THE GUISE OF YOUTH

Men say my years are few; yet I am old
   And worn with the toil of many wars,
And long for rest on some brown wind-swept wold,
   Unknown of men, beneath the quiet stars.

These greybeards prattle while I hold my tongue,
   And flaunt their callow wisdom drearily—
White-headed babes to me, whom they brand "young,"
   With knowledge gained through ages wearily.

I cannot well recall what shapes I bore,
   What spears have pierced me, or what axes gashed,
Yet through my dreams there runs the endless roar
   Of nameless battles where lost armies crashed.

Shape upon shape returning, land on land,
   Loosed by the ripping axe, the arrow's tooth,
Through endless incarnations, till I stand,
   A scarred old man, masked in the guise of youth.

MEMORIES (1)

I rose in the path of a hurtling dawn,
  and I heard the ocean say:
"When the heart is tugging to be gone,
  its best to be away."
I gripped the mane of a granite wind,
  and the stars rushed red beneath,
For the dew lay wet where the sun had set
  ere I came to a wasted heath.

The brown grass grew like a witch's nails,
  the bats wheeled stark and lone;
But shattered columns staggered there
  like a withered waste of stone.
The grass-grown pavements broke in dust
  beneath my wayward feet.
The night wind whipped a vagrant dust
  down what had been a street.

Upon a wall's low wavering line
  a cobra raised his hood.
Beside the ruins of a shrine
  I saw a white owl brood;
And in my brain the mists gave way,
  and the years came back to me,
And my laughter broke the silence grey,
  as a serpent breaks the sea.

Here in old times a city rose
  with human loves and hates,
And men came over the desert sands
  to beat at the brazen gates.
The towers broke their spears and mauls
  as a red cliff breaks the sea;
Ten thousand men beat at these walls—
  but they fell because of me.

I was the thorn that stings the flesh;
  the worm that gnaws the root;
A snaky net that might enmesh
  a nation's iron foot.
I was the thief that slipped the bolt,
  that broke the secret bars.
The red tide thundered through the wall,
  and the flames put out the stars.

Dim Time has blotted out that night
  of death and scarlet rain.
Victor and vanquished long are dust,
  but the traitor lives again.
I mock the jests that the eons brought
  in stone and the pale starlight,
And I laugh in the ruin that I wrought
  like a jackal in a night.

MEMORIES OF ALFRED

Here in old time King Alfred broke the Danes,
  And all my dreams are of that ancient war
When red-haired jarls, close locked with shouting thanes
  Bathed deep in slaughter till the even star
    Hung in the blue above the fading moon
    And silence fell like sleep on Aethandune.

They live in me again, those dead, lost days,
  And I am one with all that vanished host—
And memory of battles and forays
  Stands at my elbow like a misty ghost.
    For out of sleep that dead life is reborn
    To rise and roar and follow Guthrum's horn.

At our first charge they wavered as to break,
  But Alfred's war-cry fired their sluggish blood;
They stiffened—stood, their thirsty blades to slake,
  And both hosts rolled together like a flood.
    The spear-point kissed the heart, the word, the throat,
    And friend slew friend, not knowing whom he smote.

REMEMBRANCE

Eight thousand years ago a man I slew;
  I lay in wait beside a sparkling rill
  There in an upland valley green and still.
The white stream gurgled where the rushes grew;
The hills were veiled in dreamy hazes blue.
  He came along the trail; with savage skill
  My spear leaped like a snake to make my kill—
Leaped like a striking snake and pierced him through.

And still when blue haze dreams along the sky
  And breezes bring the murmur of the sea,
A whisper thrills me where at ease I lie
  Beneath the branches of some mountain tree;
He comes, fog-dim, the ghost that will not die,
  And with accusing finger points at me.

SHADOWS FROM YESTERDAY

Ages ago in the dawn of Time,
  I looked on a man with hate;
He fled my wrath but I followed his path,
  as grim as the hand of Fate.
Crafty he was as a jungle snake,
  but he could not 'scape from me;
I followed his trail through the fog-dim vale
  and down by the restless sea.

To the desert brown I trailed him down,
  from the mountain's craggy height.
And I speared him dead when the dawn was red
  and left him for the kite.
Down through the years strange phantom fears
  haunted my restless soul,
Strange whisperings like the far off sweep
  of the sea upon a shoal.
For the dim ghost came when the sun had set
  and shadows dusked the lea;
I heard the tread of the vengeful dead
  and his eyes would gaze upon me.
And grim they blazed when the stars were hazed
  by the fogs of the silent night,
And dim they gazed when the dawning raised,
  in the silver lifting light.

About my sleep he would glide and creep,
    weaving a magic fell;
When I would dream he would stalk and seem
    like a spectre straight from Hell.
And down the years he has haunted me,
    mocking my reddened hand,
With spectral fears he has taunted me,
    in every life and land.

Untold eons have passed away—
    for the feet of Time are fleet—
And I met the man that I slew that day,
    in a crowded city street.
A shifting glimpse of a pallid face,
    with eyes that looked me through—
And I felt the spate of my primal hate
    leap up in my veins anew.

And he knew me as I knew him,
    for his face went strange and white,
And he swiftly whirled
    through the throng that swirled
        and vanished from my sight.
Aye, he fled from me as in years gone by,
    though the reason he might not know;
He vanished away in the crowd ere I
    could speak to my ancient foe.

He fled ere I could tell my tale,
    from a memory grim and dim,
But we will meet for the years are fleet
    and I will atone to him.
For this a Truth as eld as Hell,
    changeless as cosmic rhyme,
For every sin that we revel in
    we must make right some time.

TO A FRIEND

I toiled beside you in the galley's chains
  Through long, long days of deathly toll the same.
  North born, from some far Viking land you came;
The dark Milesian fury coursed my veins.
  Then came a night of battle, blood and flame,
And we rose up and shook our tangled manes
  And wiped out days and nights of fear and shame
With a rage that laved the decks in gore and brains.

The years have stretched to eons—vanished quite
  That day we burst the grim forecastle door.
Yet let them have a care who mock our might—
  The hour may come as in those days before
When we shall rise and bellow to the night
  And plunge our hands in hot red blood once more.

WHEN DEATH DROPS HER VEIL

A thousand years, perhaps, have come and gone,
  Since I, in sight of Erin's sullen shores,
Saw Aslaf's galley burst the crawling dawn,
  And heard the water hiss beneath his oars.

The grappling irons gripped, the thrusting staves
  Were dyed in red; the arrows rent the sails;
An iron thunder shook the crimson waves—
  I met him, Aslaf, on the crunching rails.

I felt my scarlet fury surge and burn,
  I thrust and saw my reddened broadsword dart
Between his corselet's links, and felt in turn
  His blindly stabbing dagger find my heart.

177

A single aching glimpse of sky and sea,
  The white gulls wheeling in the bitter blue—
A scroll of smoke upon the distant lea—
  A dimming crash of battle—and I knew

A mist as fading life I blindly clutched—
  Close-clinched we plunged to ocean and the night
And ere the clawing sea or bodies touched
  Swift blackness brought the end of sound and sight.

A thousand years, perhaps, yet never morn
  Comes crawling white across the waters blue
But in my soul a memory is reborn,
  A misty dream of that far dawn I knew.

And as the east wind whispers sharp and cold
  I dimly sense the revel and the strife,
Those rose-red days of fire and blood and gold,
  And feel again the tang of parting life.

I envy not the singer nor the prince;
  No guerdon new may Life on me bestow,
And when Death drops her veil I shall not wince—
  I knew it all, a thousand years ago.

WHITE THUNDER

I was a child in Cornwall
   where the mountains meet the shore;
I lay on the cliffs at even
   and I heard the combers roar.

It was thunder, high white thunder,
   leaping o'er the tossing ridges;
Roaring down the jade green valleys,
   wild as Neptune and as free;
Spanning wave and shore and sky rim
   with a million unseen bridges
Till the booming cliffs re-echoed
   to the thunder of the sea.

I was a boy in London,
   timid, callow, amazed
But I heard beyond the city
   when the lights through the night fogs blazed;

Heard the thunder, high white thunder,
   booming far beyond the sky line,
Roaring up the restless vastness
   of the globe encircling sea,
Spray bejeweled, white and sapphire,
   gleaming in the topaz sky shine;
Through the mutter of the city
   high white thunder called to me.

I was a youth in Delhi and
   I left the brooding walls
For the hills that are gods of twilight
   where the wind forever brawls.

There was thunder, high white thunder,
   where the northern crags were looming,
Smiting on the reeling mountains
   with the hammer blows of Thor,
Fraught with lore of rugged ages,
   shouting wonders in its booming
Till the clashing crags re-echoed
   like a planetary war.

Now I am a man in Flanders;
   I crouch in the mire and see
The white smoke leap and billow
   to the shout of the shells that flee;

See the thunder, high white thunder
   through the screaming air come soaring,
Swirling like white clouds at even
   when the breakers rock the seas.
Let me revel in its fury,
   let me triumph in its roaring
Ere the high white thunder bear me
   into high eternities.

XV
The Road to Yesterday:
Poems Based Upon History

Howard had a deep love of history, and his particular brand of imaginative fantastic fiction, often called Sword & Sorcery, owes a debt to his deep reading about the ancient world and its history and mythology. As noted above, where Tolkien's fantasy has rightly been called "mythopoeic" [myth creating], Howard's has elements of both the mythopoeic—especially regarding the Atlantean and Cimmerian settings—and what might rightly be called the "mythomorphic" [myth shaping or reshaping]—taking the seeds of actual history, geography, and legend and growing them in new imaginatively fertile soil to metamorphose into new and amazing realms and sagas.

Nonetheless, there are many poems that connect directly to our historical records, reflecting an understanding of and profound interest in the real world of yesteryear. Often, with only slight alterations in spelling and pronunciation, the places of dim actual history appear with a new panoply of creative story.

These poems run across millennia from ancient Babylon to Rome and the Empire to Britain from Hadrian's Wall to the time of Alfred the Great through the Crusades to the English Civil War. They touch upon Attila, the Cossacks, and things as modern as a conflict between the Muscovites and Turks and the perpetual troubles of Afghanistan.

That last place, of course relevant again as it does its pendulum swing through matters of broad significance in world events is captured in one of the fine lyric poems in the English language—and certainly among Howard's best: "The Hills of Kandahar."

In the poems that follow, we see Robert E. Howard displaying his keen interest in and knowledge of the Past.

Robert E. Howard

ATTILA RIDES NO MORE

Across the silent sands we sprang
   Before the royal tent
And to our tramp the dim wind sang
   A weird accompaniment.
We flung aside the silken door
   And halted in amaze;
No wilder sight was seen before;
   Men shouldered men to gaze.

A-gibber on her throne of gilt
   The naked empress smiled
And toyed with her red dagger hilt
   As a mother with a child.
The plundered amber, gold and jade
   Gleamed round like coals of Hell
Then smoldered to a redder shade
   To swords that rose and fell.

While round the standards and the flags
   There whispered, o'er and o'er
The desert wind amid the tents:
   "King Atla rides no more."

BABYLON

For I have seen the lizards crawl
Through high Belshazzar's marble halls
When ghostly shadow petals fall
  In Babylon, dead Babylon.

And many a golden girdled spire
Like molten moonlight veined with fire,
That fell before the ages' ire
  In Babylon, far Babylon.

Have watched the star-dark, misty shades
Come down the lonely colonnades
When the grey rose of twilight fades
  In Babylon, in Babylon.

Lost since the dust dead distant noon
When Rustum heard the trumpet tune
And Tamerlane broke down the moon
And ringed the walls of Babylon.

Robert E. Howard

BABYLON HAS FALLEN

[Dreams]

"Babylon has fallen, has fallen, has fallen!
 "Babylon has fallen—" the crimson kings are dead.
The ashes sift and quiver along the bloody river;
 Babylon has fallen and all her gods are fled.

"Babylon has fallen!" Send tidings unto Egypt.
 "Babylon has fallen!" Let Israel's tribes rejoice.
Belshazzar's sword is broken, the trump of war has spoken,
 And Babylon has fallen before the trumpet's voice.

"Babylon has fallen"—Her walls were set in sapphire;
 "Babylon has fallen"—Her streets were paved with gold.
Her girls were fair as flowers—their blood is on her towers.
 Babylon has fallen; Astarte's shrine is cold.
And still in song and story, the rhymers sing her glory,
 But Babylon has fallen—oh, the regal days of old!

THE CELLS OF THE COLISEUM

Across the walls a shadow falls;
 The dreary night drags on and on.
The horses stamp within their stalls.
 I'll ride no more to meet the dawn.

Beyond this wall a sleeping Gaul
 Mutters and tosses in his sleep.
Before him maybe I shall fall
 Or in his heart my blade drink deep.

A silence falls along the halls;
 The lions mutter in the gloom.
How Time along the hours crawls
 Like some great sluggish worm of doom.

My heartbeats fall, a striking maul.
 Because my thews are hard and strong
Within the hour I must fall
 To meet the blood lust of the throng.

Along the halls a trumpet calls.
 The red arena glimmers nigh.
Thor, let me mock these fools of Rome
 And show them how a Goth can die.

Robert E. Howard

CRUSADE

Wild flying hoofs whirl up the sands
And the hot wind sings to the flashing brands.
The red lights glance from the helmet's crest
And flame on a thousand spears at rest.
White-feathered cloud the arrows whir
Flinging their scorn to the hissing spur.
Horses stumble and riders reel—
In, close in! And ply your steel.
Cursed, thrice cursed his name who flees
Though the swift shafts hum like a million bees.
Never a one would check that pace!
On they roar like a tidal-race!

Black eyes flare, dark faces leer
Scimitars thrum on the leveled spear.
On they roar like a steel-tipped wall.
Shields are shattered and turbans fall.
Mingled and broken ranks arrayed
Knight to warrior and blade to blade.
The desert rocks to the reeling hosts
And the red wind roars with a thousand ghosts.
The broadswords clamor their wild refrains
As the red rout breaks o'er the crimson plains.

An old man's fancy. The drowsy stream
Glides where the still bush-alders gleam.
Tis warm and pleasant. My race is run.
I'm only fit to drowse in the sun.
But I'd like take my sword and horse
And ride one last, wild gloried course.
To hear the thunder of fighting men
As when we shattered the Saracen.
To ride again on those wild raids,
To thrill with splendor of old Crusades.

THE CRY EVERLASTING

"A voice came out of the throng saying: 'Good rede, good rede! Slay ye the Bishop!' The bishop was forthwith slain."
— The Norman Conquest

"Good rede, good rede! Slay ye the Bishop!"
  Roaring through the gloom like a rousing tiger's snarl.
Bugle call and drum beat pale and fade before it,
  Fade before the growl of a nameless Saxon carle.

Little love I bear for the surly ceorls of England—
  A black blight befall them! The first of all my name
Breathed the breath of life in the grey Norse mountains,
  Rode with iron William when the Norman came.

Yet I burn again at that savage cry for freedom,
  Roaring down the ages at the crozier and the crown.
All the pagan eons speak in that mad bellow:
  "Slay ye the Bishop!—   the tyrant in the gown."

Freedom—freedom—freedom!
Oh, I hear the heathen ages
  Loose their pent-up fury in that one red roar!
Symbol through the Eternity,
their blind revolt shall guide us,
  That slew a Norman bishop in his own church door.

Dust, long dust are the men that heaved the axes,
  William rent their land like a blinding blast of doom,
The great Norman horses strove in blood to the fetlock,
  But their word comes down to fire us
in the twilight and the gloom.

Good rede, good rede, slay ye the bishop!
  Judge or prince or prelate, each bears a chain—
Who bars our way on the red road to freedom?
  Shatter the oppressor in the fierce red rain!

Robert E. Howard

DREAMING ON DOWNS

I marched with Alfred when he thundered forth
  To break the crimson standards of the Dane;
I saw the galleys looming in the north
  And heard the oar-locks and the sword's refrain.

And far across the pleasant Wessex downs
  The chanting of the spearmen broke the lyre,
Till where the black thorn forest grimly frowns
  We sang a song of doom and steel and fire.

Death rode his pale horse through the dreaming sky
  All through that long red summer afternoon,
And night and silence fell, when silently
  The dead men lay beneath a cold white moon.

Now Alfred sleeps with all the swords of yore,
  (But o'er the downs a brooding shadow glides)
Untrampled flowers dream along the shore,
  And Guthrum's galleys rust beneath the tides.

Now underneath this drowsy tree I lie
  And turn old dreams upon my lazy knees,
Till ghostly giants fill the summer sky
  And phantom oars awake the sleeping seas.

A DUNGEON OPENS

They let me out of my slimy cell,
  A shaking hulk of a man,
To plunge once more, ere my parting knell,
  At the throat of the Puritan.

The Stuarts may perish, buy or sell,
  Preacher or priest may toll;
I rode for my seven years in hell
  And the thought of Bloody Noll.

The hilt was good to my withered hand,
  My charger spurned the banks,
And my whitened hair was a banner there
  In the plunging royal ranks.

And ever a Face was floating before,
  And ever my broadsword bit,
And it seemed at each stroke the skull I shore
  Of the Bloody Hypocrite.

But every time when I looked down,
  To prove by better proofs,
Some nameless churl with a cloven crown
  Rolled under my horse's hoofs.

And well I knew, as my edge cut through,
  And the sour Broadbrim fell,
That the blackened soul of Bloody Noll
  Had long been locked in Hell.

I've laid my broken blade aside,
  My fury glutted full.
The blood on my hands is not yet dried,
  The edge of my hate undulled.

And I'll ride on the wings of a blackened blast
    Where the ghostly armies meet,
Till I see damned Cromwell roll at last
    Under my horse's feet.

AN ECHO FROM THE IRON HARP
[THE GOLD AND THE GREY]

Shadows and echoes haunt my dreams
    with dim and subtle pain,
With the faded fire of a lost desire,
    like a ghost on a moonlit plain,
In the pallid mist of death-like sleep
    she comes again to me:
I see the gleam of her golden hair
    and her eyes like the deep grey sea.

We came from the North as the spume is blown
    when the blue tide billows down,
The kings of the South were overthrown
    in ruin of camp and town,
Temple and shrine we dashed to dust,
    and roared in the dead gods' ears;
We saw the fall of the kings of Gaul
    and shattered the Belgae spears.

And South we rolled like a drifting cloud,
    like a wind that bends the grass,
But we smote in vain on the gates of Spain
    for our own kin held the Pass.
Then again we turned where the watch-fires burned
    to mark the lines of Rome,
And fire and tower and standard sank
    as ships that die in foam.

The legions came, hard hawk-eyed men,
    war-wise in march and fray,
But we rushed like a whirlwind on their ranks
    and swept their lines away.
Army and consul we overthrew,
    staining the trampled loam;
Horror and fear like a lifted spear
    lay hard on the walls of Rome.
Our mad desire was a flying fire
    that should burn the Roman gate—
But our day of doom lay hard on us,
    at a toss of the dice of Fate.
There rose a man in the ranks of Rome—
    ill fall the cursed day!
Our German allies bit the dust
    and we turned hard at bay.

Over the land like a ghostly hand
    the mists of morning lay,
We smote their horsemen in the mist
    and hacked a bloody way.
We smote their horsemen in a cloud
    and as the mists were cleared
Right through the legion massed behind
    our headlong squadron sheared.

Saddle to saddle we chained our ranks
    for nothing of war we knew
But to charge in the old wild Celtic way—
    and die, or slash right through.
We left red ruin in our wake,
    dead men in ghastly ranks
When fresh, unwearied Roman arms
    smote hard upon our flanks.

Baffled and weary, red with wounds,
   leaguered on every side,
Chained to our doom we smote in vain,
   slaughtered and sank and died.
Writhing among the horses' hoofs,
   torn and slashed and gored,
Gripping still with a bloody hand
   a notched and broken sword,

I heard the war-cry growing faint,
   drowned by the trumpet's call,
And the roar of "Marius! Marius!"
   triumphant over all.
Through the bloody dust and the swirling fog
   as I strove in vain to rise,
I saw the last of the warriors fall
   and swift as a falcon flies.

The Romans rush to the barricade
   where the women watched the fight—
I heard the screams and I saw steel flash
   and naked arms toss white.
The ravisher died as he gripped his prey,
   by the dagger swiftly driven—
By the next stroke, with her own hand,
   the heart of the girl was riven.

Brown fingers gripped white wrists in vain—
   blood flecked the weary loam—
The Cimbri yield no virgin-slaves
   to glut the lords of Rome!
And I saw as I crawled like a crippled snake
   to slay before I died,
Unruly golden hair that tossed
   in high barbaric pride.

Her slim foot pressed a dead man's breast,
   her proud head back was thrown,
Matching the steel she held on high,
   her eyes in glory shone.
I saw the gleam of her golden hair
   and her eyes like the deep gray sea—
And the love in the gaze that sought me out,
   barbaric, fierce and free—
Then the dagger fell and the skies fell too
   and the mists closed over me.
Like phantoms into the ages lost
   has the Cimbrian nation passed;
Destiny shifts like summer clouds
   on Grecian hilltops massed.
Untold centuries glide away,
   Marius long is dust;
Even eternal Rome has passed
   in days of decay and rust.
But memories live in the ghosts of dreams
   and dreams still come to me,
And I see the gleam of her golden hair
   and her eyes like the deep grey sea.

THE GATES OF BABYLON

The gates of Babylon stand ajar
   For traders out of the Eastern lands
Bearing sinuous dancing girls,
Silks and ivory and pearls
   Across the purple sands.

The gates of Babylon open wide
   To Eqypt's pharaoh and Sheba's queen;
The white streets echo to golden heels
And the clang of brazen chariot wheels,
   And the shields are a silver sheen.

The gates of Babylon stand ajar;
  Traders and emperors cross her sills.
She greets the men of scented breath,
But Babylon's gates are shut as death
  To the horsemen of the hills.

The gates of Babylon flare at morn
  Like an evil rose on a painted stalk,
But ever her gates are barred and shut
To the chief that rules in a herder's hut—
  The king with the eyes of a hawk.

But the lean wolves slink from the scarlet hills,
  And the kites and vultures throng the land;
And we ride full soon through a bloody dawn
O'er the shattered gates of Babylon
  With death at our left hand.

HADRIAN'S WALL

Against these stones red waves of carnage brake;
  Along these parapets Rome's armor shone.
  Here swarmed the Picts, when ghastly tribes unknown
Came trooping down from heath and mountain lake;
Here leaped the Saxon sword, red thirst to slake.
  Here sounded night on night the war-horn's drone
  Mocking the desperate Britons left alone
When 'neath her feet Rome felt her empire shake.

Still, sullen giants born of night and gloom,
Beyond, the purple, brooding mountains loom-
  Symbol of heathen gods that they sent forth,
  The ancient menace of the Northern land:
  A bulwark still, these shattered towers stand
Against the mystic hazes of the North.

THE HARP OF ALFRED

I heard the harp of Alfred
  As I went o'er the downs,
When thorn-trees stood at even
  Like monks in dusky gowns;
I heard the music Guthrum heard
  Beside the wasted towns;
When Alfred, like a peasant,
  Came harping down the hill,
And the drunken Danes made merry
  With the man they sought to kill,
And the Saxon king laughed in their beards
  And bent them to his will.
I heard the harp of Alfred
  As twilight waned to night;
I heard ghost armies tramping
  As the dim stars flamed white;
And Guthrum walked at my left hand,
  And Alfred at my right.

Robert E. Howard

THE HILLS OF KANDAHAR

The night primeval breaks in scarlet mist;
   The shadows gray, and pales each silent star,
The eastern sky that rose-lipped dawn has kissed
   Glows crimson o'er the hills of Kandahar.
   A trumpet song re-echoes from afar;
Across the crags the golden glory grows
   To drive the shades, renewing ancient war;
Now bursts full bloom the gorgeous morning rose.

These are the hills that many a sultan trod;
   Their rocks have known full many a victor's stride;
   These peaks could tell their tale of human pride—
See where they rear, each like a somber god.
   Aye, they have gazed since first the primal dawn
Fired with a wild, vague flame a bestial soul
   Who rose and stood and saw his fallen spawn
With him, somehow, part of Creation's whole,
And made himself immortal with a goal
   To be attained—this untaught simian faun.

Aye, but these peaks have known the human tread:
   The ebb and flow of dim humanity,
The restless, surging, never-ceasing tide,
   The swarming tribes that came unceasingly;
The lust of kings, the bloody war-dawn's red,
   The races that arose and ruled—and died.
They will be brooding when mankind is gone;
   The teeming tribes that scaled their barricades—
Dim hordes that waxed at dusk and waned at dawn—
   Are but as snow that on their shoulders fades.

AN INCIDENT IN THE
MUSCOVY-TURKISH WAR

Many were slaughtered in that final charge;
  Along the rail we saw the gunnels kneel,
  And then the world turned red with screaming steel,
But on we plunged, wild firing, wide and large,
Our bullies fell in rows along the marge;
  Blindly we felt deep water under heel,
  Swarmed up the anchor chains to roar and reel
With all the yelling devils of the barge.

A giant bashaw cleft eight Cossack skulls,
  And then his saber met a blade of flame—
And as his ships went down with blazing hulls:
  "Allah!" he screamed, "Thou swine—what is thy name?"
    Our captain's rapier leaped—a fire of blue.
    And "John Paul Jones!" said he, and ran him through.

Robert E. Howard

THE MASTER-DRUM

The Master beat on his master-drum,
  (Wild, roaring wild, like an unreined sea!)
Back through the fogs flew the whispering thrum,
  (Hide-covered log on a lone white lea,
  Ape-man pounding on a sounding tree.)
Primal seas with their silian scum,
Planetary chaos with the cosmic hum,
Whispered down the ages on the master-drum!

Weird echoes flying, whispering far,
  (Footprints fading on the shifting sands!)
Dim, dim song of a strange night star,
  Wild lute murmur from the Shadow-lands!
  Star gleams a-ride like spirit brands,
Chords of the night wind tuned and a-strum,
  (Vague wild music from unseen hands)
Whispered down the ages on the master-drum!

Midnight skies and a flying ghost-fire,
  Crone-faced witches, wild against the moon,
Dark, silent city, Devil-crowning spire,
Witch-fire flitting o'er the sullen mire,
  And the devil-devil secrets of the isle-wind's rune.
    Ghost fire flitting through the flying wrack,
    Flame-rid dreams of a maniac.
  Hiss of a serpent, laughter of a loon.
  And the tales of the Past on the night-wind's croon.
Tales of the Past, a-whirl and a-thrum,
Whispered down the ages with the master-drum.

NISAPUR

The day that towers, sapphire kissed,
Reeled to a Mongol sword that hissed,
And broke the silver sighing mist
　That parted doom from Nisapur.

Or when in morning shadows grey
The flying ghosts of Subotai
came galloping from far Cathay
　To trample towers of Nisapur.

Or when in midnight's star-shah'd rule
There came o'er sands like golden pools,
Bayezid riding from Stamboul
　To break the walls of Nisapur.

Ere Rustum, great fire-breathing lord
Who broke the genii with his sword,
Had fallen before the Golden Horde
　His bones are dust in Nisapur.

And he who chanted of the vine,
Spilt like a skin of Shiraz wine,
Had made that dust a thing divine—
　Divine the dust of Nisapur.

Robert E. Howard

THE RIDERS OF BABYLON

The riders of Babylon clatter forth
   Like the hawk-winged scourgers of Azrael
To the meadow-lands of the South and North
   And the strong-walled cities of Israel.
     They harry the men of the caravans,
     They bring rare plunder across the sands
To deck the throne of the great god Baal.
   But Babylon's king is a broken shell
   And Babylon's queen is a sprite from Hell;
   And men shall say, "Here Babylon fell,"
Ere Time has forgot the tale.

The riders of Babylon come and go
   From Gaza's halls to the shores of Tyre;
They shake the world from the lands of snow
   To the deserts, red in the sunset's fire;
     Their horses swim in a sea of gore
     And the tribes of the earth bow down before;
They have chained the seas where the Cretans sail.
   But Babylon's sun shall set in blood;
   Her towers shall sink in a crimson flood;
   And men shall say, "Here Babylon stood,"
Ere Time forgot the tale.

THE ROAD TO BLISS

I did not give a tinker's curse
   For the Stuarts or the Church;
They never filled an empty purse
   Or freshened beech and birch.

I fought the Puritans because
   Their sole desire was this:
To fetter man with sombre laws
   And bar them from all bliss.

They would have blacked the glowing sun,
   And damned the laughing brooks;
Ripped up the flowers one by one
   And burned all hearty books.

Now I am but a simple churl
   Who loves the kine and grass,
To watch the burning dawn unfurl,
   And the fleecy clouds that pass.

I love to dream and take my ease,
   I wish no mortal ill;
I thought to live my life in peace
   On some green Devon hill.

But when the Broad-brims stopped all play,
   And stifled fun and mirth
I roused myself and rode away
   To ride them off the earth.

The road is hard wheron I ride;
   My blade is never dry;
Of all the troopers at my side,
   There's none more grim than I.

The sour Roundheads know me well
  And little like my play:
I've sent a many one to Hell
  Since I rode out that day.

Well, boots and saddles and to horse—
  Our ranks are growing thin;
I fear the game's near run its course
  And the hunt is closing in.

Well, comrades, strike for Church or crown,
  For creed or court or king,
I'm fighting for a Devon down,
  May poles, and maids that sing.

France beckons? No, if drabness rules
  It's time for me to die;
I'll strike one blow for the joyous fools,
  The jesters such as I.

THE ROAD TO YESTERDAY

The dust is deep along the trail,
  Yet stars gleam on the way;
It knows no worldly hill nor vale,
  The Road to Yesterday.

On phantom steeds, pale-starlight shod,
  Shapes of the shadows stray,
And many a dreamer's foot has trod
  The Road to Yesterday.

He needs no whip nor spur nor goad
  To drive him on his way
Whose feet have learned to walk the road
  That runs to Yesterday.

Dim kings ride there and planets blaze
  And shadows flit for aye
Where gleams along the Age's haze
  The Road to Yesterday.

SHADOWS ON THE ROAD

Nial of Ulster, welcome home!
What saw you on the road to Rome?—
  Legions thronging the fertile plains?
Shouting hordes of the country folks
  With the harvest heaped in their groaning wains?
Shepherd piping under the oak?
Laurel chaplet and purple cloak?
  Smokes of the feasting coiled on high?
Meadows and fields of the rich, ripe green
  Lazing under a cobalt sky?
Brown little villages sleeping between?
What saw you on the road to Rome?
"Crimson tracks in the blackened loam,
  "Skeleton trees and a blasted plain,
  "A heap of skulls and a child insane,
  "Ruin and wreck and the reek of pain
"On the wrack of the road to Rome."

Nial, what saw you in Rome?—
  Purple emperors riding there,
Down aisles with walls like marble foam,
  To the golden trumpet's mystic flare?
  Dark-eyed women who bind their hair,
As they bind men's hearts, with a silver comb?
  Spires that cleave through the crystal air,
  Arch and altar and amaranth stair?
Nial, what saw you in Rome?
"Broken shrines in the sobbing gloam,
  "Bare feet spurning the marble flags,
"Towers fallen and walls digged up,
  "A woman in chains and filthy rags.
"Goths in the Forum howled to sup,
"With an emperor's skull for a drinking-cup.
"The black arch clave to the broken dome.

"The Coliseum invites the bat.
"The Vandal sits where the Caesars sat;
"And the shadows are black on Rome."

Nial, Nial, now you are home,
Why do you mutter and lonely roam?
  "My brain is sick and I know no rest;
  "My heart is stone in my frozen breast,
  "For the feathers fall from the eagle's crest
"And the bright sea breaks in foam—
  "Kings and kingdoms and empires fall,
  "And the mist-black ruin covers them all,
  "And the honey of life is a bitter gall
"Since I traveled the road to Rome."

A SONG OF THE DON COSSACKS

Wolf-brother, wolf-lover,
Over the river the kites hover
Where witch-light glimmers
And tall grass shimmers—
What dead things shall their eyes discover?
What, when the sabers sing in the gloaming,
What, when the gray wolves cease their roaming?
Wolf-lover, wolf-brother,
We are sworn to slay each other.

Gray light glances
Along our lances—
Both of us sons of our Volga mother.
Kites shall feast when ranks burst asunder
And the roar of the red tide hurls us under.
When the white steel glints and the red blood spurts—
Death in the camps and death in the yurts.
When the crimson shadows of twilight fall

We shall be feasts for the white jackal.
Wolf-lover, wolf-brother,
We be sons of the self-same mother,
Though between us flows a red-stained tide.
Horse and man
Ride we far,
You for the Kahn,
I for the czar,
Wolf-lover, Tartar-brother, ride!

A SONG OF THE LEGIONS

The crystal gong of the silence
   Shivers in shattered shards;
And the marble hall re-echoes
   To the tread of the crested guards.

Fingers pluck at the hangings,
   White in the purple gloam;
Midnight lies with the sleepers
   In the pulsing heart of Rome.

Rosy lips smile in slumber
   Arms nestle bodies white—
Rome in her silks and marbles
   Sleeps through the soft-lipped night.

Echoing down the heather
   The restless trumpets call,
Questioning each of the other
   Down the line of the winding Wall.

Eyes strain hard in the darkness,
   To the pulse of an echo blown—
Rome is of gold and iron
   But a soldier is flesh and bone.

Fires in the hills are burning,
   To the far off throb of a drum;
Through the ghostly waving heather
   What phantom figures come?

Shadows or painted warriors?
   The death drums never cease.
Stand to your watches, legion,
   That Rome may sleep in peace.

Beacons burn in the towers,
  Eyes straining hard beside,
Ears a-tune to the murmur,
  The sigh of each changing tide.

Was that the shrill of a night bird
  Where the waves are grey as steel,
Or the grind of a muffled oar-lock,
  The wash of a prowling keel?

Driftwood or sword-fanged sea-wolves,
  Not yours is rest or ease;
Stand to your watches, legion,
  That Rome may sleep in peace.

XVI

Short Measures of Joy
& The Awesome Beauty of Nature

As we find in one of Ben Jonson's odes:

> *In small proportions we just beauties see,*
> *And in short measures life may perfect be.*

So we find, I believe, some agreement with this sentiment in the work of Robert E. Howard. By all accounts he knew how to laugh and did so often, had and held fast to close friends, lived his short life passionately and deeply (even if not living it to a normal span), knew love as well as grief and despair, had hopes as well as the occasional bout with cynical hopelessness.

Howard has been seen too narrowly by his critics and commentators. The more we read of his work—especially as his complete letters and complete poetry see the light of day—the more we realize the complexity of the man. The poem "Earth-born" offers a stark contrast with the "Dark Valley" so overly emphasized by de Camp and others in what has all too often amounted to a superficial critical stance.

This section includes some of the bright poems penned by this poet of the post oaks. They show youthful exuberance and love of Life, and a deep love of the wonders of Nature.

THE AGES STRIDE ON GOLDEN FEET

The ages stride on golden feet
The stars re-echo to the beat;
   And o'er the peaks across the vales
      the sea-winds seek the dawn;
The east is tinted like the rose,
   a light breeze through the tree-tops blows
   And through the dawn the red deer goes
      to meet the timid fawn.
   Through the forest on to the smiling dawn.

THE CALL OF PAN

My heart is a silver drum tonight—
   —And the moon is red in the East—
And he drums with a rattle eery and light,
   The god with the hoofs of the beast.
Drums with a thunder gold and light,
And the silence breathes like a mist rose white,
Is it my heart that he drums tonight,
   Or the moon in the dreaming East?

His call to the sons of men at dawn
   —And they falter and halt and start—
Is the haunting wail of pipe soon gone;
Oh, they hear his pipes in the brooding dawn,
But he shouts to me and he leads me on
   With the drum that is my heart.

EARTH-BORN

By rose and verdant valley
  And silence I was born,
My brothers were the mountains,
  The purple gods of morn.

My sisters were the whirlwinds
  That broke the dreaming plains—
The earth is in my sinews.
  The stars are in my veins!

For first upon the molten
  White silver sands I lay,
And saw the ocean beckon
  With eyes of burning spray.

And up along the mountain,
  And down along the lea
I heard my brothers singing,
  The river and the tree.

And through the ocean's thunder,
  And through the forest's hush
I heard my sisters calling,
  The sea-wind and the thrush.
And still all living voices
  Leap forth amain and far,
The sunset and the shadow,
  The eagle and the star.

From caverns of the ocean
  To highest mountain tree
I hear all voices singing
  Their kinship unto me.

THE GODS I WORSHIPPED

The standards toss in pride
　As priests and prelates go,
But the gods I worshipped died
　Eight thousand years ago.

The gods of the mountain side,
　The gods of the buffalo,
The gods of the surging tide,
　The ceaseless ebb and flow.

HOPE EMPTY OF MEANING

Man is a fool and a blinded toy—
　The Fire still flickers and burns,
Though the cobra coils in the cup called Joy,
　And ever the Worm returns.

Life is a lamp with the glimmer gone,
　A dank and a darkened cave;
Yet still I swear by the light of dawn,
　And not by the grip of the grave.

ILLUSION

I stood upon surf-booming cliffs
And heard the tide-race roaring,
   roaring strong and deep and free;
  On tall wind wings the white clouds scudded by.
  Far to the east the ocean met the sky
And the booming cliffs re-echoed to the thunder of the sea.
Green are the waves and fringed with white the crest:
  Strong color contrasts, turquoise, sapphire, snow.
Tumbling the jade green billows from the west
  Roars the wild sea-wind. Keep your sea. I go.
Stranger to me the fierce red-blooded zest,
The wild beast urge, the primitive behest.
  Fierce primal impulses are thoughts I do not know.
I've ever dwelt 'mid worlds of vaguer tone,
  All tints and colors merging soft and dim,
  No garish flare of reds at the desert's rim—
The sea-winds murmur there a pleasing drone;
   The sea-fogs grace the ocean, friendly, grey.
   'Mid soft-hued woodlands shy nymphs have their play.
And so I'll none of all this garish joy,
  These blazing dawns that leap like maids o'er-bold;
These flaming greens and reds and yellows cloy,
  Barbaric tints of crimson, blazing gold.
The worlds I seek are like soft, golden chimes;
  Soft merging tints that match the breeze's croon
And no false note plays in the world-scheme rhymes—
  I seek the soft, vague plateaus of the moon.

A MOMENT

Let me forget all men a space,
  All dole and death and dearth;
Let me clutch the world in my hungry arms—
  The paramour of the earth.

The hills are gowned in emerald trees
  And the sea-green tides of grain,
And the joy, oh God, of the tingling sod,
  Oh, it rends my heart in twain.

My feet are bare to the burning dew,
  My breast to the stinging breeze;
And I watch the sun in the flaming blue
  Like a worshipper on his knees.

With the joys of the sun and love and growth
  All things of the earth are rife;
And the soul that is deep in the breast of me
  Sings with the pulse of Life.

THIS IS A YOUNG WORLD

This is a young world.
I spread my arms, I laugh.
The mountain streams are leaping
With a wildness, a laughing recklessness
That shows a kindred to my soul.
I sway with the forest sapling
And I dance with the moon-beams on the lakes.
I have shaken off musty creeds and dusty despotisms.
The universe is old but I am young.
Priests and rulers curse me for they envy my youth.
The stars are old. Their day of youth is passed.
They sit like crones and leer fruitlessly at youth.
I fling my arms to catch the fruits of youth.
The wine of youth is cool upon my lips.
The breeze whispers through the trees
And the waves laugh upon the beach.
Sap is running with the joy of living.
My blood is leaping with the laughing fury of youth.
        This is a young world.
My soul is thrilled with the laughter of youth.

XVII
The Soothing Dust: Poems on Suicide and the Subject of Death

Much has been written and said about the relevance of Robert E. Howard's suicide—so much so, that perhaps the most famous piece of poetry known to many Howard enthusiasts is one that is not even original with Howard, but, rather—as scholar Rusty Burke has shown—a verbatim gleaning and rearranging of lines from a poem by Viola Garvin:

```
All fled, all done, so lift me on the pyre.
The feast is over, and the lamps expire.
```

This pieced-together couplet, found by Dr. Howard after his son's suicide [the exact nature of the discovery of the paper with these lines is still being debated], has become the focus of much comment and discussion.

The fact of Howard's suicide, coincident with the imminent death of his mother, and the then-recent separation from Novalyne Price cannot be denied. Neither can the fact that suicide as a topic appears prominently in some of Howard's poems.

Along with Howard scholar and psychology professor Dr. Charles Gramlich, I subscribe to the belief that Howard's suicide was the result of a *reactive* rather than *clinical* depression, the result following closely upon a confluence of events forming an emotional and traumatic nexus. But there are certainly poems left us that directly address the topic—and the attraction—of suicide, evidently one theme of Howard's in his darker moods. Of these, "The Tempter" is the most well-known.

While I concur with most students of Howard in disagreeing with the de Campian mantra of Oedipal confusion and clinical depression leading to a supposedly inevitable course of events, most of the following poems do, indeed, touch upon self-destruction. The poem "The Dance With Death" is, on the other hand—as Howard scholar Paul Herman notes—in an interesting way a celebration of life and praise for the adventure-laden life that is made more full by the knowledge of Death's nearness as a close partner in "the Dance."

AMBITION

Build me a gibbet against the sky,
Solid and strong and long miles high,
Let me hang where the high winds blow
That never stoop to the world below,
And the great clouds lumber by.
Let the people who toil below
See me swaying to and fro,
See me swinging the aeons through,
A dancing dot in the distant blue.

THE DANCE WITH DEATH

The fogs of night
Fling banners red
To cloak the fading sun,
And I haste to the height
Of the mountain-head
O'er sombre valleys silently spread
Where murmur the ghosts of forgotten dead,
Through the star-gleam's glance
As I go to dance
With my mistress, The Hooded One.

Now, as the night-winds drone their dree
From the hidden caves of the ghostly sea,
And as the trees below wave dim in the vale,
And shadows flit through the star-light pale,
Weird night tunes peal
As we weave and reel
Like a maiden leal
And her cavalier.
But a grisly maid

Is the flitting shade
That sways with me through the moon-lit glade.
And the boldest knight,
Like the poorest wight,
Would flee the sight
With ghastly fear.
But on we dance 'neath an eerie sky
And light we prance, old Death and I;

Ah, beldame Death, old beldame Death!
We've tripped it many a time!
Our flying feet
Have weaved their beat
From the line to the Arctic clime.
I've felt your kiss
On the Gulf's abyss
And the swamps of the tropic slime.

Your barren bones
Gleam a dreary white
Through your lank ribs drone
The winds of the night.
An eery glimmer gleams and dies
In the empty sockets of your eyes
White and bleached as the wings of a gull
And you wear a garland upon your skull,
Ferns that grew on the swampy fen
Through the hidden bones of murdered men.
Of moss from the shores of the long-lost sea
Where the hulls of ships strew the silent lea.
First with the left foot,
Then with the right
Footing it featly through the night.
Soul to demon
And fiend to man
We've danced this dance since time began.

Around the world
Have flown our feet
In a dizzy whirl
But our lips n'er meet.
'Tis a grisly play
And I trip and sway
With her fleshless face a span away.
And her skeleton hand is on my wrist
But I swerve aside with a dexter twist
And she seeks to press
Her grim caress
Upon my lips;
And she hops and trips
And she leaps and skips.
With her bones a-clank
Over barren stone
And waving grass
And the night-winds drone
As we meet and pass
And spin again where the reeds grow rank.
Through the witch-light haze
We tread our ways
In a weird, fantastic, wizard maze.

Ah, beldame Death!
Her love is grim
And she leads to trails
That are long and dim
She is aloof
From loves and hates—
She bears my taunts
And she waits! She waits!

And a single instant
Off my guard,
A foot a-slip
On the pallid sward,

A sadle-girth loosed,
A rended sail,
And a hand that misses
A wave-lashed rail,
A reef that lifts
'Neath the plunging strakes,
A horse that falls
Or a sword that breaks;
And the music stops
And the swirl is o'er
And my feet are still
For I dance no more.

But I'll not grudge the game I trow
As I feel her kiss on my fading brow.
And I hold her measure
Above all treasure
For to dance with Death is the only joy
That thrills and leaps and fails to cloy!
And I'll only laugh as she bends to destroy.
Left foot, right foot,
We whirl and prance
And spin away on our world-long dance!

LINES WRITTEN IN THE REALIZATION THAT I MUST DIE

The Black Door gapes and the Black Wall rises;
　Twilight gasps in the grip of Night.
Paper and dust are the gems man prizes—
　Torches toss in my waning sight.

Drums of glory are lost in the ages,
　Bare feet fail on a broken trail—
Let my name fade from the printed pages;
　Dreams and visions are growing pale.

Twilight gathers and none can save me.
　Well and well, for I would not stay:
Let me speak through the stone you gave me:
　He never could say what he wished to say.

Why should I shrink from the sign of leaving?
　My brain is wrapped in a darkened cloud;
Now in the Night are the Sisters weaving
　For me a shroud.

Towers shake and the stars reel under,
　Skulls are heaped in the Devil's fane;
My feet are wrapped in a rolling thunder,
　Jets of agony lance my brain.

What of the world that I leave for ever?
　Phantom forms in a fading sight—
Carry me out on the ebon river
　Into the Night.

MINGLE MY DUST
WITH THE BURNING BRAND

Mingle my dust with the burning brand,
  Scatter it free to the sky
Fling it wide on the ocean's sand,
  From peaks where the vultures fly.

Let it drift with the drifting tide,
  And flit o'er the arctic floe,
Let it spin and ride where the snow-storms hide
  And the wild ice-field winds blow.

Let it mingle with desert sand,
  And the waves of a tropic sea,
When the roaring surge sweeps o'er the strand
  And the ocean winds shout free.

AN OUTWORN STORY

There comes long days when the soul turns sick,
  And the heart is hollow and thin and old,
  And the high-heaped clouds, grey fold on fold,
Lie like a grey shroud clammy and thick,
  And a wind blows out of them deathly cold.

Only the ghost of a dead desire
  Haunts bare woods and the muddied springs.
  Grass grows rank in the courts of kings,
And the bats brood on the broken spire
  Where the lizard crawls and the lichen clings.

Then men's thoughts turn to the soothing dust,
  Where in the end all passions drown.

And stark winds blow and men lie down
To quiet ambition and hate and lust
  In the clinging coverlets, bitter and brown.

The dim days come when in men's breast
  The heart is shriveled and dark and cold.
  The grey clouds cling like a shroud unrolled
  And men, to the brown and bitter mold,
Turn to silence and utter rest
  From an outworn story madly told.

ROMANY ROAD

Some day I'll go down a Romany Road
  But, oh, I'll go alone
Where the wind blows and the thistle grows
  And the grey moss grips the stone.
Past the grey woods where the bat broods
  Above a rain beat bone.
Its a red road and a dead road
  But a road that is all my own.
Some day I'll go down a Romany Road
  With neither lover nor friend
For my road is a high road
  And it runs to the River's bend.
And I'll go as the winds blow
  As ever I have ken'd
With Death's hand on my stirrup band
  And Hell await at the end.

Robert E. Howard

THE SANDS OF TIME

Slow sift the sands of Time; the yellowed leaves
   Go drifting down an old and bitter wind;
Across the frozen moors the hedges stand
   In tattered garments that the frost have thinned.

A thousand phantoms pluck my ragged sleeve,
   Wan ghosts of souls long into darkness thrust.
Their pale lips tell lost dreams I thought mine own,
   And old sick longings smite my heart to dust.

I may not even dream of jeweled dawns,
   Nor sing with lips that have forgot to laugh.
I fling aside the cloak of Youth and limp
   A withered man upon a broken staff.

SURRENDER [VERSION 2]

Open the window and let me go,
  I have tarried over long;
I hear the tides on the sands below
  but there is no joy in the song.
My heart is hollow with endless pain,
  my temples are growing white;
Open the window against the rain
  and let me go to the night.
Once I hailed the Tomorrow,
  I lifted a glad refrain,
But my heart is thin with sorrow
  and my eyes are blind with pain.
My wine has been the salt of tears,
  my bread is hard and stale
Close the door on the bitter years
  and let me go to the gale.
Oh, wind, sea wind on the bitter lea,
  that harries the ships with fright,
Toss me and rend me and set me free,
  mingle my soul with the night.

Robert E. Howard

THE TEMPTER

Something tapped me on the shoulder,
  Something whispered, "Come with me.
"Leave the world of men behind you,
"Come where care may never find you,
"Come and follow, let me bind you
  "Where, in that dark, silent sea,
"Tempest of the world n'er rages;
"There to dream away the ages,
"Heedless of Time's turning pages,
  "Only come with me."

"Who are you?" I asked the phantom,
  "I am Rest from Hate and Pride.
"I am friend to king and beggar,
"I am Alpha and Omega.
"I was councilor to Hagar,
  "But men call me Suicide."
I was weary of tide breasting,
Weary of the world's behesting,
And I lusted for the resting
  As a lover for his bride.

And my soul tugged at its moorings
  And it whispered, "Set me free
"I am weary of this battle,
"Of this world of human cattle,
"All this dreary noise and prattle.
  "This you owe to me."
Long I sat and long I pondered,
On the life that I had squandered,
O'er the paths that I had wandered
  Never free.

In a shadow panorama
  Passed life's struggles and its fray.
And my soul tugged with new vigor,
Huger grew the phantom's figure,
As I slowly pressed the trigger,
  Saw the world fade swift away.
Through the fogs old Time came striding,
Radiant clouds were 'bout me riding,
As my soul went gliding, gliding
  From the shadow into day.

Robert E. Howard

THE YEARS ARE AS A KNIFE

The years are as a knife against my heart.
  Of what avail the labor and the sweat,
To hammer on the anvil men call art,
  A soulless, gleaming tinsel, sparkling wet
    With drops of salty blood, black agony
    Has wrung from out the gagging soul of me.

Better the silence and the long black rest;
  Better the gray grass growing through my brain—
Far better to be done with this unrest,
  The hope, the horror, pleasure and the pain.
    Life is a liar and a drear-eyed whore—
    Death has his hand upon a silent Door.

What if I tear the wings from shifty Fame,
  Or, swine-like, wallow in a waste of gold?
Oh, hollow, hollow, hollow, men's acclaim,
  And silver never warmed a heart grown cold.
    Better the shot, the fall, the growing stain,
    Than one long blindness, shot with crimson pain.

Before I left my cradle—at my birth—
  My road was laid and every thorn was strown;
My heritage is the waste lands of the earth,
  My heart strings tuned to one long changeless groan.
    Before I saw the light of day, my cup
    With wormwood, gall and venom was filled up.

I quail with terror to the coming years—
  Oh, Christ, my way is long and gloomy-black;
Oceans I see of brine and tearing tears,
  And iron thorns that mail a bitter track.
    Better the leap, and blackness suddenly,
    Than one long road of endless agony.

I feel a wind that chills me to the bone,
   And dark the clouds that veil my reeling path;
And I must charge a citadel of stone,
   And batter Titans with a spear of lath!
     I am an ant that spins across the world,
     By heedless winds dismembered, flung and hurled.

Not only on the cross the Son of Man
   Rent blackened heavens with a futile pain—
His days of agony were short in span,
   But I am doomed to live and writhe in vain.
     But who shall gag me on the bitter crust?
     Even such brains as mine may crash to dust.

XVIII

Transience, Mutability,
Carpe Diem & *Ubi Sunt*

A few related and frequent themes in Howard's poetry formed around his central belief that all things pass, that nothing lingers long without change—usually deterioration and decay—that life is short and, therefore, ought to be experienced fully, and that, in all likelihood, true heroism and the ages of great deeds were gone forever.

Howard believed that all things are altered if not ultimately obliterated by Time. As Shelley points out in the sonnet "Ozymandias" the arrogance of the great Rameses II who believed that his works of stone would stand forever and not crumble and be lost to the sands of Time, so Howard understood that all worldly things are mutable and fleeting.

After Horace's famous advice in the ode that one should "seize the day," Howard too strove for a life full of experience and achievement—and more and more the consensus is that he succeeded in creating an interesting and important body of literary works. *Carpe Diem*, of course, can show two distince faces: it can be inspirational if interpreted as "Make the most of the time you have; fulfill your potential," but it can also be hedonistic: "Eat, drink, and be merry, for tomorrow you die."

The theme of *Ubi Sunt*: "Where have they gone?" often rephrased as Where are they now? or Where are the snows of yesteryear?" is also present. A yearning for more adventure-laden times, for both deeds and doers worthy of song, is also part of Howard's poetic and thematic landscape.

The poems in this section touch upon these themes.

AGE
[TO THE OLD MEN]

Age sat on his high throne
  And scoffed to see me ride,
But I was on the beaches
  And racing with the tide.

Age sat on his golden throne
  And named me as a fool,
But I was splashing maidens
  Nude in a forest pool.

Age sat in his corner
  And mocked my furious zest,
But I was breaking sun spears
  On my hairy chest.

Age stole from his neighbor
  Great stores of gems and gold.
Age called me from my games
  To fight for his treasure hold.

Age cowered in his castle
  And preached great deeds and high,
But I was laughing, laughing,
  As I went forth to die.

BALLADE

Shattered shards of a broken shrine
  Parted strings of an idle lyre
Yellow leaves on a whithered vine,
  Smoldered ash of a dead desire.
Shadow of golden frozen fire—
  Only shadow, the flame is gone—
The moon sets in the thorn and briar.
  Youth fades with the fading dawn.
Goblet stale with the dregs of wine,
  Fallen column and broken spire.
White mist with the tang of brine,
  Sea weed crawling ever higher.
  Sea wind cold on the sullen mire
Down where the cold sea creatures spawn
  Oh, Time, the lover, and Time the liar.
Youth fades with the fading dawn.
          Envoy
King, no brazier for the fire
  Holds the flame when the flame is gone.
The moon sets in the thorn and briar
And Youth fades with the fading dawn

DESTINY (1)

What is there real, my girl?
  Fair hair and a sparkling eye?
See, where the dust a-whirl
  Fades in a sombre sky.
What is there real, my love?
  Red lips and pearly teeth?
Ah, they are fair above,
  But a skull is grinning beneath.

DREAMS OF NINEVEH

Silver bridge in a broken sky,
  Golden fruit on a withered bough,
Red-lipped slaves that the ancients buy—
  What are the dreams of Nineveh now?

Ghostly hoofs in the brooding night
  Beat the bowl of the velvet stars.
Shadows of spears when the moon is white
  Cross the sands with ebony bars.

But not the shadows that brood her fall
  May check the sweep of the desert fire,
Nor a dead man lift up a crumbling wall,
  Nor a spectre steady a falling spire.

Death fires rise in the desert sky
  Where the armies of Sargon reeled;
And though her people still sell and buy,
  Nineveh's doom is set and sealed.

Silver mast with a silken sail,
  Sapphire seas 'neath a purple prow,
Hawk-eyed tribes on the desert trail—
  What are the dreams of Nineveh now?

EMPIRE'S DESTINY

Bab-ilu's women gazed upon our spears,
   And roses flung, and sang to see us ride.
We built a glory for the marching years
   And starred our throne with silver nails of pride.
Our horses' hoofs were shod with brazen fears:
We laved our hands in blood and iron tears,
   And laughed to hear how shackled kings had died.

Our chariots awoke the sleeping world;
   The thunder of our hoofs the mountains broke;
Before our spears were empires' banners furled
   And death and doom and iron winds were hurled,
And slaughter rode before, and clouds and smoke—
Then in the desert lands the tribes awoke
   And death and vengeance 'round our walls were whirled.

O Babylon, lost Babylon! Where now
   The opal altar and the golden spire,
   The tower and the legend and the lyre?
Oh, withered fruit upon a broken bough!
The sobbing desert winds still whisper how
   The sapphire city of the gods' desire
   Fell in the smoke and crumbled in the fire;
And lizards bask upon her columns now.

Now poets sing her golden glory gone;
And Babylon has faded with the dawn.

FOR WHAT IS A MAID TO THE SHOUT OF KINGS

For what is a maid to the shout of kings?
To the gilt parade and the host that sings?
Honor and gold and glorious raids
To he that is bold—and other maids.
Dawn gems gleam and white stars dim
By the quiet stream she watches him
Ride with the flash of shields and brands
To the battle's clash and the far strange lands.

Beyond the skyline where great kings ride,
Glory, jewels, honor and pride.
For the sap in the North must rise again
   With the wild geese winging thither;
Gay hours die and a hawk must fly
   And the rose of Spring must wither.

FUTILITY (2)

Time races on and none can stay the tread; bridal bowers
Re-echo to the flight of bats. Their garland'd towers
   Rear like gaunt specters 'gainst the dawning's red
Veiled by the fogs of time the Slayer glowers.
   Blithe Pan has passed and all the dryads fled.
We walk a dim defined and mystic vale,
   The mountains vaguely loom on either hand,
Groping we go and often lose the trail,
   Compassed by demon shapes of Shadowland.
     On either hand we hear the breakers roar,
     The shifting grey fogs close behind, before.

Mazed by the trail, and by the whole world plan,
   Drudging and toiling, never knowing why,
The Cosmic Jester of the gods is man,
   Philosophers are fools, priests jest and lie.
Nothing is real. Leaves fade and song-birds fly.

Bewildered still, our plodding ways we go,
The vagrant sport of all the winds that blow.
   And after all this toilsome fume and fret—
What ocean lies beyond? I only know
   This Universal stage is set.
The trail is placed and run that we must follow
   The Destined trail. ' Tis none of ours to choose,
     The trail that only runs from night to night
     From out the grey dawn's, cynic, and mocking light
Into the smoldering sunset's crimson wallow.
   I only know that though we win, we lose.
I only know that all conflict must cease,
That always after war, comes, somehow, peace.

THE GATES OF NINEVEH

These are the gates of Nineveh; here
   Sargon came when his wars were won,
Gazed at the turrets looming clear,
   Boldly etched in the morning sun.

Down from his chariot Sargon came,
   Tossed his helmet upon the sand,
Dropped his sword with its blade like flame,
   Stroked his beard with his empty hand.

"Towers are flaunting their banners red,
   The people greet me with song and mirth,
But a weird is on me," Sargon said,
   "And I see the end of the tribes of earth.

"Cities crumble, and chariots rust—
   I see through a fog that is strange and gray—
All kingly things fade back to the dust,
   Even the gates of Nineveh."

THE MOUNTAINS OF CALIFORNIA

Grass and the rains and snow,
   Trumpet and tribal drum;
Across my crests the people go
   Over my peaks the people come.
Girt with the pelts of lion and hare.
   Plodding with oxen wains,
Climbing the steeps on a Spanish mare,
   Soaring in aeroplanes.
Men with their hates and their ires,
   Men with their loves and their lust
Still shall I reign when their spires
   And their castles tumble to dust.

Robert E. Howard

THE NIGHT WINDS

The night winds whisper across the grass
 And sing through the dusky trees;
The night winds roar from the mountain pass
 With the tang of the distant seas.
And many a tune they pipe to the moon
 And the far-off, starlit leas.

"Nineveh crumbled and Babel fell,
 "Where are the walls of Troy?
"(Hark to the tales the night winds tell!)
 "Jove was a laughing boy
"Olympia's slopes were virgin bare,
 "Rome was a marsh snake's den
"(A sluggish and slimy adder's lair!)
 "And we were old e'en then!
"Accad's pride is the pride of dust
 "(Where is the Golden King!)
"Vanished the Persian's power and lust
 "(Hark to the winds that sing!)
"We have thundered their flags of pride
 "(We, wild winds of the world!)
"Flaunted their banners above, beside,
 "(Lastly their dust we whirled.)
"For we are old as the world is old
 "And young as Time is young
"And we have seen empires with glory and gold
 "Pass. And their tales we sung.
"Meager are men. They come, they go
 "Like the haze of dusk, like the rose of dawn,
"A ceaseless, hurrying river's flow—
 "But the winds blow on—blow on."

The winds go whispering through the vales
Harken, hark to the night winds' tales.

O BABYLON, LOST BABYLON

[notes: "Empire's Destiny variant/"Oh">"O"]

Bab-Ilu's women gazed upon our spears,
  And roses flung, and sang to see us ride;
We built a glory for the marching years,
  And fixed our throne with silver nails of pride.
Our horses' hoofs were shod with brazen fears.
We laved our bands in blood and iron tears
  And laughed to bear bow shackled kings had died.
Our chariots awoke the sleeping world,
  The thunder of our hoofs the mountains broke,
Before our spears were empires' banners furled
And death and doom and iron winds were whirled,
  And slaughter rode before, and clouds and smoke;
  Then in the desert lands the tribes awoke.

O Babylon, lost Babylon, where now
  The opal altar and the golden spire,
  The tower and the legend and the lyre?
O, withered fruit upon a broken bough.'
The sobbing desert winds still whisper how
  The golden city of the gods' desire
  Fell in the smoke and crumbled in the fire,
And lizards bask upon her columns now.
    And rhymers sing of ages gold and gone
    But Babylon has faded with the dawn.

ONLY A SHADOW ON THE GRASS

The tribes of men rise up and pass
And the very winds are gone;
Men are a shadow on the grass
But the living stars gleam on.

THE PATH OF THE STRANGE WANDERERS

They have broken the lamps and burst the camps
And they follow the roads that the wild wind tramps;
And the starlight falls on Babel's halls
And the trumpeter mounts the broken walls
And the moon comes up through the mists and damps.

"They are here today," the wild winds say,
"But who can trace the track of tomorrow?
"And who can shackle a roving heart
"That leans to the winds that waver and start,
"Or chain a soul like the ocean spray,
"Whiter than glory and brine as sorrow?"
"They are here today," the fierce winds say,
"But the east is white and the sea is grey,
"And the trumpet's blast is an empty blast
"For the winds flee and they follow fast.
"And the hall may fall and the city wall,
"And the brazen trumpet forever call,
"But the bladed rovers, where are they?"
Tower and hall and marble wall
Altar and honor and glory fall;
Grass grows in the city street—
Where are the rovers' restless feet?
Other cities waver and rise
And grow and loom before their eyes;
Topaz towers in dreaming skies.
And cities are dust upon the plain
But the wanderers come not back again.

ROAR, SILVER TRUMPETS

Roar, silver trumpets, in your pride,
   Sultans and shahs and rajahs ride
Drunken upon your wine of power;
   Yet Kismet will not be denied.

Shall plowshares turn for any flower?
   Sultans of old knew greater power,
Lusted and revelled in their hour;
   Then Azrael beckoned and they died.

TIMUR-LANG

The warm wind blows through the waving grain—
Where are the glories of Tamerlane?
The nations stood up, ripe and tall—
He was the sickle that reaped them all.
But the sickle shatters and leaves no trace—
And the grain grows green on the desert's face.

Robert E. Howard

WHERE ARE YOUR KNIGHTS,
DONN OTHNA?

Now that the kings have fallen,
  Now that the gods have fled,
Now that the cities smolder
  In a riot of ghastly red—

Where are your knights, Donn Othna?
  Where the sword that was bright?
The skies are choked with ravens—
  Where will you ride tonight?

"I left my knights in a valley
  "Far and dim in the west;
"They were weary with endless battle,
  "And I left them to their rest.

"We fed the hungry vultures
  "When we rent the ranks apart,
"And I left my good sword broken
  "In a sea-king's cruel heart.

"On a crimson couch and royal
  "Each good knight lies asleep;
"They heed not the trumpet's clamor,
  "Nor the night-wind's restless sweep.

"The hounds of Death ran howling,
  "And red the rune they bayed—
"I cannot wake my warriors,
  "I cannot mend my blade.

"But there are shields unbroken
  "And ravens yet to feed,
"And though deep-notched and crimson
  "This axe will serve my need.

"East where the ravens gather,
  "Where the death fires glimmer bright,
"Where the sea-kings roar and triumph,
    "I ride alone tonight."

XIX
Ballads & Other Narratives

One of Howard's favorite containers for his poetry was the ballad stanza and variations thereof. The folk ballad form was the dominant narrative verse form in English from the late Middle Ages through Modern times and is still very much with us in popular song (especially Country & Western music, Old Rock, and even the "common measure" of most church hymns). It's evolved form, the literary ballad, using more regular rhythms and more rhyme, has been cultivated by poets since the 18th century.

Howard was also greatly interested in the variations and transformations that the ballad allowed. One of his favorite poems was *The Ballad of the White Horse* by G. K. Chesterton. That poem, which can be viewed as the last great sustained epical narrative in English (at least meriting comparison to William Morris's *Sigurd the Volsung,* to which many would give that honor) makes use of an extended or "exploded" ballad stanza. Morris's poem, while seemingly done in irregular length sections of long-line rhymed couplets, actually compresses the normal four lines of the ballad stanza into two lines with a medial caesura. From this example and others he noted, Howard wrote several poems in both 6- and 7-accent long-lines. He also used a variation of the ballad that expanded its normal 4343 accents and ABCB or ABAB rhyme into a sestet of 434343 and ABCBDB and various other rhyme schemes.

Howard also made use of other traditional narrative forms such as blank verse (unrhymed iambic pentameter—as in Shakespeare's plays and many other important narrative and dramatic poetic works in English).

Bob Howard was one of the last narrative poets, carrying on a tradition that has sadly diminished over the past century. He should rightly be seen as one of the few great bardic voices of the last days of heroic song.

THE AFFAIR AT THE TAVERN

Trailing dusk—and a coach-and-four
Stopped in front of the tavern door.

The bell clanged and the host came out
A pudding-visaged, evil lout.

Two men stepped from the darkened coach:
"Greetings, Mark and Sir Dickon Roche."

Roche was a man of ice and steel
Rapier slim from hat to heel.
Mark was rough as a galley's keel.

"Host, is she here?" asked Dickon Roche;
"She came, my lord, in mine own coach.

"My bullies stole in her sleeping room
"Gripped her close as the clutch of doom
"And bore her off in the midnight gloom."

Mark and Dickon mount the stair,
Halt in front of a chamber there.

They enter in— in the firelight gleam
A girl springs up with a sudden scream
Stares like a creature in a dream.

"Sir Dickon Roche, what do you here?"
And her voice broke with the tang of fear.

Sir Dickon laughed and closed the door:
"The hare is caught and the chase is o'er.

"My suit was naught in your haughty sight—
"My own men brought you here tonight.

"And ere the dawn light up your face
"You shall know the best of my embrace."
Mark's roar of laughter filled the place.

Sir Dickon turned, "Your work is done.
"Return to me with the rising sun."

But Mark said, "Nay, I shared the toil.
"God's throne! Shall I not share the spoil?"

Dickon's eyes were fire slits pale;
He drummed his hilt with his finger nail.

"Must I parley, devils of Hell! with you?
"Go! Ere I run your black heart through!"
The blade leaped out like a flame of blue.

But Mark whirled round in fierce rebellion
And his lips writhed in face of a hellion.

His hanger hummed as he tore it clear
And the girl shrank back in sudden fear.

The blade whirled in a wheel of fire,
"Stand, Sir Dickon, raper and liar!
"Stand and fight for your foul desire!"

And the blades clanged in the silent room
And the blue sparks showered in the gloom.

The hanger sang through the singing air.
Mark stood weaponless and bare.

The pale girl saw his dark lips part
As the rapier sank beneath his heart.

Mark reeled as the rapier stung
Then blindly forward his body flung
Fingers wide and arms outswung.

Wasting his breath in a deathly roar.
His charge was the plunge of a wounded boar.
They crashed together on the floor.

And the blind arms locked like iron and stone
Crushing muscle and flesh and bone;
The girl stood in the room alone.

Save for the dead men on the floor
And the fire that gleamed on the chamber door.

— AND BILL, HE LOOKED AT ME AND SAID

— And Bill, he looked at me and said,
"The boat, it may hold one.
Not two.
We'll throw the dice
To see who stays, who goes.
The guy that goes,
May make the mainland."
So I looked
And now the sands stretch bare
Ocean to ocean, sea on every side.
I looked at Bill and at the boat.
I looked at Bill
And saw the beast flame in his eyes.
And knew it flamed in mine.
Our knives flashed brightly in the tropic sun.
Steel grated steel. His hand was at my throat,
My hand at his.

My mind ran back
To many a wild adventure on the sea
And land. Bill and me, pals.
But the ocean took and broke and warped our minds.
The ocean is a monster so we fought.
Bill pulled me from a drifting ice berg once and I
Rescued him from the Thugs of Delhi.
Steel rasped on steel.
I overbore him; and beastlike raised my knife.
High in the air I paused a moment.
And then Bill, gazing beyond my shoulder,
Gasped through his battered lips, "A sail!"

A LEGEND OF FARING TOWN

Her house, a moulting buzzard on the Hill,
  Loomed gaunt and brooding over Faring town;
  Behind, there sloped away the barren down
And at its foot an ancient, crumbling mill.
And often in the evening bleak and still,
  With withered limbs wrapped in a sombre gown
  And leathery face set in a sombre frown,
She sat in silence on her silent sill.

She came to Faring town long years ago—
  With her a winsome child, the ancients said,
She vanished, where, the people did not know—
  Meg mended ropes for ocean vessels' sails
  And let the people think the child was dead—
  She did not speak, but there were darksome tales.

One night the village flamed with sudden red—
  From off Meg's roof we saw the cinders stream.
  She came not forth—we entered—and in the gleam,
Saw her crouching, like a thing of dread,

Above a skeleton within her bed.
　"Child slayer!" I still hear the women scream—
　High a red and cinder spitting beam;
We hanged her and the flames consumed the dead.

A book we found, and written piteously
　In Meg's sad scrawl: "Today my darling died
　"But she shall sleep forever by my side—
"They shall not give her to the cruel sea."
　We cringed and gazed in terror and in shame
　Where still a form swung black against the flame.

MISER'S GOLD

"Nay, have no fear. The man was blind," said she.
　"How could he see 'twas we that took his gold?
　"The devil, man! I thought you were bold!"
"This is a chancy business!" muttered he,
"And we'll be lucky if we get to sea.
　"The fellow deals with demons, I've been told."
　"Let's open the chest, shut up and take a hold."
Then silence as they knocked the hinges free.
A glint of silver and a sheen of jade—
　Two strange gems gleaming from a silken fold—
Rare plunder— gods, was that a hidden blade?
　A scream, a curse, two bodies stark and cold.
With jewel eyes above them crawled and swayed
　The serpent left to watch the miser's gold.

Robert E. Howard

THE OPEN WINDOW

I remember my sister Eve
  And her supple form and her vivid eyes
And the heart that she wore upon her sleeve
  And the tales that our mother swore were lies.

Her arms were cool to a younger child,
  And wild and strange were the songs she sung,
But her hands went cold when our mother smiled
  And she said that our mother was never young.

She went in a grey and wintry dawn
  That stabbed the veil of the rainy night—
A flash in the door, and she was gone
  As a white moth flits to the candle light.

Our mother? She spoke her name no more.
  Gaunter she grew and grim and hard.
The beggar turned from our tight-lipped door
  And the flowers shrank from our leafless yard.

I saw her, Eve, in the harlot's guise.
  Her face was haggard, painted and drawn,
But the freedom, God, in her changeless eyes
  Made white my soul like a forest dawn.

THE OUTCAST

Forth from the purple and feasts of the palace
   Out through the sombre, dim wilds I must fare;
The spring of the wilderness now is my chalice,
   My viands, the spoils of the faun and the hare.

My raiment, the pelts of the wolf and the lion,
   My fareways, the paths where the green forests wave,
My comrades, the panther, the antlered deer's scion,
   My castle, the heights of a crag-frowning cave.

Friend of my youth, though the king seek to slay me,
   Driving me ever from woodland and hill,
Though swords smite me down, though torturers flay me,
   My love for thee, friend, shall abide with me still.

REBEL

I lived upon the earth of yore,
   An outlaw swart and fell,
And ankle-deep, at last, in gore
   I waded into Hell.

And where the gleaming charcoal sheened
   I dared the Devil's ire,
For man is stronger than the fiend
   And fiercer than the fire.

I swaggered through the Flaming Land
   'Mid shadows red and black
And gripped him by his taloned hand
   And smote him on the back.

"Damnation's fire!" I roared, "I trow
   "I heard the goblets clink!
"Have ye not courtesy enow
   "To bid an old friend drink?

"I served ye long upon the earth
   "Whose lands I held in fee
"And if I may not join your mirth
   "No comely host are ye!"

"Aye, I remember ye!" he spake,
   "Ye wrought full long and good.
"Come sit ye down your thirst to slake
   "In wine of Christian blood."

The fiends came marching with the feast
   Across the flaming stones.
While Satan chose a writhing priest
   I gnawed a bishop's bones.

We revelled with a savage zest
   And mocked the screeching horde
And at each fierce, sulphurous jest
   With evil laughter roared.

The red wine mounted to my head
   And fired my passion fell;
"This dare into your beard!" I said,
   "I'll gamble you for Hell!"

His laughter rose in red disdain
   Among the sooty flues.
Said he, "'Tis naught I have to gain
   "And naught ye have to lose."

"Nay, I've a girl that's worth it all,
   "I would not give nor sell,
"All golden-haired and fair and tall.
   "I'll match her 'gainst your Hell!"

"But she is of the living land!
   "Then how may this thing be?"
"If I but beckon with my hand
   "To Hell she'll follow me."

To watch the game all in a trice
   Were massed the shadow things,
While on the board we flung the dice—
   The skulls of earthly kings.

They clashed, they crashed along the board
   With sullen clank they fell.
"Ho ho! I've won!" the Devil roared,
   "Bid down your wench to Hell!"

I leaped across the flaming room
   Amid the brimstone's glare.

I heard the sullen ocean boom
   And flashed into the air.

I leaped along the old time road,
   White in the moonbeam haze,
And to her latticed window strode
   As in my boyhood days.

Across her winsome, youthful cheek
   The moonlight's silver fell.
"Rise up, rise up! And do not speak
   "But follow me to Hell."

Swift from her window then she sprung
   And never word did say
As lightly o'er my arm I flung
   And carried her away.

We whirled like phantoms through the air
   And rose a fearful yell
As through the crimson sulphur flare
   I bore her into Hell.

And Satan smacked his lustful lips
   And burning was his stare,
While to her slim and shapely hips
   Fell down her golden hair.

Then swift and sudden did I see
   That I had been a fool
And that slim girl was more to me
   Than all of Hades' rule.

And as he seized her by the hand
   I snatched from out its place
A scarlet, blazing, Hell-fire brand
   And dashed it in his face.

He staggered backward with a yell!
   I snatched her and fled fast
While on our tracks the hosts of Hell
   Came flying on the blast.

We fled like phantoms on the wind.
   Far, far and far away,
We left the flaming hordes behind
   And flashed into the day.

I dare not now the halls of Hell
   But roam about the earth,
An eery flitting phantom fell,
   A wind like unseen mirth.

But in the nighttime oft I whirl
   To a bower by the sea
And from the window steals a girl
   With golden hair, to me.

She'll be no other's love nor wife
   And here she does not err
For though for me she'd given life
   I gave up Hell for her.

THE BARON AND THE WENCH

The baron quaffed a draught of wine
  And laughed in his shaggy beard.
His eyes in the candles held a shine
  As though a mocking demon leered.

"Rare sport!" A booming laugh he roared
And on the heavy laden board
  He smote a brawny fist amain.
    "Ho, varlets!" (each in terror shook)
    "Go bring the haughty wench I took
"Prom off the galley bound for Spain!"

They haled her to the banquet hail;
  His eyes lit with a bestial blaze,
  And though she shrank before his gaze,
She proudly stood before them all.

Her hair of gold about her hips
  Fell in a silky, waving flood;
Roses would pale before her lips,
  Her slim hands showed her noble blood.
    The baron took her by the wrist
    For she seemed willing to be kissed.

SWAMP MURDER

Through the mists and damps
  The stars arise
  Like the red eyes
Of the voodoo lamps.

Alligator and frog
  Haunt the swampy stream
  And their eyes gleam.
And now the fog

Spreads its ivory scroll
  And the stars are lost
  Like crystals tossed
In the sky's blue bowl.

And deep in the glade
  A shadow slips,
  A black hand grips
A gleaming blade.

Now the red eyes
  Of the 'gator gloats
  And a body floats
And the river sighs.

SWORDS GLIMMERED UP THE PASS

Swords glimmered up the pass
Fringing the grim dark mass.
There was blood on the grass;
Red blood
But the flood
Far below lumbered on to the east and the dawn—
When all men are gone.
Shall not they,
Hill and stream,
As today
Gleam and dream,
Forgetting forever in majesty still
That men climbed the hill or died on the river.
High on the great black crags
Like hags
Brooding for death and slaughter,
We waited
With the thirst of our blades unsated
And below us rippled the water.
We two—you and I
Last to die.
At bay there we stood and the wind in our hair
Shook the iron clawed brood of the black eagle's lair.
They came in the flame of the thundering dawn
Driven and drawn
By the spate of their hate and the fate of their lust
For the glimmering dust,
They dreamed they could hold, the traitor of gold,
The breaker of thrust.
And we laughed in the bend of a curse that our blades,
they were virgin of rust
Then from his bed
The great sun clambered red;
His gleams lit up the lances and the banners of the foe;

The cohorts clambered sealing our doom
beyond repealing;
Behind our boulders kneeling we hurled our lead below.
Many a bastard there
Of that dark band
Clutched with a nerveless hand
The mocking air.
Man after man, one by one
Dropped in the eye of the sun
To the crack of the ball;
Reeled from the sombre cliff
Grim and stiff,
And the river below drank his fall.
Two men—and we laughed and we swore
In the fringe of the rifle smoke's plume,
Two men—and we laughed at the roar
Of a whole army bringing our doom.
And our rifles stammered and yammered,
Carving the air with red laces
Till our powder was burning their faces
As up to our muzzles they clambered.
You rose,
And you jeered—
In the beard
Of our foes
You hurled gold.
And some of them clutched it with screams,
and some in the clutching grew cold.
And you roared to the horde:
"Here's the price of Hell's thunder!"
And the leap of your sword
Rent a bosom a-sunder.
I swung up the stock
Of my empty gun
And the crash and the shock
Broke the brains out of one.
Then smoke veiled the sun

And blood, cliff and rock.
A reeking red carpet we made and we laid
With the crash of my gun and the slash of your blade.
Bullets jerked at us,
Knives stung;
Sword points dirked at us,
Gun stocks swung. Like reddened leopards we sprung.
And they forced us back to the lip of the pass
that over the river hung.
We were blackened with powder,
Red with blood
Ever louder we heard the flood.
Your blade was a shard on a battered hilt,
Your grip slipped on the blood you'd spilt.
From my rifle the splintered stock was rent
And the barrel was twisted, burst and bent.
The last charge came—fierce faces rose
To go blank under our last great blows.
Flame in our faces waved its sheet
And we felt the gulf yawn under our feet...
Roaring our final oaths we fell
And crashed together into Hell.

THE WITCH

We set a stake amid the stones
  That crown the headland shore,
Where wild the sea-wind ever drones
  And where the combers roar.

Then leg and ankle, wrist and hand,
  We bound her to the stake
With chains that might the fire withstand,
  And never a word she spake.

The grey gulls whirled by, light and fleet;
  Loud called the hooded tern.
We fired the fagots at her feet
  And left her there to burn.

Over her bare breasts flowed her hair,
  About her leaped the flame;
But as we turned to leave her there
  She spoke no word of blame.

I turned upon the sloping lea,
  A moment paused, alone,
Half fearful, gazing, lest I see
  The Devil claim his own.

About her breast the red fires gleamed,
  The dark smoke caught her hair,
And to my wondering eyes it seemed
  A halo floated there.

Fools! Fools! A human soul be cleaned
  By fire of Satan's taint—
'Tis we are henchmen of the Fiend!
  For we have burned—a Saint!

XX

Poems from Biblical and Hebrew Sources

Certainly among the least known of Howard's poems and even more certainly among the least commented upon by critics to date are the poems that derive from Biblical sources. While, ultimately, not subscribing to all the doctrines of the faith and being one who struck out on his own along the path toward finding the great answers, Howard, nonetheless, knew his Bible and found inspirations there—at least for his fiction and poetry and particularly in the Old Testament with all its carnage of battle and lust and savagery and sin. In this section are poems on Cain and on Lilith, the apocryphal first wife of Adam, and on Elijah.

This section also should help convince those readers and critics who have failed to see Howard's multidimensionality and that he was a far more complex man and poet than most have understood.

The last poem in this short section, "Two Men," touching upon Christ and the Crucifixion offers a far different perspective upon Howard than is commonly held. And there are other Bible-relevant poems and fragments to be found in the *Complete Poetry*.

FLIGHT

A jackal laughed from a thicket still;
   the stars were haggard pale;
Cain wiped the sweat from his pallid brow
   and hurried down the trail.
The shadows closed behind, before;
   vines hidden tripped his feet.
The trees rose stark in the pitiless dark
   and he heard his own pulse beat.
No footfalls harried the forest ways,
   no sound save his own breath,
But he clutched his spear and his own red fear
   rose in his soul like death.
Till at last he came to an unknown way
   his foot had never trod,
But now he fled from the silent dead
   and the wrathful face of God.

Red mountains loomed on every hand,
   silent as Time's first dawn,
Red ashes shifted about his feet
   as the slayer hastened on.
He passed through a valley strange and dim,
   like a nightmare place of sin
Littered with bones of ghastly things
   who rules ere the time of men.
He heard the rustle of ghostly wings,
   but never halted he
Until he stood, by a haunted wood,
   on the shore of a nameless sea.
He halted, listened; naught was there
   save the Silence at his back
And a grey sea and a red moon
   and the shadows rising black.
Till out of the ocean rose a Shape,

a monstrous thing of gloom;
And his knees were loosed and the naked Cain
  cowered before his doom.
"Come not to my red empire, Cain;
  there's blood upon your hand!
"The foremost killer of the earth
  comes not into my land!
"Down all the drifting years to come
  your fate mankind shall tell,
"That ye roamed the world for the rest of time,
  disowned by Earth and Hell!"
And the shape was gone and the moon was red
  and leaves stirred on the bough.
Cain stood alone by the unknown sea
  and the mark was on his brow.

LILITH

They hurled me from the mire
  They haled me from the silt
To desecrate the Garden
  Connive at Adam's guilt.

At Satan's bid sardonic
  I came from primal night
To tread the eons' gauntlet
  Stript naked to the light.

A dark eyed child of shadows
  I flung aside my veils—
Men cinctured me with wisdom
  And sin and serpent scales.

Staid Eve they hail Earth-mother
  Defame me to this day—
Yet Adam's hot young kisses
  They cannot take away.

Robert E. Howard

SKULLS OVER JUDAH

Oh, who comes down the mountain,
  a stalking oak at morning—
  The trail is wild by Gherith, and Carmel's crags are high!
His eyes are grim as iron, that break the people's scorning—
  Oh, who comes down from Carmel to blast and prophesy?

Alike his hairy girdle, his hardened limbs are hairy;
  Beneath his locks entangled flames cold his icy eye.
The people fall before him but naught shall make him tarry —
  Oh, who comes down from Carmel to bid a king to die?

The fury of the desert goes in the wind before him;
  He locks within his bosom the thunders of the sky.
The sages of the ages have flung their mantles o'er him—
  Oh, who comes down from Carmel
    to break the thrones on high?

The word goes out of Israel to shake the world at dawning.
  Oh, chariots of Judah, the crimson kings must die!
The hungry ravens gather and Hell's abyss is yawning.
  Elijah comes from Carmel along the morning sky!

TWO MEN

Two men stood in the gates of day
  And one man said with a kindling eye:
"The Red drums rattle, the banner sway—
  "They are bearing the Lord Christ forth to die!

"Here they must pass with our Lord, thorn crowned;
  "Here stand we with dagger bared.
"Ere the red sun sinks He shall walk unbound
  "Or we shall the salt of his doom have shared."

Spake the other: "Nay, it is sad indeed
  "That He should hang on the bloody tree,
"But the Mass hath ordered that this man bleed—
  "Shall its word be argued by such as we?

"The judge and jury sit in state
  "And the people shout that the man must die,
"And who shall question the right of His fate,
  "Or the justice thereof?—Sure not I!

"He dies today and shall be forgot.
  "Such had not been His fate, I say,
"Had He been wise and thrown His lot
  "With the great wise men who rule this day.

"Roman, usurer, Pharisee,
  "Godly men whose names shall turn
"For a thousand years on land and sea
  "When His dust forgot to the dust return.

  "He had wrought great good, this dreamy man,
"Had He chosen to go where the leaders go
  "But He sat with beggar and publican—
"And He must be wrong for the priests say so.

"He dies today, for the great Lord God
  "Doeth all things as they should be done
"Though the black blood deluge the blazing sod
  "And a million gibbets blot the sun.

"The Mass is right and must ever be right,
  "And so I shall crawl and lap at Its boots
"That I may build me a villa white
  "And boast a score of costly suits.

"Our rulers are great and godly men;
  "This man is dreamy and strange and dim.
"Greater than God is Opinion—then
  "I will not risk my future for Him."

Two men stood in the morning fog
  And one turned back to sell and buy,
And sing smooth hymns in the synagogue,
  And one went forth with his Lord to die.

*   *   *

Roman, usurer, Pharisee,
  Turned to dust with the dust of years;
Men remember their infamy
  Only because they caused Him tears.

XXI

Boxing Ballads: Poems About Pugilism

Bob Howard loved boxing—not just watching it but taking part. This trait, at least (if decidedly <u>not</u> that of prose style) he shared with Hemingway. But, as that latter scribe related in *A Farewell to Arms*: "The world breaks everyone, and afterward many are strong at the broken places." Howard strove toward acquiring that sort of strength—of body and of mind, of craft and of art.

And there's little doubt, whatever we believe about Hemingway's pronouncement of "everyone" that Howard at least suffered breaks both from and with "the world." Certainly there was that near-perpetual clash between his worlds of Art and the world of Cross Plains, Texas.

Howard's boxing stories have finally been given their due attention in recent years. It only follows that a multitalented author/poet who wrote fight stories should also write fight poems. This section presents pretty much the entirety of Howard's "boxing ballads" as I've called them. Indeed, while not all of the following poems of pugilism are ballads, several are either true ballads or expanded variants (and the allure of the nifty alliteration for the section title was too much to pass up).

I've also thrown in the one poem in the Howard corpus that touches upon wrestling. But wait! There's the bell for round one!

ALL THE CROWD

All the crowd
Meek and proud
Yellin' loud,
"Knock him out!"
Queer,
How clear
I hear
Every shout.
Sure, show!
Let 'em know
Every blow
Every clout.
First a left,
All my heft,
His guard's reft,
Great fun.
Then a right,
Full might.
My fight.
I've won.

AND DEMPSEY CLIMBED INTO THE RING
AND THE CROWD SNEERED

"And Dempsey climbed into the ring and the crowd sneered.
And Carl Morris climbed in the ring and the crowd yelled,
"Sock his damned jaw!"
And Dempsey hit Carl, by Hell!
And Carl hit the floor, by Hell!
And the crowd yelled, "You're the boy, Jack!".

"AW, COME ON AND FIGHT!"

His first was a left that broke my nose,
    His right ripped off my ear;
The red blood splashed beneath our blows
    Till we stood in a crimson smear.

He cracked three ribs with his smashing right,
    His left hooks gashed my head;
I saw the ring aswim in a light
    Hazy and dim and red.

He split my brow and the lid dropped down
    Like a curtain over the eye;
At every shove of his wet red glove
    I saw the crimson fly.

On my hands and knees in a scarlet pool
    I heard the referee toll,
And the crowd roared, "Kill the yellow bum!"
    Like the sea along a shoal.

I sprang, I struck, I crushed his skull
    With a sudden desperate swing,
He died with his eyes to the glaring lights
    And his back to the canvassed ring.

The referee counted above the dead,
    I swayed and clung to the ropes,
And the crowd roared: "Yellow! Both of 'em's bums!"
    Like the seas on the beaches' slopes.

THE CHAMP

The champion sneered, the crowds they jeered,
   And to the crowd said he,
"In all this land is there a man
   "Will go three rounds with me?"
Up then I leaped, "You bum," quoth I,
   The champion loudly jeered,
And like a crowd, full long and loud,
   The audience they cheered.

And then into the ring we came,
   And he rushed swift at me.
His nose I slammed, his jaw I whammed
   And mixed it merrily.
A swing I landed on his jaw,
   The crowd did yell and stamp,
The referee did count him out
   And I was aye the champ.

Ah, amateur, this gink hath been
   A champ before your day,
And therefore lend me fifteen cents
   And I will go my way.

THE COOLING OF SPIKE MCRUE

A parody of Robert W. Service
With Apologies to R. W. Service
and John L. Sullivan

A couple of hams were having a mill
  In Gallegher's old saloon.
With long left jabs and round house rights
  They were playing a merry tune.
One was the Bowery Terror,
  Murderous Spike McRue,
The other the pride of the whole East Side,
  Benny, the Battling Jew.

When out of the night where the fly cops were,
  Into the cheering crowd,
A stranger pummeled his way within,
  And he laughed both long and loud.
"Now who is he," said Monk McKee
  "Interferrin' wi' our sport?"
With a single clout he knocked Monk out
  And he gave a scornful snort.

He'd weigh a scant two hundred pounds,
  Yet the crowd was still as a louse
As he smashed a sledge-hammer fist on the bar
  And bellowed for drinks on the house.
And, "Boys," said he, "You dont know me,
  And I dont give a ding.
But Spike, that bloke—just watch my smoke."
  And he bounded into the ring.

Benny he ducked and the stranger swung,
  And Benny he hit the floor.
The stranger tore into Spike McRue

273

And the crowd began to roar.
Twas a left that lashed and a right that smashed,
   And a left and a right again,
And shoulders flat Spike hit the mat
   When he took it fair on the chin.

The crowd it cheered but the stranger sneered,
   As he stepped to the waiting bar,
And took a swig of whiskey, neat,
   And lighted a long cigar.
And "Boys," said he, "I dont know ye,
   And theres none of youse worth a damn,
But you all know John L. Sullivan,
   And thats the guy I am."

While knocked out flat on the trampled mat,
   Lay Murderous Spike McRue.
With his feet in the classical Yiddish face
   Of Benny the Battling Jew.

FABLES FOR LITTLE FOLKS

He was six foot four and wide as a door
  And he weighed two hundred pounds
And he laughed as he spoke, "I'll cool that bloke.
  I'll flatten him in two rounds."
Ah, the crowd they cheered, but the crowd they jeered
  When his foeman stepped in the ring;
They hissed and jowled and the giant scowled
  And rushed with a round-house swing.
Yes, he came full tilt but the beans were spilt
  For the smaller man timed him fair
And knocked him out with a left hand clout
  And the crowd gave him the air.
So the moral is this: make your foeman miss
  And never lead with your right,
But the first that you're to do is be sure
  That it's not Jack Dempsey you fight.

Robert E. Howard

IN THE RING

Over the place the lights go out,
　Except for the cluster above the ring;
The crowd begins to thunder and shout;
　At the tap of the gong I whirl and spring.
And I hear the snarl of my chargin' foe,
The Cobra Kid from Old Mexico.

And the ropes ain't there, and the crowd ain't there;
It's me and him, in the ring lights' glare;
Like cavemen foes in an age of stone,
On the ridge of the silent world, alone.

He ducks my lead as he surges in
And his left hook crashes against my chin,
And he shuts my eye with a roundhouse slam
That feels like the bunt of a batterin' ram.

The lights are swimmin' and so is the ring;
Blind I fall in clinch and cling,
The referee grunts as he tears us apart,
And I ram a left in under the heart.

And he batters me back across the ring—
Jab and uppercut, hook and swing—
A torrent of smashes that never slack—
I feel the ropes against my back.

Hard to the head he cannonades
And I hit the mat on my shoulder-blades.
My brain's full of fog, my mouth's full of brine,
But I hear the referee countin', "Nine!"

And up I reel, though my legs won't work
And the ring lights swim in a crimson murk.
The Cobra rushes, set for the spill,
Wild and wide open, blind for the kill.

And desperate, reelin', I shoot my right,
The last blind blow of a losin' fight.
And my right connects and his head goes back,
Till it looks, begod, like his neck would crack.

New strength surges through every vein
And the panther wakes in my punch drunk brain.
His knees, they buckle, his white lips part
As I blast my right in under the heart.

His jaw falls slack, his eyes, they blink,
As deep in his belly my left I sink;
Then every ounce of my beef goes in
To the right I heave to his sagging chin.

The leather bursts and the hand gives way,
But it's the end of a perfect day.
He hasn't stirred at the count of ten,
The referee lifts my hand and then
I hear the yells of the crowd again.

JACK DEMPSEY

Through the California mountains
　And many a wooded vale
The wind from sea ward whispers
　The name of the Nonpareil.
O'er many a peak snow covered
　O'er many a woodland fair
The sea-breeze murmurs the wonderful tale
　Of the lad from County Clare.
But never the wind from seaward
　And never the brooks of the vale
Can speak the half of the glory,
　The due of the Nonpareil.

Champion of all champions,
　Greatest in all times bounds,
The lad who held Fitzsimmons
　For thirteen gory rounds.
But the ring's red history passes
　In a swiftly roving tale,
And theres few who now remember
　The name of the Nonpareil.
But here's to the greatest of fighters,
　To a name that never shall fail,
To the name of the first Jack Dempsey,
　The wonderful Nonpareil.

JOHN L. SULLIVAN

Bellowing, blustering, old John L.
Fearing nothing 'tween sky and hell!
Rushing, roaring, swinging his right.
Smashing, crashing, forcing the fight.
Battering foes until they fell,
Tilt your glasses to old John L!

Mitchell he knocked, from the ring clear out!
Dropped Kilrain with a single clout!
Laflin he beat and Burke he flayed,
Knocked out the Maori Giant, Slade!
Packed in each fist, damnation and hell!
Tilt your glasses to old John L.!

Old John L.'s in town today
He's hitting it down the Great White way.
Look at his swallow tail coat, silk hat!
Mustache too, say he's on a bat!
Living it in, that you can tell,
Tilt your glasses to old John L.!

He's cleaned out the roughest, toughest saloon,
He's licked O'Rourke and Jem McClune,
Sampled every saloon on the streets,
Buying drinks for all he meets,
He's taking the bowery in pell-mell!
Tilt your glasses to old John L.!

Stick in your head in that grog-shop door,
Look at him! Listen to his roar!
"Set out the whiskey. Jimmy, ye bum!
Belly the bar, ye half bred scum!
I can lick any guy from here to hell!"
Tilt your glasses to old John L.!

The world moves on and the ring moves too
Old fighters have long given way to new.
But here's a health to the olden days,
To the wild old, mad old, bad old ways,
When a fight was a fight and not a sell,
And tilt your glasses to old John L.

KID LAVIGNE IS DEAD

Hang up the battered gloves; Lavigne is dead.
  Bold and erect he went into the dark.
The crown is withered and the crowds are fled,
   The empty ring stands bare and lone—yet hark:
The ghostly roar of many a phantom throng
Floats down the dusty years, forgotten long.

Hot blazed the lights above the crimson ring
Where there he reigned in his full prime, a king.
The throngs' acclaim roared up beneath their sheen
And whispered down the night: "Lavigne! Lavigne!"
Red splashed the blood and fierce the crashing blows.
Men staggered to the mat and reeling rose.
Crowns glittered there in splendor, won or lost,
And bones were shattered as the sledges crossed.

Swift as a leopard, strong and fiercely lean,
Champions knew the prowess of Lavigne.
The giant dwarf Joe Walcott saw him loom
And broken, bloody, reeled before his doom.
Handler and Everhardt and rugged Burge
Saw at the last his snarling face emerge
From bloody mists that veiled their dimming sight
Ere they sank down into unlighted night.

Strong men and bold, lay vanquished at his feet.
Mighty was he in triumph and defeat.
Far fade the echoes of the ringside's cheers
And all is lost in mists of dust-dead years.
Cold breaks the dawn; the East is ghastly red.
Hang up the broken gloves; Lavigne is dead.

Robert E. Howard

THEY MATCHED ME UP THAT NIGHT

They matched me up that night
  with a bird that was a fright
The Anaconda Kid from Amsterdam
His face was like a fable,
  his wrist a hawser's cable
His shoulder was a gable,
  his arm a battering ram.
He rushed me from the bell
  like a roaring ape from Hell
And I put a wicked left against his chin
But his left hand found me
  and his right swing crowned me
And the fogs closed round me
  and the ring began to spin.
A surf was roaring loud
  which I reckoned was the crowd
Gone cookoo as babies in their cribs.
At the gong my knees were knocking,
  I was weaving, ducking, blocking
I went to my corner rocking
  with a couple broken ribs.
For the second gory round
  he came roaring with a bound
Seeing he had victory in his grasp,
I let go my right and duck him—
  just above the belt it took him
And I know that I have shook him
  for he halted with a gasp.
He dropped his guard a second—
  long enough for me I reckoned—
And the crowd went crazy where they sat
For my left hand battered
  and my right hand shattered

Till the red blood splattered
   on the great grey mat.
Oh, how they did yell and whoop
   when I knocked him for a loop
Just about a couple counts before the bell.
They'd have gave as loud a bellow
   had I been the losing fellow—
God, a crowd is yellow—yellow—
   all of them can go to Hell.

TIME, THE VICTOR

Swift with your mitts and fast on your feet,
There is one battler you never can beat.
You can swing, you can dance, you can side-step and prance;
You can feint, you can lead, but there isn't a chance
To win a decision from Time.

He is the lad with the flying mitts
He knows your tricks and he knows your hits.
You may bluff, you may stall, but he's the greatest of all.

Robert E. Howard

A TRIBUTE TO
THE SPORTSMANSHIP OF THE FANS

[ed. note: and one wrestling poem for good measure]

Headlock, hammerlock, toss him on his bean again,
  Jump upon his belly and boot him in the hips,
Clamp the scissors on his neck
    and choke him till he's green again
    Get the fans wild-eyed, with froth on their lips.

Barlock, body-slam, nibble on his ears again—
  Its just like eating cabbage—and kick him in the groin,
Butt him in the belly, that brings the cheers again,
  The fans want a run for their hard-spent coin.

Flying-mare, toe-hold, twist his neck around again,
  Wrap his legs around his waist and tie them in a knot,
Stamp in his mouth so his teeth cannot be found again,
  The fans paid their money so make it good and hot.

Stranglehold, leg-split, jerk his knee-caps loose again,
  Crack his ribs and break his arms, leave him life-long lame,
Send him out on a shutter—then listen to the boos again,
  The kind fans howling that the battle was too tame.

WE ARE THE DUCKERS OF CROSSES

We are the duckers of crosses,
  We are the swingers of swings.
We count our gains and our losses
  In all of the fourth rate rings.
We are the bums and the slackers
  Swiggers of Ancient Crow.
Yet the fans pay sixteen smackers
  To see us knocked for a row.
Bout losers and bout forsakers
  They hand us a-many slams,
For we are the set-ups and fakers,
  We are the fourth-rate hams!
We are the takers of slams and blips!
  Jester and ring-side clown!
But sometimes we go with our trunks on our hips
  And jerk us a title down!
Taking bout that champs are shying,
  Where the ring gong clangs and thrums
Where the swinging mitts are flying—
  We are the fourth-rate bums!

Robert E. Howard

WHEN YOU WERE A SET-UP AND I WAS A HAM

When you were a set-up and I was a ham,
   In James J. Corbett's day
And toe to toe and blow to blow
   We mixed it in a fray
Or skitterd with many a roundhouse right
   Mid the ropes of a third rate ring
My soul was rife with the joy of strife
   As I matched you swing for swing.

And happy we swung and happy we slugged
   And happy I knocked you out
And shoulders flat you hit the mat
   With the force of that swinging clout.
And champions came and champions went
   And battled with might and main
Till we grew in might and signed for the fight
   And climbed in the ring again.

We were heavy weights, rough and tough
   But cautious at first in the fight
We sparred at ease while the crowd yelled "Cheese!"
   Or jabbed with a wary right.
Duck and side step on dancing feet,
   (Golly but you looked dumb!)
While the angry crowd in accents loud
   Remarked that we were bum.

Then happy we rushed and happy we slugged
   And happy I hit the floor
Twas a peach of a clout and they counted me out
   The while the crowd did roar.
And that was a dozen years ago
   In a ring that no man knows
Yet here tonight in a title fight
   We are matching swats and blows.

Your right is as strong as a battering ram
    Your left is a peach you bet,
Your swings are few, your gloves are new,
    Your foot work great and yet,
Your jaw is red from my rights to the head,
    Your nose from my lefts is flat
Though my jaws a sight from your lunging right,
    Five times you've hit the mat.
Then as we linger at battle here,
    With many a roundhouse slam,
Let us swing anew as in times when you
    Were a set-up and I was a ham.

XXII

The Dark Continent

Another of Howard's interests was exotic Africa. He seems to have been especially interested in the Zulus and the time of Shaka Zulu and the wars with the British. It is important for modern readers to realize the significance of the era of Howard's life and how differently the world must have seemed back then to a boy and young man living in a small town in Texas. Shaka had died only about 80 years prior to Howard's birth, and the later Zulu wars with the British and great battles like Isandlwana and Rorke's Drift had occurred fewer than three decades before. The quest by Speek and Burton for the source of the Nile and Stanley's quest to find Livingstone were still fresh.

One can conjecture about the extent of influence from writers about Africa such as H. Rider Haggard and Edgar Rice Burroughs, although Howard clearly read and absorbed both of them. Whether or not El Borak owes a nod to Allan Quatermain or Conan a nod to Tarzan, the common African setting for both earlier scribes, likely had some influence.

All this, of course, combined with the mystery and mystique of this still-being-discovered continent in Howard's mind. Even Solomon Kane ventures thither. There were still lots of vacant spaces on the maps of Africa—even into Howard's day.

Combining this with Howard's great appetite for history and geography in general, the allure of The Dark Continent was one that he had to heed.

VICTORY

Red fires in the North are glowing bright,
The tom-tom thrums through the whispering night,
And the jungle knows to the least leaf-blade
That the men of Mafu are back from the raid.
Back with the heads of a hundred braves,
Back with a hundred women slaves;
And the men for the loot are throwing lots,
And the women bend to the cooking pots.
And the night wind blows
And the jungle knows
  That the men of Mafu
Have smote their foes.

Chiefs and councillors haste to glut
At the feast in Mafu's palace-hut.
They stride through the door, and a bead of red
Unheeded falls on each feathered head;
And scarce an eye turns toward the ghastly thing
That once was the head of Goru's king:
Lord of the foes of Mafu's land,
Hung high, with a skull on either hand.
And the echoes thrum
To the roaring drum
  That boasts of the foemen
They've overcome.

And fire-light gleams on lithe forms glance
As the warriors leap in a blood-crazed dance.
The great fire roars in a crimson blast
As the naked, leaping forms spin past.
Like shadow-things in the shifting lights,
They leap in the ghastly voodoo rites,
And the fire-light gleams on white teeth bare,
Exultant fierce faces and flying hair.

And the dancers whirl.
Through the shadowy swirl
  Echoes the shriek
Of a captive girl.

Far to the East 'neath a baobab tree,
By a sullen river that runs to the sea,
Smolders a heap of ruins laid
In the midst of a ruined palisade,
Veiled by a grisly, yellow smoke,
No sound save the circling vulture's croak;
The jackals snarl o'er the cindered bones;
Unheeding, the sullen river drones.
And the river flows,
And the night wind blows,
  Sifting the ashes
Of Mafu's foes.

WHEN THE GODS WERE KINGS

Where the jungle lies dank, exuding
  The vapory swampland musk
Lurk the old ape-gods brooding
  In the dim, shade-haunted dusk.

They dream through the jungle gloaming
  Of the days of the claw and tooth,
When the whole world knew their roaming,
  When the world was strange with youth.

They ruled in an age that is vanished
  When the world was a swampland rank;
With the ages were they banished
  To the outlands dim and dank.

When the wind sighs over the meadows
  Its haunting melody brings
A tale through the jungle shadows
  Of an age when the gods were kings.

Robert E. Howard

THE ZULU LORD

This is the tale the Kaffirs tell
   as the tints of twilight melt
And the jackal jeers from the kopje's stones
   and the night-time veils the veldt;
As the cooking fires begin to glow
   and the lounging braves match tales,
This is the story the ancients tell
   in far, fire-lighted kraals:

Chaka sat in his throne of state;
   no girls that dance or sing
Bent supple forms in the palace hut
   for Chaka the Zulu king.
For Chaka the king was a man of war
   and his hands with blood were red
And never a girl could thrill his soul
   as the sight of the spear-rent dead.

But the idle assagais hung in the rack
   And idle the warring horde
For the tribes of the veldt-land bent the back
   To Chaka, the Zulu lord.

Then he formed his impis rank upon rank
   and bid them smite and slay;
Three thousand warriors of Zululand
   fell on that bloody day.
Spear clanged on shield and the squadrons reeled
   under the hot blue skies;
From his throne of state King Chaka watched
   with his gleaming, magical eyes.

And now when the dim stars light their brands
   And the night wind brings its musk
The ghosts come out of the shadowlands
   And stalk through the shuddering dusk.

They say, when the night wind stirs the leaves
   and the starlight gleams and peers,
That 'tis the rustle of unseen shields
   and the glitter of shadow spears.
And there in the dim of the ghostly night,
   far out on the silent plain,
The phantom hordes form ranks and charge,
   retreat, surge on again.

And the moon that rises above the ghosts
   And silvers the dusky land
Is Chaka, watching the spectral hosts
   That died at his command.

Robert E. Howard

ZULULAND

That is no land for weaklings,
    no land for coward or fool,
For if ever a man goes to that land,
    he learns at the greatest school
The white men in that country
    are a hardy, chosen band,
For of all the earth the place for worth
    to be proven is Zululand.

Oh, the free days under the wide free sky!
    The freedom known and felt,
The wind of the sea, the jungle for me,
    but best of it all the veldt.
Blazing under a blazing sky;
    under the sun at noon.
And weirdly white in the tropic night
    under the tropic moon.

Midnight! Hark to the roaring
    of lions miles away,
And the night birds that break your dreams
    in the first gray dawn of day.
The weird laugh of the hyena,
    as he lopes across the plain,
The scurrying fear of the wild bush-deer
    as the lion roars again.

Day, high day! With the sunlight
    flooding the veldt with gold,
And on the slope graze the antelope
    and the fluttering bush-birds scold.
And listen! Through the morning air,
    over the veldt there comes,
Bound and rebound from the sky to the ground,
    the rolling of Kaffir drums.

Leaping back from the azure sky
   to thunder in the ear,
As the grass strewn ground flings back the sound
   into the atmosphere.
Boom! Boom! Rumble and thud!
   The drums speak loud and far,
Speak without cease, a song of peace
   or a tale of bloody war.

And then the close ranked battle lines,
   where the feet beat hard packed loam,
The roar like the sea and the fierce "Sgee!"
   as the flashing spear goes home.
The ranks of tall, plumed warriors,
   warriors in stately, warlike array,
Shield held to breast, war-spear and crest,
   ready for kingly fray.

Aye, that is a land for strong men,
   and the race will never cease,
A chosen land for a chosen band
   whether in war or peace.
Then here is a toast to the strong and the true,
   a toast to that hairy band,
The Afric host, and here's a toast
   to their country, Zululand!

XXIII

Dark Fantasy & Horror

Certainly among Howard's most significant and best-known poems are those which touch upon themes and topics that fit nicely into *Weird Tales*, Lovecraft's already developing and expanding Cthulhu Mythos, and the genre of supernatural horror. Howard weaves elements of the darkly fantastic into much of his fiction and his narrative poetry. Several pieces in each of those broad genres show elements of horror, while being essentially more adventure or "Sword & Sorcery."

Howard's horror poetry shows influences from, of course, Poe and Lovecraft, but also a knowledge of folk and traditional beliefs about monstrous beings and horrific events. And the type fit nicely into the market at *Weird Tales* (and others of its ilk) that Howard had not only broken into, but at which he was succeeding admirably.

Howard was also writing at a time when this type of fiction was gaining general momentum. In American, Ambrose Bierce and Robert W. Chambers had done important work in the horror short story. In Britain, Bram Stoker and M. R. James were popular—proving as James had declared that reader's not only were seeking, but greatly enjoyed a "pleasing terror."

Howard also loved the cinema, and classics like Karloff's *Frankenstein* and Lugosi's *Dracula* were released five years before Howard's death.

So, the market was right—and Howard had found another field to "splash," another market to explore. A few poems in the following section touch upon what Lovecraft called "physical fear and the mundanely gruesome," but most have a supernatural element, something that "breaks the rules" of the world we know, the truths we depend upon to remain sane.

AGAINST THE BLOOD RED MOON
A TOWER STANDS

Against the blood red moon a tower stands;
   An everlasting silence haunts the place.
It was not reared by any human hands,
   The silent symbol of a shadowy race.
There, long ago, I stole through ancient night
   My footsteps woke strange echoes through the hour;
Strange specters walked with me through mazy light.
   I left my soul, a ghost to haunt the tower.

ALL HALLOW'S EVE

Now anthropoid and leprous shadows lope
   Down black colossal corridors of Night
And through the cypress roots blind fingers grope
   In stagnant pools where burns a witches' light.

Gaunt, scaly horrors of an Elder World
   Squat on a lone bare hill in grisly ring,
     Howling blasphemies to a red hag-moon;
And where a serpent round an oak has curled,
     And midnight shudders to a hell-born tune,
A nameless, godless shape sits slavering.

Gibbering madness slinks among the trees;
   Deep in black woods a monstrous idol nods,
And rising from the nameless Outer Seas
   Come spectres of the age-forgotten gods,

Who in blind, black infancy of earth
   Gripped howling men in their misshapen paws,
And ground, with ghastly glee and obscene mirth,
   Nude, writhing shapes between their brutish jaws.

Robert E. Howard

ARKHAM

Drowsy and dull with age the houses blink
  On aimless streets the rat-gnawed years forget—
But what inhuman figures leer and slink
  Down the old alleys when the moon has set.

AT THE BAZAAR

There breaks in bazaar of Zanzibar,
  red surge of life on life;
At eve there came through the sunset's flame
  a man with a dripping knife.
"Eunuchs a score and seven more
  I've made today," said he,
"The blood and tears of all my years
  I've caused would fill a sea.
"Search far, search far from Zanzibar
  for youths of many lands
"For my hungry steel and the glee I feel
  when they writhe beneath my hand
He laid him down where the stains lay brown
  on the floor of the gelding room,
And his gory blade as it down was laid
  clanged like a tone of doom.
In sleep he leered and clawed his beard
  with fingers black with gore;
The ghosts of dead men came from Hell
  and staked him to the floor.

BLACK SEAS

I have heard black seas booming in the night
On dim uncharted shores beneath the stars,
With reefs that never gleamed to mortal sight,
And winds that never hastened man-hewn spars.
I waver on the threshold of my choice—
Oh silver stars that gleam in oceans black!—
For through the night there sounds a nameless Voice:
"Who ride the dusky seas—they come not back."

DEAD MAN'S HATE

They hanged John Farrel in the dawn
   amid the marketplace;
At dusk came Adam Brand to him
   and spat upon his face.
"Ho neighbors all," spake Adam Brand,
   "see ye John Farrel's fate!
'Tis proven here a hempen noose
   is stronger than man's hate!

For heard ye not John Farrel's vow
   to be avenged on me
Come life or death? See how he hangs
   high on the gallows tree?"
Yet never a word the people spake,
   in fear and wild surprise—
For the grisly corpse raised up its
   head and stared with sightless eyes,

And with strange motions, slow and stiff,
   pointed at Adam Brand

And clambered down the gibbet tree,
   the noose within its hand.
With gaping mouth stood Adam Brand
   like a statue carved of stone,
Till the dead man laid a clammy hand
   hard on his shoulder-bone.

Then Adam shrieked like a soul in hell;
   the red blood left his face
And he reeled away in a drunken run
   through the screaming market place;
And close behind, the dead man came
   with a face like a mummy's mask,
And the dead joints cracked
   and the stiff legs creaked
     with their unwonted task.
Men fled before the flying twain
   or shrank with bated breath,
And they saw on the face of Adam Brand
   the seal set there by death.
He reeled on buckling legs that failed,
   yet on and on he fled;
So through the shuddering market-place,
   the dying fled the dead.

At the riverside fell Adam Brand
   with a scream that rent the skies;
Across him fell John Farrel's corpse,
   nor ever the twain did rise.
There was no wound on Adam Brand
   but his brow was cold and damp,
For the fear of death had blown out his life
   as a witch blows out a lamp.

His lips were writhed in a horrid grin
   like a fiend's on Satan's coals,

And the men that looked on his face that day,
   his stare still haunts their souls.
Such was the fate of Adam Brand,
   a strange, unearthly fate;
For stronger than death or hempen noose
   are the fires of a dead man's hate.

THE DEAD SLAVER'S TALE

Dim and grey was the silent sea,
   Dim was the crescent moon;
From the jungle back of the shadowed lea
   Came a tom-tom's eerie croon
When we glutted the waves with a hundred slaves
   From a Jekra barracoon.
Our way to bar, a man of war
   Was sailing with canvas full;
So the doomed up from the hold we bore,
   Hacked them to pieces and hurled them o'er,
And we heard the grim sharks as they tore
   The flesh from each sword-cleft skull.

Then fast we fled toward the rising sun
   But we could not flee the dead
And ever behind our flying ship
   Wavered a trail of red.

She sank like a stone off Calabar
   With all of her bloody crew.
There was no breeze to shake a spar,
   No reef her hull to hew.
But dusky hands rose out of the deep,
   And dragged her under the blue.

DESTINATION

Against the east a sombre spire
  loomed o'er a dusky, brooding wood;
Against the west the sunset's fire
  lay like a fading smear of blood.
The stranger pushed through tangled boughs;
  the forest towered stark and grim,
Fit haunting place for fiends' carouse,
  but silent in the dusk and dim.

Anon the stranger paused to hark;
  no wind among the branches beat
But bats came wheeling in the dark
  and serpents hissed beneath his feet.
Bleak stars blinked out, of leprous hue;
  the forest stretched its clutching arms;
A hag-lean moon swam up and threw
  gnarled shadows into monstrous forms.

Then of great towers he was 'ware,
  and on the sombre, crowning spire,
The moon that gibbet-etched it there,
  smote with an eery, lurid fire.
Above the forest's silent halls,
  he saw the sullen bastions frown
And o'er the towers and the walls
  strange gleams of light crawled up and down.

He scaled the steep and stood before the donjon.
  With his steel-tipped stave
He smote the huge, bronze studded door.
  (And yet his blows no echoes gave.)
The sullen door swung wide apace
  and framed in unnamed radiance dim
A grisly, horned, inhuman face
  with yellow eyes gazed out at him.

DEVON OAK

I am a Devon Oak;
   Here in the long ago
The bearded, strange eyed Druid
   Cut down the mistletoe.

Steeped in the godless past,
   Deep are my blind black roots,
They have fed on sightless things
   And subterranean fruits.

Seek not to know or guess
   To what my fibre clings;
My roots take hold on dark
   Deep hidden monstrous things.

My roots have sunken deep,
   Deeper than thought may dare—
If ye would pluck me up—
   Oh, blind to doom, beware!

Beware the shapes my roots
   Have gripped in earth and Night
Who knows what their dread grasp
   May tear into the light?

Robert E. Howard

DROWNED

My mother sat me on the cottage stair
  With steaming porridge and a pewter spoon.
  But over the purple hill there rose the moon,
Like some great silver spider from her lair.
And, breaking into shards the crystal air,
  I heard a hundred pipes burst into tune
  Among the rushes of the pool and loon:
The fairies made their music, hidden there.

My mother found my spoon and empty bowl.
  Drowned in the fen they say my body lies.
    But far below where misty blossoms shine,
I sport with elfin babe and moon-mare's foal.
  Aloft on elephantine dragon-flies,
    I quench my thirst on pomegranate wine.

A DULL SOUND AS OF KNOCKING

Who raps here on my door tonight,
  Stirring my sleep with the deadened sound?
Here in my Room there is naught of light,
  And silence locks me round.

The taste of the earth is in my mouth,
  Stillness, decay and lack of light,
And dull as doom the rapping
  Thuds on my Door tonight.

My Room is narrow and still and black
  In such have kings and beggars hid;
And falling clods are the knuckles
  That rap on my coffin lid.

THE DWELLER IN DARK VALLEY

The nightwinds tossed the tangled trees,
   the stars were cold with scorn;
Midnight lay over Dark Valley
   the hour I was born.
The mid-wife dozed beside the hearth,
   a hand the window tried—
She woke and stared and screamed and swooned
   at what she saw outside.

Her hair was white as a leper's hand,
   she never spoke again;
But laughed and wove the wild flowers
   into an endless chain.
But when my childish tongue could speak,
   and my infant feet could stray,
I found her dying in the hills
   at the haunted dusk of day.

And her darkening eyes at last were sane;
   she passed with a fearsome word:
"You who were born in Dark Valley,
   beware the Valley's lord!"
As I came down through Dark Valley,
   the grim hills gulped the light;
I heard the ponderous tramping
   of a monster in the night.

The great trees leaned together,
   the vines ensnared my feet,
I heard across the darkness
   my own heart's thundering beat.
Damned be the dark ends of the earth
   where old horrors live again.
And monsters of lost ages lurk

to eat the souls of men!
I climbed the ridge into the moon
    and trembling there I turned—
Down in the blasted shadows
    two eyes like hellfire burned.
Under the black malignant trees
    a shapeless Shadow fell—
I go no more to Dark Valley
    which is the Gate of Hell.

FAR IN THE GLOOMY NORTHLAND

Far in the gloomy Northland,
  Where the roaring north wind blows,
Driving the dim, pale for wraiths
  Over the drifting snows.

When the sleet drives fast and furious,
  And the winter north wind roars,
And the ocean, dark and sullen,
  Beats on the northern shores.

A haggard land and a barren,
  Naught to charm or allure,
A white-crested, desolate ocean,
  A gloomy, desolate moor.

Gloomy, desolate, barren,
  Feared and shunned by men,
For a phantom roams the moor,
  A spectre haunts the fen.

Men of the moors have seen it,
  Seen it and shrieked and fled,
Fleeing, half wild with terror,
  The awful thing of dread.

The thing of fright and horror,
  The thing so terribly feared,
A spectre horrible, awful,
  A thing uncanny and weird.

Robert E. Howard

THE FEAR THAT FOLLOWS

The smile of a child was on her lips—
    oh, smile of a last long rest.
My arm went up and my arm went down
    and the dagger pierced her breast.
Silent she lay—oh still, oh still!—
    with the breast of her gown turned red.
Then fear rose up in my soul like death
    and I fled from the face of the dead.
The hangings rustled upon the walls,
    velvet and black they shook,
And I thought to see strange shadows flash
    from the dark of each door and nook.
Tapestries swayed on the ghostly walls
    as if in a wind that blew;
Yet never a breeze stole through the rooms
    and my black fear grew and grew.

Moonlight dappled the pallid sward
    as I climbed o'er the window sill;
I looked not back at the darkened house
    which lay so grim and still.
The trees reached phantom hands to me,
    their branches brushed my hair,
Footfalls whispered amid the grass,
    yet never a man was there.
The shades loomed black in the forest deeps,
    black as the doom of death;
Amid the whispers of shapes unseen
    I stole with bated breath,
Till I came at last to a ghostly mere
    bordered with silver sands;
A faint mist rose from its shimmering breast
    as I knelt to lave my hands.

The waters mirrored my haggard face,
   I bent close down to see—
Oh, Mother of God! A grinning skull
   leered up from the mere at me!
With a gibbering scream I rose and fled
   till I came to a mountain dim
And a great black crag in the blood-red moon
   loomed up like a gibbet grim.
Then down from the great red stars above,
   each like a misty plume,
There fell on my face long drops of blood
   and I knew at last my doom.
Then I turned me slow to the only trail
   that was left upon earth for me,
The trail that leads to the hangman's cell
   and the grip of the gallows tree.

FORBIDDEN MAGIC

There came to me a Man one summer night,
   When all the world lay silent in the stars,
   And moonlight crossed my room with ghostly bars.
He whispered hints of weird, unhallowed sight;
I followed— then in waves of spectral light
   Mounted the shimmery ladders of my soul
   Where moon-pale spiders, huge as dragons, stole—
Great forms like moths, with wings of wispy white.
Around the world the sighing of the loon
   Shook misty lakes beneath the false-dawn's gleams;
    Rose tinted shone the sky-line's minaret;
    I rose in fear, and then with blood and sweat
   Beat out the iron fabrics of my dreams,
And shaped of them a web to snare the moon.

Robert E. Howard

THE GHOST KINGS

The ghost kings are marching;
    the midnight knows their tread,
From the distant, stealthy planets
    of the dim, unstable dead;
There are whisperings on the night-winds
    and the shuddering stars have fled.

A ghostly trumpet echoes
    from a barren mountainhead;
Through the fen the wandering witch-lights
    gleam like phantom arrows sped;
There is silence in the valleys
    and the moon is rising red.

The ghost kings are marching
    down the ages' dusty maze;
The unseen feet are tramping
    through the moonlight's pallid haze,
Down the hollow clanging stairways
    of a million yesterdays.

The ghost kings are marching,
    where the vague moon-vapor creeps,
While the night-wind to their coming,
    like a thund'rous herald sweeps;
They are clad in ancient grandeur,
    but the world, unheeding, sleeps.

THE GHOST OCEAN

There is a sea and a silent moon
  That gleams all the night with a ghostly sheen
On waves that waver in ripples dim
  From fathomless deeps of pale jade green.

Silvery waves in a silver moon,
  Like a shining, sinuous monster's scales,
And the moonbeams play on a thousand prows
  And glimmer on myriad ghostly sails.

Never a gale to shake the deep
  There has a human foot ne'er been,
But the ghost-ships ride and they do not sleep
  And they set their courses unsteered of men.

A silent sea and a silver moon
  And the ghosts of ships that have earned their rest,
They sail forever and sail for aye
  On the ghostly ocean beyond the West.

Robert E. Howard

Ju-Ju Doom

As a great spider grows to monstrous girth
   On life-blood sucked from smaller, cringing things,
   So Joab Worley, in his plunderings
Of black folk spawned in nakedness and dearth,
Grew great in all the riches prized of earth;
   Dwelling in state, a brother to black kings,
   In his great throne-hut, safe from spears and slings;
The deep black jungle echoed to his mirth.

Until he dared to go, in drunken pride,
   Alone into the ju-ju hut; all round
      The black priests trembled and the drum were beat;
At last they, on their bellies crawled inside;
   There Joab Worley lay, without a wound,
      Stone dead before the leering idol's feet.

The Last Words He Heard

The chariots were chanting in the gloom,
   The long dark banners carved the crimson sky;
   A whisper reached me as a shaft went by,
A deadly bride that sought a deathly groom.
A black tide swept us, plume on waving plume.
   The arrows filled the air like one great sigh
   The shields boomed out in one great hollow cry;
Dim pallid faces fringed that sea of doom.

Then in an instant all the loud alarms
   Died out in silence far along the plain,
      For faces gleamed bare skulls unhelmeted,
The broken spears fell down from fleshless arms.
   I cried, "My God, but all of these are slain!"
      A Voice replied, "Nay, you alone are dead."

THE LOST GALLEY

The sun was brazen in the sky,
   Like fire the sullen waves were red;
We watched the droning sea-gulls fly
   About the lurching main-mast head.
Each swaying oar against the banks
   Cadenced a steady, creaking strum.
Across the world in marching ranks
   We watched the restless surges come.
From off the waves the hell-heat flowed,
   The very sails seemed scorched and sere;
They sweated, screeched and fought, who rowed,
   As on we plied with dip and veer.

The whips began to swish and crack
   But that strange heat still fiercer flayed
More than the lash each naked back
   As o'er a blazing sea we swayed.
The oars smoked in the crimson sea,
   The gilt work melted in the flame;
The surges marched unceasingly,
   Like waves of molten bronze they came.
And when we looked to see uprise
   Some distant shore-line, there was none
The world was all of burning skies
   And flaming sea and copper sun.

There looms no beach, there lifts no shore
   For Satan spun a charm-web fell:
And so we sail forever more
   Across the molten seas of Hell.

Robert E. Howard

MOON MOCKERY

I walked in Tara's wood one summer night,
   And saw, amid the still, star-haunted skies,
   A slender moon in silver mist arise,
And hover on the hill as if in fright.
Burning, I seized her veil and held her tight:
   An instant all her glow was in my eyes;
   Then she was gone, swift as a white bird flies,
And I went down the hill in opal light.

And soon I was aware, as down I came,
   That all was strange and new on every side;
   Strange people went about me to and fro,
And when I spoke with trembling mine own name
   They turned away, but one man said: "He died
   In Tara Wood, a hundred years ago."

THE MOOR GHOST

They hauled him to the crossroads
  As day was at its close;
They hung him to the gallows
  And left him for the crows.

His hands in life were bloody,
  His ghost will not be still
He haunts the naked moorlands
  About the gibbet hill.

And oft a lonely traveler
  Is found upon the fen
Whose dead eyes hold a horror
  Beyond the world of men.

The villagers then whisper,
  With accents grim and dour:
"This man has met at midnight
  The phantom of the moor."

Robert E. Howard

ONE WHO COMES AT EVENTIDE

I think when I am old a furtive shape
  Will sit beside me at my fireless hearth,
Dabbled with blood from stumps of severed wrists,
  And flecked with blackened bits of moldy earth.

My blood ran fire when the deed was done;
  Now it runs colder than the moon that shone
On shattered fields where dead men lay in heaps
  Who could not hear a ravished daughter's moan.

(Dim through the bloody dawn on bitter winds
  The throbbing of the distant guns was brought
When I reeled like a drunkard from the hut
  That hid the horror my red hands had wrought.)

So now I fire my veins with stinging wine,
  And hoard my youth as misers hug their gold,
Because I know what shape will come and sit
  Beside my crumbling hearth—when I am old.

THE PHANTOMS GATHER

Up over the cromlech and down the rath,
Treading a dim forgotten path,
Past the ancient, vague monolith,
Out of the past of tale and myth,
Where the bat wheels silent 'round walls of might,
The phantoms gather from out the night.

THE RHYME OF THE THREE SLAVERS

Still and dim lay sea and land
  As they rowed from the sullen shore,
Their captive lay, bound foot and hand;
  His eyes gleamed as they swore:
"The men-of-war will come again
  "But you'll come never more.

"The men-of-war will come and go
  "Proud ships of the English line,
"But of our commerce they'll not know
  "And none will tell the swine;
"For you'll be fathoms down below
  "The spray of the driving brine.

"And the word shall go afield and far
  "That thus our laws are made
"And a feast for the sharks off Calabar
  "The price the traitor paid.
"And this the fate of every man
  "That hinders the white man's trade."

Far on the still bay's dusky blue
  Rocked by the drowsy tide
Their daggers pierced him through and through
  And they flung him overside.
His eyes were hells as he sank to death
  And he cursed them as he died.

They weighed their anchor and sailed at dawn
  With the souls for which they'd paid,
Three men, the vilest of Hell's red spawn,
  Fairly and Fall and Slade.
Basest of Satan's Brotherhood,
  Sharks of the slaver's trade.

And little they recked of the man they slew—
  Chief of a fetish clan—
For telling tales of their bloody crew
  To the ships of the Englishman.
(But there be deeps of the black man's soul
  No white man's eye may scan.)

They scattered far o'er the Seven Seas
  To glut each blood-stained purse;
They did foul deeds on far blue leas—
  All crimes of the Universe.
But ever there followed beneath the tides
  The ghost of a black man's curse.

For Fall was slain by a Somo chief,
  His skull was a bushman's plunder;
Fairly died on a Baltic reef
  Where his schooner crashed asunder.
And Slade was drowned off a northern sound
  And a black arm hauled him under.

THE RIDE OF FALUME

Falume of Spain rode forth amain
    when twilight's crimson fell
To drink a toast with Bahram's ghost
    in the scarlet land of Hell.
His rowels clashed as swift he dashed
    along the flaming skies;
The sunset rade at his bridle braid
    and the moon was in his eyes.
The waves were green with an eery sheen
    over the hills of Thule
And the ripples beat to his horse's feet
    like a serpent in a pool.
On vampire wings the shadow things
    wheeled round and round his head,
Till he came at last to a kingdom vast
    in the Land of the Restless Dead.

They thronged about in a grisly rout,
    they caught at his silver rein;
"Avaunt, foul host! Tell Bahram's ghost
    Falume has come from Spain!"
Then flame-arrayed rose Bahram's shade:
    "What would ye have, Falume?"
"Ho, Bahram who on earth I slew
    where Tagus' waters boom,
Now though I shore your life of yore
    amid the burning West,
I ride to Hell to bid ye tell
    where I might ride to rest.
My beard is white and dim my sight
    and I would fain be gone.
Speak without guile: where lies the isle
    of mystic Avalon?"

"A league beyond the western wind,
    a mile beyond the moon,
Where the dim seas roar on an unknown shore
    and the drifting stars lie strewn:
The lotus buds there scent the woods
    where the quiet rivers gleam,
And king and knight in the mystic light
    the ages drowse and dream."
With sudden bound Falume wheeled round,
    he fled through the flying wrack
Till he came to the land of Spain
    with the sunset at his back.
"No dreams for me, but living free,
    red wine and battle's roar;
I breast the gales and I ride the trails
    until I ride no more."

THE SEA-WOMAN

The wild sea is beating
  Against the grey sands;
The woman, the sea-woman,
  Stretches her hands.

Her eyes they are mystic
  And cold as the sea,
With slender white fingers
  She beckons to me—

There are woods in the sea
  Though the leaves are all grey,
The ocean's pale roses
  Lift dim in the spray.

I follow I follow—
  The grey sea-gull flies—
Ah, woman, sea-woman,
  There's death in your eyes.

Robert E. Howard

SHADOW THING

There was a thing of the shadow world,
  Shadow conceived and shadow born.
Who roamed through the night on silent feet
  And shunned the light of the lifting morn.

A friend of the dim and nether world,
  And the sons of man were his grisly feast,
Until one night in the forest haunts,
  This thing of the shadows met a priest.

Who by the might of the Light Above
  Walked all unscathed through
the fiend-dimmed vales.
Who saw the Way with unclouded gaze,
  And followed the lure of the dim out-trails.

Lifting souls from the marsh and mire,
  Freeing the slave, defying the king,
And bold in battle and unafraid
  He faced and conquered the shadow thing.

Conquered it, aye, but held his hand;
  Spake to the thing as it were a man,
Strongly wrought with its shadow mind,
  Until a strange, new change began.

As the desert serpent flings its skin,
  And the buffalo shakes from its hide the mire,
The thing strove strong to change its shape
  And its half-soul grew with a magic fire.

And the good priest strove with the Powers Above,
  To lift its soul from the foul to the good,
And at last prevailed, but first it must go
And for years wage war with the Devil's brood.

SHADOWS (2)

Grey ghost, dim ghost,
　　Moon and shadow spawn,
Strange are the far flung
　　Ways you have gone—
Wailing through the starlight
　　Fleeing at the dawn.

Grey ghost, dim ghost,
　　(Moon upon the hill,
Slender fingers rapping
　　At my window sill.)—

Eyes that haunt the shadows
　　Feet that shun the light—
Grey ghost, dim ghost
　　Where do you walk tonight?

SHADOWS OF DREAMS

Men sing of poets who leave their sheets
　　For the sighing dew to cool their brain
But I have tramped through the silent streets
　　Through tides of the midnight rain.
What was it drew me from my room
　　Into the rain and the night,
To the empty echoed pavements
　　And the street lamp's guttering light?
Rather the night breeze in my face
　　And the night rain in my hair,
Than the cold of a phantom ridden place
　　And the Thing that waited there.
Had I turned again to the bed where one

Slept careless in the gloom—
But I saw the empty windows frown
And the gliding shadows bore me down
   And I fled from the sleeping room.

Out in the night, the whispering night,
   And the sons of men a-bed,
What were the Shapes that met my sight
Surging close to the dimming light
That turned the rain a ghostly white,
   The lamps that glimmered red.
The Life I knew seemed strange and far,
   I tramped alone on lonely streets;
The slanting mist drowned every star.
   And echoing my footfall beats
   I heard the tramp of the dead.
The men that lived, the men that loved,
   On either side and close behind
The hard paved walks gave back their tread,
   Their whispers rode the sighing wind.

Oh, fingers steel, oh, fingers steel
   That rend the brain and heart,
Perdition born, they do not scorn
   In Hell your icy art.
Oh men that deep lie locked in sleep
   Nor dream of such abyss,
Awake, awake and see me break
   The sword of Lilith's kiss.
The roof above, the bed below,
   Your slumbering mate a-side
Oh, happy fools, what do you know
   Of this inhuman tide?
Oh sleep ye sound, your windows frowned,
   In orthodoxy wrath
At one who lost on nameless roads

Beats out his own long path.
Aye, sleep ye fools of rote and rules—
  Brains break, through naught ye deem,
And torch and steel may make ye feel
  The things whereof I dream.
I tramped along the silent streets
Through rain that fell in slanting sheets.
Tall spires arose,
  The college spires
Old sworn foes
  Of soul born fires,
Of soul born fires and fire born souls,
Grey swamps and mires mark their goals.
Beneath those trees
  Years dust and gone
Men sat on knees
  Of Life's new dawn,
Oh, men whose name are rusty.
  And men unborn shall greet the morn
  When Time has shorn my soul with scorn
And my very bones are dusty.
I saw the dreary street lamp gleam
  Through branches of the waving trees
The gutter was a coiling stream
  But curious whispers lade the breeze.
I raised on high my iron fists
  And cursed the time worn sight.
My laughter broke the sighing mists
  And rattled down the night.
And still the spires brooded high
Like Titans in the grey old sky.

Oh men that sleep, oh men that sleep,
  Come out and dance with me.
I'll show you deeper depths of Hells
  You ever dreamed could be.
I did not flee as men have fled

To seek a refuge vain.
I bared my breast to the night's unrest
   And the whip of the flying rain.
The rain was in my dank hair
   And in my face the mist
The breath of night was on my lips
   That Bast of Egypt kissed.
Oh men that sleep, oh men that sleep,
   I hear your restless sigh
And now the red of early dawn
   Makes pale the eastern sky.
Back, shadows, back into the night,
   Morn's goblet brimming full;
Back to the corners of the world
   And the dark nooks in my skull.
Oh men that sleep, awake, awake.
   The skyline glimmers white.
And I must seek again the road
   That leads to life and light.

SONG OF A MAD MINSTREL

I am the thorn in the foot,
   I am the blur in the sight;
I am the worm at the root,
   I am the thief in the night.
I am the rat in the wall,
   the leper that leers at the gate;
I am the ghost in the hall,
   herald of horror and hate.

I am the rust on the corn,
   I am the smut on the wheat,
Laughing man's labor to scorn,
   weaving a web for his feet.
I am canker and mildew and blight,
   danger and death and decay;
The rot of the rain by night,
   the blast of the sun by day.

I warp and wither with drought,
   I work in the swamp's foul yeast;
I bring the black plague from the south
   and the leprosy in from the east.
I rend from the hemlock boughs
   wine steeped in the petals of dooms;
Where the fat black serpents drowse
   I gather the Upas blooms.

I have plumbed the northern ice
   for a spell like frozen lead;
In lost gray fields of rice,
   I have learned from Mongol dead.
Where a bleak black mountain stands
   I have looted grisly caves;
I have digged in the desert sands

to plunder terrible graves.
Never the sun goes forth,
    never the moon glows red,
But out of the south or the north,
    I come with the slavering dead.
I come with hideous spells,
    black chants and ghastly tunes;
I have looted the hidden hells
    and plundered the lost black moons.

There was never a king or priest
    to cheer me by word or look,
There was never a man or beast
    in the blood-black ways I took.
There were crimson gulfs unplumbed,
    there were black wings over a sea;
There were pits where mad things drummed,
    and foaming blasphemy.

There were vast ungodly tombs
    where slimy monsters dreamed;
There were clouds like blood-drenched plumes
    where unborn demons screamed.
There were ages dead to Time,
    and lands lost out of Space;
There were adders in the slime,
    and a dim unholy Face.

Oh, the heart in my breast turned stone,
    and the brain froze in my skull—
But I won through, I alone,
    and poured my chalice full
Of horrors and dooms and spells,
    black buds and bitter roots—
From the hells beneath the hells,
    I bring you my deathly fruits.

A SONG OF THE WEREWOLF FOLK

Sink white fangs in the throat of Life,
　Lap up the red that gushes
In the cold dark gloom of the bare black stones,
　In the gorge where the black wind rushes.

Slink where the titan boulders poise
　And the chasms grind thereunder,
Over the mountains black and bare
　In the teeth of the brooding thunder.

Why should we wish for the fertile fields,
　Valley and crystal fountain?
This is our doom—the hunger-trail,
　The wolf and the storm-stalked mountain.

Over us stalk the bellowing gods
　Where the dusk and the twilight sever;
Under their iron goatish hoofs
　They crunch our skulls forever.

Mercy and hope and pity—all,
　Bubbles the black crags sunder;
Hunger is all the gods have left
　And the death that lurks thereunder.

Glut mad fangs in the blood of Life
　To slake the thirst past sating,
Before the blind worms mouth our bones
　And the vulture's beak is grating.

Robert E. Howard

THE STRANGER

The wind blew in from sea-ward,
  The day was soft and fine.
He lounged on the wide veranda
  And sipped at his Spanish wine.

Slender and darkly handsome,
  Amusedly worldly-wise,
Drawing the stars like a magnet
  With his strange inscrutable eyes.

Tolerant, an air of culture.
  The women stared, passing by.
Courteous, suave and friendly
  To a stranger—such as I.

We sat and we talked for hours,
  His evenly cadenced tone
Weaved a charm of wonder
  Till my thoughts were all his own.

Till the sun sank over the board-walk
  And the stars began to shine,
And to a toast of my wishing
  His goblet clinked to mine

* * * * *

Yonder he sits and watches
  The people who wander by,
Debonair, slim and courtly,
  With his strange inscrutable eye.

But I sit no more at his table,
  And others may hear his tales,
For I saw when he lifted his goblet
  The talons he wears for nails.

THE SYMBOL

Eons before Atlantean days
   in the time of the world's black dawn,
Strange were the kings and grim were the deeds
   that the pallid moon looked on.
When the great black cities split the stars
   and strange prows broke the tide,
And smoke went up from ghastly shrines
   where writhing victims died.

Black magic raised its serpent head,
   and all things foul and banned,
Till an angry God hurled up the sea
   against the shuddering land.
And the grisly kings they read their doom
   in the wind and the rising brine,
And they set a pillar on a hill
   for a symbol and a sign.

Black shrine and hall and cavern wall
   sank to eternal sleep,
And dawn looked down on a silent world
   and the blue unbroken deep.
Now men go forth in their daily ways
   and they reck not of the feel
Of the veil that crushed, so long ago,
   the world beneath its heel.

But deep in the seaweed-haunted halls
   in the green unlighted deep,
Inhuman kings await the day
   that shall break their chain of sleep.
And far in a grim untrodden land
   on a jungle-girded hill,
A pillar stands like a sign of Fate,

in subtle warning still.
Carved in its blind black face of stone
    a fearful unknown rune
Leers in the glare of the tropic sun
    and the cold of the leprous moon.
And it shall stand for a symbol mute
    that men are weak and blind,
Till Hell roars up from the black abyss
    and horror swoops behind.

For this is the screed upon the shaft,
    oh, pallid sons of men:
"We that were lords of all the earth,
    shall rise and rule again."
And dark is the doom of the tribes of earth,
    that hour wild and red,
When the ages give their secrets up
    and the sea gives up its dead.

THE TAVERN

There stands, close by a dim, wolf-haunted wood,
    A tavern like a monster, brooding thing.
    About its sullen gables no birds sing.
Oft a lone traveller, when the moon is blood,
Lights from his horse in quest of sleep and meal.
    His footfalls fade within and sound no more;
    He comes not forth; but from a secret door
Bearing a grisly burden, shadows steal.

By day, 'neath trees whose silent, green leaves glisten,
    The tavern crouches, hating day and light.
        A lurking vampire, terrible and lean;
        Sometimes behind its windows may be seen
    Vague leprous faces, haggard, fungus-white,
That peer and start and ever seem to listen.

THUS SPAKE SVEN THE FOOL

The night is dark; the fenlands lie asleep;
  In crimson fogs is cloaked the bloody moon.
  Afar the dreary laughter of a loon
Shakes with vague fear the slumber of the sheep.
The rushes stir like waves upon the deep.
  I do not fear, though all about me soon
  I hear the whispered tread of ghostly shoon
Glide through the night, some grisly tryst to keep.

I weary of the dusty roads of men;
  I know of beings that walk fire-arrayed,
    Whose eyes are deep with wisdom strange and hoary.
I shall go forth and live upon the fen
  And race and laugh with creatures of the shade
    And don the scarlet cloak of purgatory.

TO A WOMAN (2)

Though fathoms deep you sink me in the mould,
  Locked in with thick-lapped lead and bolted wood,
Yet rest not easy in your lover's arms;
  Let him beware to stand where I have stood.

I shall not fail to burst my ebon case,
  And thrust aside the clods with fingers red:
Your blood shall turn to ice to see my face
  Look from the shadows on your midnight bed.

To face the dead, *he*, too, shall wake in vain,
  My fingers at his throat, your scream his knell;
He will not see me tear you from your bed,
  And drag you by your golden hair to Hell.

Robert E. Howard

UP, JOHN KANE!

Up, John Kane, the grey night's falling;
The sun's sunk in blood and the fog comes crawling;
From hill-side to hill-side the grey wolves are calling:
   Will ye come, will ye come, John Kane?

What of the oath that you swore by the river
Where the black shadows lurk and the sun comes never,
And a Shape in the shadows wags its grisly head forever?

You swore by the blood-crust that stained your dagger,
By the haunted woods where hoofed feet swagger,
And under grisly burdens misshapen creatures stagger.

Up, John Kane, and cease your quaking!
You have made the pact which has no breaking,
And your brothers are eager their thirst to be slaking.

Up, John Kane! Why cringe there and cower?
The pact was sealed with the dark blood-flower;
Glut now your fill in the werewolf's hour!

Fear not the night nor the shadows that play there;
Soundless and sure shall your bare feet stray there;
Strong shall your teeth be, to rend and to slay there.

Up, John Kane, the thick night's falling;
Up from the valleys the white fog's crawling;
Your four-footed brothers from the hills are calling:
   Will ye come, will ye come, John Kane?

XXIV

The Grim Land:
Tales of Texas and the West

That Bob Howard was gravitating more and more toward narratives of and a focus upon his native state and region has been suggested by more than one Howard scholars, including Rusty Burke and James Reasoner. The great significance of his native territory on his writing has been noted quite eloquently and recently by biographer Mark Finn in his important contribution, the biography *Blood and Thunder*. Certainly, Texas and the Southwest find their way into various writings, ranging from the strictly historical essay, through the blend of Western and Horror, to include the modern humor-laden Tall Tales of Howard's wonderful answer to the Pecos Bill and John Henry and Paul Bunyan genre—Breckenridge Elkins.

Howard can be seen as one of the important laureates of Texas and the West. Certainly in poems such as "San Jacinto [version 2]" (a poem clearly derived from Tennyson's "The Charge of the Light Brigade"), we see the selfsame homage to courage and patriotic zeal that the British laureate displays.

But his poetry about "The Grim Land" as one of the several slim early poetry collections was entitled, is far broader than mere patriotic zeal or Texas bravado. It is the stuff of a poet paying homage to his land of nurture and—to some degree— his nature.

Awareness of both the Mexican and Indian contributions to the region's history are also evidenced by these poems.

The following selections shows a deep love of and life-long interest in his native soil.

Robert E. Howard

THE ALAMO

For days they ringed us with their flame
For days their swarming soldiers came
    The battle wrack was gory.
We perished in the smoke and flame,
To give the world their traitor shame
    And our undying glory.

THE BALLAD OF BUCKSHOT ROBERTS

*(Killed on the Tularosa River, New Mexico, 1878,
in the Bloody Lincoln County War)*

Buckshot Roberts was a Texas man;
(Blue smoke drifting from the pinyons on the hill.)
Exiled from the plains where his rugged life began
(Buzzards circling low over old Blazer Mill).
On the floor of 'dobe, dying he lay,
Holding thirteen men at bay.
Thirteen men of the desert's best,
True-born sons of the stark Southwest.
Men from granite and iron hewed—
Riding the trail of the Lincoln feud.

Fighters of iron nerve and will—
But they saw John Middleton lying still
In the thick dust clotted dark and brown,
Where Roberts' bullet cut him down;
So they crouched in cover, on belly or knee,
Warily firing from bush and tree.

Even Billy the Kid held hard his hate,
Waiting his chance as a wolf might wait,
His cold gaze fixed on the brooding Mill
Where the black muzzle gleamed on the window sill.

There on the floor Bill Roberts lay,
His life in a red stream ebbing away:
Weather beaten and snarled and scarred,
Grown old in a land where life was hard,
Soldier, ranger and pioneer,
Rawhide son of the Last Frontier.

Indian forays and border wars
Had left their mark in his many scars.

He had coursed with Death—and the pace was fast:
But he knew he had reached the end at last.
Shot through and through and nearly done—
Close he huddled his buffalo gun,
Propped the barrel on the window sill—
The firing ceased, and the land was still.

They knew he had taken his mortal wound,
And they waited like silent wolves around,
All but Dick Brewer who led the band:
His fury burned him like a brand;
Reckless he rose in his savage ire,
Stood in the open to aim and fire.

Roberts laughed in a ghastly croak,
His finger crooked, and the old gun spoke.
Blue smoke spat, and the whistling lead
Tore off the top of Brewer's head.

Roberts laughed, and the red tide welled
Up to his lips—the echoes belled
Clear and far—then faint and far,
Like a haunting call from a twilight star.

Robert E. Howard

The gnarled hands slid from the worn old gun;
A lark flashed up in the golden sun;
A mountain breeze went quivering past—
So he came to the long trail's end at last.

Buckshot Roberts was a Texas man
(Nightwinds sighing over Ruidosa-way)—
Heart and blood and marrow of a fighting clan!
(So the Tularosa whispers in the dawning of the day.)

BUT THE HILLS WERE ANCIENT THEN

Now is a summer come out of the sea,
　And the hills that were bare are green.
They shower the petals and the bee
　On the valleys that laze between.

So it was in the dreaming past,
　And life is a shifting maze,
Summer on summer fading fast,
　In a mist of yesterdays.

Out of the East, the tang of smoke,
　The flight of the startled deer,
A ringing axe the silence broke,
　The tread of the pioneer.

Saxon eyes in a weathered face,
　Cabins where trees had been,
Hard on the heels of a fading race,
　But the hills were ancient then.

Up from the South a haze of dust,
　The pack mules' steady pace,
Armor tarnished and red with rust,
　Stern eyes in a sun-bronzed face.

The mesquite mocked the flag of Spain,
　That the wind flung out again,
The grass bent under the pack mule train—
　But the hills were ancient then.

THE FEUD

He did not glance above the trail
  to the laurel where I lay
As he rode down to Lincoln town
  to swear my life away.
He did not look till my rifle cracked
  as the deathly ball I sped;
Then he clutched his beard as the mustang reared
  and fell from the saddle dead.

I cursed and spat at his silent form
  and left it on the trail
And climbed my way up the slopes of clay
  and the stones and sliding shale.
And as I went a strange thought grew,
  a queer and curious one:
I'd killed the man whose brother I slew
  because he killed my son.

High on a rock above the vale
  I sat till the sun went down
And thought of the corpse on the mountain trail
  that leads to Lincoln town.
The stars blinked out and the night wind blew
  and I thought how fine and fair;
Yet over the hills like a crimson fog,
  feud's shadow hovered there.

GHOST DANCERS

Night has come over ridge and hill
  Where the Bad-Lands starkly lie
Like the tortured fane of a god insane
  That mocks the brooding sky.

The last faint rose of the twilight goes
  And magic's abroad tonight;
There's an eery sheen in the lean ravine
  And witch-fire on the height.

For bleak stars blink in the dusky sky
  And glitter on shield and lance;
In bands o'er the sands of the Shadowlands
  The phantoms come to dance.

They glide, they ride, through the dim night tide,
  Warrior and chief and brave,
Whose bones are strown from the Yellowstone
  To the lake of the Little Slave.

They ride where the mesas dimly lift
  And a wind that shrills and thrills
Drones o'er the stones and the gleaming bones
  That litter the shadowed hills.

Strange and vague through the pale starlight
  Glimmers each painted face
As they creep and leap where the shadows sleep
  In the Ghost Dance of their race.

Row upon row bent low they go
  Then whirl with a sudden bound,
With a rhythmic beat of their fleet lean feet,
  To a drum that makes no sound.

And the bleak stars wave their silver brands
  In the night-sky's dusky blue,
And silence reigns o'er the barren lands
  And the ghosts of the dancing Sioux.

Robert E. Howard

THE GRIM LAND

From Sonora to Del Rio is a hundred barren miles
  Where the sotol weave and shimmer in the sun—
Like a horde of rearing serpents swaying down the bare defiles
  When the scarlet, silver webs of dawn are spun.

There are little dobe ranchoes brooding far along the sky,
  On the sullen dreary bosoms of the hills;
Not a wolf to break the quiet, not a desert bird to fly
  Where the silence is so utter that it thrills.

With an eery sense of vastness, with a curious sense of age,
  And the ghosts of eons gone uprear and glide
Like a horde of drifting shadows gleaming
    through the wilted sage—
  They are riding where of old they used to ride.

Muleteer and caballero, with their plunder and their slaves—
Oh, the clink of ghostly stirrups in the morn!
Oh, the soundless flying clatter
    of the feathered, painted braves,
Oh, the echo of the spur and hoof and horn.

Maybe, in the heat of evening, comes a wind from Mexico
  Laden with the heat of seven hells,
And the rattler in the yucca and the buzzard dark and slow
  Hear and understand the grisly tales it tells.

Gaunt and stark and bare and mocking rise the everlasting cliffs
  Like a row of sullen giants hewn of stone,
Till the traveler, mazed with silence,
    thinks to look on hieroglyphs,
  Thinks to see a carven Pharaoh on his throne.

Once these sullen hills were beaches and they saw them flee
  In the misty ages never known of men,
And they wait in brooding silence till the everlasting sea
  Comes foaming forth to claim her own again.

JOHN RINGOLD

There was a land of which he never spoke.
  A girl, perhaps, but no one knew her name,
  And few there were who knew from whence he came
For from his past he never raised the cloak.
No word he spake except to sneer or joke,
  Or, deep in drink, to curse men, life and Fate;
  Often his fierce black eyes, Hell-hot with hate,
Gleamed wolf-like through the shifting powder smoke.

His trail lay through saloon and gambling hall,
  Lone, sombre devil in a barren land.
    Perhaps, when drunk, he dreamed of mansions old,
    Ballrooms and women, proud and fair as gold—
Trail's-end, upon the strangest stage of all,
  The sun, a lone mesquite tree and the sand.

THE KIOWA'S TALE

All day I lay with the sun at my back
  As a serpent lies with a changeless stare,
My fierce eyes fixed on the single track
  That led from the woods to the cabin there.

All day, that long late summer day
  Green leaves rustled above my head
And startled song birds flitting that way
  Glimpsed the glint of my steel and fled.

Slow sank the sun and the woods were still—
  Afar there whispered a steamlet's croon—

Long had a waited to make my kill
  And the branches murmured, "Soon, ah, soon!"
He came at dusk, through the twilight red
  With the loose long stride of his swinging hips
And I drew the shaft to its gleaming head,
  And the scalp-yell hovered upon my lips.

Fair of mark in the fading day—
  My fingers quivered upon the shaft,
My red soul leaped with the lust to slay,
  My breath came swift—when a woman laughed.

From out the cabin she came to him,
  Straight and slight as an eagle's feather.
I saw them kiss in the twilight dim
  I heard them laugh—as they laughed together.

From the notch unheeded slipped the cord,
  Breaking the arrow—it fell in half.
The moon came up like a golden lord;
  As I stole away I heard them laugh.

THE LOST SAN SABA MINE

Under the grim San Saba hills
  It sleeps the years away:
    The gold that Don Miranda found
    When unnamed woods and nameless ground
    First heard the Spanish trumpets sound
  Like doom on Judgment Day.

But waving plumes and flying flame
  On shrieking winds were brought;
    Over the hills war-bonnets streamed,
    The lances flashed and the horses screamed;
    On Lipan arms the bracelets gleamed
  That Spanish hands had wrought.

Cordovan boot and tinkling spur
  The hill-paths knew no more;
    Till Bowie reeled before the flame
    That put the bursting sun to shame,
    When to the hidden cave he came,
  And stood before the door.

A grimmer sun, a redder flame
  In billowing death clouds rolled
    On Bowie and the Alamo.
    And from the north as sandstorms blow
    Burst a feathered and painted foe
  On the guardians of the gold.

Scalps with their braids in crimson dyed
  Trailed from Comanche spears.
    The hills forgot the Lipan tongue,
    But not the songs the ancients sung,
    And out of the hills the conquerors wrung
  Spoils of the vanished years.

White men and red men, breast to breast,
  In the birth throes of a state,
    Blind in the gun smoke, slashed and thrust,
    Screaming mad with the slaughter lust,
    Grappled and died in the bloody dust,
  With a frozen grin of hate.

The moccasin left a bloody track
  From shore to mountain crest;
    From roof and beam the red sparks rained;
    But the plow bit deep and the oxen strained,
    And the red warbonnets dimmed and waned
  Into the lurid West.

Like dim and ghostly caravan
  Of painted shapes astride
    Phantasmal mustangs, pass the years.
    A crest of plumes each rider rears.
    With sinking reins and drooping spears
  The phantom horsemen ride.

Scant are the relics Time has left
  To set men wondering.
    A flint by careless boot heel spurned.
    A skull by straining plow upturned.
    A shattered kiln where once was burned
  The ransom of a king.

And men forget the maddening lure
  Which cast men's lives away;
    Gaunt specters guard the gleaming tills,
    The gold which seven caverns fills,
    And under blue San Saba hills
  It sleeps till Judgment Day.

MODEST BILL

Back in the summer of '69
'Way out west on the frontier line,
There was a guy who was a fightin' fool,
He could hit a blow like the kick of a mule,
He'd been a'fightin' all o' his life,
With fists or a gun or a club or a knife.

His name was Bill Bender, (fit name as you'll see)
And he was a bear-cat, a bear on a spree.
Six foot tall and lean and spare,
Quick as a cougar and strong as a bear,
He packed two guns and a Bowie knife,
An' he was forever seeking strife.

He'd jump in the air and let out a roar,
And wave his guns and stomp on the floor,
Twirl a rope and jump through the loop,
Twist his whiskers and snort and whoop,
"I'm a shootin', hootin', rootin', scootin'
   coot from Arkansaw,
"I'm quick as a cat, smart as a rat,
   and tough as a grizzly's claw!

"Whoopee! Whoopee! Yuh listen to me,
"And see what I got to say,
"I can lick any man in the whole darn land
"Both now or any day!
"I'm a hummin', zummin' terror with a knife
"Back away, guys, er I'll hev yer life!
"Never wuz a guy as quick on the draw
"Ever come out of Arkansaw!"

Ten guys pilled on him one day,
When he was a-chantin' of his lay,

Shore they expected him to run,
But instead of his feet he used his gun.
When that was empty he used his knife
And when that broke he kept up the strife,
For he never did know when he was beat,
So he fought on with his fists and feet.

And when it was over they was all on the floor,
What hadn't gone out by the winder or door,
And Bender with torn and tattered clothes,
Was dancin' and yellin' among his foes.
"I'm a knifin', strifin', lifin', riflin' guy from Arkansaw
"And they ain't no man in the whole darn land
"Can beat me on the draw!

"I'm a whole blamed army by myself alone,
"I'm a straight hurricane and a twistin' cyclone!
"I can lick any guy from the Gulf to Powder River,
"Look a grizzly in the eye and make him shiver!
"If nerve was money I'd own a ranch."

* * * * *

Out in the middle of the Utah plain,
The Mormons surrounded a wagon train.
Fifty Mormons and twenty white,
All they could do was put up a fight,
The Mormon was worse than the blame red-skin,
And it was a cinch they'd scoop them in,
Kill every man and steal every girl.

When out of the desert there came with a whirl,
A long-whiskered guy a whoopin' and braggin',
He jumped his horse right over a wagon.
Gave a yell like a hungry wolf,
"Come on, guys! We'll run 'em to the Gulf!"
Then the rifle flashed and the bullets hummed
And the pistols cracked and the slugs zummed.

And above the crackle and the roar of the shooting,
They could hear the voice of Bender hooting,
"I'm a ramblin', gamblin', shamblin', scramblin'
    guy from Arkansaw,
"The toughest, roughest gay galoot
    that ever broke the law!
"I'm a rarin', tearin' son uh strife,
"I cut my teeth on a Bowie knife!

"I'm tougher than any other man alive,
"I trim my beard with a .45!
"I comb my hair with a circle saw
"And pick my teeth with a grizzly's claw!
"I'm a bald he-eagle from a mountain peak
"Just yuh hark to the snappin' uh my beak!

"I hate all Mormons like I hate a snake,
"I can lick the whole tribe with a picket stake!
"I'm a panther and a bear and a long gray wolf
"And I'll chase these Mormons into the Gulf!"
Then the few Mormons that was left, they run,
And Bill said, "H—l, I never have no fun!"

The Wells-Fargo stage was shooting down the line
Loaded with passengers and gold from the mine,
When down from the hills with yells and hoots,
Came a big war-party of red-skinned Utes.
They circle the stage at a flyin' run,
Slingin' arrows and bullets like fun.

There was a roar inside the stage,
And Bender jumped out in a regular rage,
Both of his gun's a blazin' of course,
He knocked a Ute over and straddled his horse.
Tore into them Utes with his guns a-flashing.
He landed on the Utes like a eagle's swoop,
Yellin' louder than they could whoop.

349

"I'm a rarin', tearin', barin', scarin'
guy from Arkansaw,
"If there's a guy that I can't lick,
that guy I never saw.
"Never saw a tree I couldn't climb,
   never saw a river I couldn't swim.
"Never saw a horse I couldn't ride,
   never saw a trader I couldn't skin.
"I'm bad on all Injuns, worse on a Ute,
"For the whole darn tribe I don't give a hoot.

"I'm as hard and tough as a hick'ry nut's hull,
"I'm a rompin', stompin' buffalo bull!
"My horns are long and sharp and keen,
"My claws are strong and powerful mean!
"I'm the guy that can make a panther shiver,
"And I'll chase these Utes across the Platte River!"

Well, the folks still say that was some battle,
But the Utes broke at last and run like cattle,
And old Bill Bender wiped his knife,
"Never had sich fun in all muh life."

     *   *   *   *   *

Bender was in a saloon one time,
Didn't have a dollar, not even a dime.
The guys they said, "He's never been on the floor,
"Never drunk enough that he couldn't drink more.
"Now, by golly, we'll all stand treat,
"And we'll drink Bill Bender off his feet."

So they bought whiskey and beer and rum,
Bill emptied the glasses fast as they come,
One by one, the guys fell on the floor,
But Bill stood up and shouted for more,
He drank ten glasses of whiskey straight,

Gulped down beer at a wonderful rate,
Of brandy he drank not less than a quart,
Tossed off a gallon of rum at a snort.
The price of licker began to mount,
At last the bartender, he lost count,
The others emptied their glasses
    as fast as he could fill
But, gosh, they couldn't keep up with Bill!

That Bill Bender was still on his shoes,
When the saloon ran out of booze.
And Bill was drunk, no doubt of that,
He couldn't hit the floor with his hat,
"I thank you kind, my friends,"says he.

Robert E. Howard

OLD FARO BILL WAS A MAN OF MIGHT

Old Faro Bill was a man of might
  In the days when the West was young,
He drank a gallon of booze each night—
  The toughest galoot unhung!
Oh, some men shrink at the sight of blood!
  Bill roomed in a cougar's lair
And for tobacco he carried a cud
  Of Mexican prickly pear!
Old Faro came of a wolfish breed,
  When he was a suckling child
He laughed at the marahuana weed
  For he said that it was too mild.
Old Faro he was a buffalo
  When it came to rough-and-tumble,
He laid the toughest battlers low
  With never a miss or fumble.
Some men stammer and halt and pause
  At the sight of lover's moons,
But Faro married a hundred squaws,
  And a couple of octaroons.

SAN JACINTO [VERSION 1]

Flowers bloom on San Jacinto,
  Red and white and blue.
Long ago o'er San Jacinto
  Wheeling vultures flew.
Long ago on San Jacinto
  Soared the battle-smoke;
Long ago on San Jacinto
  Wild ranks smote and broke.
Crimson clouds o'er San Jacinto,
  Scarlet was the haze—
Peaceful o'er calm San Jacinto
  Glide the drowsy days.

SAN JACINTO [VERSION 2]

Red field of glory
Ye knew the wild story;
Blazing and gory
  Were ye on that day!
Silence before them,
(Warriors; winds bore them!)
Red silence o'er them
  Followed the fray!

Horror was dawning!
Furies were spawning!
Hell's maw was yawning,
  Fate rode astride!
Skies rent asunder!
Plains a-reel under
Feet beating thunder!
  Death raced beside!

Doom-trumps were pealing!
Armies were reeeling!
Satan was dealing
  The cards in that game!
War-clouds unfurling!
Hell-fires were swirling,
Valkyries whirling
  Fanned them to flame!

Redly arrayed there
Glittered the blade there!
Many a shade there
  Fled to the deeps!
Wild was the glory
Down the years hoary
Still the red story
  Surges and leaps!

THE SAND-HILL'S CREST

Here where the post-oaks crown the ridge,
　　and the dreary sand-drifts lie,
I'll sit in the tangle of chaparral
　　till my enemy passes by—
Till the shotgun speaks beneath my hand
　　to my enemy passing by

(My grandfather came from Tennessee,
And a fine blue broadcloth coat wore he—
In a ragged, torn shirt I wait
For my enemy passing by.)

The drouth burned up the wheat I sowed,
　　my gaunt scrub-cattle died.
Because the winter pasture failed,
　　and the last branch-water dried.
The young corn withered where it stood
　　in the field on the bare hill-side

I had one horse to work my land—
　　one horse, and he was lame.
I hid my still in the shinnery
　　where no one ever came
I hid it deep in the thickets;
　　the corn was from my own bin,
The laws would never have found it,
　　but my neighbor turned me in

For an old spite I'd clean forgot,
　　my neighbor turned me in.

(When my grandfather was a lad,
A hundred slaves his father had;
He clothed them better than I am clad

They were sleek and fat and prime.
I've been hungry many a time
They fed full, child, man and wife.
I've been hungry most of my life.)

I found a man to go my bond—
 he knows that I won't run;
I've never been forty miles from home,
 the drouth starved all my steers
The sinking sun is shining
 on the barrel of my gun
They'd try me in the county court
 and give me seven years.

Seven years behind the bars
 because they found my still,
He showed it to the snooping laws,
 the man I'm going to kill
Then they'll give me Life or the Chair,
 according to the judge's will,
Death's not so damned hard to a man
 that's lived all his life on a post-oak hill

(When my grandfather first came West
Was never a fence on the prairie's breast.
There was a land to choose, and he chose the best,
But it slipped through his fingers like the rest,
Driving his sons to the sand-hills' crest)

The post-oaks stand up dull and brown
 against the tawny sky,
I hate them like I hate the man
 who'll soon be passing by;
At fifty feet I can not miss,
 I'm going to watch him die
Die like the dirty dog he is,
 where the drifted sand-beds lie.

SONORA TO DEL RIO

[variant of "The Grim Land"]

Sonora to Del Rio is a hundred barren miles
   Where the sotol weave and shimmer in the sun—
Like a host of swaying serpents
  straying down the bare defiles
   When the silver, scarlet webs of dawn are spun.

There are little 'dobe ranchoes,
  brooding far along the sky
   On the sullen, dreary bosoms of the hills.
Not a wolf to break the quiet, not a single bird to fly;
   Where the silence is so utter that it thrills.

Maybe, in the heat of evening, comes a wind from Mexico
   Laden with the heat of seven Hells,
And the rattler in the yucca and the buzzard dark and slow
   Hear and understand the grisly tales it tells.

Gaunt and stark and bare and mocking
  rise the everlasting cliffs
Like a row of sullen giants carved of stone,
Till the traveler, mazed with silence,
  thinks to look at hieroglyphs,
Thinks to see a carven pharaoh on his throne.

And the road goes on forever, o'er the barren hills forever,
   And there's little to hint of flowing wine—
But beyond the hills and sotol there's a mellow curving river
   And a land of sun and mellow wine.

XXV
Longer Narratives:
Howard and Epic Song

While Bob Howard wrote only a handful of longer narratives, the ones he created are impressive in sustained pace, in technical mastery, and in vivid imagery. Of these, I have included "The Ballad of King Geraint" the longest and the one closest to the heroic-epic tradition of the poets of Howard's immediately previous generations: G. K. Chesterton [*The Ballad of the White Horse*] and William Morris [*Sigurd the Volsung and the Fall of the Niblungs*] and Alfred, Lord Tennyson [*The Idylls of the King*]. As I have noted elsewhere, I also think this poem likely owes some debt—especially in its formal arrangement and section divisions—to C.K. Scott-Moncrieff's 1919 translation of the French national epic, *The Song of Roland* (which, perhaps not incidentally, considering Howard's admiration of GKC, includes an "Introduction" by Chesterton). In any event, as Chesterton points out in his introductory, *The Roland* is a poem set on "that high note of the forlorn hope, of a host at bay and a battle against odds without end...." And that is certainly the "high note" in Howard's "Geraint."

As Chesterton also maintains in that fine introduction to the *Roland*: "a man does not sing unless he has something to sing about." And Robert E. Howard both discovered and invented things about which to sing.

The other long narrative chosen for inclusion is "Eric of Norway," a poem both showing Howard's keen interest in Vikings and "the Northern Thing" as Tolkien and Lewis called it. Interestingly, it is set in a meter that is actually greatly indebted to Chesterton's *The Ballad of the White Horse*—which, of course, is a poem not only about Alfred the Great of England, but also the Viking invaders under Guthrum. With lots of rich imagery and strong alliteration—in keeping with Teutonic poetics—"Eric" is also a fine narrative feat.

THE BALLAD OF KING GERAINT

This is the tale of a nameless fight,
In a land forgot to dream and sight,
And a people lost in the gloom and night.

King Geraint ruled the western land
From the Roman Wall to Channel's sand;
The Saxons held the eastern coast
By high-beaked galley and spear-tipped host.
They reached their hands from the eastern shore
And flooded the land with fire and gore.

King Geraint marched on the Watling Road,
Along the Ouse his banners showed.
Few his warriors but fierce his lords,
Dipped and reddened their worn swords.
He had scoured the land a-near and far,
He had sold his crown for the thews of war.
Knight and warrior and man-at-arms,
Yeoman drawn from the ravished farms,
Each was armed to suit his need,
Each one rode on a goodly steed.
The hoof-beat thunder sounded far—
So Geraint rode to his last red war.

Before them all King Geraint rode,
White was the great steed he bestrode,
A gift from the Ulster king, Leoghaire;
Gold in the sun was Geraint's hair.
His grey eyes flashed 'neath the helmet's crest
Like an eagle's that stoops from his craggy nest.
Tall and graceful and fair of face,
The warrior king of a fighting race.
Conal rode at King Geraint's right,
Closest friend feast or fight;
Mighty warrior and gallant knight.

Close there rode on the king's left side,
Donal, the chieftain of Strathclyde.
Dark was he, and hard of hand
As well befitted that desperate band
That held the hills of the Cumberland
Three hundred years from the Saxon horde.
There followed close with his great black sword
Cormac of Cornwall called the Hawk,
A savage branch on an ancient stalk.
More than half a pagan, he,
Ruling alone by the western sea;
Tall and lean with a dark hawk's face.
By his side rode, pace for pace,
Angus, a chief of the northern Scot,
With King Geraint he had cast his lot.
A giant he, and his fearful blows
Wrought destruction upon his foes.

Conmac rode in his armor bright,
Never was there more noble knight.
Like the British king, he too was fair,
With a golden beard and golden hair,
Blue were his eyes and pure his heart;
He ever took the weaker's part.
Learned was he and versed in art,
Read in all of the monkish books,
And yet though mild in air and looks
Never was knight more bold than he,
Flower of British chivalry.

With his banners floating like purple sails
Rode old Cadallon, the king of Wales.
White was his beard and his flowing hair,
But grey eyes gleamed like an eagle's stare.
Lord of the savage mountaineers,
Born and bred in the crash of spears.
A fierce and crafty old wolf was he;

Now he led his men from the western sea
With the single hope: to redden his shield
Ere he left his corpse on the battlefield.

There was one with a fearsome face,
A fighting man of a strange, lost race.
He was a Pict, Dulborn by name;
Under black brows, like cold black flame
His fierce eyes blazed at all the world;
His lips in a snarl were ever curled.
Short of stature but thick of limb,
Great was the shoulder breadth of him,
Hairy and apish and wild and grim.
Never a helmet would he wear
But the tangled shock of his own black hair.
A stunted giant, most strange to see—
A shape from the grisly past was he.
His people ruled, in the dark old days,
The western isles, and their altar blaze
Lighted the land, and they alone
Reigned in the grim old Age of Stone.
Now a scant remnant, hunted forth,
Lived like wolves in the misty north.
The Pict was banished, a lone exile;
God only knows what plot or guile,
What grisly crime or what fell deed
Barred Dulborn from his own dark breed.
When they exile, who are strange and fell,
Surely the deed was born in Hell!
But Dulborn rode to Geraint's court,
And followed him ever, life and morte.
His lips were locked and the heart inside,
And with him his secret lived and died.

Uther rode there, a broken king
Reft of his crown and everything
That makes life fair in the eyes of men.

His kingdom lay on the Humber when
Anlaf, king of the Angles, came
Riving the land with steel and flame.
In one wild night he was overthrown,
Lost his castle, his queen, his throne.
He saw his stricken vassals reel,
His queen's breast bared to the reddened steel,
His son crushed under the heathen heel,
His people enslaved, his warriors dead,
A crownless, landless king he fled.
Now he gazed at the vultures in the skies
And hollows of madness were under his eyes.
Few were the words that he had spent
Since he dropped at the gate of King Geraint,
Bloody and tattered and almost dead,
In the dawn that broke so deathly red.
Few were his words, but many his deeds,
From the Channel's shore to the banks of Tweed's,
And the ravens followed him over the meads.

There followed on King Geraint's trail
Two strong chiefs of the western Gael.
Friends abroad, though foes at home,
Seeking adventures beyond the foam,
They had come before and they came again
To strike a blow for their Brython kin.

One was Nial of whom men sing
That he was brother to Ulster's king.
Tall he was, and his shoulders broad;
In his hand his ivory-hilted sword
Flashed and leaped like a living flame,
Thus sing the bards who chant his fame.
His ringlets were curled and golden red,
Like a mist of flame about his head.
Red was his steed and his armor red,
A crimson flame from heel to head.

His comrade was Turlogh of Connacht;
In days of old the twain had fought
From dawn to dark till their shields were rent,
Swords shattered and strength and fury spent.
Now like old friends, they, side by side,
Ride with Geraint to the battle tide.
Not as tall as the Ulsterman
Was Turlogh, but broader in shoulder span.

If Nial was red, Turlogh was black
Like a phantom of Death in the battle wrack.
Eyes of a hot volcanic blue
Under black brows all Erin knew,
Burned with a passion that was not quenched
Till the shield was rent and the sword red-drenched.
Black was his armor, steed and shield;
So he rode to the battlefield.
With these ten knights and a thousand men
Geraint thundered through forest and fen.

Ceawlin, king of the Saxon hordes,
Marshalled his axes and his swords.
Gathered his ealdormen and thanes
From the smoking towns and the ravished plains.
Twelve thousand warriors owned his command
And he marshalled them on either hand.
Four thousand mounted on steeds he brought,
Eight thousand more on foot that fought.
His foremost lords were four in number:
Prince Osric who ruled from Ouse to Humber,
He was a lord of the Juttish strain;
Oswald, lord of the Sussex plain;
The Wessex ealdorman, Athelstane,
And Edric of Orkney Isles, a Dane.

King Ceawlin marshalled a thousand horse
To bar King Geraint's battle course.

He put Prince Osric in command,
With five strong chiefs at either hand:
Halfgar, Frisian sea-king he,
A name of fear in the narrow sea;
He knew not mercy, pity or ruth.
The thane Otho of the Black Boar's Tooth.
Athelred, cousin to the king,
And Rognor of the golden ring.
Oswick who ravaged London town
And slew three kings on The White Horse down.
The giant brothers, berserks they,
Tostig the Ogre and Athelney.
Fearsome were they, and huge and stark,
And unlike their race, most strangely dark.
Oswy the Jut, and the Norseman Rane,
And last and greatest, the viking Swane.
Half Saxon he, half northern Dane.
His torch had lighted a hundred shores,
Rome and Egypt had heard his oars.
Proud Massilia at his thrust
Had crumpled into the bloody dust.
Broad was he, with a cruel face,
Fiercest man of a savage race.

A thousand horse Ceawlin gave
To Oswald who ruled by the Sussex wave.
Ten chiefs likewise rode at his side:
Godric, fierce in his heathen pride.
Anlaf the Angle, Wutholwine,
Wulfhere, chieftain of Horsa's line,
Aella who ruled from Tweed to Tyne.
Gulla, and Gurth and Athelfrith,
Hakon the jarl, and Jan the Lith.
To all the foot he gave command
To Athelstane of the Iron Hand.
Ealdorman of Wessex, he,
Huge and fierce in his paganry.

Edric the Red, the Orkney Dane,
Shared the command with Athelstane.
Now twice a thousand horse remain.

Over them Ceawlin's Raven flew,
His spear arose and his trumpets blew.
Ceawlin rode in his heathen pride,
With mighty warriors on either side.
His brother Ulf on his right hand,
On his left, Leofwine of Helgoland.
Godwine of Mercia, Sweyn of Kent,
Eadelberht from the banks of Trent.
Eadwig, called by men The White,
Ealdred, jarl from the Isle of Wight.
Eadmund of York with his helmet bright,
Eadward of Northumbria whose sight
Might pierce the heavens or span a gulf;
Tostig the Raven and Rane the Wolf.
The bright steel flashed in the rising sun;
He gave his orders one by one.

King Geraint passed Corinium's walls.
The country shook to the trumpets' calls.
When sudden there charged across his course
Osric the prince, with a thousand horse.
They smote the spurs, they slacked the rein—
They crashed together on the plain.
King Geraint smote Prince Osric's shield,
At the shock both mighty chargers reeled.
But the Saxon spear to splinters flew,
And the king's lance rent the shield in two,
Shivered the hauberk's scales apart,
Rent the bosom and split the heart,
Stood a yard from the Saxon's back—
Prince Osric fell in his horse's track.

Geraint hath taken another spear,
Spurring his steed in mad career.
The heathen reel to his mighty thrust,
And white steed tramples them in the dust.
Conal at Halfgar drove amain,
Hurled him dead on the bloody plain;
But the Frisian spear his corselet tore,
Into his breast he felt it gore,
And out of the wound the life blood pour.
But he spoke no word of his deathly pain,
Following close by Geraint's rein,
And the heathen fell as he smote amain.
Otho of the Boar's Tooth ran
Full career at the Cornishman.
But the spear he wielded could not avail
'Gainst Cormac's coat of triple mail,
Or the great black sword, of a hundred fights
Which grisly Druids, in the deeps of nights
Had spelled with dark, unholy rites.
And it cleft the helmet and skull beneath,
Rending apart the monstrous teeth.
Donal, the chieftain of Strath-Clyde,
At Athelred bore through the battle tide.
The Saxon shattered his shield in twain,
But his own lance pierced the Saxon's brain—
Ceawlin's cousin lay on the plain.

Angus rushed like a bear at bay
At the giant berserk, Athelnay.
The horses reel, and the riders rock,
Both lances shiver at the shock!
They reel, they stagger, they charge, they close!
Front to front, with gigantic blows.
The Scotsman's shield is rent in twain,
He flings the fragments upon the plain;
His hauberk is pierced, his helmet rent—
Now the Saxon back in his saddle is bent!

The trumpets bray and the trumpets peal!
The Scot's sword shivers in sparks of steel!
The Saxon roared and spurred his horse,
But Angus met him in full mid-course,
With a mace he snatched from a dying hand—
He smote like a wave on a windy strand,
Shattered and shivered the whistling brand,
Battered the shield to a broken wreck,
Crushed the helmet down on the neck,
Shattered the skull like an empty shell,
Headlong the horse and rider fell!

Conmac hurled down Rognor slain,
Cadallon's lance rent Oswick's brain.
Uther at Oswy rode amain.
The Juttish spear gashed Uther's thigh
But he gave no heed and his flame-lit eye
Altered not in any part
As he broke his lance in the heathen's heart.
Rane's lance broke short on Nial's crest
And Nial pierced the Norseman's breast.
Tostig the Ogre slacked his rein
At the Pict Dulborn, he rode amain.
The Pict scorned sword or lance to bear,
As he scorned a helmet save his own hair.
A great black axe was all he bore;
But Tostig's lance in twain he shore,
And the next blow down through the shoulder tore
Rent the hauberk and cleft the bone,
The giant fell from his steed like stone;
Dulborn laughed at his dying groan.

Through the battle, Swane the viking sought
For the face of Turlogh of Connacht.
An ancient feud lay red between,
A long gone day and a traitor queen,
And a crashing of galleys black and lean.

Rending helmets and hauberk scales,
The viking crashed through the ranks of Wales.
His warriors died as they crowded in
'Neath the stabbing spears of Cadallon's men;
But Swane bore on and his sword dealt doom
Till a heap of corpses gave him room.
And in a voice that roared over all that fought,
He shouted for Turlogh of Connacht.
Like a wave that breaks on the sloping shale
Was the sudden charge of the fiery Gael.
He was stained with the blood of the viking's band,
His spear had shivered in his hand,
Now he held aloft his crimson brand.
His shield the viking's broadsword turned,
Along his arm the keen edge burned.
The red drops followed the slicing steel,
Turlogh cursed in the trumpet peal,
Rose in his stirrups, spurred and smote,
Breaking the shout in the viking's throat.
Hauberk and ribs gave at the blow
And Swane fell dead from his saddlebow.

Osric and all his lords lie slain,
Their bodies litter the broken plain.
Nor have the British men-at-arms
Proven weak in the loud alarms.
Geraint and his lords have rent the foes
And their warriors have followed swift and close,
Clearing the way with mighty blows.
A hundred Britons and Welsh lie dead,
But the shattered Saxons have turned and fled,
Those who are left alive to flee;
Most of them sleep with Eternity.

King Geraint spurred his great white steed,
His army followed him over the mead,
Till Oswald of Sussex barred his way—

Now trumpets roar and the chargers neigh
And the two hosts crash in the deadly fray.
The king was a thunderbolt of stone;
Steeds and riders were overthrown;
Ceorl and eorl went down before,
Seven thanes he overbore.
Conal was ever at his side,
Staining his sword in the crimson tide.
Chief Oswald was a man of war,
Fame of his deeds was blown afar.
Now he smote on the British line,
Cleft a Briton from chin to chine,
Severed another through the spine.
From another knight he dashed the brain,
Charged from the side at the king amain.
Conal's sight was growing dim,
He saw the fight in a red haze swim.
His sword arm hung like an arm of lead,
He scarce could lift his armored head,
His life was ebbing in spurts of red.
But even as waning sight was spent
He saw the peril of Geraint.
He reined about his weary horse
And barred the furious Saxon's course.
And the blow for the back of the king was stayed
By Conal's notched unsteady blade.
Rider and steed in one overthrow
Sank beneath that fearful blow.
King Geraint wheeled and he saw the end
Of his trusted comrade and boyhood friend.
His heart went cold and his lips went pale;
He smote the Saxon like a gale,
Rent his shield and his coat of mail.
Oswald lay by Conal's side
And over them washed the battle tide.

Godric, gleaming in silver scales,
Rode full tilt at the ranks of Wales.
At old Cadallon he aimed his spear,
Shouting an insult and a jeer.
The old king grinned as a wolf might grin
As the lances clashed with a ringing din.
The Saxon's broke on the Welshman's shield
And Godric dropped on the bloody field,
The shield fell from his nerveless hand
And his brains oozed out to clot the sand.
Hakon the jarl charged in to ride
At Donal, chieftain of Strath-Clyde.
Each at the other aimed his spear,
Crashed together in full career.
Fair and full and sudden the blow,
Each dropped dead from his saddlebow.

Uther crashed on the Saxon ranks,
Breaking the spears in lofty banks.
Sudden he saw, while the lances flew,
A form remembered, a face he knew.
A terrible scream tore from his throat,
That cut like a knife through the trumpet's note.
Anlaf turned at that deathly shriek,
A pallor sucked at his bearded cheek.
And a thought in his brain reeled to and fro—
That night on the Humber, long ago.
The face of his foe, at last, at last!
Uther came like a blinding blast.
Naught he made of the upflung guard,
Naught of the shield that sought to ward.
The first blow shattered the sword and shield,
The second hurled him to the field.
Uther leaped from his saddle red,
Hewed from his shoulders the Angle's head.
Into his saddle he leaped again,
Raged like a madman over the plain.

Took deep wounds that he did not feel,
His laughter howled through the trumpet's peal.
Ever he brandished the grinning head
While on his helmet drops of red
Fell like a sluggish fall of rain,
And he screamed with a terrible mirth insane.

Cormac crashed through the Saxon line,
Full on the chieftain Wutholwine.
And the Saxon rent his shield in twain,
As the Cornish sword crashed through his brain.
The Hawk was wild with the tang of war,
His way the Saxons could not bar
For the black sword hewed through plate and crest,
Cleaving the skull and the armored breast.
Lives are snuffed like candle flame
Beneath the sword no man may tame.
Conmac, knight sans stain or blame,
Rode where he saw the white shield shine
Of Wulfhere, chieftain of Horsa's line.
They spur, they meet with a thunder shake;
The horses rear and the lances break.
Now front to front they shower blows
While the squadrons reel and the tumult grows.
From the clashing steel the blue sparks fly—
And the fury dies in Wulfhere's eye;
Under his corselet the keen blade drinks,
The charger rears and the rider sinks.

Nial smote on the pagan horse
Quenching his ivory-hilted sword
In the first and best of the Saxon blood,
The red horse raged through the clashing flood.
Ceorl and eorl and chief went down
With rended breast or cloven crown.
Aella the chieftain of the Tyne,
He clove through the shoulder and the spine.

He hacked his way to Geraint's side
Where the heathen brake like a broken tide.
Nor faltered Turlogh of Connacht;
Red the destruction that he wrought.
His red sword shore through breast and brain,
His corpses littered the trampled plain
And the red blood fell in a grisly rain.
Gulla he slew, the Juttish thane.

Dulborn smote on the shield of Gurth,
Horse and rider crashed to the earth.
Gurth arose from that deadly fall
Where dead men lie and horses sprawl.
Leaped like a tiger on his foe,
Dented his shield with a savage blow,
Gashed the shoulder that lay below.
Dulborn laughed like the twang of a bow.
Rose in his stirrups, downward smote,
Cleaving the Saxon to the throat.

Angus the giant Northern chief
Ranged like a sickle through the sheaf.
His mace was clotted and dripping red
And still it crashed through plate and head,
Crumpling iron and steel and bone.
Horses and riders were overthrown.
In the very heart of the Saxon band
Two chiefs assailed him on either hand.
Athelfrith the Kentishman
With levelled spear upon him ran.
On the other side the chieftain Jan
Heaved his axe above his head
And a terrible blow at Angus sped.
At once they smote him, breast and head.
And the horses reeled to the triple shock
But Angus sat like a man of rock.
The spear broke short on his steel-clad breast,

The red axe shattered on his crest.
And the great mace crashed through the battle wrack
An iron thunderbolt, grim and black,
A double blow, forehand and back.
The first blow shattered Athelfrith,
And the second killed chief Jan the Lith.
And men cried out to see that deed
But the maddened Angus gave no heed.
He spurred his horse at the ringing spears
And his war-cry burst the Saxons' ears.
He smote to the left and to the right;
He was gripped with a fearful need to smite.
Helmets burst and the skulls gave way
Till the Saxons broke from the bloody fray.
And still the thundering Scot pursued
Till the plain with fallen men was strewed.
And still he had followed all that fled,
Till through the mists of dark and red
King Geraint's voice pierced his brain;
Reluctant he joined his fellows again.

Of all that rode across the plain
Six hundred men alone remain;
Donal and Conal both lie slain.
Uther's armor is hacked to a shred;
Crest to heel he is grim and red.
But he holds aloft dark Anlaf's head.
Seven deep wounds now sap his life
But he heeds them not as he seeks the strife.
And he laughs a laugh so wild and grim,
His comrades glance askance at him.
Dulborn, Cormac and Angus bleed
But of their wounds they take no heed.
Now front them on the open plain,
The heavy-armed ceorls of Athelstane
With his comrade Edric the Red, the Dane.

They have locked their shields in a solid wall
Their spears a-bristle above them all.

Grimmest arm of the Saxon war,
Geraint sees his setting star.
He bunches close his thinning ranks,
An iron bolt for the iron banks.
Shoulder to shoulder, flying fast
The Britons charge in a blinding blast.
And the spears give way and the shield-walls reel
To the blast of that avalanche of steel.
Geraint and Angus, knee to knee,
Crash like a black tide from the sea.
The black mace shatters the shields apart,
Breaking the spears—into the heart
Of the stabbing host the Scotsman tore
Steeping his iron mace in gore.
Now all the Britons thunder in
And the skies are rent by the battle din.
The howling Saxons ring them close,
They rock and sway in a waste of foes,
But cleave their way with terrible blows.
Uther rushed with a laugh and scream
Like a man who rides in a nightmare dream.
He slew a thane who had his stand
Between the chiefs of the Saxon band.
And Edric smote with a reddened brand
And Athelstane on the other hand.
Horse and rider they over-bore;
Uther fell and he rose no more.
Yet his hand was locked in the ghastly red
Hair of Anlaf's severed head,
In a grip that no man born could break,
And the hardiest warrior well might quake
At the smile which his bloody lips still froze;
So Uther lay in a ring of foes.

Geraint had seen King Uther slain;
Headlong he rushed on Athelstane,
Shattered the helmet on his head,
Dashed him earthward, broken and dead.
Then he turned on Edric; but at his side
Nial had ripped through the battle tide.
And the red horse hurled chief Edric down,
And the Gaelic sword edge cleft his crown.
The British knights are torn apart,
But still they cleave through the shield-wall's heart.
Singly or in struggling groups
The Saxons league the Celtic troops.
Many a rider is overthrown;
Cormac and Angus fight alone.
Conmac and Turlogh, knee to knee,
Blast their way through the iron sea.
Life blood dying his hauberk scales
Cadallon is ringed by the swords of Wales.

Still Geraint leads with his bloody brand,
With Dulborn and Nial on either hand,
Followed close by his dwindling band.
Cormac's black sword leaped and drank
Till his dying charger reeled and sank,
Pinning his rider to the ground,
And a hedge of spears bore in around.
Bleeding from many a grisly wound,
Cormac struggled and tore him clear,
Rose through the rain of sword and spear.
He braced his feet and he smote once more
Through iron and flesh the black sword tore.
Corpses rattled against his feet;
He scarcely felt the blades that beat
Hard on his helmet. Once again
The black sword crashed and men were slain.
Battle and sky were growing black;
Around him surged the battle wrack.

The warriors shouted and crowded back.
But the thick press held them hard and stayed
Within the sweep of the Cornish blade.
Cormac with both hands gripped his sword;
Little he felt the spears that gored.
The last red ounce of his life went out
In the swing that clove through the screaming rout.
He felt the keen edge cleave through flesh,
Iron and bone and brazen mesh.
He heard the clash of falling men,
They fell at his feet like trees and then
As the sword flashed round in that deathly arc
The world wavered and all went dark.
With a ghastly laugh the blood burst red
From his pallid lips and the chief fell dead.

The horse of Angus was overthrown,
He rose in a wave of foes alone.
He hurled his shield among the brand,
Gripped his mace in his mighty hands.
The Saxons rushed like a brainless wave,
Hewing and stabbing with spear and glaive.
He loomed above them like a tower,
A man of iron in that red hour.
His great voice roared through curse and yell;
The great black mallet rose and fell.
Shield nor helmet its blows withstood,
Brass or iron or steel-braced wood.
He struck as a bolt of thunder strikes.
They thrust with spears and heavy pikes;
They hewed at corselet and crested crown,
They gripped his legs to wrestle him down.
But the spears were splintered, the swords were bent,
And they staggered back when their strength was spent.
And Angus as he broke their brands,
Shook off the grasp of their nerveless hands.

He crushed their breasts and smashed their brains,
Ceorl and eorls and jarls and thanes
Fell like leaves on that fatal spot
To the berserk wrath of the giant Scot.
But still by hundreds they crowded in,
From all sides smote with a fearful din.
From every joint of his armor ran
The blood of the terrible Northern man.
His shattered helmet fell in twain,
The blood was starting from every vein.
His armor battered, torn and rent,
But he dealt his blows without stay or stint.

A terrible harvest Angus mowed;
High heaped the corpses he bestrode.
They lay about in a ghastly ring,
Leaving a space for his mace to swing.
He stood alone in an open space
Holding on high the great black mace.
The warriors pressed back from his blows;
So Angus glared at his ringing foes.
Silent they faltered, pressing back;
Under his thick brows, heavy and black,
The terrible eyes of the chieftain blazed,
The Saxons blanched and shrank as they gazed.
But their eorls lashed them with words of fire
And they charged once more with a desperate ire.
A whirlpool of iron, a storm of steel,
Through which the shrieks of the dying peal.
A whirl of swords and over all
The terrible mace's rise and fall!
And the Saxons broke—they turned and fled
And Angus stood on a heap of dead.
He swayed above those torn mounds,
With the ebb of a score of mortal wounds.
He sought to sound his battle-cry
As he saw his foes give way and fly;

He swung his iron mace on high,
And sank on a heap of dead, to die.

The Britons have cleft through the Saxon ranks;
Few there are left of that bold phalanx.
Geraint is wounded in the knee,
Not a knight from a gash is free.
Thrice was Dulborn's charger slain
But riderless horses race the plain.
Each time the black axe hewed a course
And gained the wielder another horse.
The ranks of the men-at-arms are reft;
Scarce two hundred now are left.
But behind them the shattered Saxon horde
Reels like a dragon broken and gored.
Their leaders and half their comrades slain
They break and eddy and swirl in vain,
And stream in flight across the plain.
And now to the bray of trumpet and drum
Full two thousand riders come.
Ceawlin rides in his armor bright
With mighty men at his left and right.
His brother Ulf, his banner rears,
The Raven banner above the spears.
Leofwine, Godwine, Sweyn of Kent,
Princes from Selsey to the Trent.
Warriors from Lindisfarne and York,
Jutes and Angles, fierce and stark,
Rode in the Saxon phalanx dark.

King Geraint turned to his faithful friends:
"Here the war and my kingdom ends.
"Many have died in this red fray,
"More shall die ere the death of day.
"Turn, I beg you, your steeds toward home;
"Seek your safety beyond the foam.

"Naught is left for a crownless king
"But a kingly death where the broadswords sing.
"But there is no need for you all to die;
"Turn, I beg you, to safety fly."
Cadallon's hauberk was seeping red;
But he laughed like a wolf as he shook his head:
"I turn my back when my foes are dead.
"I am a king in my own land
"Though my only crown is a bloody brand.
"I only wish to charge and close
"And gain to the thickest of my foes."
From his battered Welsh a fierce yell rose.
Said Conmac: "With my last-drawn breath
"I follow my king to life or death."
Nial's eyes blazed with a light
Mystic, more than mortal sight.
"Never in all the world," said he,
"Is one who touches in chivalry,
"Knighthood, honor without taint,
"And kingly courage, thou, Geraint!
"Come weal or evil, time or tide,
"Shoulder to shoulder with you I ride,
"And in death I will still be at your side."
Few were Turlogh's words and brief
As well befitted a Gaelic chief:
"While Geraint lives I follow the king."
Dulborn made his black axe sing
In a whistling arc through the parting air.
He shook back his tangled mane of hair.
Fiercely laughed in the battle joy
And the primal lust to rend and destroy.
"We waste good time in words," he said,
"Let us ride in and smite them dead."
So shoulder to shoulder the warriors rein
For the last red charge on that red plain.
Oh, who the minstrel that might sing
The last great fight of the British king!

"Surely," said Ulf, "these men are mad!"
Ceawlin's eyes were fierce and sad.
He laughed with wrath and little mirth.
"Mayhap—but madmen rule the earth.
"Osric and Oswald rode in vain,
"They and all their chiefs lie slain.
"And the Britons have broken Athelstane.
"Bitter the day for me, and black.
"When Geraint rides he turns not back."
Loud laughed the Viking Leofwine:
"See how they rush upon our line!
"Deep will I quench this sword of mine!
"Turn ye, Saxons, and leave their band
"To a single sword from Helgoland!
"From this keen edge no god can save
"The Wealish thrall and the British slave."
Eadmund of York from the king turned back,
His eyes with sudden wrath were black.
"Say ye so in your brainless pride?
"You will learn this day how the Britons ride!
"Not to the Saxons is the shame
"That they fall to a thunderstorm of flame!
"This is no war of churl and slave,
"But kings and warriors tried and brave.
"This is a war where ravens fly
"As desperate men go out to die.
"We shall see if you prove your arrogant boast
"If any one of the British host,
"Chieftain or warrior, smites your sword."
With brainless laughter the heathen roared.
Tostig the Raven was short in speech;
He had rushed his galleys on many a beach,
Fiercest of all the sea-kings, he,
Name of terror on land and sea.
Now he spoke: "We shall have our fill,
"These men are charging to die—and kill!"

Ceawlin made the battle sign
And his horde rushed hard on the charging line.

The standards reel and the riders rock,
The whole earth shudders at the shock.
And the charging Britons' desperate blows
Carry them into the heart of their foes.
On every side they are leagued amain
And the battle floods the trampled plain.
King Geraint charged as a hawk might fly
Where Ceawlin's standard broke the sky.
The Viking Leofwine barred his path,
First to taste of the Briton's wrath.
Leofwine's heart was fierce and stout
But now he felt his first black doubt
As the white steed crashed through the battle rout.
Ere he could draw a single breath
They loomed upon him, a bolt of death.
One mighty stroke snapped short his brand,
Shivered the shield in his iron hand,
Dashed him dead from his saddlebow
To lie on the beaten earth below.
Ceawlin spurred to meet his foe,
But Eadmund of York on his great bay horse
Barred the Saxon monarch's course.
Forced him back, despite his wrath,
And with forty spears across his path
Hedged the way to King Geraint
Who raged like a tiger, smote and rent,
Loomed o'er the fray like a drifting cloud
Heaping dead men in a grisly crowd.

On one side Nial of Ulster crashed,
On the other Dulborn smote and slashed.
And Turlogh and Conmac followed close,
Glutting their wrath with mighty blows;

With them there smote on the dark phalanx
The men-at-arms' swift falling ranks,
Who slashed and slaughtered and slew and died;
Silent, they neither moaned nor cried.
Cadallon swayed, but he still could grin,
To the Saxon center he shattered in;
Godwine the Mercian king he slew,
Eadelberht's skull he cleft in two.
Lodbrog rushed with a terrible blow;
Horse and steed in that overthrow,
Crashed—Cadallon the king lay dead
On his dying horse in a pool of red.
And his warriors who were left to die
Rushed with a yell that tore the sky.
Like a pack of grey wolves, gaunt and grim,
They tore chief Lodbrog limb from limb.
Leaped from their horses and made a wall
Where King Cadallon met his fall,
And around the corpse of their ancient king
Died in a red unbroken ring.

Conmac crashed through the battle tide
And the ranks gave back on either side.
No man his charge might halt or stay,
To the Raven banner he hewed his way.
His helmet was gone, his head was bare,
Like a flame of gold was his golden hair.
Ulf smote as hard as a warrior may,
But Conmac tossed his shield away,
Gripped the standard in his left hand,
And the other drove his crimson brand
Rending the hauberk scales apart,
Riving the bosom and the heart.
Ulf vanished in that sea of blood;
Up in his stirrups Conmac stood,
Brandished the Raven banner high,
Blackly limned in the cloudless sky—

From all the host came a mighty cry.
Then he broke and tore it and slashed in twain
And hurled the pieces on the plain.
The Saxons were mad with shame and rage,
Nothing but death could their hate assuage.
Ceawlin sees his brother dead
And his standard lost with the torn dead.
No shield or helmet Conmac bore
But bone and iron his sword edge shore,
And many a man went down before.
Warriors fell without name or number,
Till Eadward, chieftain of Northumber,
Spurred his steed with a deathly stroke;
Conmac's sword his helmet broke,
But Eadward clove that golden head
And the Briton fell from his saddle, dead.

Dulborn saw his comrade die;
He sounded a strange dark battle cry,
And charged, his great black axe to ply.
Seven chiefs in that charge he slew,
Smiting hauberk and helmet through,
Hewing bosoms and skulls in two.
Up in his stirrups Eadward stood,
Smote as only a chieftain could.
Full on the Pict's unhelmed head,
Dulborn laughed as the blow was sped.
For the tangled shock of his thick black mane
Stayed the sword edge and saved his brain.
Though the edge bit into the scalp beneath;
Dulborn laughed through his gnashing teeth.
His black axe crashed in a singing arc
And Eadward's eyes went strangely dark.
Under his armpit fell the stroke
As a woodsman's axe falls on the oak,
Cleaving hauberk and ribs and spine,
He died with never a groan or sign.

Dulborn was mad with the battle lust,
Horse and rider crashed to dust
Before the crash of his terrible axe
That rent through iron and bone like flax.
From Osgar of Kent he dashed the brain,
Fulk of Sussex he hewed in twain.
He smote and trampled them under horse;
Tostig the Raven barred his course.
The war cry roared from each warrior's throat,
Headlong they thundered, crashed and smote.
In full mid-air the swift strokes met,
The crimson axe and the broadsword wet;
And the sword to a thousand steel sparks flew,
And the axe with never a stay went through
The brazen shield that it split in two.
But notched and strained in many a test,
It broke on the Raven's iron crest.
And each at the other his charger drove,
Close clinched they struggled, tore and strove.
Both their daggers drank deep and well
Till from their plunging steeds they fell;
Down they crashed in the rolling thunder,
And the flying horses trampled them under.

All of the British men-at-arms
Sleep at rest from war's alarms.
All of his chivalry are reft,
None of his knights is to Geraint left.
Of all that followed his gleaming train
Only the Irish chiefs remain.
All of the three are wounded sore,
Head to heel they are steeped in gore.
Their shattered shields they have thrown away,
Splendor of God, what a fearful fray!
Snapped at the hilt was Turlogh's brand,
He snatched an axe from a dying hand.

"This is the end," King Geraint said,
"All our warriors and knights are dead.
"God grant us a knightly death this day!"
"Ever we ride at your side," said they.
And the white horse, red horse, and the black
Crashed once more through the battle wrack.
Their iron-shod hoofs in pools of red
Trampled the living with the dead.
With a blinding might that caught the breath,
Like a triple thunderbolt of death,
That bursts through clouds heaped dark blue,
The three great steeds came crashing through.

Under the hoofs that spurned the wold
Headlong, horses and riders rolled.
Men saw the great white charger loom
Like a flashing thundercloud of doom,
And the great red steed like a storm of hate,
And the huge black horse like a wind of Fate.
Whole ranks go down and the long lines reel
'Neath the frantic hoofs and the lashing steel.
King Geraint aimed his fearful rush
Where Ceawlin rode in the press and crush.
His path to the Saxon king was barred
By Eadwig and Ealdred and Athelgard,
Athelwald and the Kentish Sweyn,
Asgar and Dirck the Wessex thane,
Eadmund of York and the wolfish Rane.
Into their ranks King Geraint broke,
Smote with a headlong desperate stroke.
Eadwig the White went toppling down
With a shattered shield and a cloven crown.
Through Geraint's corselet Ealdred smote
Ere the King's sword ripped the life from his throat.
Nial smote hard of Athelgard,
Hurled him dead on the bloody sward.
Turlogh's axe dashed Athelwald dead

And the next stroke split Lord Asgar's head.
Geraint slew Dirck, the Wessex thane,
Nial shore through the breast of Rane.
Eadmund of York and his comrade Sweyn
Rein against the British king,
And the house carles close in a bristling ring
Ceawlin to guard from the red sword's swing.

King Geraint has taken his mortal wound,
The battle flows in a mist around.
The world is swaying and growing dim
But he sees Ceawlin's helmet swim
There in the mist, and he charges him.
'Tween Eadmund and Sweyn he made to ride
And they assail him from either side.
But Sweyn was dashed by his arm aside.
And ere he could turn, with a war cry grim
Nial of Ulster closed with him.
Eadmund, careless of his own life,
Spurred his steed in that deadly strife.
Parried the stroke that else had sheared
Ceawlin's head to his golden beard.
And Ceawlin struck, but his sword edge turned,
On Geraint's mail; the King's eyes turned
Into the eyes of his Saxon foe,
Again he smote and again the blow
At the very throat of his king was stayed
By the parry of Eadmund's faithful blade.
Then a great black shadow over him loomed,
On his shield the axe of Turlogh boomed.
But the chiefs had seized King Ceawlin's rein
And perforce across the plain,
Out of the reach of the British king
Who raged and smote in the closing ring.

Now while the fight had thundered on
A shadow over the plain had gone,

And a strange white mist fell over all,
Veiling the plain in a mystic pall.
Men could not see for half a pace
Through the strange white shroud before their face.
Turlogh and Eadmund dealt their blows
When sudden the mist swept down to close,
Hid friends from friends and foes from foes.
In the veiling mist Turlogh smote blind
Trusting to chance his foe to find.
He felt the axe on the helmet crash
And the chief go down with a sounding clash.
He heard in the mist the ring of steel,
The shout of men and the trumpet's peal.
He heard the clash of the flying swords
Where the King and Nial fought the lords,
But all was grisly and strange and white;
Forms rose and faded in his sight.
Unseen weapons dealt him blows,
He slew in the mist invisible foes.
And all the field was white and strange
Like a plain over which dead specters range.
Men groped like blind men through the tide
And no man knows how King Geraint died.

But sudden the mist was cleared away;
On a mighty heap of dead he lay,
Last great king of the British race
There on a kingly resting place,
On a mighty couch that was red and grim;
Nial of Ulster lay by him.
Round them lay in a silent ring
The greatest chiefs of the Saxon king,
Who fell where they his way had barred:
Eadwig, Ealdred and Athelgard,
Athelwald and the wolfish Rane,
Asgar and Dirck the Wessex thane,
Eadmund of York and the Kentish Sweyn.

Silent they lay and broken and dead
Save Eadmund of York alone, whose head
Was saved from Turlogh's blinded stroke,
Though the helmet into pieces broke.
Senseless he lay upon the plain
Till his people found him among the slain.
Turlogh reined the mighty black
And the weary, torn ranks gave back
Before the charger's thundering rush,
So Turlogh crashed through the serried crush.
They saw the black steed sweeping by,
The black knight etched against the sky,
Lifting a great black axe on high.
They shrank aside, they held their breath,
They thought him a thunderbolt of Death;
The ranks gave way, they made him room,
They thought him a harbinger of Doom.
A grim black phantom of Death and Fate,
Born in the worlds of Night and Hate.
So Turlogh rode, the single knight
Left alive from that terrible fight,
And vanished from the Saxons' sight.

The word went through the British land
From the Channel's shore to the Solway's strand;
Who is the minstrel fit to sing
Of the last great fight of Britain's king?—
The song of a race swift vanishing

ERIC OF NORWAY

Eric Ranesen, the viking,
   son of the sword and spear,
Swept down the coast of England
   at the height of his wild career
Swooped down on many a village
   with his berserk, wild wolf band,
Raged along the coast like a hurricane
   with fire and sword in his hand,
Harried the coast of England
   from Severn to the Forth,
Loaded his ships with plunder,
   then sailed back to the North.

Lord of the North was Eric,
   from Salten fiord to Skye,
Lord of the wide, wild northern sea
   and many a land thereby.
He had vanquished Saxon and Welshman;
   Swede and Finn and Dane
Only one man defied him
   from Salten to Forth,
And that was Harald of Norway,
   a reaver of the North.

But he could not compare with Eric
   in dragon-ships or men,
For Harald had but one long serpent
   and Eric had five and ten.
Five long serpent vessels,
   with each an hundred men,
And half-a-score ships smaller,
   with thirty in each of the ten.
But Harald was shrewd as a grey fox
   and keen as a viking sword,

And he was born in that wild land
   that lies north of Salten fiord.

He had a friend that was tried and true,
   Hasting, a fierce North-Dane,
And they had roved the oceans
   from Iceland unto Spain.
The Dane was a mighty warrior,
   over six feet he stood,
Two hundred pounds of muscle
   and bone and wild wolf blood.
A fierce and savage warrior,
   far and wide was his fame,
No warrior in the Northland
   could stand before the Dane.

Harald was shaped like a sword-blade,
   slim and somewhat tall,
And he was a gallant chieftain
   in battle or banquet hall.
He was a foe of Eric,
   whom he hated with awful hate,
He swore that for the sea-king,
   he would open heaven's gate.
He swore that oath at Kirkness
   upon All Saints day,
And then he leaped in his serpent-ship
   and he sailed far away.

Sailed toward the isles of sunrise
   with Hasting, the North-Dane,
Avoided sheltered harbors,
   plowed through the open Main.
Into the Mediterranean,
   Harald of Norway came,
Pillaging, burning and slaying,
   gaining both gold and fame;

People of far off countries
   heard Harald of Norway's name.

Last he turned to the Northward,
   leaving the warm seas behind,
Leaving behind the warm lands
   rich with gold and with kine.
Back, yes back to the Northland
   sailed Harald, the viking bold,
With his long ship red with blood
   and weighted with gems and gold.
To Kirkness-town he sailed
   and anchored his long ship there,
With his flag, the flag of the cormorant,
   floating free to the air.

From Sigurd, the strong shipbuilder,
   he bought a long serpent-ship,
N'er such a swift strong vessel
   felt the ocean's swing and clip.
Norsemen flocked to his banner,
   Norwegian, Finn and Dane;
He bought them swords and armor
   and put to sea again.
For many a week they wandered
   over the billows' foam,
Gaining rich prize and plunder
   wherever they did roam.

Now Harald is sea-king
   with ships, a full half-score,
Three long serpents, three galleys,
   and smaller vessels, four.
Thirty score men he numbered,
   thirty score men and ten,
Berserks, sailors, vikings,
   all fierce fighting men.

And now he ranged the north sea,
    burning with years old hate,
In search of Eric the Viking,
    and his vengeance should be great.
For Eric had slain his father
    when Harald was ten years old,
He had burned his cottage above him,
    his sister he had stole.

Now on the sea of the Baltic
    have Harald and Eric met.
Ah, blades so bright at sunrise
    at night will be red and wet.
More men had Eric the Viking,
    more ships on the dark sea's spate,
But Harald's men were hard warriors
    and Harald was wild with hate.
Ship met ship with a crashing
    that shook the mighty deep;
The flicker of the war blades
    lulled many a viking to sleep.

Ship sides and decks were shattered,
    like drunkards they did reel;
War-axe clashed with buckler,
    steel rang loud on steel.
All through the fierce battle
    raged Harald and Hasting the Dane;
Their keen and bloody sword blades
    were many a warrior's bane.
They boarded one of Eric's long serpents,
    to slay and burn and wreck;
Ten vikings closed on Hasting,
    he left them dead on the deck.

Harald engaged the captain,
    the viking Sven the Red;

He ran Sven through the body
   and cleft Jens Larsen's head.
His foes went down before him
   like chaff before the blast;
With a rush he gained the quarterdeck
   and hewed down the tall main-mast.
The long ship raised her battered side
   and sank beneath the main,
But Harald and his vikings
   were on their own ship again.

All day long raged the battle
   and as night was beginning to fall,
Harald's ship crashed with Eric's,
   the greatest of them all.
The steering wheels were deserted,
   the grappling irons were filled,
And the two ships, locked together,
   drifted upon the tide.
And on the sides of the long ships,
   the battle waxed grim and great,
For Harald at last went berserk
   with the force of his mighty hate.

His spear was bloody and broken,
   he drew his red-stained sword.
With a rush he joined his vikings
   that sought Eric's ship to board.
For Eric's ship was taller
   by the width of a huge bull's hide,
And Harald's vikings tried in vain
   to climb the slick wet side.
And arrows by Eric's archers
   and pots of boiling lead,
And crossbow bolts and javelins
   rained down upon their head.

Harald sprang on Hasting's shoulder
  and leaped with might and main,
He caught the edge of the taffrail,
  slipped, and caught again.
A viking rushed to smite him,
  an arrow struck him down,
And then Harald was over the side
  and on the deck with a bound.

Eric and Eric's warriors
  were coming like a blast,
But Harald hurled a rope overside
  and made one end of it fast.
Then like a wolf at bay he turned
  to meet his foeman's band
And Tien, the god of battle,
  guided the blade in his hand.

Five warriors fell before him,
  ah, deep his long sword bit,
And he strove to come near Eric
  but the press was too great for it.
But there were many against him
  and they bore down his brand,
When over the side came Hasting
  with his broadsword in his hand.
And after him, Harald's vikings,
  warriors four score and five,
Swarmed over Eric's taffrail
as bees swarm from a hive.

Now of all the bloody conflicts
  that had been fought that day,
This was the bloodiest battle,
  this the most furious fray.

Ten score men there battled,
   five score on each side, led
By Hasting and Harald of Norway,
   by Ragnar and Eric the Red.
Harald, viking of Norway
   and Hasting the fierce North Dane,
Eric, sea-king of Norway
   and Ragnar the giant thane.

Fierce and uncertain the battle,
   deep-dyed was blade and mace,
Till at last on the quarterdeck, Harald
   and Eric met face to face.
Hakon, the noble jarl,
   fought at Eric's right hand,
On the left, Ragnar the giant,
   and none before him could stand.
Hakon aimed a blow at Harald,
   a terrible blow aimed he,
But Hasting gripped the jarl by the throat
   and hurled him into the sea.

Harald crossed swords with Eric
   without a thought of the thane,
Who turned in time to save himself
   from the silent rush of the Dane.
Sven thought to stab Hasting
   but Olaf struck him dead,
And Aylbrand slew Black Egil
   who struck at Harald's head.
And Rane the hard old sea-wolf
   and Ulf and Lodbrog the Bear,
Stood close so that none of Eric's men
   should rescue their chieftain there.

On the red deck paused the battle,
   as gathered the shades of night,

The warriors on each side lowered arms
   to watch their chieftains fight.
Eric was larger than Harald,
   taller by a head,
But Harald pressed the sea-king
   so hard that more than his hair was red.

It was a battle of giants
   'twixt Ragnar and the Dane,
Their blades rang like Thor's hammer,
   from each the red blood came,
O'er breastplate and bearskin corselet
   the blood began to run,
The whole wild scene was reddened
   by the rays of the setting sun.
Ragnar lost his footing
   and slipped on the slippery board,
And his mighty brand was wrenched from his hand
   by a twist of the Danish sword.

Great Ragnar staggered backward
   and stood like a beast at bay.
And Hasting laughed a roaring laugh
   and threw his sword away.
With his bare hands sprang toward Ragnar,
   who met him, nothing loath,
Like bears they wrenched and wrestled
   and down on the deck went both.
Upon his back lay Hasting,
   with Ragnar on his chest,
The thane drew a long dagger
   and struck at Hasting's breast.

But Hasting caught him by the wrist,
   "I had fought ye fair," gasped he,
"Yes, fought you fair, with my hands bare,
   but ye used the steel on me."

Then came a mighty struggle
    such as of man ne'er wrote,
And there on the deck lay Ragnar
    with Hasting's dirk in his throat.

Meanwhile Harald and Eric
    had wielded their blades like men,
Blue steel clashed with blue steel,
    warlike was the din.
Eric's arm went high in the air
    and a terrible blow struck he;
Harald's guard was beaten down
    and he fell to his knee.
Down came the mighty blade again,
    to sever Harald's neck,
But he sprang aside and the great blade
    sank a hand's breadth in the desk.

Before he could wrench his sword free,
    Harald was on his foe,
With his point against Eric's bosom,
    where death would follow the blow.
"Now yield ye," said Harald of Norway.
    "Yield ye, Eric the Red!"
"Yield? To die by the headsman's axe
    or the hangman's noose?" he said.
Like the leap of a fiery comet
    was the dart of Harald's sword,
But Eric had hurtled backward,
    tearing his steel from the board.

Yet Harald's blade found his bosom
    and it bit deep and sharp,
A shaft's width more and Eric
    had passed to the long dark.
Half-mad with pain and fury,
    Eric charged again and again.

He backed Harald 'gainst the taffrail
   and pressed him with might and main.
His point pierced Harald's shoulder;
   his edge found Harald's head,
And Eric laughed, for it seemed to him
   that Harald would soon be dead.

Harald leaned against the taffrail
   and gripped it with his hand;
The blood streamed from his arm and head,
   and he could scarcely stand.
When Eric saw his foeman's plight,
   with laughter loud he roared,
Like a buffalo bull he charged to meet—
   the point of Harald's sword!
For Harald's strength for an instant returned
   and he put it all in a thrust:
To the hilt it sank in Eric's breast
   and Eric bit the dust.

Over the hilt and pommel
   the red life blood did run,
And the star of Eric of Norway
   went down with the setting sun.
Hasting stood by a stanchion
   with Ragnar at his feet,
And deep in his heart he had believed
   that Eric could ne'er be beat.

Years a score and seven
   had Hasting roamed the sea,
But long as he lives he'll ne'er forget
   the sight he then did see.
The great ships locked together,
   shattered at rail and side,
Drifting, aimlessly drifting,
   drifting upon the tide.

Harald's ship deserted,
   battered, almost a wreck,
And a band of blood-stained
   warriors standing on Eric's deck.

In hold and scuppers, rolling,
   the bodies of the dead,
And on his blood-splashed quarterdeck,
   Eric, Eric the Red.
And Harald stanching above him,
   arm dropped and head drooped low;
As Hasting watched, he tottered
   and fell across his foe.

Upon the coast of Norway,
   the night was going down
And the grey dawn was gathering
   over old Kirkness-town.
The watcher in the tower
   aroused him from his sleep,
And yawned and stretched and gazed afar
   over the rolling deep.
He sweeps the sea from north to south—
   something has caught his eye—
A two-mast sail that gleams snow white
   against the azure sky.

Another sail, another yet,
   before the breeze they run,
And from the bed of ocean
   leaped up the great red sun.
The lonely watcher started,
   from the tower hurried down,
To shout his news in the market place
   and rouse the waking town.
And this was the message he shouted,
   these the words that he said,

"The ships of Harald are coming!
    Of Harald and Eric the Red!"
Then the people rushed from their houses,
    they rushed out into the street,
Men and women and children,
    for they wanted the ships to meet.
And some there were for Harald,
    and some for Eric the Red,
But one and all they rose up
    and left their warm beds,
And hastened to the long wharves
    and stood upon the quay
To watch the grim long serpents
    come sailing into the bay.

First came the ship of Harald;
    then seven other ships
With battered and splintered decks and sides
    and sails full of tears and rips
Broken, shattered, half-sinking,
    they reeled on the waterway
And a long fierce shout of welcome
    went up from the crowded quay.
Closer came the vessels,
    sailing across the bay,
And "Whose flag on Eric's vessel?"
    the folk on the wharfs say.

Nearer, the hearts beat faster,
    hands shaded starry eyes,
And "Great Thor, is it Eric's or Harald's?"
    was breathed like a hundred sighs.
Then from the throng upon the wharf
    rose up a mighty cry,
For all could see the cormorant
    flashing against the sky.

And hanging far below it,
    marred by tear and stain,
The black flag of the raven
    that would never fly again.

So Harald rose in greatness,
    in wealth and mighty fame,
And over all the nation
    spread Harald the Viking's name.
High he rose in fame and power
    and stood beside the king.
And he was an earl of Norway
    and wore King Olaf's ring.

And far, far, far to the northward,
    beside the Iceland strand,
Lies Eric in his tomb of ice,
    with spear and shield in hand.
Locked fast in a drifting iceberg
    doth Eric of Norway lie,
So will he drift forever
    under the great white sky.
Lying in state as a king should,
    until the judgment day,
In warlike, regal splendor
    sleeps Eric of Norway.

The fortunes of Harald and Eric
    rang loud in Hasting's brain,
For the fine soul of a poet
    hid in the savage Dane.
He could read as well as pillage,
    could write as well as slay,
And he wrote this saga of Eric the Red
    and Harald of Norway.

XXVI

Pirate Tales

Bob Howard was intrigued by pirates and their lore. So to craft fictions about Black Vulmea and Bêlit was by no means sufficient to whet Howard's appetite for the buccaneers and tales of raiding and pillaging on the high seas.

Likely his love of the sea helped make tales of privateering and piracy even more inviting.

Reavers and rogues form a goodly portion of Howard's repertoire of characters. These poems also nicely parallel the section on the Vikings in a later section of this book.

The second poem in this section, "Buccaneer Treasure" might well have qualified as a longer narrative—albeit nowhere near as long as "Geraint" or "Eric." But its topic places it more solidly in this section, I think.

Here follows a good sampling of pirate poems—several of them among Howard's finest historical, pseudo-historical, and fictional narrative verses.

A BUCCANEER SPEAKS

I've broken the laws of man and God,
  I've flung my gauntlet forth to the world.
I've turned from the ways that in youth I trod—
  Yonder the Skull Flag flies unfurled.

I laugh at Death and I mock at Life.
  Through seas of blood I have steered my prow.
I've known the glories of crimson strife
  And I've tattooed the cross-bones on my brow.

I've bared my breast to the sea-wind's force;
  Sailed red ways beyond seamen's ken.
I've scattered red ruin along my course,
  Of ravished women and slaughtered men.

I've steered in the teeth of bloody dawns
  And I've raced the sun-set o'er crimson seas.
I've sailed where abyss-red Hell yawns,
  And I've battled the bergs where the star beams freeze.

I've seized my wish at the hilt of the sword
  And held my own by the point of the blade,
Spite of the foe or my own wild horde,
  Were it gold of man or beauty of maid.

I've had my pleasure in slaughter and wreck,
  And all undaunted my end shall be,
With the broken sword on a bloody deck
  Or the raven's croak on the gallows tree.

BUCCANEER TREASURE

This is a story that I heard
    from the lips of a drunken tramp
Down by the wharfs in Mike's saloon,
    in the light of the smoky lamp.
From his tousled hair his strange eyes stared,
    glimmering, shot with blood;
His rags hung loose and his tattered shoes
    were caked with the wharfside mud.

With his twitching hands and his rasping laugh
    he gazed like an idol grim
With a drunken leer o'er the stein of beer
    that I had bought for him.
"Look here," said he, "I'll tell you a tale—
    a strange story, d'ye hear?
No man has heard it from me before;
    I've held it many a year.

"Some twenty years ago it was,
    I found myself a-float
From the shattered deck of a fog-bound wreck,
    at sea in a sailless boat.
Me and the mate—the other boats
    they lost us in the fog.
Still was the day and grim and grey,
    the sea like curdled grog.

"The silence shuddered o'er the waves,
    we scarcely dared to speak.
We might have rowed for half a day;
    it might have been a week.
The mate had got the water-keg
    and kept it to his hand,
A pistol resting on his knee
    to keep him in command.

"He sat unmoving in the bows,
   his gaze an insane stare.
At first he'd let me have a drink
   and then he wouldn't share.
I rowed until my strength gave out
   and as he sat he slept;
I shipped the oars; as he dozed
   closer to him I crept.

"My thirst was like a raging fiend;
   I leaped with lifted knife;
He woke—his pistol grabbed—too late;
   my dagger drank his life.
I seized the keg—gods! it was good!—
   I guzzled long and deep,
Then flung my victim overside,
   lay down and fell asleep.

"I might have slept for half a day,
   I might have slept a year,
But when I woke the fog had broke,
   the sea was sapphire clear.
The sea was clear and strange to me;
   it lay like a girl asleep.
Though strange it be yet I could see
   uncounted fathoms deep.

"As I were mazed I lay and gazed
   through emerald depths untold.
The eastern sky was rosy red,
   the sun was rising gold.
The lazy waves they swung the bow
   with a gentle sway and lift.
I laid the oars across the thwarts
   and the boat I let it drift.

"I watched and saw strange shadows stray
    for fathoms down below;
Like shimmery, gossamer things of dreams
    I watched them come and go.
And then sometimes, like fairy chimes
    or a golden Chinese gong,
Strange music echoed across the sea
    like tones of a wordless song.

"Through the golden day as mazed I lay,
    like jade without a flaw,
The sea lay clear to my wondering eyes
    and strange were the sights I saw.
I gazed on wonders of ages gone
    as my boat went drifting o'er
Gem-set towers and strange sea flowers
    a-bloom on the ocean floor.

"Galleys of cities long forgot,
    dragon-ships and triremes;
Beneath the bows of my drifting boat
    they glided like hazy dreams.
Spires and castles swam into view,
    lost cities met my glance
And ever the shadows swayed and fled
    like things of a deep sea dance.

"At last I saw them plain and clear
    and I swear I do not lie!
The shadows were mermaids, that I saw,
    beautiful, swift and shy.
Their hair was wavy and long and gold,
    their bodies whiter than snow;
Through the wondrous sheen of the ocean green
    they sported to and fro.

"The sun was close to the western sea
   when the fairest maid of the mer
Swam by me, beckoning with her hand,
   and I set my course by her.
I scarcely needed to touch an oar,
   in a merry laughing throng
The sea-girls swarmed on every hand
   and hurried my boat along.

"The sun was touching the western sea,
   gold on a sea of blue,
When riding the green waves motionless,
   a galley loomed to view.
Barnacles crusted her ancient stakes,
   her tall mast held no sail;
I found a rusty anchor chain
   and clambered across the rail.

"So ancient was she I gaped and gazed
   in wonder, craning my neck;
Skeletons sat at the rotting oars
   and lay on the sun-warped deck.
A steel-bound chest on the main bridge stood
   and a skeleton lay thereon.
From the size of the bones he must have been
   a giant of thews and brawn.

"All in and out among his ribs
   the clinging sea moss twined
And decked the bare, sea-rotting skull
   that once had held a mind.
Those bones were old as Time itself,
   sun-warped, broken and grey.
I flung them down upon the deck
   and the chest's lock pried away.

"But I knew by the sword cuts and the marks
    as I flung back the lid
I had found the treasure that seamen seek,
    the treasure of Captain Kidd!
Glimmers of diamonds met my eyes,
    rubies that shone like stars;
Gleam and glitter of virgin gold,
    shimmer of silver bars.

"I thrust my hands in the kingly hoard
    where the doubloons rare lay massed—
When an icy breath like a thing of Death
    like a shadow whispered past.
I turned me round, my eyes a-blink,
    half-blind from the treasure shine—
The short hair prickled at my neck
    and a cold hand touched my spine.

"For I will swear that I saw there
    a sight to cold the blood,
The skeleton like a living man
    before me rose and stood!
The fleshless, toothless jawbones moved
    and yet he spoke no word,
But they upon the deck uprose
    and the bones of the rowers stirred.

"The rotten oars began to creak
    and sway each in its groove,
The arm bones creaked and bent and swayed—
    the galley began to move!
The galley leaped like a fleeing dear,
    straight into the west she sped
As the scarlet sun in a sea of blood
    sank with a blaze of red.

"The crimson waves cleft to her prow
   and in behind her spun.
And I saw a world of lurid flames
   behind the setting sun.
In wild amaze I watched them blaze,
   leap up and die and flare
Beyond the rim of the fiery sea
   like things of a wild nightmare.

"No worldly fires could fling such flame
   and I knew what befell—
As faster and faster the galley sped—
   she was bearing me into Hell!
Shrieking I hurled me across the rail,
   I clambered into the boat,
With shaking hands I loosed the chain
   and pushed her far afloat.

"But the galley altered not her pace,
   'twas as she fled the night,
Marvelling there I watched her fly,
   fast dwindling from my sight.
Till far away like some foul bird
   she stood against the flare,
Then vanished in the red sunset
   and Hell that waited there.
The stars came blinking o'er the sea,
   slow came a slender moon,
And I found that I clutched in my shaky hand
   a tarnished gold doubloon.

"The blue waves barely rocked the boat
   beneath the silver moon,
All night she drifted with the tides
   as I lay half in swoon.
And sometimes 'tween the dusk and dawn,
   after the moon had slid

Across the skyline, there came to me
    the ghost of Captain Kidd.

"He wore his pistols and great sea boots
    as when he trod the deck,
But shackles clung to his hairy arms
    and the noose was on his neck.
And he told me how, as a living man,
    he had sailed to unknown climes
And had found that galley upon the sea,
    adrift since ancient times.

"And put thereon his chest of loot
    and a grisly bargain made
With Satan himself, and with men's blood
    he sealed his part of the trade.
And Satan guards his servant's gold
    with a magic grim and fell
And none may seize that blood-stained loot
    lest they be hurled into Hell.
From his bearded lips I had the tale,
    ere the weary stars had fled,
And he faded like a wisp of smoke
    before the dawn broke red.

"How many days my boat did drift,
    I swear I cannot say,
But I came to upon the deck
    of a trader from Bombay.
I told them not my weird tale,
    they would have deemed me crazed.
Indeed I scarce believe myself
    all was so strange and mazed.

"But sure it was not lunacy,
    no daftness of the moon,
For in a pocket of my clothes

I found the gold doubloon.
For many a year I've sailed the seas,
   but nevermore have seen
That frightful galley all afloat
   upon that sea of green.

"Around the world for twenty years
   I've sailed the driving brine,
Some day I'll sight that ship again
   and her plunder will be mine.
I'm weary, worn, bent by toil,
   I've neither wife nor friends,
But never shall I quit the trails
   that lead to far sea ends.
That treasure haunts my restless dreams;
   I see the gleaming hoard.
A tramp? Ha! Ha! Some day I'll live
   like some blue-blooded lord."

This was the story that he told,
   that drunken, strange-eyed tramp
And as he finished, a thing that gleamed
   in the light of the smoky lamp
He laid upon the drink-stained bar.
   Before each curious stare
A glittering thing of Spanish gold,
   a dubloon glinted there.

Robert E. Howard

DRAKE SINGS OF YESTERDAY

On Devon downs I met the ghost of Drake;
His sigh was like a wind that whispered past.

The barnacles encrust the rotting stroke
And sea-weed shrines the fallen mizzen-mast.
   The sword of glory long has turned to rust,
And shattered now the prows that years of yore
   Beat up the sunset through the blinding gust
That lashed us off the magic Carib shore.

The glory and the glamor and the glee,
   The raiding and the roving and the rage,
Have faded like the smoke upon the sea,
   And History turns down another page.

Where are the bawcocks and the bullies hold,
   The swaggerers, the rufflers, all of they
Who strutted on the deck and filled the hold
With silk and spice and yellow Spanish gold,
   The loot of Indies, Darien and Cathay?

Oh, frown upon their deeds if so ye will,
   And name them crimson handed, black of heart
They braved the unknown world and had their fill
Of death and danger where the sunsets spill
   Unrecokoned perils; and they took their part
Of cannonade and cutlass, wind and rack.
   They paved the way for ye who were to come,
And ye who followed rode a beaten track
   Oh, winds that set our rigging all a-hum!
Oh, tides that gripped our prow, on unmapped seas!
   Oh, galleons that loomed against the dawn!
Oh, battle-thunder off the wide, white leas,
   Oh, hissing cutlass hacked by English brawn!
   Oh, plunder from the shattered cargoes drawn!

Boats of Cordovan leather, silken sash,
  Damascus steel, doubloons and silver plate;
Rough carven gems to match the starlight's flash,
  And gold moidores and many a piece-of-eight.

Tons of brown ale and barrels of black rum,
  And many a pipe of sharp Canary wine;
Toledo blades that shimmer, gleam and hum,
  And bales of spice and gods of strange design.

Oh, dreams that grip and cut me like a knife!
  Let others rest in slumber and in death
I cannot sleep: I need the sting of life.
The pounding of the wins, the fire, the strife.
  The slashing spray, the sea-wind's blasting breath'
    The joy, the pain, the peril, heat and snow,
    The tavern, and the ale at Plymouth Hoe.

I may not rest in Nombre Dios Ray
  Up through the emerald fathoms I arise
When night reels up to drink the dying day
  And stars are silver daggers in the skies.
    And night on night, I live it all again
    My boyhood, manhood, Devon and the Main!

I met the ghost of Drake one Devon night;
  And sang of sail and sword and rover's bench——
And in his eyes there gleamed the Magic Light
  Of Deathless Life not even Death can quench.

Robert E. Howard

A DYING PIRATE SPEAKS OF TREASURE

Lash me two round shot hard to my ankles;
  Over the rail let me slide to the deep;
I'll never see Bristol; the crack of a pistol
  Has weighted my eyelids wi' coming o' sleep.

The prize it was ours, its crew all a-lying
  Face down in the scuppers and dead on the deck;
When spat! came the ball of the mate who lay dying,
  Cheating the gallows, mayhap, o' my neck.

You'll take a new captain and share all the plunder
  And sail for Tortuga or ever it's morn,
And maybe you'll drink for him that lies under
  The tides that come creeping around from the Horn.

Give you a map o' the treasure I've taken?
  Tell where the gems and the doubloons are hid?
Why hiding of treasure's the custom and pleasure
  Of Drake and of Morgan, of Flint and of Kidd.

Of the twenty-odd years I've sailed on the ocean,
  On the Red Sea Trade with the Main's Brotherhood,
By all the winds shaken, great loot I ha' taken
  And mainly considered it splendid and good.

So clap on all sails and steer for the sunset,
  If ever my treasure you're wishful to find —
Where white combers thunder you'll find rarer plunder
  Than out o' Golconda there ever was mined.

For I've hidden my loot in the winds and the surges,
  Where the keel breaks the waves and soft surges croon,
It's the gems o' the skyline where sea and sky merges,
  It's the gold o' the sun and the silk o' the moon.

It's the silver o' starlight, the mist o' the morning
  All gossamer webs, and the deep coral caves,
The winds and the wonder o' reef-riven thunder,
  The emerald sheen o' the snow-crested waves.

The gold that I gathered that mankind had minted,
  It slipped through my fingers like sands on the beach;
But the silver o' starlight was ever unstinted,
  And the gold o' the sunset was ever in reach.

Oh, the sea is my love, though my fingers be crimson,
  The treasure I've hidden, you hunt for in vain;
So sail ye for plunder till Judgment Day's thunder—
  But I'll go to my Treasure House under the Main.

FLINT'S PASSING

Bring aft the rum! Life's measure's overfull
  And down the sides the splashing liquor slops
    To mingle in the unknown seas of Doubt.
    Bring aft the rum! The tide is going out;
The breeze has lain, the tattered mainsail drops
Against the mast. And on the battered hull
    I hear the drowsy slap of lazy waves
And through the port I see the sandy beach,
And sullen trees beyond, a swampland dank
    I've known the isles the furtherest tide surge laves—

Now like a stranded hulk I come to die
Beside a shore mud-foul and forest-rank
Bring aft the rum! And set it just in reach.
  I've sailed the seven seas, long, bloody years
I've seen men die and ships go reeling down—
    I might have robbed my fellow man in style
    But I was long on force and short on guile—

415

So 'stead of trade I chose the buccaneers—
Rig aft a plank there, damn you! Sink or drown!—
Life is a vain, illusive, fickle thing—

Now nearly done with me—it could not hold
  Allurement to allay my thirst—for rum
  Steps on the main companion? Let them come.
Here is the map, let Silver have the gold.
Gems, wenches, rum—aye, I have had my fling
  I guzzled Life as I have guzzled rum.
    Run up the sails—throw off the anchor chain—
The courses sway, the straining braces thrum.
The breezes lift, the scents of ocean come—
  Bring aft the rum! I'll put to sea again.

A PIRATE REMEMBERS

From the scarlet shadows they come to me,
   Shades of the dust-dead past,
Like drifting fogs of the restless sea
   From the silent Nameless Vast.
Ghostly and grey in the dying day
   Their spectral ranks are massed.

With their lank, dank hair, and their eery stare,
   Fantom and fiend and ghost—
Skeletons limned in a haunted sky,
Footfalls light where the dim bats fly,
Stealthy shadows—yet none but I
   Am 'ware of the weird host.

Their light tread whispers on every hand
   When I walk through the shadows' rack
And I hear the mumble of fleshless jaws
   In the dark behind my back.

Red shades of many a buccaneer
   Whose bones rust in the sea,
Grisly phantoms who gape and leer
   That died on the gallows tree.
And they haunt my brain with their dim refrain:
   "As we are, thou shalt be."

Robert E. Howard

A Song of the Anchor Chain

Let down, let out the anchor chain,
  The gulls are dipping low,
A faint wind rattles stays in vain—
  Oh, let the anchor go.
A yellow mist is lying,
A broken wind is sighing
And Captain Gower's dying—
  Oh, let the anchor go!

Carven with ivory rough and rare
  Warped with the sea salt spray
Glowered the captain's cabin where
  The dying buccaneer lay.

He sought to dream of flying ships
  And winds that waver and dart,
But the rattle of death was under his lips
  And Hell was in his heart.

And ever the vision rose and fled—
  A craft on the outward tack.
And a ghostly skipper who swayed and said—
  "No man of our crew came back."

And ever a vision followed fast—
  A ship with a tattered tail
Idly flapping a broken mast—
  And a plank was over the rail.

Gower dreamed of the gallows-tree—
  In a sloop like a lurching gull
He sailed a weird white haunted sea
  Where each wave was a skull.

Gower clutched at a flask of rum,
   And dreamed of a bloody moon,
And he heard the evilly muttering drum
   In the jungle baccaroon.

He heard the whimper of naked slaves
   And the crack of the driver's whip
And the wailing of women and brawny braves
   Pent in the hold of the ship.

He dreamed of low long ships that run
   From the guns of a man-o'-war,
And a crimson road from the rising sun
   To the coast of Calabar.

He saw on the waste of a windy sea,
   Strange death lights glimmer and slant
And he sailed for the port of Eternity
   With the sailor's echoed chant—

"Let down, let out the anchor chain,
   "The wind is rising slow,
"Its far to Rio and the Main,
   "Oh, let the anchor go.
"Oh, turn her bows for Gades
   "To greet the wharf side ladies,
"And Gower's gone to Hades.
   "Oh, let the anchor go."

XXVII

Poems Relevant to the Prose Fiction

Following the tradition of the epigraph to introduce prose fiction with poetic fragments relevant to the story to follow—or to intersperse such poetic snippits into the text of a prose narrative, Howard accompanied many of his prose tales with poetic flourishes. These were occasionally borrowed and quoted from others—Chesterton and *White Horse* for one—but such infusions were more often poetry of his own device. One likely influence for this tendency in Howard was the writing of Talbot Mundy, whom Howard read and admired. Most readily apparent in all the *Tros of Samothrace* novels, Mundy's epigraphs for chapter headings are often well-wrought and story-relevant poetry or prose poems.

In addition to these short and fragmentary verses, Howard also did his readers a great service by composing whole poems on important characters from his prose fiction: Solomon Kane, Kull, and Bran Mak Morn in particular. Unfortunately for us who would have delighted in more, the only poetic piece relevant to Conan seems to be the great poem "Cimmeria"—even if only tangentially relevant, not about Conan directly, but rather the inspiration for his native land. Of course the character Am-ra in the first poem has been viewed as a proto-Conan.

Also included in this section is one group of poems that might just as easily be placed in the earlier chapter on ballads and narratives or in the later chapter on poetic sequences and cycles. But as Deuce Richardson has aptly pointed out, the Zukala poems not only form a nice poetic cycle, but fit with the prose-relevant poems; hence, their inclusion here.

The poems in this section add a richness and a texture and an extra touch of verisimilitude to the narratives to which they relate. They often serve as "pretended authorities" as Lin Carter called such pseudo-sources: things like Lovecraft's *Necronomicon* or Robert W. Chambers' *The King in Yellow*.

AM-RA THE TA-AN

Out of the land of the morning sun,
  Am-ra the Ta-an came.
Outlawed by the priests of the Ta-an,
  His people spoke not his name.
Am-ra, the mighty hunter,
  Am-ra, son of the spear,
Strong and bold as a lion,
  Lithe and swift as a deer.
Into the land of the tiger,
  Came Am-ra the fearless, alone,
With his bow of pliant lance-wood,
  And his spear with the point of stone.

He saw the deer and the bison,
  The wild horse and the bear,
The elephant and the mammoth,
  To him the land seemed fair.
Face to face met he the tiger,
  And gripping his spear's long haft,
Gazed fearless into the snarling face,
  "Good hunting!" cried he, and laughed!
The bison he smote at sunrise,
  The deer in the heat of day,
The wild horse fell before him,
  The cave-bear did he slay!

A cave sought he? Not Am-ra!
  He lived as wild and free,
As the wolf that roams the forest,
  His only roof a tree.
When he wished to eat he slaughtered,
  But not needlessly he slew,
For he felt a brother to the wild folk,
  And this the Wild Folk knew.

The deer they spoke to Am-ra,
  Of kin by the tiger slain,
Am-ra met the tiger,
  And slew him on the plain!

A youth in the land of the Ta-an,
  A slim, young warrior, Gaur,
Had followed Am-ra in the chase,
  And fought by his side in war.
He yearned for his friend Am-ra
  And he hated the high priest's face,
Till at last with the spear he smote him,
  And fled from the land of his birth race.
Am-ra's foot-prints he followed,
  And he wandered far away,
Till he came to the land of the tiger,
  In the gateway of the day.

Into the land of the tiger,
  There came an alien race,
Stocky and swart and savage,
  Black of body and face.
Into the country of Am-ra,
  Wandered the savage band,
No bows they bore but each carried
  A stone-tipped spear in his hand.
They paused in Am-ra's country,
  And camped at his clear spring fair,
And they slew the deer and the wild horse,
  But fled from the tiger and bear.

Back from a hunt came Am-ra,
  With the pelt of a grizzly bear,
He went to the spring of clear water
  And he found the black men there.
More like apes than men were they,
  They knew not the use of the bow,

They tore their meat and ate it raw
For fire they did not know.
  Then angry waxed bold Am-ra,
Furious grew he then,
  For he would not share his country
With a band of black ape-men …

THE BELL OF MORNI

There's a bell that hangs in a hidden cave
  Under the heathered hills
That knew the tramp of the Roman feet
  And the clash of the Pictish bills.

It has not rung for a thousand years,
  To waken the sleeping trolls,
But God defend the sons of men
  When the bell of the Morni tolls.

For its rope is caught in the hinge of hell,
  And its clapper is forged of doom,
And all the dead men under the sea
  Await for its sullen boom.

It did not glow in an earthly fire,
  Or clang to a mortal's sledge;
The hands that cast it grope in the night
  Through the reeds at the fen-pool's edge.

It is laden with dooms of a thousand years,
  It waits in the silence stark,
With grinning dwarves and the faceless things
  That crawl in the working dark.

And it waits the Hand that shall wake its voice,
  When the hills shall break with fright,
To call the dead men into the day,
  And the living into the Night.

THE BLACK STONE

They say foul beings of Old Times still lurk
In dark forgotten corners of the world,
And Gates still gape to loose, on certain nights,
Shapes pent in Hell.

THE BLOOD OF BELSHAZZAR

It shone on the breast of the Persian king,
  It lighted Iskander's road;
It blazed where the spears were splintering,
  A lure and a maddening goad.
And down through the crimson, changing years
  It draws men, soul and brain;
They drown their lives in blood and tears,
  And they break their hearts in vain.
Oh, it flames with the blood of strong men's hearts
  Whose bodies are clay again.

CIMMERIA

I remember
The dark woods, masking slopes of sombre hills;
The grey clouds' leaden everlasting arch;
The dusky streams that flowed without a sound,
And the lone winds that whispered down the passes.

Vista upon vista marching, hills on hills,
Slope beyond slope, each dark with sullen trees,
Our gaunt land lay. So when a man climbed up
A rugged peak and gazed, his shaded eye
Saw but the endless vista—hill on hill,
Slope beyond slope, each hooded like its brothers.

It was gloomy land that seemed to hold
All winds and clouds and dreams that shun the sun,
With bare boughs rattling in the lonesome winds,
And the dark woodlands brooding over all,
Not even lightened by the rare dim sun
Which made squat shadows out of men; they called it
Cimmeria, land of Darkness and deep Night.

It was so long ago and far away
I have forgotten the very name men called me.
The axe and flint-tipped spear are like a dream,
And hunts and wars are like shadows. I recall
Only the stillness of that sombre land;
The clouds that piled forever on the hills,
The dimness of the everlasting woods.
Cimmeria, land of Darkness and the Night.

Oh, soul of mine, born out of shadowed hills,
To clouds and winds and ghosts that shun the sun,
How many deaths shall serve to break at last
This heritage which wraps me in the grey
Apparel of ghosts? I search my heart and find
Cimmeria, land of Darkness and the Night.

Robert E. Howard

THE DRUMS OF PICTDOM

How can I wear the harness of toil
And sweat at the daily round,
While in my soul forever
The drums of Pictdom sound?

THE GREY GOD PASSES

O, Masters of the North, we come
with tally of remembered dead,
Of broken hearth and blazing home,
and rafters crashing overhead.
A single cast of dice we throw
to balance, by the leaden sea,
A hundred years of wrong and woe
with one red hour of butchery.

The war was like a dream; I cannot tell
How many heathen souls I sent to Hell.
I only know, above the fallen ones
I heard dark Odin shouting to his sons,
And felt amid the battle's roar and shock
The strife of gods that crashed in Ragnarok.
— *Conn's Saga*

THE HOUR OF THE DRAGON

The Lion banner sways and falls
   in the horror haunted gloom;
A scarlet Dragon rustles by,
   borne on winds of doom.
In heaps the shining horsemen lie,
   where the thrusting lances break,
And deep in the haunted mountains
   the lost, black gods awake.
Dead hands grope in the shadows,
   the stars turn pale with fright,
For this is the Dragon's Hour,
   the triumph of Fear and Night.

KELLY THE CONJURE-MAN

There are strange tales told when the full moon shines
  Of voodoo nights when the ghost-things ran—
But the strangest figure among the pines
  Was Kelly the conjure-man.

KINGS OF THE NIGHT

The Caesar lolled on his ivory throne—
   His iron legions came
To break a king in a land unknown,
   And a race without a name.
         — *The Song of Bran*

Robert E. Howard

THE KING AND THE OAK

Before the shadows slew the sun
    the kites were soaring free,
And Kull rode down the forest road,
    his red sword at his knee;
And winds were whispering round the world:
    "King Kull rides to the sea."

The sun died crimson in the sea,
    the long gray shadows fell;
The moon rose like a silver skull
    that wrought a demon's spell,
For in its light great trees stood up
    like specters out of hell.

In spectral light the trees stood up,
    inhuman monsters dim;
Kull thought each trunk a living shape,
    each branch a knotted limb,
And strange unmortal evil eyes
    flamed horribly at him.

The branches writhed like knotted snakes,
    they beat against the night,
And one great oak with swayings stiff,
    horrific in his sight,
Tore up its roots and blocked his way,
    grim in the ghostly light.

They grappled in the forest way,
    the king and grisly oak;
Its great limbs bent him in their grip,
    but never a word was spoke;
And futile in his iron hand,
    a stabbing dagger broke.

And through the tossing, monstrous trees
   there sang a dim refrain
Fraught deep with twice a million years
  of evil, hate and pain:
"We were the lords ere man had come
   and shall be lords again."

Kull sensed an empire strange and old
   that bowed to man's advance
As kingdoms of the grass-blades
   before the marching ants,
And horror gripped him in the dawn
   like someone in a trance.

He strove with bloody hands against
   a still and silent tree;
As from a nightmare dream he woke;
   a wind blew down the lea
And Kull of high Atlantis
   rode silent to the sea.

THE LION OF TIBERIAS

He rides on the wind with the stars in his hair;
   Like Death falls his shadow on castles and towns;
And the kings of the Caphars cry out in despair,
   For the hoofs of his stallion have trampled their crowns.

Robert E. Howard

MEN OF THE SHADOWS

From the dim red dawn of Creation,
  From the fogs of timeless time
Came we, the first great nation,
  First on the upward climb.

Savage, untaught, unknowing,
  Groping through primitive night,
Yet faintly catching the glowing,
  The hint of the coming Light.

Ranging the lands untraveled,
  Building our land-marks of stone.
Vaguely grasping at glory,
  Gazing beyond our ken
Mutely the ages' story
  Nearing on plain and fen.

See, how the Lost Fire smolders,
  We are one with the eons' must.
Nations have trod on our shoulders,
  Trampling us into the dust.

We, the first of the races,
  Linking the Old and the New—
Look, where the sea-cloud spaces
  Mingle with ocean-blue.

So we have mingled with ages,
  And the world-wind our ashes stirs,
Vanished ore we from Time's pages,
  Our Memory? Wind in the firs.
Stonehenge of long-gone glory,
  Sombre and lone in the night,
Murmur the age-old story
  How we kindled the first of the light.

Speak, night-winds, of man's creation,
  Whisper o'er crag and fen,
The tale of the first great nation,
  The last of the Stone Age men.

THE ONE BLACK STAIN

Sir Thomas Doughty, executed at St. Julian's Bay, 1578

They carried him out on the barren sand
  where the rebel captains died;
Where the grim grey rotting gibbets stand
  as Magellan reared them on the strand,
And the gulls that haunt the lonesome land
  wail to the lonely tide.

Drake faced them all like a lion at bay,
  with his lion head upflung:
"Dare ye my word of law defy,
  to say that this traitor shall not die?"
And his captains dared not meet his eye
  but each man held his tongue.

Solomon Kane stood forth alone,
  grim man of a sombre race:
"Worthy of death he well may be,
  but the court ye held was a mockery,
"Ye hid your spite in a travesty
  where Justice hid her face.

"More of the man had ye been, on deck
  your sword to cleanly draw
"In forthright fury from its sheath,
  and openly cleave him to the teeth—
"Rather than slink and hide beneath
  a hollow word of Law."
Hell rose in the eyes of Francis Drake.
  "Puritan knave!" swore he,

"Headsman, give him the axe instead!
  HE shall strike off yon traitor's head!"
Solomon folded his arms and said,
  darkly and somberly:

"I am no slave for your butcher's work."
  "Bind him with triple strands!"
Drake roared in wrath and the men obeyed,
  hesitantly, as men afraid,
But Kane moved not as they took his blade
  and pinioned his iron hands.

They bent the doomed man to his knees,
  the man who was to die;
They saw his lips in a strange smile bend;
  one last long look they saw him send
At Drake, his judge and his one-time friend,
  who dared not meet his eye.

The axe flashed silver in the sun,
  a red arch slashed the sand;
A voice cried out as the head fell clear,
  and the watchers flinched in sudden fear,
Though t'was but a sea-bird wheeling near
  above the lonely strand.

"This be every traitor's end!"
  Drake cried, and yet again;
Slowly his captains turned and went,
  and the admiral's stare was elsewhere bent
Than where cold scorn with anger blent
  in the eyes of Solomon Kane.

Night fell on the crawling waves;
  the admiral's door was closed;
Solomon lay in the stenching hold;
  his irons clashed as the ship rolled,

And his guard, grown weary and overbold,
  laid down his pike and dozed.
He woke with a hand at his corded throat
  that gripped him like a vise;
Trembling he yielded up the key,
  and the somber Puritan stood up free,
His cold eyes gleaming murderously
  with the wrath that is slow to rise.

Unseen to the admiral's cabin door
  went Solomon from the guard,
Through the night and silence of the ship,
  the guard's keen dagger in his grip;
No man of the dull crew saw him slip
  in through the door unbarred.

Drake at the table sat alone,
  his face sunk in his hands;
He looked up, as from sleeping—
  but his eyes were blank with weeping
As if he saw not, creeping,
  Death's swiftly flowing sands.

He reached no hand for gun or blade
  to halt the hand of Kane,
Nor even seemed to hear or see,
  lost in black mists of memory,
Love turned to hate and treachery,
  and bitter, cankering pain.

A moment Solomon Kane stood there,
  the dagger poised before,
As a condor stoops above a bird,
  and Francis Drake spoke not nor stirred,
And Kane went forth without a word
  and closed the cabin door.

THE PHOENIX ON THE SWORD

Chapter II

When I was a fighting-man, the kettle-drums they beat,
The people scattered gold-dust before my horse's feet;
But now I am a great king, the people hound my track
With poison in my wine-cup, and daggers at my back.
    —*The Road of Kings.*

Chapter III

Under the caverned pyramids great Set coils asleep;
Among the shadows of the tombs his dusky people creep.
I speak the Word from the hidden gulfs
    that never knew the sun—
Send me a servant for my hate, oh scaled and shining One!

Chapter IV

When the world was young and men were weak,
    and the fiends of the night walked free,
I strove with Set by fire and steel
    and the juice of the upas-tree;
Now that I sleep in the mount's black heart,
    and the ages take their toll,
Forget ye him who fought with the Snake
    to save the human soul?

Chapter V

What do I know of cultured ways,
    the gilt, the craft and the lie?
I, who was born in a naked land
    and bred in the open sky.
The subtle tongue, the sophist guile,
    they fail when the broadswords sing;
Rush in and die, dogs—
    I was a man before I was a king.
    —*The Road of Kings.*

THE POOL OF THE BLACK ONE

Into the west, unknown of man,
Ships have sailed since the world began.
Read, if you dare, what Skelos wrote,
With dead hands fumbling his silken coat;
And follow the ships through the wind-blown wrack—
Follow the ships that come not back.

QUEEN OF THE BLACK COAST

Believe green buds awaken in the spring,
  That autumn paints the leaves with somber fire;
Believe I held my heart inviolate
  To lavish on one man my hot desire.
          —*The Song of Bêlit.*

In that dead citadel of crumbling stone
  Her eyes were snared by that unholy sheen,
And curious madness took me by the throat,
  As of a rival lover thrust between.
          —*The Song of Bêlit.*

Was it a dream the nighted lotus brought?
  Then curst the dream that bought my sluggish life;
And curst each laggard hour that does not see
  Hot blood drip blackly from the crimsoned knife.
          —*The Song of Bêlit.*

The shadows were black around him,
  The dripping jaws gaped wide,
Thicker than rain the red drops fell;
But my love was fiercer than Death's black spell,
Nor all the iron walls of Helli
  Could keep me from his side.
          —*The Song of Bêlit.*

Robert E. Howard

RED BLADES OF BLACK CATHAY

Trumpets die in the loud parade,
  The gray mist drinks the spears;
Banners of glory sink and fade
  In the dust of a thousand years.
Singers of pride the silence stills,
  The ghost of empire goes,
But a song still lives in the ancient hills,
  And the scent of a vanished rose.
Ride with us on a dim, lost road
  To the dawn of a distant day,
When swords were bare for a guerdon rare—
  The Flower of Black Cathay.

THE RETURN OF SIR RICHARD GRENVILLE

One slept beneath the branches dim,
 Cloaked in the crawling mist,
And Richard Grenville came to him
 And plucked him by the wrist.
No nightwind shook the forest deep
 Where the shadows of Doom were spread,
And Solomon Kane awoke from sleep
 And looked upon the dead.
He spake in wonder, not in fear:
 "How walks a man who died?
"Friend of old times, what do ye here,
 "Long fallen at my side?"
"Rise up, rise up," Sir Richard said,
 "The hounds of doom are free;
"The slayers come to take your head
 "To hang on the ju-ju tree.
"Swift feet press the jungle mud
 "Where the shadows are grim and stark,
"And naked men who pant for blood
 "Are racing through the dark."
And Solomon rose and bared his sword,
 And swift as tongue could tell,
The dark spewed forth a painted horde
 Like shadows out of Hell.
His pistols thundered in the night,
 And in that burst of flame
He saw red eyes with hate alight,
 And on the figures came.
His sword was like a cobra's stroke
 And death hummed in its tune;
His arm was steel and knotted oak
 Beneath the rising moon.

But by him sang another sword,
   And a great form roared and thrust,
And dropped like leaves the screaming horde
   To writhe in bloody dust.
Silent as death their charge had been,
   Silent as night they fled;
And in the trampled glade was seen
   Only the torn dead.
And Solomon turned with outstretched hand,
   Then halted suddenly,
For no man stood with naked brand
   Beneath the moon-lit tree.

THE ROAD OF AZRAEL

Towers reel as they burst asunder,
   Streets run red in the butchered town;
Standards fall and thee lines go under,
   And the iron horsemen ride me down.
Out of the strangling dusts that blind me
   Let me ride for my hour is nigh,
From the walls that stifle, the hoofs that grind me,
   To the sun and the desert wind to die.

RUNE OF THE ANCIENT ONE

Gods of heather, god of lake,
Bestial fiends of swamp and brake;
White god riding on the moon,
Jackal-jawed, with voice of loon;
Serpent god whose scaly coils
Grasp the Universe in toils;

See the Unseen Sages sit;
See thee council fires alit.
See I stir thee glowing coals,
Toss on manes of seven foals.
Seven foals all golden shod
From thee herds of Alba's god.

Now in numbers one and six? ,
Shape and place the magic sticks,
Scented wood brought from afar,
From the land of Morning Star.
Hewn from limbs of sandal-trees,
Brought far o'er thee Eastern Seas.

Sea-snake fangs, see now I fling,
Pinions of a sea-gull's wing.
Now the magic dust I toss,
Men are shadows, life is dross.
Now the flames crawl, ere they blaze,
Now the smokes rise in a haze.

Fanned by far off ocean blast
Leaps the tale of distant past.
Dimly, dimly, glimmers thee starlight,
  Over thee heather-hill, over the vale.
Gods of the, Old Land broodo'er the far night,
  Things of the darkness ride on the gale.
Now while the fire smolders,while smoke enfolds it,
  Now ere it leaps in clear, mystic flame,
Harken once more (else the dark gods withold it)
Hark to the tale of the race without a name.

Robert E. Howard

THE SCARLET CITADEL

They trapped the Lion on Shamu's plain;
They weighted his limbs with an iron chain;
  They cried loud in the trumpet-blast,
  They cried, "The Lion is caged at last!"
Woe to the cities of river and plain
If ever the Lion stalks again!
           —*Old Ballad.*

  Gleaming shell of an outworn lie;
    fable of Right divine—
  You gained you crown by heritage,
    but Blood was the price of mine.
  The throne that I won by blood and sweat,
    by Crom, I will not sell
  For promise of valleys filled with gold,
    or threat of the Halls of Hell!
           —*The Road of Kings.*

The Lion strode through the halls of Hell;
Across his path grim shadows fell
  Of many a mowing, nameless shape——
  Monsters with dripping jaws agape.
The darkness shuddered with scream and yell
When the Lion stalked through the halls of Hell.
          — *Old Ballad.*

A long bow and a strong bow, and let the sky grow dark!
The cord to the nock, the shaft to the ear,
  and the king of Koth for a mark!
           —*Song of the Bossonian Archers.*

SOLOMON KANE'S HOMECOMING

The white gulls wheeled above the cliffs,
   the air was slashed with foam,
The long tides moaned along the strand
   when Solomon Kane came home.
He walked in silence strange and dazed
   through the little Devon town,
His gaze, like a ghost's come back to life,
   roamed up the streets and down.

The people followed wonderingly
   to mark his spectral stare,
And in the tavern silently
   they thronged about him there.
He heard as a man hears in a dream
   the worn old rafters creak,
And Solomon lifted his drinking-jack
   and spoke as a ghost might speak:

"There sat Sir Richard Grenville once;
   in smoke and flame he passed.
"And we were one to fifty-three,
   but we gave them blast for blast.
"From crimson dawn to crimson dawn,
   we held the Dons at bay.
"The dead lay littered on our decks,
   our masts were shot away.

"We beat them back with broken blades,
   till crimsom ran the tide;
"Death thundered in the cannon smoke
   when Richard Grenville died.
"We should have blown her hull apart
   and sunk beneath the Main."
The people saw upon his wrist

the scars of the racks of Spain.
"Where is Bess?" said Solomon Kane.
   "Woe that I caused her tears."
"In the quiet churchyard by the sea
   she has slept these seven years."
The sea-wind moaned at the window-pane,
   and Solomon bowed his head.
"Ashes to ashes and dust to dust,
   and the fairest fade," he said.

His eyes were mystical deep pools
   that drowned unearthly things,
And Solomon lifted up his head
   and spoke of his wanderings.
"Mine eyes have looked on sorcery
   in dark and naked lands,
"Horror born of the jungle gloom
   and death on the pathless sands.

"And I have known a deathless queen
   in a city old as Death,
"Where towering pyramids of skulls
   her glory witnesseth.
"Her kiss was like an adder's fang,
   with the sweetness Lilith had,
"And her red-eyed vassals howled for blood
   in that City of the Mad.

"And I have slain a vampire shape
   that sucked a black king white,
"And I have roamed through grisly hills
   where dead men walked at night.
"And I have seen heads fall like fruit
   in a slaver's barracoon,
"And I have seen winged demons fly
   all naked in the moon.

"My feet are weary of wandering
    and age comes on apace;
"I fain would dwell in Devon now,
    forever in my place."
The howling of the ocean pack
    came whistling down the gale,
And Solomon Kane threw up his head
    like a hound that sniffs the trail.

A-down the wind like a running pack
    the hounds of the ocean bayed,
And Solomon Kane rose up again
    and girt his Spanish blade.
In his strange cold eyes a vagrant gleam
    grew wayward and blind and bright,
And Solomon put the people by
    and went into the night.

A wild moon rode the wild white clouds,
    the waves in white crests flowed,
When Solomon Kane went forth again
    and no man knew his road.
They glimpsed him etched against the moon,
    where clouds on hilltop thinned;
They heard an eerie echoed call
    that whistled down the wind.

Robert E. Howard

SOMETHING ABOUT EVE

Bugles beckon to red disaster,
  Dead men gnaw at the coffined sod,
And we who ride for the One Black Master
  Are leagued in the lists with the knights of God.

SONG OF THE PICT

Wolf on the height
Mocking the night;
Slow comes the light
Of a nation's new dawn.
Shadow hordes massed
Out of the past.
Fame that shall last
Strides on and on.
Over the vale
Thunders the gale
Bearing the tale
Of a nation up-lifted.
Flee, wolf and kite!
Fame that is bright.

A SONG OF THE RACE

High on his throne sat Bran Mak Morn
    When the sun-god sank and the west was red;
He beckoned a girl with his drinking horn,
    And, "Sing me a song of the race," he said.

Her eyes were as dark as the seas of night,
    Her lips were as red as the setting sun,
As, a dusky rose in the fading light,
    She let her fingers dreamily run

Over the golden-whispered strings,
    Seeking the soul of her ancient lyre;
Bran sate still on the throne of kings,
    Bronze face limned in the sunset's fire.

"First of the race of men," she sang,
    "Far from an unknown land we came,
From the rim of the world where mountains hang
    And the seas burn red with the sunset flame."

"First and the last of the race are we,
    Gone is the old world's gilt and pride,
Mu is a myth of the western sea,
    Through halls of Atlantis the white sharks glide."

An image of bronze, the king sate still,
    Javelins of crimson shot the west,
She brushed the strings and a murmured thrill
    Swept up the chords to the highest crest.

"Hear ye the tale that the ancients tell,
    Promised of yore by the god of the moon,
Hurled on the shore a deep sea shell,
    Carved on the surface a mystic rune:"

"'As ye were first in the mystic past
  Out of the fogs of the dim of Time,
So shall the men of your race be last
  When the world shall crumble,' so ran the rhyme."

"'A man of your race, on peaks that clash,
  Shall gaze on the reeling world below;
To billowing smoke shall he see it crash,
  A floating fog of the winds that blow.'"

"'Star-dust falling for aye through space.
  Whirling about in the winds that spin;
Ye that were first, be the last-most race,
  For one of your men shall be the last of men.'"

Into the silence her voice trailed off,
  Yet still it echoed across the dusk,
Over the heather the night-wind soft
  Bore the scent of the forest's musk.

Red lips lifted, and dark eyes dreamed,
  Bats came wheeling on stealthy wings;
But the moon rose gold and the far stars gleamed,
  And the king still sate on the throne of kings.

THE SOWERS OF THE THUNDER
The Ballad of Baibars

Iron winds and ruin and flame,
  And a Horseman shaking with giant mirth;
  Over the corpse-strewn, blackened earth
Death, stalking naked, came
Like a storm-cloud shattering the ships;
  Yet the Rider seated high,
Paled at the smile on a dead king's lips,
  As the tall white horse went by.

THE THING ON THE ROOF

They lumber through the night
  With their elephantine tread;
I shudder in affright
  As I cower in my bed.
They lift colossal wings
  On the high gable roofs
Which tremble to the trample
  Of their mastodonic hoofs.

Robert E. Howard

THE ZUKALA POEMS:
A NARRATIVE CYCLE

THE TOWER OF ZUKALA

Far and behind the Eastern wind
   Beyond the hinterlands
Where strange shores lift and strange stars drift
   Zukala's tower stands.

Zukala's sendings go abroad
   Beyond all worlds' ends,
But no man knows Zukala's foes
   And no man knows his friends.

For far and strange and wide the range
   Zukala's mystic power;
He slays each year with a ghostly spear
   In the dim of the midnight hour.

He sits alone on a moon-pale throne,
   In clouds and stars arrayed;
He sits a-dream and his strange eyes gleam
   Like sapphire set in jade.

Each ghostly night from wan starlight
   The dim dew falls a-shower,
And the restless ghosts of by-gone hosts,
   They throng Zukala's tower.

Silent they come when the twilight goes
   And the drifting shadows fall;
Their pale lights flare on the unlit stair
   And gleam in the dusky hall.

Lost years are there, and vanished dreams,
   And every by-gone hour;
The dead days creep where the shadows sleep
   In chamber and hall and bower.

The phantoms glide through the twilight tide,
   They slip through the wan starlight;
The eery shine of the Phantom Nine
   Gleams through the whispering night.

Wandering shades of the long gone past
   With their haunting, luminous eyes,
They glide and lurk in the shadows murk
   As the shuddering night-wind sighs.

Through the dusty halls of Zukala's tower
   Dim specters haunt the dusk,
And the strange night-wind that sometimes blows
   Carries the ages' musk.

When the midnight brings her gliding fears
   To fright the wailing loon,
Zukala's tower starkly rears
   Against a blood-red moon.

The yellow stars, like eyes of cats,
   Gaze through the weird hour,
And silently the spectre bats
   Flit round Zukala's tower.

Robert E. Howard

ZUKALA'S HOUR

High in his dim, ghost-haunted tower
   Zukala sits alone;
Like a spider, spinning his webs of power
   Upon his moon pale throne.

All through the long, star-spectral night
   The tower knows no tread,
Save for, sometimes, the eery, light
   Swift footfalls of the dead.

He does not sleep and his eyes are deep
   As the Seas of Falgarai;
And he moves his sceptre but to sweep
   The dim stars out of the sky.

And when the wind is out of the east
   And the bent moon's silver gleam
Makes pale the stars like ghosts at feast,
   Zukala sits a-dream.

But when the wind is out of the north
   And the grey light lifts for morn
Zukala harries his Sendings forth
   To know if a child be born.

And the babe that is born in that mystic hour,
   In the time of the paling light,
Is cursed with the gift of Zukala's power—
   The gift of second sight.

For an unseen web from the mystic shores
   Upon his soul is thrown
And though his brothers may number scores
   That babe must walk alone.

He shall walk in lands that are dim and grey,
    Yet never shall he take fright,
Though ghosts shall whisper to him by day
    And walk at his side by night.

His brothers may sing to the echoing sky,
    Proud lords of the Universe,
But he shall see with an unveiled eye,
    For that is Zukala's Curse.

He shall see that the world is fog and dust,
    Blind Destiny all that rules;
The gold that he gains shall be as rust
    And his brothers empty fools.

Ambition shall be but a broken goad;
    Hollow shall be his mirth.
The pathway of ghosts shall be his road
    And the wastelands of the earth.

Empty shall be the cheers of hosts
    Though he win to all heights of power.
For he is destined to walk with ghosts
    That is born in Zukala's Hour.

ZUKALA'S JEST

The gods brought a Soul before Zukala,
 A Soul that had been wandering in Space;
"A babe is to be born at the coming of the morn,
"And this soul is chosen for the place."
 Down from his throne looked Zukala
With his strange eyes a-glitter from his face.
 "The babe shall be a girl," said Zukala,
 "With every tooth a pearl," said Zukala;
"A woman strangely fair with wondrous golden hair
"Men's souls shall she ensnare," said Zukala.
 "She shall raise mankind to wrath," said Zukala;
 "Blighted love shall haunt her path," said Zukala;
"Men for her their souls will sell for her destiny is fell,
"And her feet are set toward Hell," said Zukala.

Then spake the Soul to Zukala,
 To Zukala on his throne of gleaming jade:
"Nay, my lord, but is it just, dooming to a life of lust,
"That just fashioned from the dust, lord Zukala?
"Thus my destined trail is laid ere I am in flesh arrayed,
"Then shall men my sins upbraid, not Zukala."
 From his throne of gleaming jade spake Zukala:
"Human forms were made to fade," said Zukala;
 "But the soul must stand the test
 "And the gods must have their jest
 "Else Creation held no zest," laughed Zukala.
Long and loud from his throne laughed Zukala.

ZUKALA'S LOVE SONG

Along the sky my chariot ran,
    And the star-things ran before.
I raced the breeze over star-lit seas
    Till the very wind gave o'er;
But my soul grew lone, and my heart grew sad,
    Sad as the sighing sea,
For there was never a girl or lad
    To laugh in the skies with me.

I hid my wings in a scarlet cloak,
    I lowered my burning eyes,
And I went on foot with a lilting lute,
    A beggar from the skies.
I tuned my lute to a song of love,
    I edged my song with mirth,
And my feet drank deep of the waving grove
    And deep of the dust of earth.

And maidens flung me silver coins,
    And women praised my voice,
And when dawn was past, I found at last
    The rose-white girl of my choice.
She flung me a rose when I sang to her,
    And its roots sank in my breast;
But oh, she flung me a deathly rose
    When she put my love to jest.

I sang her songs like a dew drop's fall
    And songs like a bugle peal;
But her heart was cold, and the world grew old,
    And the heart of me turned to steel.
I rent to shreds my scarlet cloak,
    I raised my terrible eyes,
I spread my wings till they hid the sun,
    And mounted again to the skies.

I left my scarlet cloak to lie
    Like a rift of blood on the sward,
But I did not break the lute I bore,
    For that was the soul of a bard.
Then from the blue empirean deeps
    Where Nothing conquers All,
I raised a hand to the tiny world
    As a giant grasps a ball;

And I seized the woman that I loved,
    She screamed in my embrace;
And I brought her to me, white and still
    From the fear of that rush through space.
She lay in the hollow of my hand
    And shrieked to hear the truth:
That I who laughed to see her writhe
    Was one with the beggar youth.

Then into the bowl I flung her soul,
    And the stars in glittering dress
Laughed, crowding in with their cosmic sin,
    To jeer at her nakedness;
For the golden plates that hid her breasts
    And the silk that covered her loins
I rent and flung to the trailing mist
    As a drunkard scatters coins.

Blue and dim on the topaz rim
    Where the silence drinks the night,
Forgotten moons like crazy loons
    Hovered into her sight;
And out of the deep where shadows sleep
    That never knew the sun,
Strange eyes aflame, the dark stars came,
    Whispering, one by one.

And with burning eyes that hid her thighs
    As fire-flies cover a tree,
They kissed her face in a hot embrace,
    And she whimpered upon her knee.
Then I swept the band with a jade-nailed hand,
    And the slim of her waist I gripped,
And the stars fell out of her hair like moths
    And through my fingers slipped.

High on a lone sapphirean throne
    I sat me down with a laugh,
And in wild alarm she clung to my arm,
    In fear she clutched at my staff.
A million miles beneath her seat
    Rippled the topaz seas,
And there were stars below her feet
    And moons between her knees.

XXVIII

Viking Tales

As he loved stories about pirates, so Howard loved the sagas of those Medieval plunderers and world travelers, the Vikings. Secondary only to his self-perceived Celtic roots, his questionably-attested connections to Norse lineage was, at least, an important element in his persona—if not in his person by bloodlines and accurate genealogy. It is likely enough to say that he felt a kinship with things both Celtic and Norse—at least with the worlds they commanded in his imagination.

While, of course, "Eric of Norway" could easily be placed in this grouping, it seemed more significant to place it among the long narratives—especially since there are ample shorter Viking poems, as the following selections attest.

I believe that there was considerable influence upon Howard by two of the most prominent translators and literary figures of the nineteenth century: Henry Wadsworth Longfellow and William Morris. The American is quoted from in the letters and Howard even uses some Longfellow in his epistolary eulogy for his friend Herbert Klatt. The possible influence of Morris's *Sigurd the Volsung* and other sagas like *Nial* and *Grettir* and *Vinland*—and, quite probably, the English *Beowulf* (about a Swedish Viking who comes to the aid of a Danish Viking chieftain)—are all things for the critic to consider. And Guthrum who figures into the story of Alfred the Great and the Battle of Ethandune in Chesterton's *White Horse*, but also figure in.

The following medley of poems demonstrates Howard's keen love of Viking history, culture, and lore. CHANGES HERE - see 6 x 9

THE OUTGOING OF SIGURD THE JERUSALEM-FARER

The fires roared in the skalli-hall,
  And a woman begged me stay—
But the bitter night was falling
And the cold wind calling
  Across the moaning spray.

How could I stay in the feasting-hall
  When the wild wind walked the sea?
The feet of the winds drew out my soul
To the grey waves and the cloud's scroll
Where the gulls wheel and the whales roll,
  And the abyss roars to me.

Man the sweeps and bend the sail—
  We need no oars tonight,
For the sharp sleet drives before the gale
That dashes the spray across the rail
To freeze on helmet and corselet scale,
  And the waves are running white.

I could not bide in the feasting-hall
  Where the great fires light the rooms—
For the winds are walking the night for me
And I must follow where gaunt lands be,
Seeking, beyond some nameless sea,
  The dooms beyond the dooms.

Robert E. Howard

THE RETURN OF THE SEA-FARER

Thorfinn, Thorfinn, where have you been?
    And whence do you come, in the rain and the night?
The grey ocean surges have swallowed your men
    And your dragon-ship sleeps where the wolf-waves roll white.
On your corselet is crusted the salt of the sea,
    And the blown spray is frozen to ice in your hair,
Your keen sword is broken, and still hauntingly
    Your eyes like a fey-woman's distantly stare.

Were there figures unnamed in the seas of the West,
    Were there scale-crusted dragons that shattered your ships?
Were there ocean-fiends riding the dark billows' crest,
    Or icy sea-women with death on their lips?

"Bare stretch the seas to the set of the sun
    "No mermaid or kraken opposes the keel
"Of the lies of women and priests are they spun,
    "To naked winds only the blue billows reel.

"West, ever west like a sea-gull we fled,
    "The wind in our sails and the spray in our teeth,
"And the moon or the sun a cold radiance shed
    "Through the fathomless fathoms that thundered beneath.

"Then at last rose in wrath the monster we dared,
    "The winds' maddened stallions neighed death all around,
"The white fangs of the hounds of the ocean were bared—
    "And we tossed like a rat in the teeth of the hound.

"Lashed into blindness, we staggered in flight,
    "We reeled to the rush of the howling white host,
"And then like a phantom born out of the night,
    "Through the fury and madness, I glimpsed a strange coast.
"Eastward and eastward the gale hurled us on,

"And the dragon-ship staggered at each stroke and strain,
"Till she sank like a stone in a frenzy of dawn,
  "And the sea cast me forth from her bosom again.

"I am haunted by dreams that are stronger than ghosts,
  "They lift me and thrill me with weird second sight,
"Who can rest or be still who has seen nameless coasts,
    "Has glimpsed a new world in the storm and the night?"

Robert E. Howard

THE RHYME OF THE VIKING PATH

Serpent prow on the Afric coast,
 Doom on the Moorish town;
And this is the song the steersman sang
 As the dragon-ship swept down:

I followed Asgrimm Snorri's son
 around the world and half-way back.
And 'scaped the hate of Galdjerhrun
 who sank our ship off Skagerack.
I lent my sword to Hrothgar then;
 his eyes were ice, his heart was hard;
He fell with half his weapon-men
 to our own kin at Mikligard.

And then for many a weary moon
 I labored at the galley's oar
Where men grow maddened by the rune
 of row-locks clacking ever more.
But I survived the reeking rack,
 the toil, the whips that burned and gashed,
The spiteful Greeks that scarred my back
 and trembled even while they lashed.

They sold me on an Eastern block;
 in silver coins their price was paid;
They girt me with a chain and lock;
 I laughed and they were sore afraid.
I toiled among the olive trees
 until a night of hot desire
Blew me a breath of outer seas
 and filled my veins with curious fire.

Then I arose and broke my chain
 and laughed to know that I was free,

And battered out my master's brain
  and fled and gained the open sea.
Beneath a copper sun adrift,
  I shunned the proa and the dhow,
Until I saw a sail uplift,
  and saw and knew the dragon prow.

Oh, East of sands and sunlit gulf,
  your blood is thin, your gods are few;
You could not break the Northern wolf
  and now the wolf has turned on you.
The fires that light the coasts of Spain
  fling shadows on the Eastern strand.
Masters, your slave has come again
  with torch and axe in his red hand!

Robert E. Howard

SINGING HEMP

Aslaf sat in the dragon bows
  And smote on his soulless harp,
And he sang of the winds and the cold sea-path
  And the sword-edge bitter and sharp.

"Ravens whetting their iron beaks,
  "Black in the blood-red dawn,
"And the quenchless fire of the mad desire
  "That drives the Viking on.

'The wind that blows to the night-black gulfs
  "It bears the Southland's groans;
"We turn not back on the red sea-track
  'Til the white sea has our bones.

"Sons of the frost—the cold blue souls
  "Of the cloud-rack, torn and whirled,
"Are the fires that rise in the Viking's eyes,
  "Oh, blind black wolf of the world!"

THE SONG OF HORSA'S GALLEY

From the Baltic Sea our galleys sweep
   To South and West and East,
We bring our bows from the Northern snows
   That the great grey wolves may feast.

To the outmost roads of the plunging sea
   Our dragon ships are hurled,
We have broken the chains of the Southern Danes
   And now we break the world.

Out of the dark of the misty north
   We come like shapes of the gloam
To harry again the Southland men
   And trample the arms of Rome.

The ravens circle above our prows
   And our chant is the song of the sea.
They hear our oars by a thousand shores
   And they know that the North is free.

Robert E. Howard

VIKING'S TRAIL

From the sullen cliffs and the grim fiords
   Where the naked shorelines frown
We turned our prows toward the sun-spun south
   Where a weak king held the crown;
Past the scarlet sand of Helgoland
   The dragon-ships swept down.

In the restless seas of the Hebrides
   The sun in the cold clear blue
Shone on the decks of red-stained deal,
   Raven-banner and plunging keel,
Bronze boar-helmet and grey sword-steel
   And the beards of each berserk crew.

The warning fires leaped up at dawn
   As the Southland coast we raised
From looming headland and barren dune
   The beacon signals blazed.

But it was no beacon smoke that hung
   A-sway in the evening breeze
For the smoldering towns on the fertile downs
   And the wrecks along the leas
Marked red the trail of the Serpent sail
   And told that we swept the seas.

VIKING'S VISION

A white sea was flowing,
   a bitter wind was blowing,
Our chanting shook the cormorants
   that wheeled about the bows,
South—Deathward we were sailing,
   and Aslaf gripped the railing,
A hungry dagger at his hip,
   a scowl upon his brows.

We roared for red tomorrows
   to bring the Southland sorrows
In sunken ship and plundered town
   and wives and daughters raped.
We sang of castles falling,
   gold lost beyond recalling,
Till Aslaf wheeled and cursed at us
   till every mouth there gaped.

"Go tell your lusts to devils,
   you ape-faced swine of evils!
"Or save the breath you waste today
   for shout and battle shock!"
And as he ceased to thunder,
   I caught my breath in wonder
To see a tremor in that hand
   that might have crushed a rock.

Fire smote the Southland beaches
   'mid women's wails and screeches.
We drove the bees to cover,
   and we broke them from their hives.
Where blades their blue sparks showered
   and maidens shrank and cowered,
We plunged our souls in glory,
   and we plunged our swords in lives.

In armor rent and battered
   lay dead men still and scattered.
The light that lit the burning towns
   shone red on gems and gold;
And for each man's desire
   were girls as fair as fire—
But Aslaf's frown was on his brow
   as if his heart were cold.

We came all drunk and roaring,
   gold coins and gems a-pouring
Into his lap—the fairest girls,
   and praises and acclaim.
With wolfish snarl of anger,
   he cursed our drunken clangor,
And tossed the loot upon the earth—
   his eyes were icy flame.

"Swine of the tavern benches!
   What boot these naked wenches?
"These twinkling stones and yellow guads,
   what mean them all to me?
"A weird is come upon me,
   the hand of Fate is on me,
"And over all the clamor
   sounds the calling of the sea.

"I have no rest in sleeping,
   I hear strange waters sweeping
"Long beaches where no Viking's foot
   has ever trod before.
"I take in ale no pleasure,
   for still I hear the measure
"Of long and even waves that break
   upon an unknown shore.

"West where lost winds are sighing,
 a new strange world is lying!
"Its vales and mountains fill my dreams,
 its calling breaks my sleep;
"And dust is battle glory,
 the while a mystic story
"Each west wind brings to haunt my heart
 across the roaring deep.
"My prow has plowed the Baltic,
 and where these rocks basaltic
"From high above the narrow gates
 that lock the Middle Sea;
"And that dark Afric river
 that feeds the sea forever,
"And I have seen the waters break
 on high Byzantium's lea.

"But there are seas unparted,
 and there are coasts uncharted,
"And o'er the waves a whisper comes
 that I am first to go.
"The hour of doom is striking
 the twilight of the Viking!
"To ship! We seek the Fate that waits
 beyond the sunset's glow."

XXIX

Poetic Sequences

Included herein are three poetic sequences: *Black Dawn*, *Sonnets out of Bedlam*, and *Voices of the Night* [aka *The Iron Harp*]. Not only was there a likely influence upon Howard from Lovecraft, whose own *Fungi from Yuggoth* series began its run in *Weird Tales*, there is little doubt that Howard simply wished to extend his poetic reach by attempting one of the usual accomplishments generally attributed to those who wish to be considered a "true poet." Sequences of sonnets, such as the *Bedlam* poems and other poetic sequences are generally considered an imperative somewhere in the overall opera of a poet's achievement—a test to be passed, an indication of poetic prowess.

The other important thing about sequences of poems is the sustained thematic and tonal resonance of the group taken as a whole. One poem can impress and focus, but a group that sustains some intended theme or message or worldview and portrays a broader panorama of themes is more like a symphony than a single poem can hope to be.

BLACK DAWN

1. SHADOWS

A black moon nailed against a sullen dawn
  Shakes down dark petals of a sombre rose;
    The long lank shadows, sons of solitude,
     Slink to the hills that silent, crouch and brood.
    Across the East a grisly radiance grows,
And in the West the last grim star is gone.
Sons of the glaring idols of the night,
  There still are groves amid the ebon crags,
In silent valleys, far from human sight,
  Where horror slinks and doom, and sunlight lags.
There still are caves which know no mortal foot
  And crawling rivers, blind and ghastly still,
And rocks that grip the oak tree's twining root—
  The asphodel still blooms beneath the hill.

I know your faces leering through the dark,
  Your mumbling lips that fail of human speech.
The winds of night enfold you, swift and stark,
  Unhallowed phantoms, whispering each to each.
    You thrill with horror subtle, nameless, blind—
    But grimmer shadows haunt the human mind.

2. CLOUDS

The gods have said: "Life is a mystic shrine"
   My laughter rattles down to break the night;
   Gods holy and unholy lend your sight,
And for a certain symbol and a sign
   My groping brain to steel and sapphire turn,
   And give me opal eyes that brood and burn
And mock the stars for mystery and shine.
And on a pedestal amid a grove
   Set me to stand while eons drift away,
While worshippers come bowing drove on drove
   And worship me with rose and harp and lay.
And write my name with suns and silver rods:
"One more false god amid a waste of gods."

3. SHRINES

Mohammed, Buddha, Moses, Satan, Thor!
  I lifted fanes to each of you betimes,
And proved your worth by murder, rape and war
  And bloody whips and chants and pious rhymes.
My sacrificial smoke put out the sun;
  I shook the world to give the gods a feast.
I read their kinship plain in every one—
The mullah, the evangelist, the nun,
  The voo-doo dancer and the mumbling priest.
I knew you when you raised a dabbled beard,
  And shook the gory dagger in the sky,
While trumpets crashed and horses neighed and reared
  And victims on the altars sank to die.
I knew you when you brought the virgin bride
  And stripped her in the temple of the god,
And set her on his marble thighs astride
  And found her womb with his cold phallic rod.
I knew you in the darksome Middle Age,
  A monster brooding in decay and dust;
You called on God but turned the Devil's page,
  And made your gown a screen to cloak your lust.
I saw you when the Salem witches burned,
  (The stars were glowing cinders in the heat)
  And when, hard bound across the cart's rough seat
With writhing buttocks naked and upturned
  You whipped the Quaker women through the street.

4. THE IRON HARP

They sell brown men for gold in Zanzibar,
   And screaming youths still feel the knife's caress
   And hear the brutish jeers at their distress.
Dark shadows haunt the harem sill and bar;
   A buyer lifts a dark eyed dancer's dress
To see the treasure he is paying for.
Kites haunt the trail from grim Nyanza Lake,
   The trail hard beaten out by fear and doom,
They swing, they dip, their iron beaks to slake—
It is not fruit that their red gullets take;
   Against the night the silent jackals loom.
Their feasts? They lie like milestones built of hate,
   Where last the whip caressed or dagger kissed;
And now the vulture's searching talons grate
   On shackles that still grip the leg and wrist.
But ah, men say, the bloody trail is far
From grim Nyanza's shore to Zanzibar.
   Look not for mercy in the Eastern lands,
   For blood must ever drip from dusky hands,
But Light is birthright of the Sons of Thor.
   And yet, proud striding races of the North,
How long since your white hands have gripped the hilt,
   How long since death and carnage bellowed forth,
And Nordic blood by Nordic hands was spilt?
No longer youths are sold in London town
   To writhe beneath the grinning gelder's hands,
   No longer in the Roman market stands
A shackled woman with a lifted gown.
   But only yesterday a nightmare dream
   Brought doom and fire and death and woman's scream.
And in the East again the death fires grow
And red winds out of Hell begin to blow.

5. INVOCATION

Break down the world and mold it once again!
  A jest chaotic that has run its time.
It had its birth in Hell and death and pain,
  And iron tears and blood and burning slime.
Not one white pebble on the crawling beach
  But has a destiny as great as man,
Who down the years has sought, but cannot reach,
  The stars that mock him and the gods that ban.
Break down the world; the sun is growing old,
  And Life is weary and the moons are far.
Break down the world, and of its scattered gold
  Beat out a single gem to crown a star.
    Or let it float for all Eternity
    A single star-mote in the endless sea.

Robert E. Howard

SONNETS OUT OF BEDLAM

1. THE SOUL-EATER

I swam below the surface of a lake
  And found myself within a curious hall,
  Lined with bronze columns, somber-black and tall;
On them I heard the evil gray waves break.
Sudden the granite floor began to shake;
  A monster strode from out an iron stall;
  Before his gryphon feet I reeled, to fall
As one who, dreaming, struggles to awake.

Upon my lips he set his grisly mouth
As to allay some fierce, demoniac drouth.
  A broken shell, I tread the earth in vain;
    My comrades are the goblin and the troll,
  Since One in that forgotten, sunken fane
    In evil hunger sucked from me my soul.

2. THE LAST HOUR

Hinged in the brooding west a black sun hung,
And Titan shadows barred the dying world.
The blind black oceans groped; their tendrils curled
   And writhed and fell in feathered spray, and clung,
   Climbing the granite ladders, rung by rung,
Which held them from the tribes whose death-cries skirled.
Above, unholy fires red wings unfurled—
   Gray ashes floated down from where they swung.

A demon crouched, chin propped on brutish fist,
   Gripping a crystal ball between his knees;
    His skull-mouth gaped, and icy shone his eye.
   Down crashed the crystal globe—beneath the seas
The dark lands sank—lone in a fire-shot mist.
   A painted sun hung in a starless sky.

3. THE SINGER IN THE MIST

At birth a witch laid on me monstrous spells,
   And I have trod strange highroads all my days,
   Turning my feet to gray, unholy ways.
I grope for stems of broken asphodels;
High on the rims of bare, fiend-haunted fells,
   I follow cloven tracks that lie ablaze;
   And ghosts have led me through the moonlight's haze
To talk with demons in the granite hells.

Seas crash upon dragon-guarded shores,
   Bursting in crimson moons of burning spray,
And iron castles ope to me their doors,
   And serpent-women lure with harp and lay.
The misty waves shake now to phantom oars—
   Seek not for me; I sail to meet the day.

4. HAUNTING COLUMNS

The walls of Luxor broke the silver sand
  When stars were golden lepers in the night,
  And, granite monsters in the pallid light,
They lurched like drunken Titans through the land,
With giant strides, most terrible and grand.
  They ringed me when the slender moon was bright,
  And gazing up their cold, inhuman height,
I shrieked and writhed and beat them with my hand.

Then dawn spread far her amaranthine gleam,
  And I could feel my brain to opal turn
That on the iron hinges of the dream
  Shattered to glowing shards that freeze and burn.
    God grant my bones lie silver on the plain
    Ere yet the walls of Luxor come again.

5. THE DREAM AND THE SHADOW

I dreamed a stony idol striding came
  Out of the shadows of a brooding land,
  And drew me, with unspoken, grim command
Into the dark. He named a monstrous Name,
And when I shrank with more than earthly shame,
  He raised me high, gripped in his granite hand,
  And crushed me—then to stain the silver sand,
My blood dripped down in jets of crimson flame.

I woke, and cold with horror of this dream,
  Rose in my bed, crossed white with moonlight's bars.
    Sudden a monstrous shadow seemed to loom
Above my bed; I lay and could not scream.
    Across the sky a shadow passed like doom,
  And for an instant, blotted out the stars.

VOICES OUT OF THE NIGHT
[THE IRON HARP]

1. OUT OF THE DEEP
[THE VOICES WAKEN MEMORY]

The blind black shadows reach inhuman arms
  To draw me into darkness once again;
The brooding night wind hints of nameless harms,
  And down the shadowed hill a vague refrain
    Bears half remembered ghosts to haunt my soul—
    Like far-off neighing of a nightmare's foal.
But let me fix my phantom-shadowed eyes
  Hard on the stars ñ pale points of silver light;
Here is the border-land ñ here reason lies—
  There, vision, gryphons ñ Nothing, and the Night.
Down, down, red specters! Down! And rack me not!
  Out, wolves of Hell! Oh, God, my pulses thrum—
The night grows fierce and blind and red and hot,
  And nearer still the grim insistent drum.
I will not look into the shadows—No!
  The stars shall grip and hold my frantic gaze—
But even in the stars black visions grow,
  And dragons writhe with iron eyes ablaze.
Oh, gods that raised my blindness with your curse,
  And let me see the horrid shapes behind
All outward veils that cloak the universe,
  The loathsome demon-spells that blind and bind,
    Since even the stars are noisome, foul and fell,
    Let me glut deep with memory dreams of Hell.

2. BABEL

Now in the gloom the pulsing drums repeat,
  And all the night is filled with evil sound;
I hear the throbbing of inhuman feet
  On marble stairs that silence locks around.

I see black temples loom against the night,
  With tentacles like serpents writhed afar,
And waving in a dusky dragon light
  Great moths whose wings unholy tapers char.
Red memory on memory, tier on tier,
  Builds up a tower, time and space to span;
Through world on world I rise, and sphere on sphere,
To star-shot gulfs of lunacy and fear—
  Black screaming ages never dreamed by man.

Was this your plan, foul spawn of cosmic mire,
To freeze my soul to stone and icy fire,
To carve me in the moon that all mankind
May know its race is futile, weak and blind—
A horror-blasted statue in the sky,
    That does not live and nevermore can die?

3. LAUGHTER IN THE GULFS

Ten million years beyond the sweep of Time,
　Ten million leagues from bound and measured Place
I hear vast monsters in the cosmic slime
　That mock the pallid glow of my dim face.
Here scum is quick and crawling filth alive
　And nameless, shapeless horrors breed and crawl,
And serpent-things horrific writhe and thrive—
　But through the nauseous muck I hear the Call—
There still are deeper Hells of Time to plumb,
　Dark demon shapes more terrible and vast—
Unheard, unguessed, un-dreamed of, broods the drum,
　That crouch along the sky-line of the Past.
Great taloned fingers grope from out the Deeps
　And fearful eyes are gleaming in the gloom,
Dismembered limbs that lie in moldering heaps
　Start up and strive to drag me to my doom,
　　And I with laughter of a man insane
　　Am wading through a cloud that is a Brain.

4. MOON SHAME

The great black tower rose to split the stars
In all the world below there was no light,
But other towers fringed the sky like spars
To mark that silent city of the night.
On one high altar nearest to the cold
Hard pallid moon that broke the velvet sky,
With waving plumes and mask of beaten gold
A grim nude figure stood ñ the priest was I.
The worshippers lay round in one dim ring
And on the altar's face that blackly shone,
A naked woman, cold and white and prone,
Lay silent to my frightful whispering.
My low, grim chanting ceased ñ like men who sinned
The worshippers about us caught their breath
And through my plumes I heard the night-born wind
Whisper a wordless monotone of death.
From hidden lutes there broke a grisly tune;
I reached an arm that plumbed the pulsing skies,
And tore from out her place the frosty moon
And laid it between those heavy naked thighs.
Then swift the change in fashion, form and shape,
I saw a faint mist shift and fade away -
And there a woman with a woman lay,
In shameful passion and unnatural rape.
Strange were her eyes, icy deep and icy cold
With passions human soul could never hold;
More cold and white than rarest ivory were
Her upturned, surging buttocks and her thighs,
And firm full breasts; her strange pale moonlight hair
Floated about her shoulders like a cloud;
No whisper broke the silence; still and cowed,
The people cringed before her icy eyes.
Beneath her thighs the woman whimpered twice
Then hid her eyes before those eyes of ice.

5. A CROWN FOR A KING

A roar of battle thundered in the hills;
  All day our iron blades drank deep in blood;
Till lighted with the flame the sunset spills
  We saw against our backs the river's flood.
Among its rocks the waters screamed and raced,
  We had our choice, we wild rebellious slave,
To die beneath the horrors that we faced
  Or die amid the horror of the waves.
Aye, we were men who gathered at the marge,
  And spear and insult at our foemen hurled -
They were not men who gathered for the charge,
  But demons of a blood-black elder world.
But even risen slaves may have a king -
  We had a king like some great iron tower,
And bloody now he faced the closing ring
  And leaned on his red sword in that red hour.
The life blood trickled down his hairy breast;
  His eyes were blazing suns of deathless hate,
He shook his hair back like a lion's crest,
  And staggered out, sword high, to meet his fate.
Aye, breast to breast that final charge we met,
  And blind with blood and slaughter, smote and slew;
Our broken swords were ghastly red and wet,
  But still the bat-like pinions beat and flew,
And fearful talons dragged us to our doom,
And fiendish eyes flamed through the deepening gloom.
  Still in the west there burned a fading flame,
When I rose reeling in a field of red.
  And searching for our warrior king I came
And found him dead upon a heap of dead.
  Demon and man, they silent lay, and still;
With cloven skull, rent heart and torn breast.
  And now the moon was rising on the hill,
And now the light was dying in the west.

Aye, I alone of all that mighty horde,
Still held my life; into a rough rude ring
  I bent with waning strength a broken sword,
A diadem to crown a warrior king.
    And on his red brow set the bloody crown,
    Then Life gave up the ghost as night came down.

Prose Poems
XXX

Howard's sequence of prose poems, published as *Etchings in Ivory*, is a fitting representation of this mode of which Howard made little use. The opening selection in this book is "Proem," which I take to be a fitting start, since it directly addresses the reader of the works and words to follow.

One of the problems inherent in both free verse (*verse libre* as the French dubbed it originally) and, to a greater extent, of the *prose poem* is the difficulty with many works in either mode to distinguish the language from prose. This has caused confusion, not only among lay readers of poetry, but also among critics.

Perhaps the formal distinctions are best to begin with. Free Verse is poetic <u>in form</u> due to the simple fact that, like regular verse poetry which is metered (has <u>measured</u> rhythms) and usually rhymed (at least in the Occidental traditions), <u>the poet determines the length of lines and exactly where the line will break and "turn"</u> (Latin: <u>*verso*</u>). With prose, of course, well exemplified by digital text or web pages, the divisions are paragraphs and sentences, but the text "reflows" to fit the margins, and the prose writer cares not exactly where the return ("turn") happens. That being said, the simple arrangement of prose into lines does not make it poetic in the sense of content or essence.

A "prose poem," on the other hand is a work arranged formally upon the page like prose, but which has, ideally, some poetic essence or merit stemming from the language itself.

But the fact that many writings have been <u>highly poetic prose</u> [Take, for example, the "Gettysburg Address" or Donne's "Meditation XVII"—and Howard's fiction includes much of this, with a poet's "ear" and flair and nuance], and it is difficult to separate from the work intended to be a "prose poem."

Both poetic prose and prose poems are richer in other, usually poetic, features: figurative language, compactness of message, archaic vocabulary, "poetic license," sound emphasized as much as sense, "music" as much as meaning. This makes them difficult to differentiate. Where does one end, the other begin?

The reader can decide where the following works fit.

ETCHINGS IN IVORY

PROEM
[SEE PAGE 1 FOR THIS TEXT]

FLAMING MARBLE

This is a dream that comes to me often. Not in the lazy, illusive haze of day-dreaming, but clear and vivid to my sleeping world.

I stood in a room whose carven lapis lazuli ceiling reared up on pillars of cold pure marble. The floor beneath my sandals was marble and the walls which glimmered frostily through the forest of the columns were likewise of marble. Somewhere a fountain tinkled musically and, as if in accompaniment, a lyre sighed a love song of Sappho.

I stood in the center of this room and I was I. I stood and was and lived, having no cognizance of any other personality; yet I saw myself as a man gazes at his image in a great luminous mirror. Truly, I was a man. A great, huge-shouldered, deep-chested brute of a man, with powerful knotted legs and heavy arms. I was dark, with heavy sombre brows lowering over volcanic eyes, and black unruly hair that topped a low, broad forehead. Save for the sandals on my feet and a loincloth of silk, I was naked.

A woman reclined on a luxurious couch before me. This woman, lounging like a slim and supple leopardess on the furs and silk, partook of the quality of her surroundings. Like marble she was, with the iciness of frozen fire, and I know as I look at her, that her white flesh is cold to the touch—cold and smooth.

And in my waking hours I wonder—in what lost empire, in what ancient city was that room in which I stood? Who was I? And who was this woman? Was it Athens or Rome? Was it Aspasia, Thais, Messalina or Lais who lay before me?

The columns of the room were Corinthian, carved with the symbol of acanthus. The frieze work along the scrolls of the ceiling suggested the Ionian. The exotic luxury of the silken hangings, the lush rugs, and the voluptuous divans hinted of the Orient—not the Orient of Today, but the Orient of Yesterday, before the Ottoman came out of the East to defile ancient shrines. But what proofs therein? That might have been a room of the latter Athenian days, or of Rome during her Augustan Age. For during her decadence, Athens borrowed the best of her neighbors, and Rome had never an artistry of her own, but ravished Greece and the Eastern lands for rarities.

As for the woman, her hair which shimmered like frozen gold was cut in the Egyptian manner and differed therein from the hair style of women of today. A thin silken scarf covered her curving breasts, and a sach [sic] of the same material was bound loosely about her voluptuous hips. An armlet of green gold, coiled like a serpent with ruby eyes, formed her single ornament.

Now her fine, scintillant grey eyes flashed like white flame under ice, and she lashed me with words like silver daggers and diamond-pointed spears. The language she spoke I do knot know, for the sound of it was as familiar to me then as is the language I speak in my waking life, and whether she reviled me in classic Latin, purring Ionian, clashing Doric, or sibilant Egyptian, I do know. Nor do I remember what she said, or I scarcely heard, as I stood there scornful, with arms folded on my mighty breast—for my eyes were devouring the beauty of her marble limbs, the cold splendor of her haughty face, regal now like a goddess in her wrath.

Oh, be sure I was her slave—but little of the slave I seemed then, harkening to her tirade with a half-smile toughing [sic] my grim lips, and answering, when I did answer, in a deep, untamable rumble.

The cold, grey eyes flashed with a fiercer light, and suddenly, with the lithe volcanic suddenness of a leaping tigress, my mistress was on her feet and her round white arm swept on high a slender whip with a jade hilt. But before its stinging lash ever touched my great shoulders, I tore it from her hand with a laugh that roared like the stinging salt sea, and crushed her to my breast.

She fought like a wild woman as I swept her off the floor and held her, cursing and helpless, and I felt her cool limbs and body writhing against mine as I crushed her scarlet, rose-leaf mouth with fierce and violent kisses. A moment she fought against her fate, and then the marble limbs caught fire from my passion, and the round arms went around my massive neck. I held in my arms a woman of flaming marble who gave back fierce kiss for savage kiss.

Then—I saw her eyes blaze wide as she glanced across my shoulder—she screamed—and I felt an icy and intolerable coldness under my left arm. I released the woman and reeled in a drunken half-circle as I turned. Lights and shadows of lights flared and flickered before me, and red and sapphire flames criss-crossed in slender spears. Staggering in the topaz gloom which had suddenly engulfed me, I sensed vaguely a human form before, and lurching headlong upon it, gripped it in my blindly clutching hands and crushed it while, afar off, creams shattered the crystal gong of the silence into million vibratory shards. Then the night flowed in red waves of darkness over me.

Now who was the woman I owned as mistress in that dim day? Who was I, slave and barbarian, that I might clasp the naked body of my aristocratic mistress in my sword-hardened arms? Who killed the barbaric slave in the marble woman's room so long ago, and who was she who loved the slave that, dying, slew his slayer? Who knows? Strange-eyed Life strides on with mask and staff, etching his art against the sky like statues on Arcadian hills.

Only in dreams do men see the face of Life, without the mask.

SKULLS AND ORCHIDS

Surely it was in decadent Athens--In marble-throned Athens of Sophocles in the Periclean Age. For fluted columns rose about me, and glancing between and beyond them, I could see a whitely paved street; upon the other side a temple, whose pillars bore the Ionic capital and whose frieze and pediment were glorious with figures which could have come into pulsing marble life only under the godlike hand of Phidias.

I stood in a chamber which must have corresponded to the usual gynaeconitis, save that I saw no spindle nor any implement of female household employment. The hangings and couches were of the finest make and fabric, and the rugs on the marble floor were ankle deep. And hereby was a strangeness, and the columns and the ceilings were symbolic of another, younger, and simpler age, and were of Spartan comeliness and Spartan straightforwardness. The pillars were Doric with the simple capital instead of the usual scrolled ram's-head, Ionian type, and on the entablature, the metopes between the jutting triglyphs were etched with a workmanship which hinted of no other than Ictinus How strange to see this Peloponnesian culture in Athens of the myrtle crown! Were it not for the furnishings of the room and the glory of the Acropolis shimmering yonder in the distance, I would wonder if it were not in truth, the house of some taciturn soldier of Lacedaemon.

I stood and held out my hands to a tall, handsome young man who stood before me, clad in the skirt and mantle of the Athenian citizen. His was the true patrician face, and his black hair was bound by a fillet of gold. His gold-banded arms were heavy and smoothly muscled. And I loved this man, for I was a woman, slim and lethal and passionate.

I wore little except sandals on my slim white feet, and a wide sash flung carelessly about my form, and my hair, half restrained by a cloth of gold stephane, fell in black waves about my agile shoulders, And I was beautiful.

As in my dreams, all this I know without conscious thought; I see with-out detaching my ego from that other dream-self--I am a double entity, an absolute unity, without reason or logic as men know them, but possessed of the knowledge of those other lives.

So I know that I was beautiful, just as I saw both the interior and the exterior of that room in the mind's eye of the woman I was then. I knew, without thinking, just how the outer frieze and cornice looked and transmitted that knowledge to my sleeping self of today, even while my dream-self plead with the young Grecian.

"You are handsome as Apollo himself, today," I said, "Demetrius, take me to hear Aristophanes' latest drama, will you not?" He sighed as if in weary resignation,

"Astaihh," he said, "you are wasting your time with me-- have I not told you that all is over between us? Go you your way, girl, there are many men who desire your love. Menander the poet would sell his soul into Hades for a single smile from you."

That idler, that scribbler of airy nothings?" my red lips curled, "Demetrius--"I glided close to him sinuously, and my round arms went about his neck.

Demetrius," I coaxed, "you loved me once! From the hard life of a soldier I led you in my arms and taught you the wonders and mysteries of luxuries and arts--and other things beside.

"I am younger than you, I Demetrius, and in all Athens there is none other more beautiful arid accomplished. Aspasia herself can boast of no greater skill on the lyre, and even that cold calculator Herodotus has praised my iambic verses-- written in honor of you, Demetrius! Phidias thought enough of my body to enthrone it forever in the Parthenon, and Menander has written me a thousand poems, unknown to the world who laughs at his comedies.

"Demetrius, do you owe me nothing? Remember, I left the gynaeconitis forever to follow the life of a "companion," losing my Athenian citizenship thereby, and all because of you. For you are a Spartan after all. Demotrius, and no Athenian gentlewoman may many a foreigner, even though he be a Hellene and high in Athens' ranks. I cared not; I never loved the monotonous and ignorant drudgery of the Athenian home, and while you were true to me, I was happy,"

"You might be happy with another," he said patiently. "It is not as if you were destitute--"

"I have everything but the love I desire," I answered, clinging to him, "Denetrius, no woman has come between us, more shame to you! We were happy until you listened to the philosophers, until you delved into the secret cults of Apollo."

His face darkened, and he put my arms from about him with unnecessary roughness. I was angered,

"Pent from the herd, the bull grows fierce and hard and tosses the wolf and the lion," I sneered. "But let him to the herd once more! So the Spar-tan in his barren land persuades himself that he is exalted above all men in his stupid self-denial, rejoices in his slaying prowess only, and boasts of the slavery he names freedom! But let him taste the joys of other, brighter, and more cultured lands, and he forswears all the trials of the camp for the silken couch and the wine--and even forswears natural delights. "He scowled darkly.

"Girl, be silent! I would not lay upon you in anger the hands that caressed you aforetime, but go your way and let me go mine!"

At that moment another entered. A slim, golden-haired boy, whose limbs were caned of ivory and whose rose-leaf mouth carved in a happy smile, whose fair cheeks blushed as he saw Demetrius. The Spartan's face softened, and with a war-hardened arm, he drew the boy gently to him, uptilting that girlish face for a kiss. While I stood by, my nails sinking into the palms of my hands between rage, shame, and jealousy.

"Demetrius, my lover," said the boy, "will thou not read to me the verse of Sappho wherein she sings of the silver shoulders of Anacreon?"

"That I will, child," said Demetrius tenderly. "Await ye here while I procure the manuscript."

He left the room, after a meaning glance at me, and I gazed at the boy with the morbid interest and repellent fascination with which a woman views a strange reptile. Truly, it was no wonder that the rulers of the city were tearing their beards and scouring the Aegean ports for beautiful woman, if this sort of condition existed. The boy eyed me ingenuously, yet I fancied I could detect a faint hint of triumphant malice in the curve of his wonderful lips. I stepped toward him as a cat stalks a mouse, though my own mouth was sailing.

"My child, said I. laying a hand on his smooth womanish arm and drawing him nearer me, "Many a woman might envy those lips of yours--"

Ha He staggered! His lips had been instinctively raised for my kiss, but the kiss was a deathly one. I wrenched the slim dagger free as he fell, and stepped back, my eyes wide with a kind of horror. He dropped to his knees, blood spurting from between the fingers with which he covered his wound. His rose-leaf lips opened and a broken cry escaped; then with a loose, flexing motion of his limbs, he slid prostrate and lay still.

I whirled, and the dagger, falling from my suddenly weak fingers, tinkled a silver rhyme on the marble floor. Demetrius stood in the wide doorway, and there was death in his eyes. I shrank back, my hands outstretched as though to fend off my doom, but in one stride he reached me. His hand gripped my breast and hurled me against a column where he held me as in a vise, whimper-Inv. and writhing vainly. I saw his right hand sink to him girdle and cone up again with a long glitter of white steel, and then a brand of frozen fire sank between my young breasts, and a sudden hot flow drowned the beseeching wails that trembled in my mouth. He stepped away from me, flinging the sword aside with a loathing gesture, and the red drops flew from the cruel bladelike rubies shaken from a white comet's train. I reeled two steps from the column and fell at his feet, striving even then to kiss his skirt. But he drew his garments from me, and as I lay there at the cold foot of that Doric column, more salt than death to me was the sight of Demetrius as he lifted the dead youth tenderly in his arms and kissed his dead lips. Then striding in the misty haze that had somehow enveloped the room, he turned away and went down a long and monstrous corridor of jade and opal shadows which wavered and closed behind him.

I struggled up in a sitting posture, one hand clutching my deathly wound, the other outstretched in hunger. Demetrius! Demetrius!"

But only the empty caverns of the great room gave back my cry, and I fell upon my face as a wave of weakness swept over se. Chaotic nightmare visions raced before me, and then I felt myself lifted in gentle arms. Through the mists a kindly, serious face looked at me,

"Astaihh? Who has done this? That Spartan? By Hades, I will drown him in his own blood!"

"Menander!" how weak my voice sounded. "No, harm him not. I slew myself. he touched me not. He loved me, Menander,"

What a pitiful touch to ease hurt vanity! Long streamers of purple and lavender swept across my view, and my weakness waxed. Seas, surging and restless, shone before me, lit by hard icy stars. I trembled, for how was Ito voyage those unknown oceans?

Astaihh!" Menander's voice broke in a great sob, "Oh, girl, go not from me! Oh, Zeus and Hera! Take her not from me! Have ye not beauty enow in your Elysian Fields that ye should covet the heart of my bosom!"

Now a wan fragrance stole over me, and my limbs relaxed with an almost sensuous ease. I felt no hurt, and my very weariness was restful; peace was upon me, and my arms stole weakly about Menander, 'Menander - I - have - loved - you - always, "Let him glean a little happiness if he could. His hungry lips, wet with the salt of tears, pressed mine, but my last thought was of Demetrius. I loved with a woman's love. Life, strange-eyed Life, your staff and your mask!

MEDALLIONS IN THE MOON

There is a gate whose portals are of opal and ivory, and to this gate I went one silent twilight when the amber sky was deepening to pale blue on the world rim and the great unlighted houses were basaltic monsters carved in the sky.

This gate I opened with a key forged from the silver of a dream, and entered the garden which lay beyond the gate. Once within this garden, the outer world ceased to exist for a space. I walked amid cameos of unguessable beauty, old as youth and young as Time. Undefiled and unchanged through the eons, this garden dreams along the sky nor may any invading foot crush a single flower therein; for only they may enter it, to whom each flower is a god.

Night had stolen upon it, flinging a tinkling veil of dark gossamer and through the shadows the great white faces of the nameless flowers nodded at me, and & shower of snowy petals floated down from the vines that embraced the musk-breathing trees.

Fountains gurgled and flung their sheens of silver high in the perfume-laden air, and the night breeze bore tome the hint of myrrh and aloes, jasmine and rose, rare spices and exotic flowers, and the blossoms of strange garden fruits.

Then the soon came slowly up ever the garden, liming boldly the solid black clusters of trees, revealing unthought-of valleys and winding silver rivers, fringed with nodding ferns and slim birches,

Afar I caught the glimmer that hinted of mystic lakes, haunted with dim islands, and the strange cry of the loon woke the echoes with unwonted desire.

The moon topped the dark eastern world-rim and stood above in splendor like a crimson shield of blood. And from somewhere a great bat came flying and for a moment stood out against the moon, wings outstretched. So, for an instant, the moon was a great , exotic, blood~red medallion, whose etching was the black shape of a huge bat.

THE GODS THAT MEN FORGET

The tang of winter is in the air and, in the brain of me. Old age comes upon me prematurely, like a mist from the cold sea, and deep and dreary in the gulfs of my soul, stir old ghosts of dreams. For the love of winter is not my love, and ever the desire burgeons in me for green trees and grass bursting in jade tides up through the pulsing sod. And the love of slow rivers sleeps in my bosom like a babe beneath his mother's heart. of slow lazy rivers and leaf gowned branches bending close to their bosoms. And warm winds and blazing stars when the nights are still and the good lush earth caresses my careless limbs with her warmth.

But the wind is out of the east and winter comes striding on brittle and sounding feet. What glory in the grey rain and the slanting sleet, the sullen ice and the brooding north winds? I have risen at dawn n the days of summer's desire and gazed at the nodding grass when each blade was a flaming gem in the morning fire of the dew. When the cold winds come and the sleet is sharp in the air, when the fogs drift grey and frost glimmers; then the desire of me wings south and the song of the wild geese is a threnody which shatters my brittle heart with fierce longing.

Oh, seas and the ghosts of seas beneath the Southern Cross! I have sailed them in my dreams and in my dreams I have races, springy-thewed and brown-limbed, along the wide white beaches between the palm trees and the lazy surf, my arms outstretched for a laughing golden-skinned nymph with a flaming hibiscus in her flying hair.

For far beyond the glimmer of these cold stars, over the amethyst rim of the world, there lies an island, a lazing gem set in the restless aquamarine of the main. Living I have never looked upon it, but sleep with its gossamer wings has borne me to its mystic bosom and there through long drowsy hours I have listened t0 the whisperings of the palm-tree leaves or the long sweeping intonations of the emerald, snow edged waves.

Or I have tumbled in sport upon the clear fragrance of the said, hearing quick breathless musical laughter like the tinkle a silver lute, feeling, like the breath of satin, the soft swift touch of round limbs against mine; crushing laughing protests as I sank my eager lips between youthful breasts that were like twin domes of burning ivory.

We were very old people on the island, old as races are measured but man had come before us.

One day I climbed the leafy green fastness of the dreaming and mysterious hills where no man ever went. Higher and higher I climbed where the silence brooded like a sleeping god and I went on wary toes lest I should wake the drowsing leaves which carved out the tourmaline (SP?) shadows. And at last I stood against the topaz sky and saw the coiling green serpent that men call the seas spread beneath me from horizon to horizon, and the distant white sails that hung against the skyline like a splash of white flame on a turquoise girdle. And the dusky jade-gowned slopes stretched beneath my feet far down to the beaches where the distance caned the bays and inlets into little clear-cut stencils that winked like sapphires set in a green mitre.

And there I cane upon a shrine of sard and calcite and an old forgotten god. Sunk and lost in the white-faced flowers and the lush grass were the marble paves which once girded his fane. Vines crawled like shimmering green serpents across his pedestal of red-veined onyx, and orchids flung about him their fragrance like an invisible white mist.

Prom great, strange magic eyes of carven rubies he looked at me and the jade and amber of his face glimmered ghostily in the purple shadows of the leaves. Not by word nor by sign did he speak to me, but the brooding invocation of the silence spoke to me.

"Ages ago (said the lost god) was I born from the flaming dew and the deep blue caverns of the sea; and from the shimmering fleece of golden cloud and the drifting dust of the stars. Here in the shrine of the sea came worshipper and neophyte, laden with silver jars of nectar, and purple and scarlet plumes from birds that haunted the jungles of the moon, and veils of star-woven silk, and ambergris.

"To my feet danced ivory-limbed girls, crowned with chaplets of asphodel and myrtle, to bedeck me with heliotrope and rose, orchid and iris and orange blossom. My altar smoked on amaranthine mountains,

"Where now are the lute-voiced neophytes, the wonder-cinctured acolytes, who sung before me the feast songs and the wine songs, the song of the seasons and the chant of the nuptials? The purple fog and the crimson fog drift before the sea breeze. And the races of men fade like visions of forgotten glory. All have vanished, worshipper and priest, silver-sceptered emperor and train-bearing slave. Youth with its blaring trumpets, its smoke of incense-billowing censers; the pride and the splendor! Men are fickle and let no god think within his heart, 'I am forever,' Gods and women are one with men who forgot them."

BLOODSTONES AND EBONY

I knelt in a great cavern before an altar which sent up in everlasting spirals a slender serpent of white smoke. Behind this altar brooded a vast and intangible Shape in the fragrant gloom, like a black tower seen through the mists of sleep. No reflection thereof waved back from the red dark surface of the altar, yet therein I gazed as though to read the answer of dark mysteries. On each side of me stretched away into the shadows, shimmering lines of worshippers like myself, kneeling, their naked bodies glistening a vague white.

Now from the silence and the darkness in front of me case the clear flat tones of a black jade gong, in even and regular cadence, and now the bodies of the worshippers swayed and bent. As one, the great throng rocked to the rhythm of the sound and the din ranks undulated in long, sweeping waves, like silver-white birches bending before the wind.

Now the gong fell silent, and the ranks froze into stone. Above, the great roof was lost in the darkness, upheld by great walls like black, red~veined cliffs which swept up and up until they merged with the black shadows. Here the sword-edged echoes of the gong vibrated a moment and then died in the pulsing silence.

Now a golden voice began where the gong had ceased and rose on a pure, slow scale. At the first sound, a slow fire began to steal through my veins and my blood turned to singing wine. Higher and higher the melodious chant crept, and a voluptuous dizziness carried me on its crest, as if borne on a satyr's shoulders; I mounted a ladder of black roses up through the dark and glittering ocean of the stars.

Now gulfs of jet purple and abysses of billowing mists lay beneath me and I swung dizzily up through incredible distances and colossal, undreamable heights, until the stars glittered like diamond points myriad leagues below my feet. And still that vibrant golden voice carried me on and on.

As in a sensual half-swoon whose incredible exultation was almost a hurt, I floated through realms beyond and outside all human ken, and the drifting emerald and crimson plumes of star-dust caressed my naked limbs with soft tan-human lips. Now the chant whirled up to heights unbearable, and I was hurled into a black void of utter night, whose darkness was hard and icy-smooth to my touch--and then it was shot through by long lances of hard-edged red, and through black and crimson bars I floated down.

Through the scented gloom of the great cavern the voice sank to a lulling refrain, and the silken and velvet hangings rustled in its harmony. There whispered in its golden chords, hints of untold mysteries and eon-haunting magic. The altar glowed darkly like a living ruby, and I heard the sweep of nighty [sic] bat-like wings. I felt the presence of ancient demons whose bodies were of burning jet and whose eyes were as caverns of red flame in the night.

Eerie footfalls whispered across the heavy air, and I sank down, spreading my limbs in pleasurable abandon. The scent of the incense smoke filled my nostrils, and the golden chant wove for me a patterned weave of bloodstones and ebony rowing fainter and farther away as I sank in an overpowering fragrant sea of misty purple and scarlet waves which drowned my senses in the rich, wan luxury of its perfumed tide.

Index of Titles

501

Index of First Lines

Form-Finder Index
(locate poems by genre and form)

NOTE 1: When two or more poems begin on the same page, the order in which the poems appear on the page is shown by a hyphen after the page number followed by the order number. Example: 137-1, 137-2.

NOTE 2: Robert E. Howard often used variations of the ballad stanza and other forms in the construction of longer stanzas by the simple technique of compressing shorter stanzas together to form longer groups. This technique is indicated in the following index by an asterisk* following the page numbers of the respective poems.

BALLAD VARIETIES (HOWARD'S FAVORITE STANDARD AND EXPERIMENTAL FORMS):

BALLAD (ABCB/DIMETER (2-BEAT LINES)
321

BALLAD EXPANDED — VARIABLE STANZAS
ABCBDB EXPANDED 6-LINE BALLAD
464
ABCBDB (COMPRESSED INTO TRIPLETS)
310, 428
VARIOUS GROUPINGS OF 4/3
21-2, 282*, 417

BALLAD — "HOWARDIAN" LONG-LINE BALLAD (7-BEAT LINES ARE REALLY 4-3 AS IN THE BALLAD; SEEMS LIKE LONG LINE COUPLETS, ACTUALLY STANDARD BALLAD IMITATION; OCCASIONALLY 6-BEAT LINES, IMMITATIVE OF THE SHORT BALLAD)
29, 31 (WITH INTERNAL RHYMES), 49*, 69-1, 104-2*, 105*, 107*, 114*, 120 (COMPRESSED AS OCTAVES), 123, 172, 175-2* (WITH INTERNAL RHYMES IN THE EVEN LINES), 179 (ALTERNATING LONG-LINE BALLAD AND SYNCOPATED TETRAMETER QUATRAIN STANZAS), 190* (WITH MUCH INTERNAL RHYME), 263*, 292*, 294*,

BALLAD—"HOWARDIAN" LONG-LINE BALLAD (CONT.)

298-2* (MUCH INTERNAL RHYME), 299-2*, 305*, 308*, 319*, 331*, 340-1*, 355 (VARIABLE SECTIONS), 389* (VARIOUS GROUPS OF 6 BEAT LINES, REPLICATING THE RHYTHMS OF THE SHORT BALLAD), 404*, 426-2 (FOLLOWED BY COUPLETS), 427-1*, 431*, 434-ALL FOUR CHAPTER HEADINGS, 440-2*, 440-4, 441*, 465 (WITH INTERNAL RHYMES)

BALLAD STANZA (LITERARY SHORT BALLAD — ABAB/3333)

62-2, 65, 67*, 91, 94, 97*, 101, 110-2, 138-2 (WITH FEMININE RHYMES IN THE EVEN LINES), 142, 144-2, 148-1, 201, 203, 212-1, 232-2*, 252, 278*, 285*, 291, 327*, 330, 430, 447-2*

BALLAD STANZA (LITERARY STANDARD BALLAD — ABAB/4343 OR LITERARY LONG BALLAD ABAB/4444)

11, 12 (OPENING LINES),18, 19, 21, 28 (WITH ONE EXPANDED BALLAD STANZA OF ABCCCB), 33, 37, 53*, 55, 71*, 74, 76, 77, 96*, 98*, 99 (WITH RHYTHMIC VARIATIONS), 100, 109-1, 110-3*, 121-1, 133, 140-4, 154-1 (WITH INTERNAL RHYME IN THE ODD LINES), 167, 168 (WITH CONCENTRATED ACCENTS), 182*, 185, 187 (WITH SYNCOPATED RHYTHM), 189, 212-2, 221 (WITH DIMETER VARIATION IN THE LAST LINE), 222-1, 223* (MUCH INTERNAL RHYME), 225*, 233 (WITH SEVERAL ACEPHALOUS ["HEADLESS," LACKING A FIRST SYLLABLE] LINES), 237-1, 237-2*, 240-1, 250, 251 (WITH MUCH ANAPESTIC VARIATION), 256 (WITH "EXPANDED BALLAD" SIX-LINE SECTIONS: AABCCB AND ABABCC, RESPECTIVELY), 261, 267, 271, 284 (WITH SYNCOPATED RHYTHM), 301*, 302*, 304-2, 313*, 339, 342 (ANAPESTIC AND SYNCOPATED METERS), 343-2, 352*, 353*, 357 (SYNCOPATED RHYTHMS), 403, 418, 424-2, 427-2, 427-3, 429 (ANAPESTIC METER), 436*, 437*, 438-1*, 444-1, 445, 450, 458

HEPTASTICH (7-LINE STANZA)
ABAAAAB/TETRAMETERS AND DIMETERS
148-2

HEROIC OCTAVE (ABABCDCD/PENTAMETER)
40-2, 297-1, 299-1

HEROIC QUATRAIN (ABAB/PENTAMETER)
9-2, 35-1, 35-2, 95, 115-1, 122, 140-2, 171, 177-2, 188, 297-2, 298-1

HEROICS (VARIABLE STANZAS OF IAMBIC PENTAMETER, MANY ABAB GROUPS)
196 (ED. NOTE: PERHAPS HOWARD'S FINEST LYRIC POEM - TIMELESS), 471, 472, 477, 478, 480, 481,

HEXASTICHES (SIX-LINE STANZAS)
ABABCB/TRIMETER
6
ABABCB/"HEADLESS" [ACEPHALOUS] TETRAMETER
85
AABBCC/HEXAMETERS
25
ABCBDB
90 (TRIMETER WITH TETRAMETER VARIATION), 115 (TRIMETERS)
ABCCCB (ANOTHER FORM OF EXPANDED BALLAD)
113, 345, 435-5, 457
ABCAAB (ANOTHER FORM OF EXPANDED BALLAD)
144-1
AABCCB/DIMETERS
158
AABCCB/TRIMETERS
336-1
VENUS AND ADONIS STANZA — ABABCC/PENTAMETERS
174-1, 228

OCTAVES (EIGHT-LINE STANZAS/IRREGULAR)
ABACBACC/TETRAMETER
   4
AAABCCCB/TETRAMETER (WITH LINES 4 AND 8
TRIMETER)
   129
AAABCCCB / DIMETER (DACTYLIC METER – IN IMITATION
OF TENNYSON'S "CHARGE OF THE LIGHT BRIGADE")
   354
ABBACCDD
   140-1
ABCBDBEB/PENTAMETERS
   143-1
ABABAABB/PENTAMETERS
   145-1
ABBACDCD/PENTAMETERS
   147
ABBACDCD/TETRAMETERS
   447-1

PENTASTICHES (FIVE-LINE STANZAS)
ABCCB/TETRAMETER
   193 (TRIMETERS IN LAST LINES OF STANZAS),
ABBAB/TETRAMETER
   222-2

PROSE POEMS
   1, 484, 487, 492, 493, 496

QUATRAINS (FOUR-LINE STANZAS/IRREGULAR)
UNRHYMED
   3-1,
BRACE STANZAS ABBA/DIMETER (2-BEAT LINES)
   257
ABAB (TRIMETERS AROUND PENTAMETERS)
   140-3

QUATRAINS (FOUR-LINE STANZAS/IRREGULAR) CONT.

ABAA/PENTAMETERS
   145-2
AAAB/TETRAMETERS
   183 (WITH REFRAINS), 199 (WITH REFRAINS)
ABCB/HEXAMETERS
   184 (WITH INTERNAL RHYME IN SOME LINES)
ABAB//HEXAMETERS
   266
RUBAIYAT STANZA (AABA) FOLLOWED BY BBBC
   241-1

SONNETS (HOWARD'S SECOND FAVORITE FORM OF POEM, TYPICALLY ITALIAN/PETRARCHAN OR SOME VARIATION THEREOF)

SONNET IN BALLAD METER (INTERESTING BLEND OF TWO FORMS—EXPERIMENTAL)
   27, 93, 323-1 (ABCBDB AEFE GHAH) SHORT LINES AND SYNCOPATED)

SONNET (ITALIAN/PETRARCHAN) [THE ORIGINAL FORM: ABBAABBA IN THE OCTAVE AND VARIABLE SESTETS, NEVER ENDING IN A COUPLET – HOWARD'S SONNET FORM OF CHOICE]

CDEDEC SESTET
   41
CCDEDE SESTET
   86-2, 474
CDECDE SESTET (ONE OF THE TWO STANDARD FORMS)
   102-1, 143, 160, 304-1, 312-1, 312-2, 314, 333-2
CDEDCE SESTET
   102-2, 475-1
CDCDCD SESTET (THE OTHER OF THE TWO STANDARD FORMS)
   127, 128-1, 174-2, 249, 475-2

Sonnet (Irregular/Experimental)
ABABCDCDEFEFGHGHII (18 lines/English Sonnet extended by an extra quatrain, but keeping the pattern)
479

Sonnet (Couplet Sonnet/tetrameters)
235 (with irregular sestet: AABBCCDD octave, EE<u>FGHG</u>)

Sonnets as Stanzas (Italian/Petrarchan Base – a Double Sonnet)
ABBAABBA / CDCEDE / FGGFFGGF / HIIHJJ
248

Sonnet (Couplet Sonnet/hexameters with heptameter variation)
AABBCCDD EEFFGG
152

Sonnet (English/Shakespearean)
ABABCDCDEFEFGG
473 (Howard's only English/Shakespearean sonnet)

Syncopated Rhythm
14 (in some stanzas)
Tetrameters/much anapestic variation
155, 161
Tetrameters/dactylic and trochaic
165-2

Tercets (3-line stanzas)

Terza Rima (compressed — ABABCB hexains)
317 (another way to expand the short ballad),

TERCETS (3-LINE STANZAS) CONT.

TRIPLETS
HEXAMETER
66,
MOCK TRIPLETS (ARRANGED IN THREES, BUT
ACTUALLY A LITERARY SHORT BALLAD)
83,
TETRAMETER
334 (WITH DOUBLE RHYMES)

TROCHAIC TETRAMETERS (AS IN LONGFELLOW'S "HIAWATHA" OR THE HALF-LINES OF POE'S "THE RAVEN")
163, 226 (WITH SOME CATALECTIC LINES [LINES
LACKING THE FINAL REGULAR SYLLABLE), 438-2

VARIABLE RHYMES/MIXED STANZAS
56-2, 58 (A BLEND OF COUPLETS AND LITERARY
BALLAD), 62-1, 81, 125, 126, 134 (VARIOUS 4-, 5-, AND 6-
LINE STANZAS), 153, 198 (SYNCOPETED RHYTHMS,
VARIABLE RHYMES), 204, 205, 210-1, 213 (VARIABLE
RHYMES AND LINE LENGTHS), 217-2, 236, 239 (SEEMS
LIKE AN EXTENDED SONNET EXPERIMENT), 240-2 (WITH
MUCH ANAPESTIC VARIATION), 258 (RANDOM RHYMES
AND LINE LENGTHS), 283, 323-2, 412
(PENTAMETERS/VARIABLE HEROIC STANZAS), 415
(PENTAMETERS/VARIABLE HEROIC STANZAS), 452 (WITH
MUCH FALSE RHYME)
69-2

VILLANELLE
(19 LINE FRENCH FIXED FORM – THIS ONE A VARIANT,
RHYMES CORRECT, NORMAL REFRAINS LACKING)
159

www.ingramcontent.com/pod-product-compliance
Lightning Source LLC
Chambersburg PA
CBHW051054030726
47504CB00006B/1627